Figure 36.

BOOK OF THE HOPI

There is no such thing as a little country. The greatness of a people is no more determined by their number than the greatness of a man is determined by his height.

—Victor Hugo

FIGURE 55. MALE-FEMALE PÁHO

OPPOSITE: FIGURE 43. POTTERY MOUND
SKUNK PAINTING

BOOK OF THE
HOPI

BY FRANK WATERS

Drawings and source material recorded by

OSWALD WHITE BEAR FREDERICKS

NEW YORK: THE VIKING PRESS

FOREWORD

LAURENS VAN DER POST, gifted writer and perceptive student of humanity, has deplored the loss to our society of the "whole natural language of the spirit," with the result that we no longer have a certain basic sense of proportion. The wisdom of this observation will be apparent to readers of *Book of the Hopi,* wherein an ancient people, living in our midst today, are attempting to preserve what may be lost to us forever. Lacking that sense of proportion, we are endangered by a false set of values that may make our "Road of Life" very rough indeed. With all the teachings of our recorded history, with all the finely developed tools of the mind, with the scientific revelations of centuries of experience at our fingertips, will we fumble the ball when the moment of decision arrives? To our constant horror, we find ourselves stumbling along the brink of conflict. We search for truth, but somehow in a moment of crisis it eludes us.

This *Book of the Hopi* is the story of a people. It is a story of success and failure, but the story of success so outweighs that of failure that it deserves our most earnest attention; for here, I believe, may be the answer we seek. Here we discover the "natural language of the spirit" speaking in loud, clear tones. Here we find the sustaining power of the religious sense and the clue to understanding. Here we may find our salvation. As so often happens, the clue was in our own back yard all the time.

This story is one never before expressed in any written form. The fact that this book exists is the result of countless fortuitous circumstances. As Frank Waters states, "This great cooperative effort could not have been obtained before, nor could it be obtained now." Being in the right place at the right time has won many battles. In this case, another battle has been won. A great people (now few in number indeed) speaks to us, and we are the richer for it if we but have the necessary degree of humility to listen.

It has been our sincere desire to provide some opportunity for a remarkable group of our fellow citizens to tell us in their own words of the infinite source of their strength. Through this revelation we trust that they may regain in the eyes of their community some of the status which they so richly deserve in their hour of extremity, which, because of their traditional and deep sense of humility, may otherwise be denied them. In assisting and encouraging them to give the magnificently beautiful story of their "Road of Life" to the world, we feel that we may have taken the first step to delay the fulfillment of their most fearful prophecy.

FREDERICK H. HOWELL, Director,
Charles Ulrick and Josephine Bay Foundation

FIGURE 36. EAGLE CLAN LEADER

OPPOSITE: FIGURE 61. CORN MURAL

CONTENTS

PHOTOGRAPHS

X · PHOTOGRAPHS

FIGURE 62. EAGLE CLAN SYMBOLS

FIGURE 59. RELIGIOUS LEADER, AWATOVI

INTRODUCTION

This is a strange and wonderful book. Its spokesmen are some thirty elders of the Hopi Indian tribe in northern Arizona.

The Hopis regard themselves as the first inhabitants of America. Their village of Oraibi is indisputably the oldest continuously occupied settlement in the United States. It and most of the other villages cling to six-hundred-foot-high escarpments of three rocky mesas rising abruptly out of the desert plain: Hano, Sichomovi, and Walpi on First Mesa; Mishongnovi, Shipaulovi, and Shongopovi on Second Mesa; Hotevilla, Bakavi, and Oraibi on Third Mesa; and Moencopi lying fifty miles to the west. No part of the vast arid plateau

XI

embracing parts of New Mexico, Arizona, Colorado, and Utah is more in-hospitable than the Hopi Reservation of nearly four thousand square miles, itself completely surrounded by the twenty-five-thousand-square-mile wilderness of the Navajo Reservation. Men have had to walk ten miles each day to tend their little patches of squaw corn. Women have trudged interminably up the steep cliff-sides with jars of water on their heads. This is their immemorial homeland, the desert heartland of the continent.

Most of their spokesmen here are old men and women with dark wrinkled faces and gnarled hands. They speak gutturally, deep in their throats and almost without moving their lips, their voices rising out of the depths of an archaic America we have never known, out of immeasurable time, from a fathomless unconscious whose archetypes are as mysterious and incomprehensible to us as the symbols found engraven on the cliff walls of ancient ruins.

What they tell is the story of their Creation and their Emergences from previous worlds, their migrations over this continent, and the meaning of their ceremonies. It is a world-view of life, deeply religious in nature, whose esoteric meaning they have kept inviolate for generations uncounted. Their existence always has been patterned upon the universal plan of world creation and maintenance, and their progress on the evolutionary Road of Life depends upon the unbroken observance of its laws. In turn, the purpose of their religious ceremonialism is to help maintain the harmony of the universe. It is a mytho-religious system of year-long ceremonies, rituals, dances, songs, recitations, and prayers as complex, abstract, and esoteric as any in the world. It has been the despair of professional anthropologists, ethnologists, and sociologists.

The great pioneer ethnologist Alexander M. Stephen, who first recorded the details of Hopi ceremonialism in the 1890s, was led to exclaim irritably in his classic journal: "Damn these tantalyzing whelps, to the devil with all of them! I have been bamboozled from pillar to post all day, have received no scrap of information!" He came to the conclusion that Hopi ceremonialism was so abstract that it would take longer than a man's lifetime to understand it, and that it required a sixth sense of the Hopis themselves.

J. Walter Fewkes later was equally baffled. He wrote: "There is much mysticism in the proceedings which thus far the writer fails to understand. . . . In many instances these native explanations in which much esotericism appears to enter, have not been understood. . . ."

Today, more than a half-century later, almost every Hopi ceremony has been reported with painstaking accuracy by a host of professional observers. Yet their studies are limited to minute exoteric descriptions of ritual para-phernalia and how they are used. The esoteric meanings and functions of the ceremonies themselves have remained virtually unknown. This is not wholly due to traditional Hopi secrecy. Professional scientific observers themselves have never granted validity to those aspects of Hopi ceremonialism that border the sixth-sense realm of mysticism. Indeed the rationalism of all the Western world vehemently refutes anything that smacks of the unknown or "occult." Hence Hopi belief and ceremonialism have been dismissed as the crude folk-lore and erotic practices of a decadent tribe of primitive Indians which have no relationship to the enlightened tenets of modern civilization.

The word "Hopi" means "peace." As a People of Peace the Hopis have tacitly ignored this outside view of themselves, suffering American domination with aloofness and secrecy, and keeping at bay the technological civilization swirling about them. But now the bow is bending. Their long-repressed resentment is breaking out against ethnologists and anthropologists who have discounted their beliefs, commercial agents who would exploit them, and the national government itself which has betrayed them. Greater tremors of unrest and resentment against the imposition of our rational materialism are shaking the Sierra Madres and the Andes. The psychic chasm separating us from all red America, black Africa, yellow Asia, and the brown Middle East grows ever wider. Who can doubt the signs that a transition to another great new age has begun?

That these Hopis have revealed their conceptual pattern of life to us now, for the first time, imparts to their gift a strangeness unique in our national experience. For they speak not as a defeated little minority in the richest and most powerful nation on earth, but with the voice of all that world commonwealth of peoples who affirm their right to grow from their own native roots. They evoke old gods shaped by instincts we have long repressed. They reassert a rhythm of life we have disastrously tried to ignore. They remind us we must attune ourselves to the need for inner change if we are to avert a cataclysmic rupture between our own minds and hearts. Now, if ever, is the time for them to talk, for us to listen.

This, then, is their book of talk. It is not a professional paper—neither a sociological or psychological study nor an anthropological report. It is the presentation of a life-pattern rooted in the soil of this continent, whose growth is shaped by the same forces that stamp their indigenous seal upon its greatest mountain and smallest insect, and whose flowering is yet to come. The Hopis do not set themselves apart as human entities from this pattern. They are as sure of the future as they are of the past.

Beginning with their Genesis, and carrying through their Old Testament of previous worlds and their New Testament of the present to the Revelation of their esoteric ceremonialism, the tenets of this book are as sacred to the Hopis as the Judaic-Christian Bible is to other peoples. Many of these will find it impossible to concede that the Hopis, according to Hopi belief, were also a Chosen People. Nor will the Hopi view of the universe as an inseparably interrelated field or continuum be quite palatable to those who tacitly accept the role of man as a rational entity created to stand apart from nature in order to control its politically ordered cosmology with an imperialistic mechanization. They will prefer still to regard it rather as the strange and naïve myth of a still primitive tribe of Indians, facing possible extinction because of lack of adaptation. This will make its profound sense of wholeness no less wonderful to others, who see their own culture uneasily reflecting the cataclysmic split between the spiritual and the material, the conscious and unconscious. For this message of peace, this concern with helping to preserve the inherent harmony of the universal constituents of all life, reaffirms for all of us everywhere man's imperishable belief in the fullness and richness of life granted him by his creative forces, if he can but find a way of self-fulfillment.

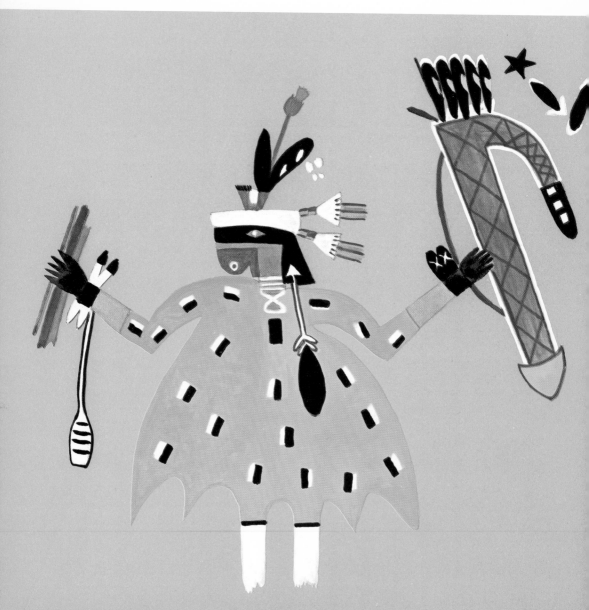

FIGURE 37. QUALETAQA

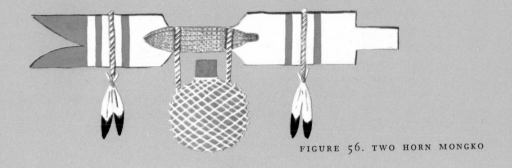

A note about the compilation of the book:

Grateful acknowledgment is made of financial support by charitable funds, made possible by the Charles Ulrick and Josephine Bay Foundation, Inc., and my sincere thanks go to Mr. Frederick H. Howell, who conceived the project during a trip to the Hopi country several years ago. He then initiated the work and has directed it with unflagging interest and encouragement through many periods of trial.

Work on the project required nearly three years. Much of this time I lived on the Reservation in a little Hopi house below Pumpkin Seed Point, taking meals with my research co-worker, Oswald White Bear Fredericks, and his wife, Naomi, who lived a half-mile away. Our enforced intimacy under trying conditions I look back upon with warmth and gratitude.

One after another, through the months, the discourses of our Hopi spokesmen were taken down in Hopi on a tape recorder by White Bear, who later translated them into English with the aid of his wife. White Bear was especially qualified to record and translate this source material. A full-blood Hopi born in Oraibi, a member of the Coyote Clan, and a nephew of the late Wilson Tawákwaptiwa, Village Chief of Oraibi, he attended Haskell Institute in Lawrence, Kansas, and Bacon College, Muskogee, Oklahoma.

All the Hopi spokesmen willingly and freely gave the information they were qualified to impart by reason of their clan affiliations and ceremonial duties; none of them was paid informant fees in the manner customarily followed by professional researchers gathering information for scientific studies. Each regarded the compilation of this book as a sacred task—a monumental record that would give their children and their children's children a complete history of their people and their religious belief. This great cooperative effort could not have been obtained before, nor could it be obtained now; already some of the older spokesmen have died. Their traditions come to us by the dictate of fate we call fortuitous chance, at the time when we, as they, most need them.

The spokesmen include: the late Wilson Tawákwaptiwa (Sun in the Sky), Bear Clan, Village Chief of Oraibi; Charles Fredericks, Tuwahoyiwma (Land Animals), Bear Clan, New Oraibi; Mrs. Anna Fredericks, Tuvengyamsi (Land Beautiful with Flowers), Coyote Clan, New Oraibi; Dan Qöchhongva (White Cloud above Horizon), Sun Clan, Hotevilla; Mrs. Bessie Sakmoisi (Chasing One Another on Green Field), Side Corn Clan, Bakavi; John Lansa (Lance), Badger Clan, Oraibi; De Witt Sahu (Yucca Food), Hawk Clan, Oraibi; Baldwin Polipko'ima (Male Followed by Butterfly Maiden), Badger Clan, Hotevilla; Johnson Tuwaletstiwa (Sun Standing Up), Bow Clan, New Oraibi; Bert Sakwaitiwa (Animals Run on Green Pasture), Bear Clan, Moencopi; Ralph Silena (Place in Flowers Where Pollen Rests), Sun Clan, Shongopovi; Joseph Chölö (Raindrop), Snake Clan, Oraibi; Claude Kawanyuma, Bear Clan, Shongopovi; Earl Pela, Sun Clan, Shongopovi; Sequaptewa, Deep Well Clan, Hotevilla; Paul Siwingyawma (Corn That Has Been Rooted), Eagle Clan, Hotevilla; the late Otto Pentiwa (Painting Many Kachina Masks), Kachina Clan, New Oraibi; Sam Paweki, Rabbit Clan, Oraibi; Tom Mutchku, Water Clan, Oraibi; Stewart, Reed Clan, Walpi; Earl Mumriwa, Cloud Clan, Walpi; Sakhongva (Green Corn Standing), Hotevilla; Jack Pokunyesva (Man before Altar), Hotevilla; Ralph Tawangyaoma, Hotevilla; Elizabeth White, New Oraibi; Bob Adams, Walpi; and Robert, Badger Clan, Oraibi.

From their rough source material, so often unavoidably incomplete and contradictory, supplemented by answers to specific questions, personal observation of all ceremonies, and field trips to all sites mentioned, with additional historical research, I have written the text presented here.

Oraibi always has been regarded as the parental home of Hopi ceremonialism. Hence the interpretation of the ceremonies follows as closely as possible the traditional Oraibi pattern, noting the deviations in other villages during recent years.

For the same reason, the Oraibi dialect has been adhered to in preference to the different dialects of other villages. Although the Scriptures have been published in Hopi, Hopi is not yet a commonly written language; perhaps because of the extreme difficulty of translation, as pointed out by Benjamin Lee Whorf, who has made a profound analysis of the language. All Hopi words used here have been spelled according to a system worked out by Mr. Charles Hughes of Columbia University, to whom thanks are given for his help.

Particular thanks are due to Mrs. H. R. Voth and her daughter Mrs. P. A. Dyck for permission to reproduce photographs from the rare collection taken by the Reverend H. R. Voth during his residence at Oraibi a half-century ago. The caption material also has been supplied by Mrs. Voth.

To all the other persons, too numerous to mention, who aided us in so many ways, I can only say, *"Kwakwai! Kwakwai!"*

In arranging the material so vast in scope and detail, I have borne in mind that it virtually constitutes a Hopi Bible. Hence it is presented in chronological order, beginning with the Creation, akin to our own Genesis, and the people's successive Emergences from the three previous worlds to the present Fourth World. Part Two, which may be viewed as a Hopi Exodus, then recounts the prehistoric migrations of the clans over this continent until they arrived at their predestined homeland, whose center is present Oraibi. Here was initiated the great annual cycle of religious ceremonies still carried on as described in Part Three. Part Four then summarizes the historical period from the arrival of the first white men in 1540 to the present time.

It was wished that the book serve the practical purpose of helping to solve current Hopi problems of local self-government, factional disputes, land claims against the Navajo tribe and the national government, and other political and economic controversies. The arrangement of the text best meets this obligation by presenting these problems in Part Four, as all Hopi secular life is so based on the religious that these current problems cannot be properly viewed without the perspective of long tradition. Indeed, the whole history of the Hopis *vis-à-vis* the United States—as does the relationship of the Indian and the White throughout all the Americas—tragically illustrates our ignorance of and lack of interest in learning the traditional beliefs of the peoples we have dominated. It is fervently hoped that this book will be of great assistance to representatives of the Indian Bureau, National Park and Forest Service, state and court officials, and private industry in their future dealings with the Hopis.

As a final word I must reiterate that this book is an expression by Hopis of the traditional viewpoint. All the material in it, save my own obvious commentaries, was supplied by our Hopi spokesmen and approved as transcribed in manuscript form. Its aim as a free narrative was to achieve the full spirit and pattern of Hopi belief, unrestricted by detailed documentation and argumentative proof. As such it conflicts in innumerable instances with the scientific views of the Hopis held by outside academic observers. The documentary scholar may question whether an ancient primitive people could have evolved such a rich belief and preserved its full tradition for generations by word of mouth. He may assert that the interpretations of the myths, legends, and ceremonies are largely my own speculations. He will certainly deny that invisible spirits manifest themselves as described. To these doubts and denials my only answer is that the book stems from a mythic and symbolic level far below the surface of anthropological and ethnological documentation. That it may not conform to the rational conceptualization ruling our own beliefs does not detract from its own validity as a depth psychology different from our own. It stands for itself as a synthesis of intuitive, symbolic belief given utterance for the first time.

This then is the *Book of the Hopi,* as its title implies, given to us with the hope we will receive it in the same spirit of universal brotherhood that impelled its compilation.

PART ONE

THE MYTHS:

Creation of the Four Worlds

1

Tokpela: The First World

The first world was Tokpela [Endless Space].

But first, they say, there was only the Creator, Taiowa. All else was endless space. There was no beginning and no end, no time, no shape, no life. Just an immeasurable void that had its beginning and end, time, shape, and life in the mind of Taiowa the Creator.

Then he, the infinite, conceived the finite. First he created Sótuknang to make it manifest, saying to him, "I have created you, the first power and instrument as a person, to carry out my plan for life in endless space. I am your Uncle. You are my Nephew. Go now and lay out these universes in proper order so they may work harmoniously with one another according to my plan."

Sótuknang did as he was commanded. From endless space he gathered that which was to be manifest as solid substance, molded it into forms, and arranged them into nine universal kingdoms: one for Taiowa the Creator, one for himself, and seven universes for the life to come. Finishing this, Sótuknang went to Taiowa and asked, "Is this according to your plan?"

"It is very good," said Taiowa. "Now I want you to do the same thing with the waters. Place them on the surfaces of these universes so they will be divided equally among all and each."

So Sótuknang gathered from endless space that which was to be manifest as the waters and placed them on the universes so that each would be half solid and half water. Going now to Taiowa, he said, "I want you to see the work I have done and if it pleases you."

"It is very good," said Taiowa. "The next thing now is to put the forces of air into peaceful movement about all."

This Sótuknang did. From endless space he gathered that which was to be manifest as the airs, made them into great forces, and arranged them into gentle ordered movements around each universe.

Taiowa was pleased. "You have done a great work according to my plan, Nephew. You have created the universes and made them manifest

3

in solids, waters, and winds, and put them in their proper places. But your work is not yet finished. Now you must create life and its movement to complete the four parts, Túwaqachi, of my universal plan."

SPIDER WOMAN AND THE TWINS

Sótuknang went to the universe wherein was that to be Tokpela, the First World, and out of it he created her who was to remain on that earth and be his helper. Her name was Kókyangwúti, Spider Woman.

When she awoke to life and received her name, she asked, "Why am I here?"

"Look about you," answered Sótuknang. "Here is this earth we have created. It has shape and substance, direction and time, a beginning and an end. But there is no life upon it. We see no joyful movement. We hear no joyful sound. What is life without sound and movement? So you have been given the power to help us create this life. You have been given the knowledge, wisdom, and love to bless all the beings you create. That is why you are here."

Following his instructions, Spider Woman took some earth, mixed with it some túchvala (liquid from mouth: saliva), and molded it into two beings. Then she covered them with a cape made of white substance which was the creative wisdom itself, and sang the Creation Song over them. When she uncovered them the two beings, twins, sat up and asked, "Who are we? Why are we here?"

To the one on the right Spider Woman said, "You are Pöqánghoya and you are to help keep this world in order when life is put upon it. Go now around all the world and put your hands upon the earth so that it will become fully solidified. This is your duty."

Spider Woman then said to the twin on the left, "You are Palöngawhoya and you are to help keep this world in order when life is put upon it. This is your duty now: go about all the world and send out sound so that it may be heard throughout all the land. When this is heard you will also be known as 'Echo,' for all sound echoes the Creator."

Pöqánghoya, traveling throughout the earth, solidified the higher reaches into great mountains. The lower reaches he made firm but still pliable enough to be used by those beings to be placed upon it and who would call it their mother.

Palöngawhoya, traveling throughout the earth, sounded out his call as he was bidden. All the vibratory centers along the earth's axis from pole to pole resounded his call; the whole earth trembled; the universe quivered in tune. Thus he made the whole world an instrument of sound, and sound an instrument for carrying messages, resounding praise to the Creator of all.

"This is your voice, Uncle," Sótuknang said to Taiowa. "Everything is tuned to your sound."

"It is very good," said Taiowa.

When they had accomplished their duties, Pöqánghoya was sent to the north pole of the world axis and Palöngawhoya to the south pole, where they were jointly commanded to keep the world properly rotating. Pöqánghoya was also given the power to keep the earth in a stable form of solidness. Palöngawhoya was given the power to keep the air in gentle ordered movement, and instructed to send out his call for good or for warning through the vibratory centers of the earth.

"These will be your duties in time to come," said Spider Woman.

She then created from the earth trees, bushes, plants, flowers, all kinds of seed-bearers and nut-bearers to clothe the earth, giving to each a life and name. In the same manner she created all kinds of birds and animals—molding them out of earth, covering them with her white-substance cape, and singing over them. Some she placed to her right, some to her left, others before and behind her, indicating how they should spread to all four corners of the earth to live.

Sótuknang was happy, seeing how beautiful it all was—the land, the plants, the birds and animals, and the power working through them all. Joyfully he said to Taiowa, "Come see what our world looks like now!"

"It is very good," said Taiowa. "It is ready now for human life, the final touch to complete my plan."

CREATION OF MANKIND

——— So Spider Woman gathered earth, this time of four colors, yellow, red, white, and black; mixed with *túchvala,* the liquid of her mouth; molded them; and covered them with her white-substance cape which was the creative wisdom itself. As before, she sang over them the Creation Song, and when she uncovered them these forms were human beings in the image of Sótuknang. Then she created four other beings after her own form. They were *wúti,* female partners, for the first four male beings.

When Spider Woman uncovered them the forms came to life. This was at the time of the dark purple light, Qoyangnuptu, the first phase of the dawn of Creation, which first reveals the mystery of man's creation.

They soon awakened and began to move, but there was still a dampness on their foreheads and a soft spot on their heads. This was at the time of the yellow light, Síkangnuqa, the second phase of the dawn of Creation, when the breath of life entered man.

In a short time the sun appeared above the horizon, drying the dampness on their foreheads and hardening the soft spot on their heads. This was the time of the red light, Tálawva, the third phase of the dawn of Creation, when man, fully formed and firmed, proudly faced his Creator.

"That is the Sun," said Spider Woman. "You are meeting your Father the Creator for the first time. You must always remember and observe these three phases of your Creation. The time of the three lights, the dark purple, the yellow, and the red reveal in turn the mystery, the breath of life, and warmth of love. These comprise the Creator's plan of life for you as sung over you in the Song of Creation:

SONG OF CREATION

The dark purple light rises in the north,
A yellow light rises in the east.
Then we of the flowers of the earth come forth
To receive a long life of joy.
We call ourselves the Butterfly Maidens.

Both male and female make their prayers to the east,
Make the respectful sign to the Sun our Creator.
The sounds of bells ring through the air,
Making a joyful sound throughout the land,
Their joyful echo resounding everywhere.

Humbly I ask my Father,
The perfect one, Taiowa, our Father,
The perfect one creating the beautiful life
Shown to us by the yellow light,
To give us perfect light at the time of the red light.

The perfect one laid out the perfect plan
And gave to us a long span of life,
Creating song to implant joy in life.
On this path of happiness, we the Butterfly Maidens
Carry out his wishes by greeting our Father Sun.

The song resounds back from our Creator with joy,
And we of the earth repeat it to our Creator.
At the appearing of the yellow light,
Repeats and repeats again the joyful echo,
Sounds and resounds for times to come.

The First People of the First World did not answer her; they could not speak. Something had to be done. Since Spider Woman received her power from Sótuknang, she had to call him and ask him what to do. So she called Palöngawhoya and said, "Call your Uncle. We need him at once."

Palöngawhoya, the echo twin, sent out his call along the world axis to the vibratory centers of the earth, which resounded his message throughout the universe. "Sótuknang, our Uncle, come at once! We need you!"

All at once, with the sound as of a mighty wind, Sótuknang appeared in front of them. "I am here. Why do you need me so urgently?"

Spider Woman explained. "As you commanded me, I have created these First People. They are fully and firmly formed; they are properly colored; they have life; they have movement. But they cannot talk. That is the proper thing they lack. So I want you to give them speech. Also the wisdom and the power to reproduce, so that they may enjoy their life and give thanks to the Creator."

So Sótuknang gave them speech, a different language to each color, with respect for each other's difference. He gave them the wisdom and the power to reproduce and multiply.

Then he said to them, "With all these I have given you this world to live on and to be happy. There is only one thing I ask of you. To respect the Creator at all times. Wisdom, harmony, and respect for the love of the Creator who made you. May it grow and never be forgotten among you as long as you live."

So the First People went their directions, were happy, and began to multiply.

THE NATURE OF MAN

With the pristine wisdom granted them, they understood that the earth was a living entity like themselves. She was their mother; they were made from her flesh; they suckled at her breast. For her milk was the grass upon which all animals grazed and the corn which had been created specially to supply food for mankind.* But the corn plant was also a living entity with a body similar to man's in many respects, and the people built its flesh into their own. Hence corn was also their mother. Thus they knew their mother in two aspects which were often synonymous—as Mother Earth and the Corn Mother.**

In their wisdom they also knew their father in two aspects. He was

---

* See Part Two, Chapter 1.

** The personification of the same two identical aspects the Aztecs called Tonantzin, which means "Our Mother." The Spaniards later called her, in the Christian Church, the Virgin of Guadalupe, still the Christian patroness of all Indian America.

the Sun, the solar god of their universe. Not until he first appeared to them at the time of the red light, Tálawva, had they been fully firmed and formed. Yet his was but the face through which looked Taiowa, their Creator.

These universal entities were their real parents, their human parents being but the instruments through which their power was made manifest. In modern times their descendants remembered this.

When a child was born his Corn Mother * was placed beside him, where it was kept for twenty days, and during this period he was kept in darkness; for while his newborn body was of this world, he was still under the protection of his universal parents. If the child was born at night, four lines were painted with cornmeal on each of the four walls and ceiling early next morning. If he was born during the day, the lines were painted the following morning. The lines signified that a spiritual home, as well as a temporal home, had been prepared for him on earth.

On the first day the child was washed with water in which cedar had been brewed. Fine white cornmeal was then rubbed over his body and left all day. Next day the child was cleaned, and cedar ashes were rubbed over him to remove the hair and baby skin. This was repeated for three days. From the fifth day until the twentieth day, he was washed and rubbed with cornmeal for one day and covered with ashes for four days. Meanwhile the child's mother drank a little of the cedar water each day.

On the fifth day the hair of both child and mother was washed, and one cornmeal line was scraped off each wall and ceiling. The scrapings were then taken to the shrine where the umbilical cord had been deposited. Each fifth day thereafter another line of cornmeal was removed from walls and ceiling and taken to the shrine.

For nineteen days now the house had been kept in darkness so that the child had not seen any light. Early on the morning of the twentieth day, while it was still dark, all the aunts of the child arrived at the house, each carrying a Corn Mother in her right hand and each wishing to be the child's godmother. First the child was bathed. Then the mother, holding the child in her left arm, took up the Corn Mother that had lain beside the child and passed it over the child four times from the navel upward to the head. On the first pass she named the child; on the second she wished the child a long life; on the third, a healthy life. If the child was a boy, she wished him a productive life in his work on the fourth pass; if a girl, that she would become a good wife and mother.

Each of the aunts in turn did likewise, giving the child a clan name from the clan of either the mother or father of the aunt. The child was

* An ear of perfect corn whose tip ends in four full kernels.

then given back to its mother. The yellow light by then was showing in the east. The mother, holding the child in her left arm and the Corn Mother in her right hand, and accompanied by her own mother—the child's grandmother—left the house and walked toward the east. Then they stopped, facing east, and prayed silently, casting pinches of cornmeal toward the rising sun.

When the sun cleared the horizon the mother stepped forward, held up the child to the sun, and said, "Father Sun, this is your child." Again she said this, passing the Corn Mother over the child's body as when she had named him, wishing for him to grow so old he would to have lean on a crook for support, thus proving that he had obeyed the Creator's laws. The grandmother did the same thing when the mother had finished. Then both marked a cornmeal path toward the sun for this new life.

The child now belonged to his family and the earth. Mother and grandmother carried him back to the house, where his aunts were waiting. The village crier announced his birth, and a feast was held in his honor. For several years the child was called by the different names that were given him. The one that seemed most predominant became his name, and the aunt who gave it to him became his godmother. The Corn Mother remained his spiritual mother.

For seven or eight years he led the normal earthly life of a child. Then came his first initiation into a religious society, and he began to learn that, although he had human parents, his real parents were the universal entities who had created him through them—his Mother Earth, from whose flesh all are born, and his Father Sun, the solar god who gives life to all the universe. He began to learn, in brief, that he too had two aspects. He was a member of an earthly family and tribal clan, and he was a citizen of the great universe, to which he owed a growing allegiance as his understanding developed.

The First People, then, understood the mystery of their parenthood. In their pristine wisdom they also understood their own structure and functions—the nature of man himself.

The living body of man and the living body of the earth were constructed in the same way. Through each ran an axis, man's axis being the backbone, the vertebral column, which controlled the equilibrium of his movements and his functions. Along this axis were several vibratory centers which echoed the primordial sound of life throughout the universe or sounded a warning if anything went wrong.

The first of these in man lay at the top of the head. Here, when he was born, was the soft spot, *kópavi*, the "open door" through which he received his life and communicated with his Creator. For with every breath the soft spot moved up and down with a gentle vibration that was communicated to the Creator. At the time of the red light, Tálawva, the last phase of his creation, the soft spot was hardened and the door was closed. It remained closed until his death, opening then for his life to depart as it had come.

Just below it lay the second center, the organ that man learned to think with by himself, the thinking organ called the brain. Its earthly function enabled man to think about his actions and work on this earth. But the more he understood that his work and actions should conform to the plan of the Creator, the more clearly he understood that the real function of the thinking organ called the brain was carrying out the plan of all Creation.

The third center lay in the throat. It tied together those openings in his nose and mouth through which he received the breath of life and the vibratory organs that enabled him to give back his breath in sound. This primordial sound, as that coming from the vibratory centers of the body of earth, was attuned to the universal vibration of all Creation. New and diverse sounds were given forth by these vocal organs in the forms of speech and song, their secondary function for man on this earth. But as he came to understand its primary function, he used this center to speak and sing praises to the Creator.

The fourth center was the heart. It too was a vibrating organ, pulsing with the vibration of life itself. In his heart man felt the good of life, its sincere purpose. He was of One Heart. But there were those who permitted evil feelings to enter. They were said to be of Two Hearts.

The last of man's important centers lay under his navel, the organ some people now call the solar plexus. As this name signifies, it was the throne in man of the Creator himself. From it he directed all the functions of man.*

---

* Tibetan and Hindu mysticisms, like Hopi mysticism, postulate a similar series of centers of force or psychophysical centers in the human body, in which psychic forces and bodily functions merge into each other. These *cakras*, as described, coincide with those of the Hopis. They correspond roughly with the physical centers but they function psychically rather than solely physiologically.

The highest and most important center described by Eastern mysticism lies, like that of the Hopi, at the crown of the head. Known as the *Sahasrara-Padma*, the Thousand-Petaled Lotus, it is associated with the pituitary gland of the brain. It is so important as a seat of psychic consciousness that it is regarded as of a higher order than the other centers. As in the Hopi belief, it is the "door to the Creator," through which consciousness enters and leaves.

Below it, centered between the eyebrows, lies the *Ajna Cakra* which corresponds to the *medulla oblongata* of modern physiology, forming the basis of the brain and controlling the sympathetic nervous system.

The *Visuddha Cakra* is the throat center. It corresponds to the physical *plexus cervicus* of the cerebro-spinal system and is associated with the respiratory system.

Below these higher centers lie two more centers which are also identical with those of Hopi mysticism. The first of these is the heart center, the *Anahata Cakra*, corresponding to the heart plexus of the *sympaticus* which controls the heart and blood vessels.

Below this lies the *Manipura Cakra*, the Navel Lotus and the Hopi "Throne of the

The First People knew no sickness. Not until evil entered the world did persons get sick in the body or head. It was then that a medicine man, knowing how man was constructed, could tell what was wrong with a person by examining these centers. First he laid his hands on them: the top of the head, above the eyes, the throat, the chest, the belly. The hands of the medicine man were seer instruments; they could feel the vibrations from each center and tell him in which life ran strongest or weakest. Sometimes the trouble was just a bellyache from uncooked food or a cold in the head. But other times it came "from outside," drawn by the person's own evil thoughts, or from those of a Two Hearts. In this case the medicine man took out from his medicine pouch a small crystal about an inch and a half across, held it in the sun to get it in working order, and then looked through it at each of the centers. In this manner he could see what caused the trouble and often the very face of the Two Hearts person who had caused the illness. There was nothing magical about the crystal, medicine men always said. An ordinary person could see nothing when he looked through it; the crystal merely objectified the vision of the center which controlled his eyes and which the medicine man had developed for this very purpose. . . .

Thus the First People understood themselves. And this was the First World they lived upon. Its name was Tokpela, Endless Space. Its direction was west; its color *sikyangpu*, yellow; its mineral *sikyásvu*, gold. Significant upon it were *káto'ya*, the snake with a big head; *wisoko*, the fat-eating bird; and *muha*, the little four-leaved plant. On it the First People were pure and happy.

Creator," which corresponds to the *solar plexus* of the sympathetic system, controlling the conversion of inorganic into organic substances and the transmutation of organic substances into psychic energies.

Eastern mysticism describes two more centers below these which are not included in the Hopi series, the *Muladhara Cakra*, the Root Center at the base of the spinal column, corresponding to the *sacral plexus* and *plexus pelvis*, which stands for the whole realm of reproductive forces. The negative functions of rejection and elimination of elements that cannot be assimilated are associated with the *Svadhisthana Cakra*, lying just above it and corresponding to the *plexus epigastricus*. These two centers are often combined into one.

These seven centers are always enumerated in ascending order to that at the crown of the head, as they become successively less gross in nature and function. The four lower centers, it should be noted, represent successively the four gross elements that comprise man's body: earth, water, fire, and air. According to Hopi belief, the body of the earth and the body of man were both constructed of these same gross elements, in this same order. It may be briefly stated here that both Eastern and Hopi mysticism equate the bodies of man and the earth, and the centers within man with the seven universes.

Sources: The Tibetan series, translated and edited by W. Y. Evans-Wentz, London: Oxford University Press, 1927–1957; *The Serpent Power*, translated from the Sanskrit by Sir John Woodroffe, Madras: Ganesh & Co., 1953; and *Foundations of Tibetan Mysticism* by Lama Anagarika Govinda, New York: E. P. Dutton & Co., 1960.

2

Tokpa: The Second World

So the First People kept multiplying and spreading over the face of the land and were happy. Although they were of different colors and spoke different languages, they felt as one and understood one another without talking. It was the same with the birds and animals. They all suckled at the breast of their Mother Earth, who gave them her milk of grass, seeds, fruit, and corn, and they all felt as one, people and animals.

But gradually there were those who forgot the commands of Sótuknang and the Spider Woman to respect their Creator. More and more they used the vibratory centers of their bodies solely for earthly purposes, forgetting that their primary purpose was to carry out the plan of Creation.

There then came among them Lavaíhoya, the Talker. He came in the form of a bird called Mochni [bird like a mocking bird], and the more he kept talking the more he convinced them of the differences between them: the difference between people and animals, and the differences between the people themselves by reason of the colors of their skins, their speech, and belief in the plan of the Creator.

It was then that animals drew away from people. The guardian spirit of animals laid his hands on their hind legs just below the tail, making them become wild and scatter from the people in fear. You can see this slightly oily spot today on deer and antelope—on the sides of their back legs as they throw up their tails to run away.

In the same way, people began to divide and draw away from one another—those of different races and languages, then those who remembered the plan of Creation and those who did not.

There came among them a handsome one, Káto'ya, in the form of a snake with a big head. He led the people still farther away from one another and their pristine wisdom. They became suspicious of one another and accused one another wrongfully until they became fierce and warlike and began to fight one another.

All the time Mochni kept talking and Káto'ya became more beguiling. There was no rest, no peace.

But among all the people of different races and languages there were a few in every group who still lived by the laws of Creation. To them came Sótuknang. He came with the sound as of a mighty wind and suddenly appeared before them. He said, "I have observed this state of affairs. It is not good. It is so bad I talked to my Uncle, Taiowa, about it. We have decided this world must be destroyed and another one created so you people can start over again. You are the ones we have chosen."

They listened carefully to their instructions.

Said Sótuknang, "You will go to a certain place. Your *kópavi* [vibratory center on top of the head] will lead you. This inner wisdom will give you the sight to see a certain cloud, which you will follow by day, and a certain star, which you will follow by night. Take nothing with you. Your journey will not end until the cloud stops and the star stops."

So all over the world these chosen people suddenly disappeared from their homes and people and began following the cloud by day and the star by night. Many other people asked them where they were going and, when they were told, laughed at them. "We don't see any cloud or any star either!" they said. This was because they had lost the inner vision of the *kópavi* on the crown of their head; the door was closed to them. Still there were a very few who went along anyway because they believed the people who did see the cloud and the star. This was all right.

After many days and nights the first people arrived at the certain place. Soon others came and asked, "What are you doing here?" And they said, "We were told by Sótuknang to come here." The other people said, "We too were led here by the vapor and the star!" They were all happy together because they were of the same mind and understanding even though they were of different races and languages.

When the last ones arrived Sótuknang appeared. "Well, you are all here, you people I have chosen to save from the destruction of this world. Now come with me."

He led them to a big mound where the Ant People lived, stamped on the roof, and commanded the Ant People to open up their home. When an opening was made on top of the anthill, Sótuknang said to the people, "Now you will enter this Ant kiva, where you will be safe when I destroy the world. While you are here I want you to learn a lesson from these Ant People. They are industrious. They gather food in the summer for the winter. They keep cool when it is hot and warm when it is cool. They live peacefully with one another. They obey the plan of Creation."

So the people went down to live with the Ant People. When they were all safe and settled Taiowa commanded Sótuknang to destroy the world. Sótuknang destroyed it by fire because the Fire Clan had been its leaders. He rained fire upon it. He opened up the volcanoes. Fire came from above and below and all around until the earth, the waters, the air, all was one element, fire, and there was nothing left except the people safe inside the womb of the earth.

This was the end of Tokpela, the First World.

EMERGENCE TO THE SECOND WORLD

While this was going on the people lived happily underground with the Ant People. Their homes were just like the people's homes on the earth-surface being destroyed. There were rooms to live in and rooms where they stored their food. There was light to see by, too. The tiny bits of crystal in the sand of the anthill had absorbed the light of the sun, and by using the inner vision of the center behind their eyes they could see by its reflection very well.

Only one thing troubled them. The food began to run short. It had not taken Sótuknang long to destroy the world, nor would it take him long to create another one. But it was taking a long time for the First World to cool off before the Second World could be created. That was why the food was running short.

"Do not give us so much of the food you have worked so hard to gather and store," the people said.

"Yes, you are our guests," the Ant People told them. "What we have is yours also." So the Ant People continued to deprive themselves of food in order to supply their guests. Every day they tied their belts tighter and tighter. That is why ants today are so small around the waist.

Finally that which had been the First World cooled off. Sótuknang purified it. Then he began to create the Second World. He changed its form completely, putting land where the water was and water where the land had been, so the people upon their Emergence would have nothing to remind them of the previous wicked world.

When all was ready he came to the roof of the Ant kiva, stamped on it, and gave his call. Immediately the Chief of the Ant People went up to the opening and rolled back the *núta*. *"Yung-ai!* Come in! You are welcome!" he called.*

Sótuknang spoke first to the Ant People. "I am thanking you for doing your part in helping to save these people. It will always be remembered, this you have done. The time will come when another world will

---

* The *núta* is the straw thatch over the ladder-opening of modern Hopi kivas. This is the ritual procedure followed when a *kachina* enters a kiva.

be destroyed; and when wicked people know their last day on earth has come, they will sit by an anthill and cry for the ants to save them. Now, having fulfilled your duty, you may go forth to this Second World I have created and take your place as ants."

Then Sótuknang said to the people, "Make your Emergence now to this Second World I have created. It is not quite so beautful as the First World, but it is beautiful just the same. You will like it. So multiply and be happy. But remember your Creator and the laws he gave you. When I hear you singing joyful praises to him I will know you are my children, and you will be close to me in your hearts."

So the people emerged to the Second World. Its name was Tokpa (Dark Midnight). Its direction was south, its color blue, its mineral *qöchásiva,* silver. Chiefs upon it were *salavi,* the spruce; *kwáhu,* the eagle; and *kolíchiyaw,* the skunk.

It was a big land, and the people multiplied rapidly, spreading over it to all directions, even to the other side of the world. This did not matter, for they were so close together in spirit they could see and talk to each other from the center on top of the head. Because this door was still open, they felt close to Sótuknang and they sang joyful praises to the Creator, Taiowa.

They did not have the privilege of living with the animals, though, for the animals were wild and kept apart. Being separated from the animals, the people tended to their own affairs. They built homes, then villages and trails between them. They made things with their hands and stored food like the Ant People. Then they began to trade and barter with one another.

This was when the trouble started. Everything they needed was on this Second World, but they began to want more. More and more they traded for things they didn't need, and the more goods they got, the more they wanted. This was very serious. For they did not realize they were drawing away, step by step, from the good life given them. They just forgot to sing joyful praises to the Creator and soon began to sing praises for the goods they bartered and stored. Before long it happened as it had to happen. The people began to quarrel and fight, and then wars between villages began.

Still there were a few people in every village who sang the song of their Creation. But the wicked people laughed at them until they could sing it only in their hearts. Even so, Sótuknang heard it through their centers and the centers of the earth. Suddenly one day he appeared before them.

"Spider Woman tells me your thread is running out on this world," he said. "That is too bad. The Spider Clan was your leader, and you were making good progress until this state of affairs began. Now my Uncle, Taiowa, and I have decided we must do something about it. We are going to destroy this Second World just as soon as we put you people who still have the song in your hearts in a safe place."

So again, as on the First World, Sótuknang called on the Ant People to open up their underground world for the chosen people. When they were safely underground, Sótuknang commanded the twins, Pöqánghoya and Palöngawhoya, to leave their posts at the north and south ends of the world's axis, where they were stationed to keep the earth properly rotating.

The twins had hardly abandoned their stations when the world, with no one to control it, teetered off balance, spun around crazily, then rolled over twice. Mountains plunged into seas with a great splash, seas and lakes sloshed over the land; and as the world spun through cold and lifeless space it froze into solid ice.

This was the end of Tokpa, the Second World.

EMERGENCE TO THE THIRD WORLD

For many years all the elements that had comprised the Second World were frozen into a motionless and lifeless lump of ice. But the people were happy and warm with the Ant People in their underground world. They watched their food carefully, although the ants' waists became still smaller. They wove sashes and blankets together and told stories.

Eventully Sótuknang ordered Pöqánghoya and Palöngawhoya back to their stations at the poles of the world axis. With a great shudder and a splintering of ice the planet began rotating again. When it was revolving smoothly about its own axis and stately moving in its universal orbit, the ice began to melt and the world began to warm to life. Sótuknang set about creating the Third World: arranging earths and seas, planting mountains and plains with their proper coverings, and creating all forms of life.

When the earth was ready for occupancy, he came to the Ant kiva with the proper approach as before and said, "Open the door. It is time for you to come out."

Once again when the *núta* was rolled back he gave the people their instructions. "I have saved you so you can be planted again on this new Third World. But you must always remember the two things I am saying to you now. First, respect me and one another. And second, sing in harmony from the tops of the hills. When I do not hear you singing praises to your Creator I will know you have gone back to evil again."

So the people climbed up the ladder from the Ant kiva, making their Emergence to the Third World.

3

Kuskurza: The Third World

Its name was Kuskurza, its direction east, its color red. Chiefs upon it were the mineral *palásiva* (copper); the plant *piva*, tobacco; the bird *angwusi*, crow; and the animal *chöövio*, antelope.

Upon it once more the people spread out, multiplied, and continued their progress on the Road of Life. In the First World they had lived simply with the animals. In the Second World they had developed handicrafts, homes, and villages. Now in the Third World they multiplied in such numbers and advanced so rapidly that they created big cities, countries, a whole civilization. This made it difficult for them to conform to the plan of Creation and to sing praises to Taiowa and Sótuknang. More and more of them became wholly occupied with their own earthly plans.

Some of them, of course, retained the wisdom granted them upon their Emergence. With this wisdom they understood that the farther they proceeded on the Road of Life and the more they developed, the harder it was. That was why their world was destroyed every so often to give them a fresh start. They were especially concerned because so many people were using their reproductive power in wicked ways. There was one woman who was becoming known throughout the world for her wickedness in corrupting so many people. She even boasted that so many men were giving her turquoise necklaces for her favors she could wind them around a ladder that reached to the end of the world's axis. So the people with wisdom sang louder and longer their praises to the Creator from the tops of their hills.

The other people hardly heard them. Under the leadership of the Bow Clan they began to use their creative power in another evil and destructive way. Perhaps this was caused by that wicked woman. But some of them made a *pátuwvota* [shield made of hide] and with their creative power made it fly through the air. On this many of the people flew to a big city, attacked it, and returned so fast no one knew where they came from. Soon the people of many cities and countries were making *pátuwvotas* and flying on them to attack one another. So corruption and war came to the Third World as it had to the others.

This time Sótuknang came to Spider Woman and said, "There is no use waiting until the thread runs out this time. Something has to be done lest the people with the song in their hearts are corrupted and killed off too. It will be difficult, with all this destruction going on, for them to gather at the far end of the world I have designated. But I will help them. Then you will save them when I destroy this world with water."

"How shall I save them?" asked Spider Woman.

"When you get there look about you," commanded Sótuknang. "You will see these tall plants with hollow stems. Cut them down and put the people inside. Then I will tell you what to do next."

Spider Woman did as he instructed her. She cut down the hollow reeds; and as the people came to her, she put them inside with a little water and *hurúsuki* (white cornmeal dough) for food, and sealed them up. When all the people were thus taken care of, Sótuknang appeared.

"Now you get in to take care of them, and I will seal you up," he said. "Then I will destroy the world."

So he loosed the waters upon the earth. Waves higher than mountains rolled in upon the land. Continents broke asunder and sank beneath the seas. And still the rains fell, the waves rolled in.

The people sealed up in their hollow reeds heard the mighty rushing of the waters. They felt themselves tossed high in the air and dropping back to the water. Then all was quiet, and they knew they were floating. For a long, long time—so long a time that it seemed it would never end—they kept floating.

Finally their movement ceased. The Spider Woman unsealed their hollow reeds, took them by the tops of their heads, and pulled them out. "Bring out all the food that is left over," she commanded.

The people brought out their *hurúsuki;* it was still the same size, although they had been eating it all this time. Looking about them, they saw they were on a little piece of land that had been the top of one of their highest mountains. All else, as far as they could see, was water. This was all that remained of the Third World.

"There must be some dry land somewhere we can go to," they said. "Where is the new Fourth World that Sótuknang has created for us?" They sent many kinds of birds, one after another, to fly over the waters and find it. But they all came back tired out without having seen any sign of land. Next they planted a reed that grew high into the sky. Up it they climbed and stared over the surface of the waters. But they saw no sign of land.

Then Sótuknang appeared to Spider Woman and said, "You must continue traveling on. Your inner wisdom will guide you. The door at the top of your head is open."

So Spider Woman directed the people to make round, flat boats of the hollow reeds they had come in and to crawl inside. Again they entrusted themselves to the water and the inner wisdom to guide them. For a long time they drifted with the wind and the movement of the waters and came to another rocky island.

"It is bigger than the other one, but it is not big enough," they said, looking around them and thinking they heard a low rumbling noise.

"No. It is not big enough," said Spider Woman.

So the people kept traveling toward the rising sun in their reed boats. After awhile they said, "There is that low rumbling noise we heard. We must be coming to land again."

So it was. A big land, it seemed, with grass and trees and flowers beautiful to their weary eyes. On it they rested a long time. Some of the people wanted to stay, but Spider Woman said, "No. It is not the place. You must continue on."

Leaving their boats, they traveled by foot eastward across the island to the water's edge. Here they found growing some more of the hollow plants like reeds or bamboo, which they cut down. Directed by Spider Woman, they laid some of these in a row with another row on top of them in the opposite direction and tied them all together with vines and leaves. This made a raft big enough for one family or more. When enough rafts were made for all, Spider Woman directed them to make paddles.

"You will be going uphill from now on and you will have to make your own way. So Sótuknang told you: The farther you go, the harder it gets."

After long and weary traveling, still east and a little north, the people began to hear the low rumbling noise and saw land. One family and clan after another landed with joy. The land was long, wide, and beautiful. The earth was rich and flat, covered with trees and plants, seed-bearers and nut-bearers, providing lots of food. The people were happy and kept staying there year after year.

"No. This is not the Fourth World," Spider Woman kept telling them. "It is too easy and pleasant for you to live on, and you would soon fall into evil ways again. You must go on. Have we not told you the way becomes harder and longer?"

Reluctantly the people traveled eastward by foot across the island to the far shore. Again they made rafts and paddles. When they were ready to set forth Spider Woman said, "Now I have done all I am commanded to do for you. You must go on alone and find your own place of Emergence. Just keep your doors open, and your spirits will guide you."

"Thank you, Spider Woman, for all you have done for us," they said sadly. "We will remember what you have said."

Alone they set out, traveling east and a little north, paddling hard day and night for many days as if they were paddling uphill.

At last they saw land. It rose high above the waters, stretching from north to south as far as they could see. A great land, a mighty land, their inner wisdom told them. "The Fourth World!" they cried to each other.

As they got closer, its shores rose higher and higher into a steep wall of mountains. There seemed no place to land. "Let us go north. There we will find our Place of Emergence," said some. So they went north, but the mountains rose higher and steeper.

"No! Let us go south! There we will find our Place of Emergence!" cried others. So they turned south and traveled many days more. But here too the mountain wall reared higher.

Not knowing what to do, the people stopped paddling, opened the doors on top of their heads, and let themselves be guided. Almost immediately the water smoothed out, and they felt their rafts caught up in a gentle current. Before long they landed and joyfully jumped out upon a sandy shore. "The Fourth World!" they cried. "We have reached our Place of Emergence at last!"

Soon all the others arrived and when they were gathered together Sótuknang appeared before them. "Well, I see you are all here. That is good. This is the place I have prepared for you. Look now at the way you have come."

Looking to the west and the south, the people could see sticking out of the water the islands upon which they had rested.

"They are the footprints of your journey," continued Sótuknang, "the tops of the high mountains of the Third World, which I destroyed. Now watch."

As the people watched them, the closest one sank under the water, then the next, until all were gone, and they could see only water.

"See," said Sótuknang, "I have washed away even the footprints of your Emergence; the stepping-stones which I left for you. Down on the bottom of the seas lie all the proud cities, the flying *pátuwvotas*, and the worldly treasures corrupted with evil, and those people who found no time to sing praises to the Creator from the tops of their hills. But the day will come, if you preserve the memory and the meaning of your Emergence, when these stepping-stones will emerge again to prove the truth you speak."

This at last was the end of the Third World, Kuskurza [an ancient name for which there is no modern meaning].

4

Túwaqachi: The Fourth World

"I have something more to say before I leave you," Sótuknang told the people as they stood at their Place of Emergence on the shore of the present Fourth World. This is what he said:

"The name of this Fourth World is Túwaqachi, World Complete. You will find out why. It is not all beautiful and easy like the previous ones. It has height and depth, heat and cold, beauty and barrenness; it has everything for you to choose from. What you choose will determine if this time you can carry out the plan of Creation on it or whether it must in time be destroyed too. Now you will separate and go different ways to claim all the earth for the Creator. Each group of you will follow your own star until it stops. There you will settle. Now I must go. But you will have help from the proper deities, from your good spirits. Just keep your own doors open and always remember what I have told you. This is what I say."

Then he disappeared.

The people began to move slowly off the shore and into the land, when they heard the low rumbling noise again. Looking around, they saw a handsome man and asked, "Are you the one who has been making these noises we have heard?"

"Yes. I made them to help you find the way here. Do you not recognize me? My name is Másaw. I am the caretaker, the guardian and protector of this land."

The people recognized Másaw. He had been appointed head caretaker of the Third World, but, becoming a little self-important, he had lost his humility before the Creator. Being a spirit, he could not die, so Taiowa took his appointment away from him and made him the deity of death and the underworld. This job Below was not as pleasant as the one Above. Then when the Third World was destroyed, Taiowa decided to give him another chance, as he had the people, and appointed him to guard and protect this Fourth World as its caretaker.

He was the first being the people had met here, and they were very respectful to him. "Will you give us your permission to live on this land?" they asked.

"Yes, I will give you my permission as owner of the land."

"Will you be our leader?" the people then asked.

"No," replied Másaw. "A greater one than I has given you a plan to fulfill first. When the previous parts of the world were pushed underneath the water, this new land was pushed up in the middle to become the backbone of the earth. You are now standing on its *átvila* [west side slope]. But you have not yet made your migrations. You have not yet followed your stars to the place where you will meet and settle. This you must do before I can become your leader. But if you go back to evil ways again I will take over the earth from you, for I am its caretaker, guardian, and protector. To the north you will find cold and ice. That is the Back Door to this land, and those who may come through this Back Door will enter without my consent. So go now and claim the land with my permission."

When Másaw disappeared, the people divided into groups and clans to begin their migrations.

"May we meet again!" they all called back to one another.

This is how it all began on this, our present Fourth World. As we know, its name is Túwaqachi, World Complete, its direction north, its color *sikyangpu,* yellowish white. Chiefs upon it are the tree *kneumapee,* juniper; the bird *mongwau,* the owl; the animal *tohopko,* the mountain lion; and the mixed mineral *sikyápala.*

Where all the people went on their migrations to the ends of the earth and back, and what they have done to carry out the plan of Creation from this Place of Beginning to the present time, is to be told next by all the clans as they came in.

5

Commentary: The Symbol of the Emergence

The whole myth and meaning of the Emergence is expressed by one symbol known to the Hopis as the Mother Earth symbol. There are two forms, the square and the circular, as shown in Figure. 1.

Figure 1. Mother Earth symbol

There are one circular and five square symbols ranging from four to six inches in diameter carved on a rock just south of Oraibi, and one circular form about nine inches in diameter carved on a rock south of Shipaulovi.* A combination of the two forms is also carved on a wooden stick which is planted in front of the One Horn altar in the Kwani kiva at Walpi during the Wúwuchim ceremony.

The symbol is commonly known as Tápu'at [Mother and Child]. The square type represents spiritual rebirth from one world to the succeeding one, as symbolized by the Emergence itself. In this drawing the straight line emerging from the entrance is not connected with the maze. Its two ends symbolize the two stages of life—the unborn child within the

---

* Another is carved on the inside wall of an upper story of the ruin of Casa Grande near Florence, Arizona.

womb of Mother Earth and the child after it is born, the line symbolizing the umbilical cord and the path of Emergence. Turning the drawing so that the line stands vertical, at the top of the page, you will see that the lower end is embraced by the U-shaped arm of the maze. The inside lines represent the fetal membranes which enfold the child within the womb, and the outside lines the mother's arms which hold it later.

The circular type differs slightly in design and meaning. The center line at the entrance is directly connected with the maze, and the center of the cross it forms symbolizes the Sun Father, the giver of life. Within the maze, lines end at four points. All the lines and passages within the maze form the universal plan of the Creator which man must follow on his Road of Life; and the four points represent the cardinal or directional points embraced within this universal plan of life. "Double security" or rebirth to one who follows the plan is guaranteed, as shown by the same enfoldment of the child by the mother. The additional meaning this circular type offers is that it also symbolizes the concentric boundaries of the land traditionally claimed by the Hopis, who have secret shrines planted along them. During Wúwuchim and other ceremonies the priests make four circuits around the village to reclaim this earth ceremonially in accordance with the universal plan.

A structural parallel to this Mother and Child symbol is the kiva, itself the Earth Mother. The *sipápuni,* the small hole in the floor, represents the womb, the Place of Emergence from the preceding world; and the ladder leading out through the roof for another Emergence to the succeeding world is the umbilical cord. Enactment of the Emergence is given during Wúwuchim, when initiates undergo spiritual rebirth.

The symbol is said to have substantially the same meaning to other Indian tribes in North, Central, and South America. The Pimas call it the House of Teuhu, Teuhu being the gopher who bored the spiral hole up to the surface of the earth for the Emergence, thus being the Spirit of the Placenta. The Cunas in Panama assert that the cross in it is the Tree of Life, the umbilical cord and fetal membranes of the Earth Mother when she gave birth to her children.*

It is curious that the symbol has been long known throughout the world, being identical with the diagram of the Labyrinth of Daedalus which appeared on early Cretan coins.** The Labyrinth was said to have

---

* According to Dr. Clyde Keeler, Medical Geneticist of the Milledgeville, Georgia, State Hospital, who is making a study of its history and distribution.

** In addition to Dr. Keeler, the anthropologist Harold Sterling Gladwin, in *Men Out of Asia* (New York: McGraw-Hill, 1947), also states that the maze carved on the wall of Casa Grande is identical with the Minoan labyrinth shown on coins from Knossos, Crete, at a date of 200 B.C. Both of these men suggest that the symbol was introduced into prehistoric America by explorers from southern Asia.

been built by Daedalus in Crete to hide the Minotaur, the result of the unnatural union of Queen Pasiphaë with a sacrificial bull. The Egyptian ancestors of this Cretan labyrinth—especially the Osireion of Menes—were water labyrinths entered by boat and serving as burial places. Hence they were essentially maps of the wanderings of the soul in the afterlife until it found rest and rebirth at the Tree of Life in the center, and this religious meaning has adhered to the symbol during its spread throughout the world.

Although the basic meaning of the Hopi creation myth and the symbol which expresses it is subjective, we cannot ignore the literal interpretation—that the Hopis came to America from the west, crossing the sea on boats or rafts from one "steppingstone" or island to the next. A similar interpretation can be made of the myth of the ancient Quiché Maya, which relates that the waters parted and the tribes crossed on steppingstones placed in a row over the sand—"Stones in a Row, Sand under the Sea." *

The Hopis with this sacred tradition knock on the head the popular anthropological belief that the Hopi *sipápuni* or Place of Emergence was Grand Canyon, ninety miles west of Oraibi. The Hopis simply use the Colorado River as a symbol for the water to the west, and the precipitous wall of Grand Canyon to symbolize the mountainous wall extending throughout the Fourth World of America.

The tradition also refutes the popular theory that the Hopis, like all Indians, emigrated from Asia to America by way of the Bering Strait land bridge. Yet it gives no clue to the many rational questions long asked. From what ancient race of world mankind did the Hopis spring? What and where was the now submerged Third World of the Hopis? When did they emigrate to America?

Since the time of Plato there has persisted a belief in the antediluvian existence of such continents during past geologic periods. Certainly the land masses on this planet have not always held the same shape and location. Data obtained during the International Geophysical Year tend to prove that other continents did exist. Scientific credence is now given to the theory proposed by Alfred Wegener, a German geologist, that our present continents have broken away from greater land masses and are slowly drifting to ever-new positions on the face of the earth. Their movements are caused by convection currents set in motion by radioactivity in the center of the earth, making the earth a great gyroscope forever spinning at a fixed angle. This is a modern restatement of the Hopi view in which Pöqánghoya and Palöngawhoya personalize the

---

* *Popul Vuh, the Sacred Book of the Ancient Quiché Maya* (Norman, Okla.: University of Oklahoma Press, 1950).

opposite polarities of the great magnetic circuit which keeps the earth rotating and the land masses of its upper crust shifting. We now know that, with continental drifts, there are different directions at different times for north, magnetic north having once been in the middle of the Pacific and then in the Southwest of the United States. The Hopi creation myth parallels this finding in its assertion that the polar center of the earth shifted from the now vanished Third World to the Hopi homeland on this present Fourth World. Zoological and botanical evidence supports the geological with many examples of animal and plant life that were brought, as the Hopi creation myth asserts, from the previous "world."

Whether or not the Hopi creation myth is regarded as a record of prehistoric events, there is no question of the value of the esoteric mysticism it reveals, despite its superficial simplicity. Man is created perfect in the image of his Creator. Then after "closing the door," "falling from grace" into the uninhibited expression of his own human will, he begins his slow climb back upward. Within him are several psychophysical centers. At each successive stage of his evolution one of these comes into predominant play. Also for each stage there is created a world-body in the same order of development as his own body, for him to become manifest upon. When each succesive period of development concludes with catastrophic destruction to world and mankind, he passes on to the next. The four lower centers, as they successively descend in man, decrease in purity of consciousness and increase in grossness of physical function. In the fourth stage of development he reaches the lowest and mid-point of his journey. The Fourth World, the present one, is the full expression of man's ruthless materialism and imperialistic will; and man himself reflects the overriding gross appetites of the flesh. With this turn man rises upward, bringing into predominant function each of the higher centers. The door at the crown of the head then opens, and he merges into the wholeness of all Creation, whence he sprang. It is a Road of Life he has traveled by his own free will, exhausting every capacity for good or evil, that he may know himself at last as a finite part of infinity.

How appallingly simple it seems in this Hopi creation myth! Only its closest parallel, the Tantric teachings of Tibetan and Hindu mysticism, reveal in meticulous detail the profundity of its premise. As specific footnotes in this narrative suggest, they elucidate the functions of man's centers and describe in full the stages of mankind's development. Quite obviously we of the West view the psychical achievements of the East with a suspicious alarm comparable to that with which the East views our hydrogen bombs, interceptor missiles, and space rockets. Mysticism has its own dangers—from which the Hopis themselves have suffered acutely, as we shall see; and pragmatic Western science has bestowed immeasurable blessings upon all mankind. It is merely a matter of choosing different goals and the means of achieving them. The contrast of the two systems is mentioned here because this pathetically small and misunderstood minority group, the Hopis, are so strangely attuned to the precepts of another hemisphere rather than to the technological civilization engulfing them.

From the same mysticism the peoples of the Far East have created an empirical science, the Hopis a cosmic drama. The whole multi-world universe is its stage; the cataclysmic epochs of geological change provide the props; and its characters are the Hopis themselves, masked as all the races of mankind. This alone recommends our earnest attention. For seldom has any cast attempted to play simultaneously two different roles— that of the cosmic spirit of mankind and that of temporal man.

The characters have now emerged to the vast continental stage of this new Fourth World. Let us follow their wandering migrations.

PART TWO

THE LEGENDS:

Migrations of the Clans

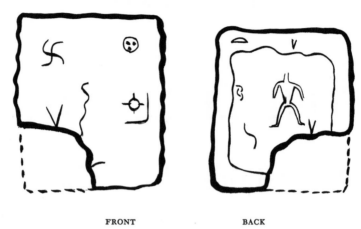

FRONT   BACK

Figure 2. Fire Clan tablet

FRONT   BACK

Figure 3. First Bear Clan tablet

1

The Four Migrations

Upon their Emergence to this new Fourth World, the people were told that they could not simply wander over it until they found a good place to settle down. Másaw, its guardian spirit, outlined the manner in which they were to make their migrations, how they were to recognize the place they were to settle permanently, and the way they were to live when they got there. All this was symbolically written on the four sacred tablets given them.

THE SACRED TABLETS

One of the tablets Másaw gave to the Fire Clan. As shown in Figure 2, it was very small, about four inches square, made of dark-colored stone, and with a piece broken off from one corner. On one side were marked several symbols, and on the other the figure of a man without a head. Másaw was the deity of the Fire Clan; and he gave them this tablet just before he turned his face from them, becoming invisible, so that they would have a record of his words.

This is what he said, as marked on the tablet: After the Fire Clan had migrated to their permanent home, the time would come when they would be overcome by a strange people. They would be forced to develop their land and lives according to the dictates of a new ruler, or else they would be treated as criminals and punished. But they were not to resist. They were to wait for the person who would deliver them.

This person was their lost white brother, Pahána, who would return to them with the missing corner piece of the tablet, deliver them from their persecutors, and work out with them a new and universal brotherhood of man. But, warned Másaw, if their leader accepted any other religion, he must assent to having his head cut off. This would dispel the evil and save his people.

The deity of the Bear Clan, Söqömhonaw, then gave three stone tablets to the Bear Clan, which was to be the leading clan on this Fourth World. The first of these (Figure 3) was small, with a strange pattern scratched on one side. This, he said, was the land pattern around the permanent village where they would settle, showing the land holdings to be apportioned to all clans supporting the religious ceremonies. On the other side of the tablet were marked two bear tracks, indicating that all the land beyond these religious land holdings was to be held in the custody of the Bear Clan, which was to reserve it for the animal kingdom upon which the people depended for food.

 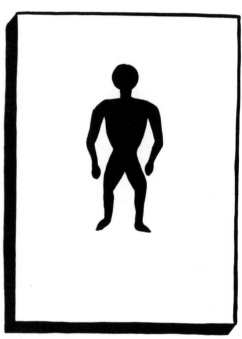

FRONT   BACK

Figures 4 and 5. Second Bear Clan tablet

The front of the larger, second Bear Clan tablet (Figure 4), was marked with a cornstalk in the center, around which were grouped several animals, all surrounded by two snakes; and in each corner was the figure of a man with one arm outstretched. The two snakes symbolized the two rivers that would mark the boundaries of the people's land.* The outstretched arms of the four men signified that they were religious leaders holding and claiming the land for their people; no one should cross the boundary rivers without permission, or destruction would come

---

* The Colorado and the Rio Grande Rivers.

upon them. The back of the tablet (Figure 5) showed a man who represented the leader or village chief, who was always to be of the Bear Clan.*

There was still a third tablet which Söqömhonaw gave to the Bear Clan. On the front (Figure 6) six men, arms folded across belly and crotch, were enclosed within the borders of two rectangles. The double-lined borders of the rectangles again symbolized the rivers enclosing the land; and the six men represented the leaders of the most important clans. Along the left side, whose edge was notched with tiny cuts, were

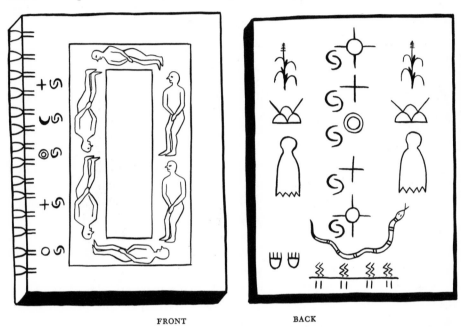

FRONT   BACK

Figures 6 and 7. Third Bear Clan tablet

marked sun, moon, stars, and the *nakwách* symbol of brotherhood. The back (Figure 7) was covered with a maze of symbols: corn, cloud, sun, moon, star, water, snake, *nakwách*, spirit of the Creator, and bear tracks.**

---

* There is currently some confusion about this figure. Some informants state that the man is headless, prophesying, like the Fire Clan tablet, that a time would come when the leader would sacrifice himself by having his head cut off in order to save his people.

** This third Bear Clan tablet was shown to the writer in December 1960 by John Lansa's wife, Myna, of the Parrot Clan, in Oraibi, who now has it in custody. The tablet was approximately 10 inches long, 8 inches wide, and 1½ inches thick. The stone resembled a dull gray marble with intrusive blotches of rose. It was very heavy, weighing about 8 pounds. The markings on it were as described. There was no means of estimating how old it or the markings were.

All the tablets are said to be still in the possession of the Hopis, although some of them have disappeared and are not to be seen. They have figured importantly throughout the history of Hopi dealings with other tribes and the United States Government, and are of great significance at the present time.

The use made of them, the manner of the disappearance of some of them, and their probable location at present, are related in Part Four, Chapter 6.

THE MAGIC WATER JAR

To each clan Másaw then gave a small water jar. In the years to come, he said, they would be slowly migrating over the earth, and many times there would be no water where they settled. They were then to plant this jar in the ground and, thereafter, for as long as they remained there, water would keep flowing out of this *pá'uipi* [Water Planted place].

"One certain person," went on Másaw, "must be ordained to carry this water jar for the whole clan. He must be a holy person whose life is perfect in every way. Four days before you are ready to move on, this water carrier must go without salt and he must pray. Then he will carry the jar until you arrive at the next stop on your migrations. For four days more he will pray and fast and go without sleep before planting the jar again. Then again the water will start flowing, and he may take up his normal life."

Másaw now instructed them what to do if the jar should be broken or should need to be replaced.

"You must go through a purification ceremony for four days. Then a woman who belongs to the same family as the water carrier must gather clay, shape and fire a new jar. The water carrier or a young unmarried man of perfect character will be given the jar and an eagle feather to carry in his left hand and the wing tip of an eagle to carry in his right hand. He must go to the largest body of water, preferably the ocean. He will go by that power which you still possess.

"At the ocean shore he will kneel, place his prayer feather at the water's edge, and draw a line with cornmeal in the direction of his people. When the wave recedes and little bubbles appear in the sand where the *paváwkyaiva* (water dogs) are, he must dig them out with the wing tip of his eagle and put them in his jar. After this he will put in the seaweed, the *páwisavi* (water mucous or slime), a tiny sea shell, some sand from the ocean floor, and the *páchayanpi* (water sifter) which skates on the surface. Finally he will put in the jar some water from the ocean itself.

"Thus when the jar is planted on a high mountain or in a sandy desert or near a village where there is no water, the materials in the jar will draw water from the distant ocean to supply you without end. The time will come when the villages you establish during your migrations will fall into ruins. Other people will wonder why they were built in such inhospitable regions where there is no water for miles around. They will not know about this magic water jar, because they will not know of the power and prayer behind it."

THE FOUR MIGRATIONS

And now before Másaw turned his face from them and became invisible, he explained that every clan must make four directional migrations before they all arrived at their common, permanent home. They must go to the ends of the land—west, south, east, and north—to the farthest *páso* (where the land meets the sea) in each direction. Only when the clans had completed these four movements, rounds, or steps of their migration could they come together again, forming the pattern of the Creator's universal plan.

That is the way it was. Some clans started to the south, others to the north, retraced their routes to turn east and west, and then back again. All their routes formed a great cross whose center, Túwanasavi [Center of the Universe], lay in what is now the Hopi country in the southwestern part of the United States, and whose arms reached to the four directional *pásos*. As they turned at each of these extremities they formed of this great cross a swastika, either clockwise or counter-clockwise, corresponding to the movement of the earth or of the sun. And then when their migrations slowed as they reached their permanent home, they formed spirals and circles, ever growing smaller. All these patterns formed by their four migrations are the basic motifs of the symbols still found today in their pottery and basketware, on their *kachina* rattles and altar boards.

Often one clan would come upon the ruins of a village built by a preceding clan and find on the mound broken pieces of pottery circling to the right or to the left, indicating which way the clan had gone. Throughout the continent these countless ruins and mounds covered with broken pottery are still being discovered. They constitute what the people call now their title to the land. Everywhere, too, the clans carved on rocks their signatures, pictographs and petroglyphs which identified them, revealed what round of their migration they were on, and related the history of the village.

Still the migrations continued. Some clans forgot in time the commands of Másaw, settling in tropical climates where life was easy, and developing beautiful cities of stone that were to decay and crumble into ruin. Other clans did not complete all four of their migrations before settling in their permanent home, and hence lost their religious power and standing. Still others persisted, keeping open the doors on top of their heads. These were the ones who finally realized the purpose and the meaning of their four migrations.

For these migrations were themselves purification ceremonies, weeding out through generations all the latent evil brought from the previous

Third World. Man could not succumb to the comfort and luxury given him by indulgent surroundings, for then he lost the need to rely upon the Creator. Nor should he be frightened even by the polar extremities of the earth, for there he learned that the power given him by the Creator would still sustain him. So, by traveling to all the farthest extremities of the land during their four migrations, these chosen people finally came to settle on the vast arid plateau that stretches between the Colorado and Rio Grande Rivers.

Many other people today wonder why these people chose an area devoid of running water to irrigate their sparse crops. The Hopi people know that they were led here so that they would have to depend upon the scanty rainfall which they must evoke with their power and prayer, and so preserve always that knowledge and faith in the supremacy of their Creator who had brought them to this Fourth World after they had failed in three previous worlds.

This, they say, is their supreme title to this land, which no secular power can refute.

2

North to the Back Door

Hay-ya, ha-ya, mel-lo . . . .

So the people began their migrations, climbing up a high mountain. They were accompanied by two insect people resembling the katydid or locust, the *máhu* [insect which has the heat power]. On top they met a great bird, the eagle. One of the *máhus,* acting as a spokesman for the people, asked the eagle, "Have you been living here very long?"

"Yes," replied the eagle, "since the creation of this Fourth World."

"We have traveled a long way to reach this new land," said the *máhu.* "Will you permit us to live here with you?"

"Perhaps," answered the eagle. "But I must test you first." Drawing out one of the arrows he was holding in his claws, he ordered the two *máhus* to step closer. To one he said, "I am going to poke this arrow into your eyes. If you do not close them, you and all the people who follow you may remain here."

Whereupon he poked the point of the arrow so close to the *máhu's* eye it almost touched, but the *máhu* did not even blink. "You are a people of great strength," observed the eagle. "But the second test is much harder and I don't believe you will pass it."

"We are ready for the second test," said the two *máhus.*

The eagle pulled out a bow, cocked an arrow, and shot the first *máhu* through the body. The *máhu,* with the arrow sticking out one side of him, lifted the flute he had brought with him and began to play a sweet and tender melody. "Well!" said the eagle. "You have more power than I thought!" So he shot the other *máhu* with a second arrow.

The two *máhus,* both pierced with arrows, played their flutes still more tenderly and sweetly, producing a soothing vibration and an uplift of spirit which healed their pierced bodies.

The eagle, of course, then gave the people permission to occupy the land, saying, "Now that you have stood both tests you may use my feather any time you want to talk to our Father Sun, the Creator, and I will deliver your message because I am the conqueror of air and master of height. I am the only one who has the power of space above, for I represent the loftiness of the spirit and can deliver your prayers to the Creator."

Ever since then the people have used the feathers of an eagle for their prayer-feathers or *páhos,* and sing to a sick child, knowing that the sweet power of music will help to heal him. The locust *máhu* is known as the Humpbacked Flute Player, the *kachina* named Kókopilau, because he looked like wood [*koko*—wood; *pilau*—hump] (Figure 8). In the hump on his back he carried seeds of plants and flowers,* and with the music of his flute he created warmth. When the people moved off on their migrations over the continent they carved pictographs of him on rocks all the way from the tip of South America up to Canada, and it was for these two *máhus* that the Blue Flute and Gray Flute clans and societies were named.

Blue Flute   Gray Flute   Spirit or *kachina*

Figure 8. Kókopilau

Having obtained the eagle's permission to occupy the land,** the people now divided into four groups, each going a different direction. With those going to the north was the Blue Flute Clan, accompanied by one of the two *máhus.* Every so often this Humpbacked Flute Player would stop and scatter seeds from the hump on his back. Then he would march on, playing his flute and singing a song. His song is still remembered, but the words are so ancient that nobody knows what they mean.

---

* The Kókopilau or Kokopeli *kachina* is often made with a long penis to symbolize the seeds of human reproduction also.

** The national emblems of the United States and Mexico both contain the eagle.

The song goes like this:

Ki-tana-po, ki-tana-po, ki-tana-po, ki-tana-PO!
Ai-na, ki-na-weh, ki-na-weh
Chi-li li-cha, chi-li li-cha
Don-ka-va-ki, mas-i-ki-va-ki
Ki-ve, ki-ve-na-meh
HOPET!

The Spider Woman led this group going northward. It comprised five clans: the Spider Clan named after her, the Blue Flute Clan, the Ghost or Fire Clan, the Snake Clan, and the Sun Clan. They traveled slowly up the length of the continent on the west side of the mountain wall. Going was easy in the tropical country, where it was warm and there were plenty of fruits and vegetables to eat. Then the land became drier and colder. Sometimes they stopped for a year or more to plant and harvest some of the corn they carried with them. They would make homes by digging holes in the ground and roofing them with brush and poles—which people now describe as "pit houses." Then the star which was guiding them moved on, and they packed up again to follow it. The remains of these pit houses and the rock writings they made on their way are the "flags" and "footprints" marking their long journey.

Northward and still northward the star kept leading them until they came to a land of perpetual snow and ice. At night they burrowed into snowbanks and kept warm with the power of heat they were able to evoke. For water they planted the little jar of water they always carried; it became a spring which gushed forth water here just as it had in the dry deserts they had crossed to the south. They also carried a little bowl of earth. Into this they planted seeds of corn and melon; and as they sang over it, the seeds grew into plants and the plants bore corn and melons. Such were the powers they possessed because they were still pristinely pure on this new Fourth World.

At last they reached what is now the Arctic Circle. "It is as far as we can go," they said to one another. "The way is blocked by a mountain of snow, a sea of ice. Clearly this is the Back Door of this Fourth World, which Sótuknang said was closed to us."

Spider Woman, however, urged them to go on. "You have the magic powers given you. Use them. Melt this mountain of snow, this sea of ice."

The Spider Clan agreed at once, persuading the others to pool their magic powers to melt the closed Back Door—the Blue Flute Clan using the Humpbacked Flute Player to play his flute to bring tropical warmth;

the Fire Clan summoning the fire deep inside the earth; the Sun Clan invoking the heat of the sun; and the Snake Clan trying to crack the mountain of snow and the sea of ice with mighty vibrations, the snake having the power to utilize the vibrations sent along the world's axis by the two Twins because he lives deep underground. Four times they tried, but failed to break through the closed Back Door.

Sótuknang then appeared to Spider Woman and said sternly, "If my Uncle, the Creator, and I, his Nephew, had allowed you to open this Back Door, disaster would have come. The melted mountain of snow and sea of ice would have flooded this new Fourth World and forever changed its shape from the way we ordained it to be. You have done wrong. Because you helped to create these people and have aided them in all their Emergences, we have allowed you to remain young and beautiful. But now because you have disobeyed our wishes I am going to let your own thread run out. We are not going to cut it off. Just let it run out until you are an ugly old woman. Now something more. Because the Spider Clan named after you also encouraged the people to use their sacred powers wrongly, I ordain that the Spider Clan hereafter will breed wickedness and evil. That is what I had to say. Now I have said it."

So all the clans turned back from the north and returned southward along the east side of the wall of mountains until they came to Pisísvaiyu, now known as the Colorado River. The Spider Clan, separating from the others, then continued on south to the place from which they all had started. The other four clans, the Fire, Blue Flute, Snake, and Sun Clans, turned eastward and traveled until they came to the Atlantic Ocean. Then they turned back and began their slow migration to the western limit of the land.

THE SERPENT MOUND

On the great prairies they stopped again. The Snake Clan especially wanted to leave its footprint here, but there were no cliffs on which to mark the picture writing. So the people left their signature in the shape of a great mound of earth resembling a snake (Figure 9).

Some contemporary Hopis believe that the great Serpent Mound near Louden, Ohio, may have been constructed by their ancestors. The largest serpent effigy in the world, it is an earth embankment nearly one-fourth of a mile long, twenty feet wide, and five feet high, grown over with grass that has prevented it from erosion. It represents a serpent whose body is extended in seven deep curves. Its jaws are open, the walls forming them being about sixty feet long and seventeen feet wide. Between them is a large oval mound, commonly believed to be an egg which the serpent is swallowing.

Whatever its origin may be, a member of the Snake Clan interpreted the meaning of the serpent mound, according to Hopi tradition, from a photograph and drawing of it. As there was no rock in the area, the village where the people lived, the burial mounds nearby, and the serpent mound itself were made of plastered mud—*chochmo* [mud mound]. The oval mound represents the village. It was placed within the jaws of the snake to show that it was protected by the snake's power. Its extension, sticking out in front, shows that the snake has the power to draw light. The two small round mounds on each side of his head represent his eyes

Figure 9. Serpent Mound

as well as the circular markings on his body. The great length of his body indicates that he is the longest snake known to the people. He faces west because the people were traveling west when they built this mound, although he is the guardian snake of the east and would continue to protect them until they reached the wall of mountains separating east from west. His name is Tókchi'i [Guardian of the East].*

There are five other snakes of the directions. Pálulukang [Water Snake] is the Guardian of the South, who protected the people when they were in that area.** Masichu'a [Gray Horned Snake] is the snake of the north. Káto'ya [Black Snake] is the guardian of the west and night. Táwataho [Sun, Flying, or Whip Snake] governs the Above, being able to fly and never touching the ground. Tuwáchu'a [Sand or Sidewinder] is the snake of the Below, from whom we receive the vibrations of the earth and the knowledge of the movement of things that inhabit the earth.***

---

* There is a shrine for him southeast of Oraibi called Kouknupovi, and it is said a similar shrine was placed for him on the Atlantic Coast.

** This is the snake who in puppet form dances in the kiva during the Night Kachina Dances.

*** Of these six directional snakes only those of the Below, North, and West are used during the Snake-Antelope Ceremony, these being the only ones whose power man can control.

Continuing their migrations west, the people crossed the wall of mountains that separate east from west, being the axis of the continent, along which the Twins at either end send out their vibrations. They were now under the protection of Káto'ya. Eventually they reached the shore of the sea to the west, turned back east again, and recrossed the mountains. Their movement became progressively slower as the star began to guide them in a great circle over a high, dry plateau whose center is now known as the Four Corners, being the only point in the United States where four States touch. Here it stopped over Chaco Canyon in northwestern New Mexico.

THE RACE TRACKS AT CHACO CANYON

Chaco Canyon, now a national monument, contains the finest remains of an ancient civilization north of Mexico. In the canyon, eight miles long and two miles wide, are found eighteen major ruins, including Pueblo Bonito, Chettro Ketl, and Pueblo del Arroyo, and hundreds of smaller sites. Pueblo Bonito is the largest single ruin yet found. Covering three acres, it was five stories high and contained thirty-two kivas and eight hundred rooms, housing a population of twelve hundred people. Built more than a thousand years ago, the walls of this great pueblo were constructed of alternate layers of large rocks and small stones fitted together so tightly that no mortar was necessary.

This great crossroads of all clans figures so prominently in the migration legends that we made two trips to Chaco Canyon, taking Hopi informants with us. John Lansa on the last trip made some interesting discoveries.

Hundreds of artifacts had been found during the excavations: stone tools, bone implements, baskets, pottery, cotton cloth, and turquoise beads. Among these were seashells, the skeletons of fourteen macaws in one room, and the feathers of tropical birds commonly believed to have been brought in over ancient trade routes. According to our Hopi friends, they confirm the migration route of the Flute Clan, which still uses the heads of macaws and feathers of tropical birds in the Flute Ceremony, and of the Snake Clan, which uses seashells. Displayed in the museum were two other artifacts identified as a neckpiece and an inlaid earring, the túoinaka (stacked-up-corn ear jewel), worn by the Flute Maidens in the Flute Ceremony. In addition to these, hundreds of fragments were excavated at Tetra Chetl and taken to the repository in Globe, Arizona, for restoration and assembly. Among these we later identified fragments

of wooden parrots such as are still used on the altar of the Blue Flute
Society.

At Chaco one whole cliff wall was covered with pictographs, including a row of Kokopilau figures and the signatures of many other
clans: the Snake, Sun, Bear, Sand, Coyote, Lizard, Eagle, Water, Parrot,
Spider, and Bow. John was sure that there were certain shrines nearby.
Park officials knew of none but graciously took us in a four-wheel-drive
truck up to the high plateau behind unexcavated Pueblo Alto and overlooking Esgavada Wash to the north. After an hour's patient search, John
found one shrine. Although he had never been there before, he sighted
from this and located a second—a pile of rocks under which he dug out
three circular stones. From these two shrines he sighted the location of
a third across the wash.

These three shrines,* he told us later, marked the courses of three
race tracks. The one to the west he believed had been used by the Flute
Society during the Flute Ceremony. Ceremonial races are still held during
the Flute and Snake-Antelope Ceremonies—the only Hopi ceremonies
which include races. The *pohoki* to the east, where the three circular
stones were found, was a shrine of the sun; the three stones symbolizing
the three previous worlds to which life was imparted by the sun. It was
the southern terminus of a long race track that extended northward to
the sun temple at Mesa Verde, some three or four days' travel by foot; a
faintly discernible trail is still visible by plane.

A feature of contemporary Flute and Snake races is the small jar of
sacred water which, captured by the winning runner from the priest
carrying it, brings rain to his family's fields.** According to tradition the
same ritual was followed here at Chaco for many years. Then as more
and more clans came in, building up the vast pueblos and creating rivalry
between them as tillable land became more scarce, the races deteriorated
into mere sporting events held by competing clans and pueblos. As a
result of this, rain became more and more scarce and the springs began
to dry up. A secret meeting of the two branches of the Flute Clan was
now called. The dominant Blue Flute group admitted it had used its
power wrongly in attempting to melt the Back Door to the continent and
that its ceremonies here were being corrupted. Accordingly it gave up
its leadership to the Gray Flute Clan, whose leaders ordered both groups
to leave Chaco to resume their migrations.

Behind them follow the Snake, Fire, and Sun Clans. South of Chaco
Canyon the Flute Clan separated from the others, traveling to Suyátupovi

---

* *Pohoki* (prayer standing house), also known as *tútuskya* (shrine in open).
** As described in Part Three.

(Where the Soil is Soft), now known as Canyon de Chelly. After several years they went westward to the Colorado River, south, and then east again to settle at Pavi'ovi. For a while they lived at Awatovi but could not get along with the people in this big village. So they took up their march to establish a new village, Ötöpsikvi (Valley of the Strong Plant), now a ruin in Canyon Diablo.

All this time they had been without an altar, conducting their ceremonies only with their *tiponi* or clan fetish. Here they built a new altar like the one they had been forced to leave behind at Chaco Canyon. The priests carved the wooden *kyaro* [parrot] with great care, for the feathers of this bird bring the warmth necessary for germination. The clan then moved to Shongopovi before eventually settling in Oraibi.

BETATAKIN AND KEET SEEL

Some people say that the Snake, Fire, and Sun Clans also went to Canyon de Chelly before they parted from the Flute Clan. At any rate, they soon migrated west to a wild and beautiful region marked by great arched caves in the high cliff walls. Here at Kawéstima [North Village] each of the three clans established a village of its own.

The village to the south, Betatakin, is situated down in a gloomy box canyon a 1½-mile walk from the top of the canyon. It is built in a huge cave whose arch rises 236 feet high in the 500-foot wall of a red sandstone cliff, and it contains nearly 150 rooms. It was built by the Fire Clan. In the rock writings nearby are two interesting figures, among others (Figures 10a and 10b).

The man in Figure 10a is said to be Taknokwunu, the spirit who controls the weather. It is easy to see why his figure with the rainbow stripes inside the shield was marked on the wall, for Figure 10b, with three quadrants painted red, shows that three-fourths of the surrounding area had dried up for lack of rain. This seems substantiated by tree-ring dating, which indicates that Betatakin was occupied between 1242 and 1300, embracing the period of the Long Drought. The four handprints to the left of Figure 10a show that the Fire Clan had completed its four-directional migration and was on its way to Oraibi.

For centuries the Fire Clan always looked back on Betatakin as its ancestral home. After the disastrous split of 1906 at Oraibi when one quarreling faction moved out, it was with the intention of returning to Betatakin. Even today some dissidents in Hotevilla talk of going back to Betatakin, though it is now under government control.

The village to the north, an 11-mile horseback ride from Betatakin, is the largest cliff pueblo in Arizona, containing more than 160 rooms. It is equally spectacular, lying in a similar large cave. Its name is Keet Seel,* and it was built by the Spider Clan.

The third village, built by the Snake Clan, is now known as Inscription House; it lies 30 miles west and contains about 75 rooms.

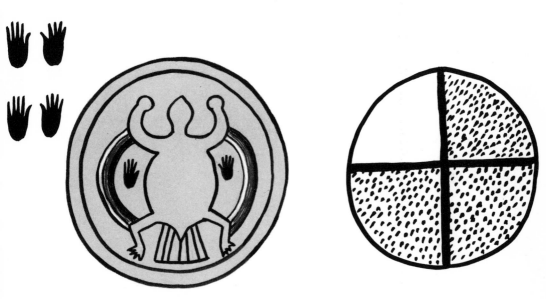

Figure 10a. Figure 10b.

Rock writings near Betatakin

It is ironic that all Kawéstima, called "North Village" because it lay north of Oraibi, now comprises the Navajo National Monument; and the builders of its three villages—ancestors of today's Hopi Snake, Fire, and Sun Clans—are known only as Anasazi, a Navajo name for the "Ancient Ones" who preceded them. There is nothing at all Navajo about the villages and their traditions.

Abandoning these spectacular villages, the three clans moved south to build a new village on a point above present-day Moencopi. The Spider and Snake Clans carved markings on a stone near the spring. About 1870 a Mormon named Ashie cut out the portion of the rock containing the markings and mounted it over the doorway of the home which had just been built by Tuvi, for whom Tuba City is named. Here it was seen for years.

---

* Or Kiet Siel, which in Navajo means "broken pottery." It was abandoned in 1286 in a peaceful, orderly withdrawal after many rooms had been carefully sealed.

For a long while the Fire Clan remained near Moencopi. The Snake Clan moved down along the Little Colorado, establishing a new village at Móngpatuiqa [Owl Point Water]. The Spider Clan traveled along Moencopi Wash to Talastema [Praise of Pollen], now known as Blue Canyon, where they built a village whose ruins are still visible. The clan then migrated to build a new village at Keleva [Sparrow Hawk Shrine].

Finally, after centuries of migration, all three clans moved to Oraibi, camping below the cliffs next to the Kachina Clan until they were accepted in the village.

3

The Badger and the Sacred Spruce

The Badger Clan is one of the four most important Hopi clans. It is custodian of the sacred spruce, the most powerfully magnetic of all trees. During Niman Kachina, when a member of each of the four clans takes position about the kiva to represent one of the four cardinal directions, it is a Badger who stands to the north. Yet the story of the Badger Clan begins far down in the tropical south.

A number of clans led by the Bear Clan began their migrations by going southward to the land's end. After reaching the *páso* at the tip of South America, the groups separated on their way back, some deciding to go east and others west. When they were in the warm country a small girl in one group became ill. No one could make her well. So the oldest member, the *wu'ya,* went into the forest to seek the wisdom or power that might cure her. Following a strange track, he came upon a stranger.

"Yes. These are my tracks," said the stranger. "I am Honani, the Badger. How can I help you?"

The old man related the trouble. Honani promptly dug up a herb, telling him to take it home, boil it, and give the child the liquid to drink, which would cure her. Then he showed the old man more herbs and plants and trees to cure all the illnesses that might beset his people. "Pray also and I will help you," he said. "Medicine must always be accompanied by prayer and good thoughts."

After returning to his people, the old man prepared the herb as he had been directed, and the little girl was cured. "In return for the help and knowledge this spiritual being has given us, let us from now on be known as the Badger Clan," he said.

They continued their migration northward, stopping near Palátkwapi [Red House or Red Land, believed to be somewhere in Mexico]. Here they found evidences of other clans who had preceded them and hurried on. But somewhere north of there they had to stop for some time to lay in a supply of food. This place they called Honinyaha [Badger Earth Dam]. Resuming their travel, they reached the Rio Grande River and moved northward up the west bank until they found suitable land for planting and harvesting two crops. Their next stop was near Chi-yá-wi-pa [Narrow Hair Bang People, now known as the pueblo of San Felipe]. Still moving northward, they reached mountains so cold and high it was impossible to live there, turned back toward Toko'navi [Hard Rock Mountain, now known as Navajo Mountain], and proceeded westward to the shore of the Pacific.

Here they planted their shrine and stayed four days. Then they moved eastward across the continent to the Atlantic Coast, where they planted another shrine and watched the sun come up four times. Returning westward, but north of their eastward route, they slowed as they reached the mountains in what is now southern Colorado.

During all these years and generations the Badger Clan had been increasing. There were now separate groups calling themselves the Brown Badger, Gray Badger, and Black Badger Clans. The latter, the original clan, still held the leadership, but its leader or *wu'ya* was getting old and weak.

"We have completed our migrations to the four ends of the earth," he told his people. "Clearly it is time for us to settle down, build a village, and await the sign that will direct us to our final destination."

The leaders of the Brown and the Gray Badger Clans grumbled, but they obeyed. They found a beautiful canyon and a huge cave in the cliff in which they began to build houses and storerooms and kivas—a whole village. It kept getting bigger and bigger, for the Badger Clan was soon joined by the Butterfly Clan and other clans which also wandered in from their own migrations. But also dissension kept increasing until the rains no longer came and the snow stopped falling. The corn withered. Game vanished. The people began to suffer hunger.

Then the old *wu'ya* called the people together. "Clearly it is time to leave. Your quarreling has brought misfortune. Now you must go your separate ways," he told them sadly. "I myself am too old and feeble to go with you. Listen now to my last instructions. Leave me here. But in four years come back and look for me in the important places—the kivas, the shrines, the springs. If I have been to blame in any way for the quarreling and the misfortune which besets you, you will not find me, my body, or any sign of me. But if my heart has been true you will find a sign and you will know what to do. Go now and remember what I have told you."

So all the people abandoned the village, separated, and continued their migrations. But in four years the Badger Clan leaders returned as they had been directed. The old *wu'ya* had left a sign which all could read clearly. His heart had been pure, his power great. In his dying hour he had gone down to the spring below the village and transformed himself into a spruce tree. There it was for all to see. The dried-up spring was gushing forth again, and at the water's edge was a small spruce tree four years old.

From that time on the people perpetuated his memory. Every year at the time of Niman Kachina they sent a messenger to plant prayer feathers at the spruce, asking the spirit of the old *wu'ya* to participate in their ceremony, and they brought back spruce in token of his assent. Salavi [Spruce] was his name, and Salapa was the name of the village where they had left him.

"I do not know just where this Salapa is: I have never been there," said John Lansa of the Badger Clan, Old Oraibi. "I know only that it is somewhere to the northeast, too far to go nowadays. For years, ever since I can remember, we have taken our prayer feathers to a Salapa just outside Oraibi to the northeast. This is not the real Salapa. It is only a shrine to symbolize it. No, I do not know where the ancient village of Salapa is, with its spring and the spruce which grew out of the body of Salavi."

How strange is the thing we call coincidence. From my boyhood days in Colorado I had been fascinated by the spectacular ruins in the canyons of Mesa Verde in southwestern Colorado, particularly by the mysterious structure ambiguously called the Sun Temple, whose function has never been known; and the great cliff-dwelling of 114 rooms and 8 kivas built in a large cave, which Richard Wetherill and Baron Gustaf Nordenskiold in 1891 named Spruce Tree House after a large spruce nearby, estimated to be at least two hundred years old.

Could it be possible that this was the ancient Salapa, curiously re-named in our language Spruce Tree House? And was the great spruce still standing near a spring below it the spruce, or its descendant, said to have grown out of the body of Salivi? What could account for such a preposterous coincidence?

I asked White Bear to take John Lansa, who had never been there, up to see if he could find anything to substantiate the ancient legend.* It was all there on the wall of the cliff at Pictograph Point, down the canyon from Spruce Tree House. A maze of rock writing, as shown in Figure 11, confirming the oral traditions of his own Badger Clan. Details and inter-pretations of a few of the pictographs follow.

---

* A second trip with other Hopi informants cleared up the mystery of Sun Temple whose meaning is explained in Chapter 9.

Figure 11. Rock Writing at Pictograph Point

Figure 12 shows the old *wu'ya,* Salavi, leader of the Badger Clan. His arms are upraised because he is an important, holy man and has nothing

Figure 12. Salavi   Figure 13. Stylized butterfly

to hide. He keeps good thoughts and is on guard against evil, day and night, as shown by the symbols of the sun and moon over his head.

Figure 13 is a stylized butterfly, a signature of the Póvolnyam or Butterfly Clan.

In Figure 14 the old chief, Salavi, is pictured horizontally to show that he has passed away. The jagged line above him denotes water, which ends in a spring to the right, and out of this grows the spruce tree into which he transformed himself at death. The arms or branches of the

Figure 14. Salavi's death

spruce are upraised because the spruce is holy, the most magnetic of all trees, its branches forming a throne for the clouds to rest upon. The symbol below represents Salavi's lifeline; it rises at birth from Mother Earth, extends horizontally at ground level during his life span, sinks down at death, and then comes back in spirit form into the roots of the spruce directly above. The footprint is the mark of the people on their migration.

On the rock also are drawn four small circles about a larger circle, as shown below in Figure 15.

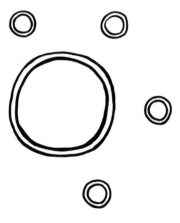

Figure 15. Pattern of kivas

The same pattern is formed by one large kiva and four smaller ones about it near one of the first ruins seen as one enters Mesa Verde. The small kivas indicate the presence of the four most important Hopi clans of the present time—the Bear, Badger, Eagle, and Parrot. The large kiva also symbolizes the gathering of the chiefs of these four clans, the Nalöönangmomwit [Four Religious Chiefs United Together], in their directional positions about the Mong [Chief] kiva on the last morning of Niman Kachina.

Figure 16. Sáviki

Figure 17. Bow Clan villages

The other pictographs sketch the history of additional clans and the quarrel among them before they separated. Figure 16 represents Sáviki, deity of the evil Bow Clan, and Figure 17 shows the number of the villages it established before arriving at Mesa Verde. Figure 18 is another form of the *nakwách* symbol of brotherhood also formed when the priests clasp hands in the same manner during the public dance of Wúwuchim today.

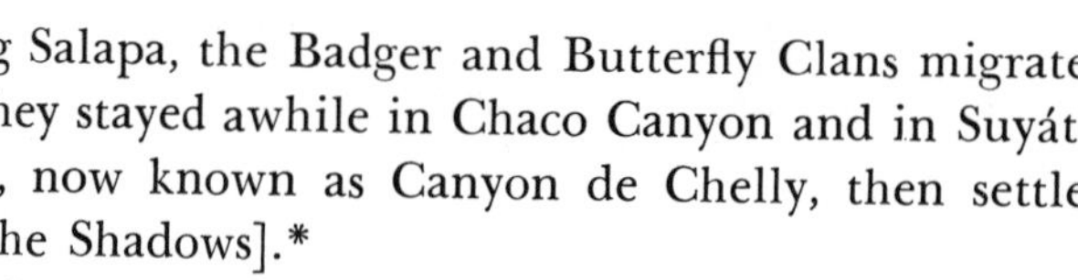

Figure 18. Nakwách symbol

Leaving Salapa, the Badger and Butterfly Clans migrated southward together. They stayed awhile in Chaco Canyon and in Suyátupovi [Loose Sand Place], now known as Canyon de Chelly, then settled at Kísiwu [Spring in the Shadows].*

After a long time the Butterfly Clan moved to Awatovi. The Badger Clan then dispatched a runner to the Bear Clan at Oraibi, asking permis-

---

*This is a very sacred place. To it the pilgrimage for spruce is made every year at the time of Niman Kachina. See Chapter 6, Part Three.

sion to settle with them. The chief of the Bear Clan sent word that the chief of the Badger Clan must himself ask permission. So the chief of the Badger Clan moved his people to Third Mesa, settling at Cha'aktuika [Crier's Point]. Here he planted two spruce trees, a male and a female. They grew very fast, soon reaching a height of several feet. The Badger Clan chief then went to ask the Bear Clan chief for permission to settle in Oraibi.

"These two spruce trees are the proof of our power and the gift we will make if you admit us to Oraibi," he said. "They are a sign that all the high places around the village will be covered with spruce trees whose power you may use in your ceremonies."

The Bear Clan chief refused. At that moment the two spruce trees at Crier's Point fell down. Ever since then the Hopi people have been obliged to go to Kísiwu after spruce for their ceremonies. The Badger Clan then settled at Túwanasavi [Center of the Universe], near Oraibi.

Many years passed, each dryer than the last. The crops failed, the people of Oraibi began to suffer. The Bear chief then called upon the Badger chief.

"I refused you admittance to our village because I knew of the quarrels dividing the people of the Badger Clan," he said. "But now I must ask you to help us with your ceremonies to bring back fertile times. Now I must ask you to come to Oraibi."

"We will come," answered the Badger chief. "But we will come only in the procession, in order to bring blessings to your people."

Great preparations were made. Corn and beans and squash were planted; the masks and costumes were readied for the *kachinas;* new songs were composed. When all was ready the Badger chief sent word for the Bear chief to meet his people at Kákchintueqa [Kachina Point]. The Bear chief did so and escorted the Badger Clan into Oraibi in a great procession that entered Oraibi from the north.

This is the great procession that now takes place during Pachávu at the time of the Powamu ceremony. And during Niman Kachina, on the morning after the Home Dance, when a member of each of the four most important clans takes position about the kiva to represent one of the four cardinal directions, a Badger always stands to the north, for that is the direction from which his clan entered Oraibi.

4

Migrations of the Bird Clans

The parrot is the symbol of fertility and the fruitful south, figuring significantly on the Blue Flute and Gray Flute altars. The Parrot Clan is also recognized as the symbolic mother of all Hopi clans. It stands next to the Bear Clan in line of succession, and one of its members always designates the south.

This is how it derived its name and importance.

The people in the Parrot Clan began their migration in the warm country far to the south. There were very few of them. An old man and woman, fearful that their clan would die out, wandered into the jungle to seek a power that would make them a fertile people who would multiply enough to carry on their migrations.

Soon they met a stranger, who took them to his home, where a beautiful woman welcomed them. "I heard your prayers for the power of fertility," she told them. "So I sent my messenger to bring you here. Now I will give you this blessing."

She led the old couple to a large nest in the corner, containing many eggs of beautiful colors. "Kneel down and put your right hand on these eggs," she told the woman first and then the man. "Pray now for the blessing you want."

The old couple did so. After a time they felt the movement of life within the eggs.

"Good!" said the beautiful woman. "Now you may take your hands off the eggs, knowing that they are parrot eggs and that you are now Kyáshwungwa, Parrot Clan people. You will be fruitful and multiply, you will have the power of fertility. In time to come other clans and people will ask you for the power of increase. You must never deny them this power, for you are Yumuteaota, Mother People. Remember me and what I say, for I am the one who takes care of all bird people."

The old couple returned happily to their people, and they took up their long migration, multiplying as they went.

54

They went northward through Pusivi [Big Cave] near Nogales, turned west, and came to the Pacific. Going eastward toward the Atlantic, they stopped at Kyashva [Parrot Spring] in Grand Canyon, and at Sawyava [Bat Cave] in Walnut Canyon, which had been settled by the Chosnyam [Blue Jay people]. After turning northwest, they passed several small ruins on the flat prairies [in Nebraska or Iowa of today], and followed up the east side of the Great Divide through Canada toward the Back Door. They then came down on the west side, stopping at several places: Túwi'i [Terrace] near the pueblo of Santo Domingo, which still today reveres parrots; Wénima; Pavi'ovi [Water on High Place] and Chosóvi [Blue Bird Hill], both near Tonto ruins; Walnut Canyon; Wupatki [Tall House] near Flagstaff; and finally Shongopovi and Oraibi.

Among the clans not admitted when they first reached Oraibi was the Bow Clan. Resentful because they were refused admittance, the Bow Clan leaders planted at Masvösö [Ghost Cove Valley] the most destructive of all snakes, the red-bellied water snake, to test out the power of the Bear Clan. The snake, rising out of the valley, began to sway its head back and forth. All the land began to vibrate; rocks and boulders began to tumble from the cliffs.

Having no power to stop it, the chief of the Bear Clan called in his kiva a meeting of all clans. "You see what is happening. The vibration of this evil snake is bringing an earthquake that will destroy all our village and our people. The only way to stop it is to sacrifice a life. We, the Bear Clan, will offer the life of a young boy. Which clan among you will offer the life of a young girl?"

Till midnight the clans pondered and argued. Finally the Parrot Clan, Mother of the Clans, assented to the sacrifice. Preparations began at once. The little Parrot girl's hair was washed and in it was tied a fluffy eagle feather. She was dressed in a red and white ceremonial cape and given a plaque full of cornmeal. The little Bear boy's hair was also washed and left to hang free with an *ómawnakw* [cloud feather] tied to it. Across his nose and down his cheeks was drawn a line of *yalaha* [red earth paint]. He was dressed in a *saquavitkuna* [blue kilt] and given a plaque of cornmeal to carry.

By dawn all the songs had been sung, the *páhos* made. In a long procession the clan chiefs conducted the two children to Masvösö. The red-bellied water snake was still swaying its head, and now all around its body water was gushing out.

"Listen to us!" said the Bear chief. "We have come to offer you the lives of these two children. Please accept this and do not destroy us."

The little boy and girl, having been told that this was the only way their people could be saved from destruction, walked fearlessly up to the snake. Slowly he wrapped his coils about the children and gave a last mighty shake. Instantly a great body of water erupted, and in it the monster snake disappeared with the children.

Almost immediately the water stilled. The village chief of Oraibi then walked through the water and placed four coiled plaques over the hole into which the snake had sunk. For many years the great pool of water remained, but the red-bellied snake never again appeared to threaten the village.

Because of its noble sacrifice of a little girl, the Parrot Clan today is next in line of leadership to the Bear Clan, symbolizes the south as one of the four most important Hopi clans, and is considered the mother of the people.*

THE EAGLE CLAN MIGRATIONS

The three branches of the Eagle Clan—the Condor, Eagle, and Gray Eagle—were among the last to arrive on this Fourth World. They moved south along the high mountains in South America and settled with the two branches of the Sun Clan—the Forehead and the Sun—which had preceded them. Here they all built up a great city of stone. The two chief deities were the sun and the condor, whose images and symbols were used everywhere.

In time the two clans began to quarrel, the Sun Clan claiming that the sun was more powerful than the Eagle Clan deity, Kwátoko; and the Eagle Clan asserting that the Sun Clan could not send its prayers to the sun without using eagle feathers or *páhos*. Finally, when it became obvious that the two clans could no longer live together, the leaders agreed that they would postpone proving their power to each other until they met again at their permanent place of settlement.

The conditions were these: If the Sun Clan during its long migration used the power of the sun for evil purposes, the Eagle Clan could claw out the eyes of the Sun chief and claim the power of the sun. Conversely, if the Eagle Clan during its journey ever inflicted the disease of the eagle, *kwána'pala* [twitching of the head and body], upon others, the Sun Clan would blind the Eagle chief and claim the power of the eagle.

---

* The Bear Clan, a member of which always serves as Village Chief, is regarded as the father of Oraibi, just as the Parrot Clan is considered the mother. The late Chief Tawák-waptiwa of the Bear Clan was married to a woman of the Parrot Clan. Hence this couple was symbolically the father and mother of Oraibi. According to Hopi prophecy, this was the last couple to unite the two clans. With the chief's death in 1960, Oraibi was left without proper parents—an omen of the end of Oraibi.

Receiving from Kwátoko the sign that they were to move out first, the Eagle Clan migrated northward. Their first settlement was near what is now Mexico City. At Qahápqol [Willow Springs], south of present Santa Rosa, New Mexico, they turned eastward to the Atlantic Ocean, where they built a shrine, *tútuskya* [stones in circle, opening to east, feathers inside].

Westward across the continent they migrated to their third *páso* on the shore of the Pacific.

Returning eastward they settled at Húkpivi [Windy Valley], near St. George, Utah. They then turned north until Kwátoko appeared and told them to make a shrine here for their last *páso*.

Moving slowly south now, they met other clans, with whom they settled at Wúpovakavi [Large Reed Field] near Ganado, at Awatovi, and finally at Pösövi [Sharp Corner], east of Oraibi. The Eagle chief then went to the Bear chief to request admittance into Oraibi.

Asked the Bear chief, "Have your people ever used the power of your deity against other people?"

"No," replied the Eagle chief. "We have done only as we were directed to do by our guardian spirit, Kwátoko."

"If you are permitted to settle in our village and become one of our family of clans, what ceremony or power can you contribute for the good of all?"

"Kwátoko commands all the upper air. He is the master of height. He is the watchful eye that will keep a lookout for the approach of people who would try to overpower us and take away our knowledge. His are the feathers that carry our thoughts and prayers to our father Sun, the *páhos* you may use in all your ceremonies."

"Good!" said the Bear chief.

"But in return for these powers," asked the Eagle chief, "what land will you give my people for their cultivation?"

"All the land north of Oraibi in the valley west of Savútuika [Chopped Rock Point]," the Bear chief said promptly. "It shall be known as Kwávasa [Eagle Land] from this time on."

So the Eagle Clan moved into Oraibi. Thereafter it served as the watchful eye for the village, giving warning of the approach of the Tavasuh [One Who Pounds an Enemy's Head, the Hopi name for Navajos] when they came to destroy the crops. Also it permitted use of eagle feather for *páhos* in all ceremonies.

After many years the Sun Clan came to Oraibi, requesting admittance. Remembering the quarrel and the agreement between their two clans at the beginning of their migrations, the Eagle Clan exercised its duty of keeping a watchful eye on the meetings between the Sun and

Bear chiefs. At last the Eagle chief said, "We have found out that the Sun Clan during its migration used the power of the sun wrongly and to gain advantage over other people.* We will not claw out the eyes of the Sun chief and claim the power of the sun, as our forefathers agreed. But the Sun Clan has lost its true power. It must lose all the advantages it has gained over other people. This we say."

That is the way it was. The Sun Clan was admitted into Oraibi, but given inferior and hilly land far south of the village. And never since then has the Sun Clan exercised a great power in any ceremony.

So it is that the Eagle Clan represents the east, with the Bear Clan standing to the west, the Parrot Clan to the south, and the Badger Clan to the north. These are the four most important Hopi clans today.

---

* In attempting to melt the Back Door as related in Part Two, Chapter 2.

5

Wénima and the Short Rainbow

The Short Well (or Cistern) and the Deep Well Clans, branches of the Water Clan, settled for a short time in a village near Globe, Arizona, when they were slowly migrating from the south. Differences arose between two brothers who were the respective leaders of the two clans. In order to choose which should be the chief of the village, the people arranged for a public demonstration of their powers. Corn was planted by each of the brothers, and when it came up each prayed to his clan deity to send rain. Rain came, falling on the corn of the younger brother, who prayed to Panaiyoikyasi, but not on the corn of the older brother. This made the older brother so angry that he demanded that the younger brother leave. So the younger brother and his followers migrated northeast to the village of Wénima, taking with them the *wu'ya* or *tiponi* of their deity Panaiyoikyasi.

Panaiyoikyasi means "Short Rainbow." This is why he is the deity of the Water Clan and his image is painted with vertical rainbow stripes of orange, green, blue, and black. Modern Hopis say that when it rains the Short Rainbow stands over Tútukwi [Volcanic Butte], southeast from Oraibi in the direction of Wénima. Short Rainbow links the sky and earth, having power over the atmosphere when the sun is shining and power over the earth when rain falls upon it. With this beneficent power he gives beauty and pollen to the plants and flowers upon which insects depend for life. Figure 19, showing an insect drawn within a flower, illustrates this beneficent aspect of Panaiyoikyasi's power. It also symbolizes Kuwánlelenta [To Make Beautiful Surroundings], the guardian spirit of sunflowers and deity of the Sunflower Clan. Sunflowers are important to the Hopis. In the women's ceremony, Owaḳlt, two maidens come into the plaza with faces painted with the ground petals of sunflowers. Hence the face is round, representing its female aspect. This is also the meaning of the decorative symbols shown in Figure 20, which were painted on a pottery bowl found within the ruins. They are sunflower maidens, for sunflowers are living persons imbued with life by the deities and our Father Sun, just as we are.

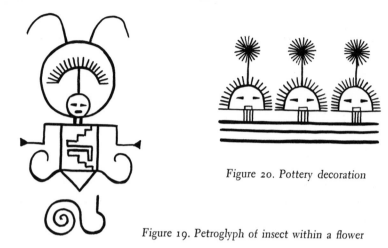

Figure 20. Pottery decoration

Figure 19. Petroglyph of insect within a flower

Eventually it came time for the clans to abandon Wénima and continue their migrations. Figure 21 shows a snake in the center, identifying

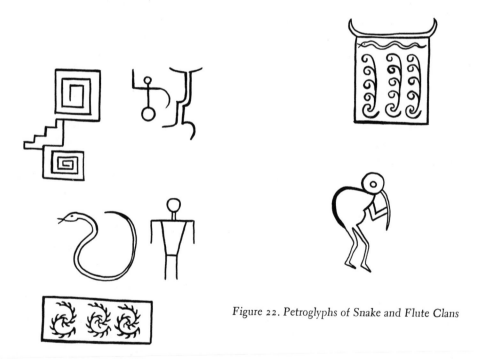

Figure 22. Petroglyphs of Snake and Flute Clans

Figure 21. Petroglyphs of Snake and Water Clans

the Snake Clan. In the oblong below are depicted three waves of water, revealing that the Water Clan was on the third "round" of their migrations, having gone to the shores of the ocean three times. The two figures on the right represent the two branches of the Water Clan, the larger man representing the Deep Well Clan and the smaller man the Short Well Clan. Separating without trouble, the Snake Clan went southward and the Deep Well Clan northward, the latter finally entering Oraibi from the northeast. This is shown by the petroglyph carved above the snake. The center broken line represents the terraced walls of the village, the maze to the north the route of the Deep Well Clan, and that to the south the direction taken by the Snake Clan.

Figure 22 again substantiates tradition that the Snake Clan had been associated with the Water Clan, as shown by the snake on the upper part of the oblong. Within it are plants representing a plentiful food supply. Below this is pictured the well-known humpbacked flute player, Kóko-pilau, who of course belongs to the Flute Society. Kókopilau suggests that the Flute and Sun Clans were also present in Wénima, for the two clans work together in those rituals which help the sun to turn back at the times of the winter and summer solstices.

Figure 23 shows the marking of a spider and one of the offspring which it hatches, indicating the presence of the Spider Clan. The eleven cross bars on the line in Figure 24 indicate the number of years that the people stayed in Wénima, and the two branches at the end show the separation of the clans when they departed. With the Deep Well people went the spirit of their deity, Panaiyoikyasi, shown hanging over their heads, arms upraised. But behind them they left his image lying face down, as shown, to give the deserted village spiritual protection. Such figures were always left as "cornerstones" to attest the village's occupancy by Hopi clans and to welcome them back if they ever returned.

According to tradition wu'yas were left in abandoned villages located near the four highest points surrounding Oraibi. A line drawn from Wénima to Oraibi and extended northwest indicates Toko'navi [Hard Rock Mountain] or Navajo Mountain. Somewhere near here there is said to be another ruin formerly occupied by the Fire or Ghost Clan and containing its wu'ya. Similarly another line drawn through Oraibi at a right angle designates Mesa Verde to the northeast, in one of whose ruins was buried the wu'ya of the Eagle Clan; and the San Francisco peaks to the southwest, former home of the Kachina Clan. These four highest points are the Cloud Houses of the directions—Wénima, as we have stated, being also known as Paláomawki or Red Cloud House—the wu'yas left in the ruins about each guarding the land about the central point of Oraibi.

Panaiyoikyasi possessed, in addition to his beneficent power, a great destructive force. Some people say this derives from his power to link sky and earth, which magnetically attract each other during storms. Other people say it is in the form of an invisible poisonous gas. Hence his image was laid face down in the crypt, for if it had been left face up the time

Figure 23. Petroglyphs of the Spider Clan

Figure 24. Petroglyphs of departure from Wénima

would have come when the two most powerful peoples on the earth faced each other with this terrible destructive force. In addition to this safeguard, Panaiyoikyasi's right arm was broken off so that the Hopi people could never use his destructive power.

Left with his image was a water jar, symbolic of the oceans reached by the Water Clan during its migrations. In it were beads of shell which also came from the seas, symbolizing the hearing aids by which one invokes their power. With these were also left beads of turquoise, given to all deities as tokens of honor and respect, for such *chosposi* [bluebird eye] signifies spiritual understanding between two beings.

Having sealed up the crypt in the kiva, the people abandoned Wénima and resumed their migration. After wandering to many places, they arrived at Oraibi, where they were permitted to build a permanent home. The site picked by the leader of the Water Clan was on the southeast edge of the village near the Típkyavi [Womb] used in all important ceremonies. Here a special kiva was built, and on all four walls were painted murals for use in Water Clan rituals. When this was done, the leader went to a high place at evening and looked toward the southeast. In a little while Panaiyoikyasi revealed himself as a short rainbow, signifying that he had heard the people's prayers and would always bring moisture for their fields. . . .

On August 11, 1960, national news syndicates reported the discovery of a small stone image near Vernon, Arizona, as "one of the important discoveries of the twentieth century in Southwestern archaeology." The find was announced by the Chicago Natural History Museum upon receipt of a message from Dr. Paul S. Martin, its chief curator of anthropology, at the excavation site.

The image was nine inches high, carved from sandstone, painted with vertical stripes of orange, green, blue, and black, and with its right arm missing. It was found in a secret crypt within one of the largest rectangular kivas ever excavated in the Southwest. The figure, estimated to be about seven hundred years old, was believed to be a *kachina* similar to those still being carved of wood by modern Hopi Indians. "To my knowledge," Dr. Martin said in his message, "no one has ever before found a *kachina* of either wood or stone in a kiva. As far as I can determine, the image is unique."

White Bear and I, upon reading of the discovery, felt that it was indeed important, but not for the reason given. A *kachina* is a spirit of any kind—a star, mountain, plant, animal, or invisible force. So also is the man who impersonates the spirit during ceremonials, wearing the sacred mask and costume which invests him with its power. The small image, like a doll carved of cottonwood and given to children so that they may become familiar with the many different *kachinas*, is popularly known now also as a *kachina*. But it is not invested with sacred power; it is not used in ceremonies; and it is not preserved in the kiva. Hence we did not believe the Vernon image was a *kachina*.

From the circumstances surrounding the find, we believed it to be a *wu'ya* or *tiponi*. A *wu'ya* is a clan deity, and a *tiponi* is a fetish of stone or wood representing the deity and belonging to the clan. Thus the *tiponi* is seldom brought out into the open and is not generally known, being reserved for ritual use in the kiva. In common usage the names of *wu'ya* and *tiponi* are often synonymous, the oldest member of the clan and keeper of the *tiponi* also being called a *wu'ya*.

To identify the image, we made two trips to the excavation site. During White Bear's first trip Dr. Martin kindly exhibited the image and the small jar containing several beads of stone, jet, shell, and turquoise found with it. A photograph of it was then shown to several Hopis, who identified the image at once as Panaiyoikyasi. Several weeks after the excavating party had left, we returned to explore the area more thoroughly.

The ruins of the village lay on a small knoll in a valley only four miles from Springerville, rather than close to Vernon about twenty-five miles away. The kiva was approximately fifty feet long and forty-seven feet wide, and the secret crypt was in the floor on the south side. A quarter-mile to the north another unexcavated portion of the village or a different settlement occupied a rocky butte.

Examination of the original walls of the ruin seemed to indicate that the village was the site of three different settlements. The walls consisted of successive layers of large stones alternating with small stones, the same construction as the walls of the ruins at Chaco Canyon. On the large stones were several signatures of the Water Clan, as shown in Figure 25. The one on the left, representing water, is also found in color at Chaco Canyon.

Figure 25. Signatures of the Water Clan

The figure with a protruding tail, shown to the right, represents a tadpole before it drops its tail to become a frog, a symbol of the Water Clan.

Among numerous petroglyphs found on the cliffs just across the valley, those shown in Figure 26 are particularly interesting.

The drawing to the upper left represents a cloud reflected in the water below. In the drawing to the upper right, the cloud terrace symbol formed by the figure's upraised arms is repeated upside down by his legs in the same manner as in the cloud to the left. The figure represents Panaiyoikyasi, deity of the Water Clan. The drawing under them shows four large waves of water, indicating the four migration routes to be completed by the Water Clan.

All these markings indicated that the Water Clan was one of the principal clans which occupied the village. At a later time other Hopi clans occupied the village, which is still known as Palaómawki [Red

Cloud House] because it lies to the southeast, east being symbolized by red. The area is also well known to the Zuñis, who have a shrine nearby and regard it as the ancestral home of the Koyemski or Mudheads. Today both Hopis and Zuñis more commonly know the village as Wénima, a name combining a Hopi and a Zuñi word; *nima* in Hopi means "going home." The village thus derives its name from the fact that it was settled by Hopi and Zuñi clans during their migratory "way home" to permanent settlement in Oraibi and Zuñi.

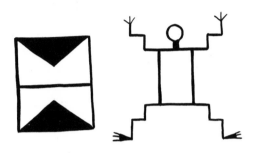

Figure 26. Petroglyphs of the Water Clan

It seemed apparent to our Hopi spokesmen that from oral tradition and all the petroglyphs, as pictured above, we had identified the ruins of the village and the image found within it. More satisfactory proof loomed up in one last carving on a cliff several miles away from the ruin. Depicting the village of Wénima, it is reproduced in Figure 27.

The small figures at the bottom indicate the people who lived there, the corn which supplied their food, and the horizontal footprints of several clans who stayed with the Short Well and Deep Well Clans. Vertical footprints would have indicated they had gone on, north or south. The large figure in the center is that of Panaiyoikyasi establishing a spiritual tie with the people. If archaeologists had discovered this picture writing and had been able to read it, they would have known where to find his stone image without excavating the whole ruin. The small black square on the right (south) side shows the location of the secret crypt.

Figure 27. Petroglyph of village of Wénima

To substantiate further all these rock carvings and oral traditions, we ascertained from one of the few remaining members of the Deep Well Clan that Panaiyoikyasi was still its deity. Its *wu'ya* or *tiponi* he remembered well. It was a small image carved of wood and painted with vertical rainbow stripes of orange, green, blue, and black—just like the Vernon image. During the Oraibi Split of 1906, when the Deep Well Clan moved out of Oraibi, its members left it buried in a secret crypt, where it still remains, perhaps to be unearthed by future archaeologists when Old Oraibi is finally and completely abandoned. Ten years later, in 1916, the paintings in the Water Clan kiva at Oraibi were found and re-traced, and there are many wonderful legends about them and Panaiyoikyasi still told today.

A member of the Water Clan living in another village also told us that its *tiponi,* a wooden image of Panaiyoikyasi, was still planted in front of the One Horn altar during the Wúwuchim ceremony in which he participated.

The great importance of the Vernon discovery is that it confirms the rock writing and the great body of living tradition about it, and without that confirmation the image itself would be comparatively meaningless. It establishes a link between the Hopis and still another prehistoric ruin, illustrating how Southwest archaeology may be read in light of the living ceremonialism that exists today.

6

The Mysterious Red City of the South

Far in the tropical south, no one knows where, lay the mysterious Red City of the South, Palátkwapi [Red House]. Perhaps it was in Mexico, perhaps in Central or South America. Wherever it was, it is still an important landmark in the geography of Hopi legend. Clan after clan included it in their migrations. Hundreds of tales are told about it. With all their variations and contradictions, the Kachina Clan version may come closest to the truth, for it was the *kachinas* who built Palátkwapi.

Upon their Emergence a number of clans, headed by the Bear Clan, and including the Coyote and Parrot Clans, chose to go south. They were accompanied by a number of *kachina* people. These *kachina* people did not come to the Fourth World like the rest of the people. In fact, they were not people. They were spirits sent to give help and guidance to the clans, taking the forms of ordinary people and being commonly regarded as the Kachina Clan.*

Having reached the southern *páso* and left their signatures, the clans returned north until they reached the red-earth place where the *kachina* people instructed them to settle and build. From a small village it grew into a large city, a great cultural and religious center, the mysterious Red City of the South.

Under the supervision of the *kachina* people, Palátkwapi was built in three sections. Completely surrounded by a high wall, the first section was reserved for ceremonial purposes; the second section, adjoining it, contained storage rooms for food; and the third section comprised the living quarters for the people of all clans. Underneath all three sections ran the river.

The ceremonial section was the most important. There were no kivas then, as there are today, divided to accommodate initiates and cere-

---

* A fuller explanation of the *kachina* concept is given in Part Three.

monial participants. Instead, there were two buildings, one for initiates and one for ceremonial purposes. The ceremonial building was four stories high, terraced like the pueblos we see today. The main door opened to the east, and there were two smaller doors facing north and south.

On the first or ground floor the *kachina* people taught initiates the history and meaning of the three previous worlds and the purpose of this Fourth World to which man had emerged. On the second floor they taught the structure and functions of the human body and that the highest function of the mind was to understand how the one great spirit worked within man. The spirit or *kachina* people taught this so that the people would not become evil again and this Fourth World be destroyed like the first three.

In the third story initiates were taught the workings of nature and the uses of all kinds of plant life. Although the people were still relatively pure and there was little sickness, some evils would come, bringing resultant illnesses; and for each one there was a plant remedy for the people to remember.

The fourth story was smaller than the three below, making the ceremonial building resemble a pyramid. To this top level were admitted only initiates of great conscience who had acquired a deep knowledge of the laws of nature. Here they were taught the workings of the planetary system, how the stars affected the climate, the crops, and man himself. Here too they learned about the "open door" on top of their heads, how to keep it open, and so converse with their Creator.*

---

* This description of Palátkwapi was given by the late Chief Tawákwaptiwa several years before his death in 1960.

No one knows where Palátkwapi might have been. Some of our Hopi spokesmen, who are able to read Hopi meanings from symbols and pictographs carved on Mayan stelae and temple walls, believe that the center of the Mayan Old Empire, Palenque, in Chiapas, Mexico, was the Hopi legendary city of Palátkwapi.

Others, to whom I have described the plan and ruins of Casas Grandes in Chihuahua, Mexico, recognize many similarities between it and Palátkwapi as described by Chief Tawákwaptiwa. Covering 237 acres, the immense walled city of Casas Grandes was divided into a ceremonial section and a residential section divided by a great open plaza. In the ceremonial precinct have been excavated an immense ball court, a truncated pyramid, and great mounds respectively shaped like a parrot, a serpent, and a cross. The dwelling area contained hundreds of rooms, many with T-shaped doorways, and pens for confining both parrots and turkeys. Inside the city was a large reservoir filled by a ditch run from the river a few miles to the north. From this reservoir rock-walled underground ducts led throughout the city. They possibly served as both a water system and a sewage system.

These great ruins have been unearthed only within the last two years by the Amerind Foundation of Dragoon, Arizona, and the National Institute of Anthropology and History of Mexico. They are not yet completely excavated and a report on them has not yet been published. This lends additional interest to the interpretation by our Hopi spokesmen of the use of the mounds.

According to them, Casas Grandes was occupied by Hopi clans, whether or not it was the legendary Palátkwapi. This tends to confirm the fact that it shows an amalgamation of a

The two chief spirits of the *kachina* people giving these instructions were Eototo and Áholi. Eototo worked especially with the Bear Clan, and Áholi undertook to give special instructions to the Corn Clan and its branch, the Side Corn Clan. The Corn Clan was told it was to be very important in the future. For when the people had reached their permanent settlement there would come three other races of people which would be identified by the colors of the corn they raised—the black, the yellow, and the white. They themselves were represented by the red corn, whose color symbolized the west from which they had come to this Fourth World. Hence the Corn Clan was instructed to see that all the clans did not fail to raise corn of all four colors—the red, black, yellow, and white—to insure the coming of all races to live in brotherhood in this new world.

As a token of their leadership, the Bear Clan and the Corn Clan were each given a scepter or chief's stick called a *mongko* [from *mongwi*, chief, and *koko*, stick] to carry when performing their religious duties. This *mongko* is the supreme symbol of spiritual power and authority and is still carried during Hopi rituals.*

The Coyote Clan was also assigned its proper place among the clans, being designated to come last to "close the door." There were two divisions. The Water Coyotes' main duty was to inspect the route of the migration to be followed in order to know the nature of the country the clans were to traverse. They were given special powers enabling them to

---

cultural stream northward from the Valley of Mexico and another southward from the Southwest, indicating that it lay on a migratory route between them.

The Parrot mound was used by the Parrot Clan for a special ceremony conducted every spring. The Parrot Clan, as we know, was the Mother Clan, which possessed the power of reproduction. Hence the parrot-shaped mound, made out of earth, represented the Mother Earth. To fertilize it each spring, a Parrot Clan member, a young girl of twelve, was ceremonially garbed in a dress and headdress made of parrot feathers and given an egg made out of cornmeal. Carrying this on a plaque to the mound at sunrise, she would deposit it in an opening on the east side where the first ray of the rising sun would strike it. The cornmeal egg in Mother Earth would thus be fertilized by Father Sun and give forth crops of corn symbolizing the mother-milk food of mankind.

The Snake mound was similarly used by the Snake Clan in a blessing rite for the six directional snake deities, there being no kivas in Casas Grandes. The same ritual is now conducted in the kiva at Oraibi, where there are symbolic representations of six shrines placed some distance away from the village. Hence there should be found six directional shrines somewhere about Casas Grandes.

The pyramid and the cross mound were the most important, for they were used by the Kachina Clan. The cross mound, whose arms were oriented to the four primary directions, pointed to the four worlds: the west being the First World; south, the Second World; east, the Third World; and north, the present Fourth World. At the end of each arm was a round platform. These symbolized the four worlds and the unleavened bread tied to the thorny branch carried by the Kachina Clan people during the morning after the Niman Kachina ceremony.

Pictograph signatures of Hopi clans have been found on the east side of the great divide running through Chihuahua. It will be interesting to learn if the excavators of Casas Grandes find more near the great ruins to confirm these interpretations.

* Pictured and described in Part Three, Chapter 2.

cross great rivers and lakes. When the clans settled at one place for a long period, a member of the Coyote Clan called a Qaletaqa [Guardian] always acted as guard. A Qaletaqa also brought up the rear of every ceremonial procession to guard against evil.

So Palátkwapi grew and prospered. No crops were left unattended, no food was wasted. The great storage rooms in the second section of the city were kept filled at all times. As the clans came in, they were assigned quarters in the third section. The young men and women were taught crafts and were given religious instruction before they resumed their migrations.

The time came, however, when evil entered. Perhaps it was because the people found life too easy and did not resume their migrations. Other people lay the blame on the Spider Clan, which had returned from the back door to the north, where they had used their power wrongfully. According to the Bear Clan version, the Spider Clan was refused admittance to Palátkwapi for this reason. So one early dawn the clan attacked the city.

One of the *kachina* women, Héhewúti, had just got up and was putting up her hair when the attack came. Immediately she threw on her clothes, grabbed up a bow and arrows, and rushed out to help defend the city. That is why the Héhewúti [Warrior Mother] Kachina in Hopi rituals today wears part of her hair loose and her clothes are so untidy.* Another *kachina*, Cha'kwaina, gasped out "hu-hu" as he was shot by enemy arrows—the only sound the Cha'kwaina Kachina now makes during Hopi rituals.

Day after day the people resisted the Spider Clan's attack. The walls were strong, the gates stout. But still they were driven out of the third section of the great city. Then they were driven out of the second section, where all their surplus food was stored. Finally they made their last stand in the ceremonial section, across one corner of which ran a small river. And now a terrible thing happened. The Spider Clan began to cut off the river to deprive the defenders of water.

Immediately a council meeting was called in the barricaded city. It was decided to dig a tunnel underneath the river, through which all clans could escape. Immediately all men were put to work, and in several days the tunnel was completed. That night another meeting was held to plan the escape of the clans.

"This is the way it will be done," said the *kachina* leader. "The Bear Clan will go through first. Then the Corn Clan and the Parrot Clan. The Coyote Clan will go last, as always. As each clan emerges on the other

---

* As described in Part Three.

side of the river it must resume its migration immediately in the direction ordained for it. The day will come when your migrations are completed and you are all united again. So remember all that we have taught you, properly observe your ceremonies, and keep the doors on top of your heads open.

"Now we, the *kachina* people, will remain here to defend the city, while you make your escape in the darkness. The time for us to go to our far-off planets and stars has not come yet. But it is time for us to leave you. We will go by our powers to a certain high mountain, which you will know, where we will await your messages of need. So whenever you need us or our help, just make your *páhos*. Now another thing. We are spirit people, and we will not be seen again by you or your people. But you must remember us by wearing our masks and our costumes at the proper ceremonial times. Those who do so must be only those persons who have acquired the knowledge and the wisdom we have taught you. And these persons of flesh and blood will then bear our names and be known as the Kachina Clan. Now it is dark. The time has come. Go quickly."

The escape began in the order prescribed. But in the hurry and bustle the leader of the Side Corn Clan forgot to take with him his *mongko* or Law of Laws. So it was that Áholi did not carry a *mongko* when he arrived at Oraibi long afterward. So, too, is it a prophecy that Kachina Dances will be the last Hopi rituals to be done away with, when all else taught the people is forsaken and forgotten.

After making their escape, the clans resumed their migrations. The Kachina Clan reached the *pásos* of the directions and made many settlements before arriving at Oraibi. These include: Soycheopu [Cliff Along Cedar Ridge]; the ruins now south of Meuvatukovi [Snow Cap Mountain] in Oak Creek Canyon; Quanevi, near the two peaks north of Snow Cap Mountain; and Wupatki. The real *kachinas,* as we know, are spirits from other planets and stars, but the high mountain to which messages are directed to them is San Francisco Mountain, southwest of Oraibi, near Flagstaff.

7

The Journey of the Twins

The legend of the journey of the little twins contains another version of the destruction of Palátkwapi; ties together the two chief *kachinas*, Eototo and Áholi, and the Water Clan and the Side Corn Clan; and the Hopis believe it is illustrated by several murals on the walls of the kiva in the great ruin along the Rio Grande now known as Kuaua.

For a long time the Water Clan lived at Palátkwapi, that mysterious Red City of the South, helping to build it into a great cultural and religious center. They were able to do this because their two guardian spirits or deities helped them. Eototo was the deity of the Bear Clan, and still today he is the supreme chief of all the *kachinas* who come each year to bring blessings to the Hopi people. He is always accompanied by the Áholi *kachina* dressed in his strange conical head-mask and tropical-colored shoulder cape, for Áholi was the tutelary deity of the Water Clan and custodian of the magic water jar.

After many years Eototo and Áholi warned the people that they were breaking the law by remaining at Palátkwapi; they must migrate to the four *pásos* before settling down permanently. Yet the people kept staying. They liked their great Red City, the tropical climate and rich land that made life easy for them. So the two deities ordered the Water Clan to destroy the city.

This is how it was done. The chief called his son, a sixteen-year-old boy, into his kiva and instructed him to get up early every morning, run toward the mountain, and then plant a stick in the ground where he stopped. The boy did so, planting the stick a little farther each day as he became stronger.

The chief again called him into the kiva. "You are gaining strength and endurance. Now here are four masks—a black one, a red one, a brown one, and a white one. Each morning put on a different one when you run. Then come back to me at the end of four days."

On the fourth day he was instructed to put on all four masks, one on top of the other. The chief then dressed him in a ceremonial kirtle, painted his body, and said, "Go to a different quarter of the city each night, groan and make noises."

Hearing the strange noises and groans as the city began to rumble, the people began to worry. The fastest runners tried to catch the young man, but he was too swift for them. Then the chief told his son, "You have awakened our people to their wickedness. Tonight you must let them catch you. Only in this way, perhaps, can we save our people."

That night the young runner allowed himself to be caught and brought back to a great fire in the center of the village. By its light the elders took off his masks, one by one, only to recognize the son of their chief. "Why have you done this to us?" they demanded angrily.

"So you will admit your wickedness before it is too late," he replied. "But I see I have failed to lead you out of the city. Now you will kill me, this I know. But be sure you bury me here in the plaza so you will see still more signs."

The elders killed him with a flint knife and buried him in the plaza. Next morning one of his fingers was sticking up out of the grave, and every morning still another finger stuck up. On the fourth morning a serpent rose out of the grave, and as he moved his coils the earth shook and a few buildings toppled. By noon half the great city had fallen, hundreds of people had been killed, and the rest of them in great panic were fleeing the smoking ruins.

One house remained untouched. It was the home of a couple who had twins, a boy and a girl. Twins, as everybody knows, have a special power and are called *chöviohóya,* young deer. The mother and father had gone out into the fields that morning. Believing their children had been killed in the destruction of the city, they joined the fleeing refugees. The twins, however, remained in their house all that dreadful day and night. Next morning when they came out they found the city in ruins and all the people gone. Deciding to follow their tracks, the little boy packed some food in a blanket, secured his bow and arrows, and took up the trail with his sister.

Traveling was difficult. Their food gave out. The little girl cried. But the little boy kept trailing a deer and finally shot it. The deer, who was not dead yet when the boy reached it, said, "Your people have traveled so far ahead, and your sister is so weak, you will never catch up with them. So I came here to help you. Now listen to my instructions. When I die, cut off some meat and cook it for your supper. But do not break any of my bones. Save the back part of the hind leg bone from the lower joint to the hoof. Shape it into a *móchi* [awl]. With this you can make yourselves new clothes from my skin to keep you warm. But always carry the *móchi* around your neck. I will come every night then and carry you on my back."

Eventually the twins arrived at a prosperous big village far to the north along the Rio Grande River. Its name was Kowáwaimave [Kachina House]. For a long time the twins stayed there, and for many years afterward the Rio Grande villages called them and their people Mochis or Awl People—a name that the Spaniards later distorted into Moquis, which means Dead People.

THE KUAUA MURALS

Kowáwaimave is now known as the prehistoric pueblo of Kuaua, whose ruins lie on a high bluff overlooking the Rio Grande just west of Bernalillo, New Mexico. One of its rectangular kivas has been restored, with beautiful mural paintings in full color on the walls. According to our Hopi informants, a series of them depicts the story of the little twins who fled from the mysterious Red City of the South.*

Figure 28. The twins

---

* The pueblo contained 1200 rooms and 6 kivas, and was inhabited from 1300 to 1600 A.D. It was excavated in 1934 by the University of New Mexico, Museum of New Mexico, and School of American Research. The walls of the "Painted Kiva" bore 85 layers of adobe plaster, and 17 layers of brilliant frescoes depicting 364 individual figures. Dr. Bertha P. Dutton of the Museum of New Mexico interprets these murals differently from the Hopis, whose account is given here.

Figure 28 represents the twins. The dark half of the body with the hand holding a ceremonial cane or rod represents the boy. The light side, with a hanging breast and a hand holding feathers, represents the girl. The circle joining them at the solar plexus indicates they are of the same blood. They are soon to meet the deer, as shown by the hands imprinted above the deer tracks.

Figure 29. Killing of the deer

Figure 29 depicts how they met and killed the deer. The boy's arrow passes through the deer's body. The dots flowing from the deer's mouth to the children's hand outstretched for help indicate the instructions the deer gave them. The two hands holding the deer's back legs show that the boy followed instructions to take the bone from the deer's lower back leg and make an awl from it. The children then leave, their footprints showing they traveled toward the northwest, as this mural figure was painted on the west wall of the kiva.

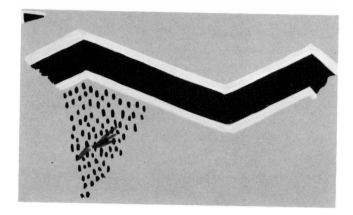

Figure 30. The Rio Grande

The Rio Grande River, which they reached, is shown in Figure 30, drawn on the north wall. Here the children were called the Móchi or Awl People, the beginning of the Awl Clan. This clan has died out, but a branch of it is known as the Tepnyam [Thorny Stick] Clan, which now carves its ceremonial awl from hard wood.

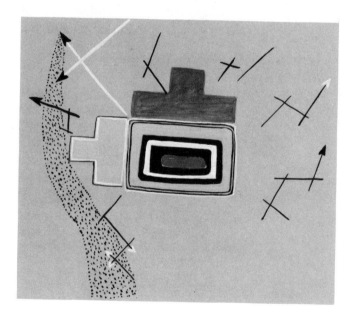

Figure 31. The sipápuni

Figure 31 symbolizes the *sipápuni,* the Place of Emergence. The dark cloud terrace above represents the male power possessed by the boy twin, and the light cloud terrace to the left, the female power possessed by the girl.

Figure 32. Girl in Awl Clan ritual

The *sipápuni* is shown again in Figure 32 at the feet of the girl who is carrying out part of the ritual developed by the Awl Clan.

Figure 33. Boy in ritual with water jar

The boy also participates in the ritual, as shown in Figure 33. To the right is the *móngwikoro*, the magic water jar which the leader plants in the ground. It is pointed at the bottom for this purpose. The water it produces is represented by the sprinkling to the left. The woman's ceremonial water jar, in Figure 34, is rounded on the bottom.

Figure 34. Woman's water jar

Figure 35. Red Hawk Clan leader

Figure 35 clearly depicts the leader of the Kelnyam [Red Hawk]
Clan, as shown by the dotted markings on his legs and the Red Hawk
standard he is holding. He uses this standard only during the Wúwuchim
ceremony and, at its conclusion, carries it to the Mong [Chief] kiva.

Figure 36. The Nalöönangmomwit

The Nalöönangmomwit, the four directional and spiritual leaders of the four major clans—Bear, Parrot, Eagle, and Badger—are shown in Figure 36. The religious chief of the Bear Clan stands at the extreme right in front of a cloud-terrace altar to perform a ceremony which brings moisture to the soil below for the growth of the cornstalks shown between all figures.

Figure 37 depicts Qaletaqa, the traditional Hopi guardian. He carries a *hótango* [quiver of arrows] and wears a deerskin. A portion of his white knitted leggings is shown. These *namósasavu* [shin coverings] are worn only by members of the Coyote Clan.

The birds in Figure 38 are swallows, whose feathers the Hawk Clan uses to send out their messages and prayers during Wúwuchim, because the swallow is the swiftest of all birds. The one on the left is ascending

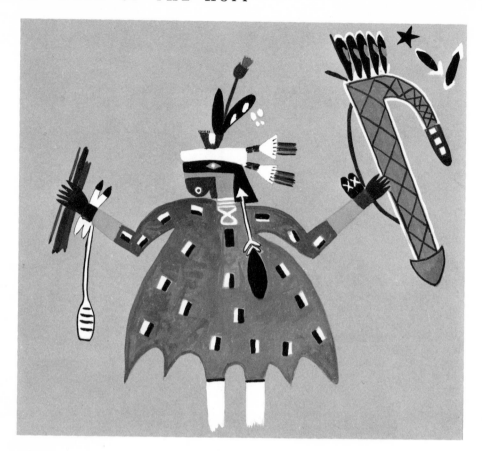

Figure 37. Qaletaqa

Figure 38. Swallows

its path before complete darkness covers all the earth, as shown by the short horizontal line across its path. The seven dots near the swallow's beak represent the seven stars in the Pleiades; the nine larger dots, the nine stars in Corona or Lakón [also the name of the women's society and its ceremonial]; and its three inner dots or stars, the feminine Qaletaqa and the two throwers whom she leads into the circle of dancers during the ceremony.*

The swallow on the right shows that the ceremony has progressed past midnight. The cross line is darker and longer, and the distance from it to the swallow's beak is shorter. Also the nine stars in Lakón have moved up to the swallow's beak, and the Pleiades have vanished. This illustrates that the kiva ceremonies at ancient Kuaua, as those in modern Hopi kivas, were timed by the position of the stars.

Figure 39. Pöqánghoya

Figure 39 represents one of the Hero Twins, Pöqánghoya.** At the time of Creation he was given the duty of solidifying the earth. Hence he is always painted in dark earth-colors, and carries the makwanpi, the

* Fully described in Part Three.
** See Part One.

rounded stick with which he pointed to the soft earth and said, "You shall become solid." For protection against evil he carries the white shield called *pátuwvotah*. The dotted lines mean rain; the cloud terrace above him and the lightning coming down to the water jar denote power.

Figure 40. Head of the Corn Clan

Figure 40 is the head of the Corn Clan, whose power extends over all the directional-colored corn—the red, yellow, white, and black—the white in his hand being the purest in nature.

ORIGIN OF THE SIDE CORN CLAN

Meanwhile the people fleeing from Palátkwapi reached northern Mexico. Here the two clans separated, Eototo leading the Bear Clan to the northwest, and Áholi guiding the Water Clan northeast to settle for a time near the site of the present Silver City, New Mexico. The Water Clan then turned east and went to the Atlantic, leaving along its route pieces of pottery marked with a spiral turning counterclock- wise. On their way back to the Pacific their settlements were marked with spirals turning clockwise.

After coming back to the Divide, they turned north until they were blocked with ice and snow. Having migrated south, they settled at Mesa Verde with a number of other clans and then traveled on with the Side

Corn Clan to Masípa [Gray Spring], near present Zuñi, and then to a village in Salt River Canyon.

By this time the two clans had intermarried, and two young men, having different mothers but the same father, began to quarrel over which was to be leader. They agreed to settle the matter with a contest, each planting a field of corn and praying for rain. The younger brother's corn received the rain. He was declared the leader, and his followers were given the privilege of naming their children after both the Water Clan and the Side Corn Clan. When the older brother's corn dried up, it was just beginning to have *pikyas* [side corn] on the stalks. Therefore his followers could not give their children water names; they could name them only after corn.

The group under the younger Water Clan leader went west; the Side Corn people went northeast. For a long time the Water Clan stayed at Pavowkyiva [Swallow Spring], near present Montezuma Castle and Well. Then they built a village on top of Gray Mountain; lived near Moencopi; settled near Kísiwu; and finally came to Savútuika [Rock Point Hammered], about seven miles north of Oraivi [Rock Place on High].

Recognizing Oraivi or Oraibi as their permanent place of settlement, and finding out that the Bear Clan had already arrived, they sent word that they were now ready to reunite with their forefathers' brothers. Great preparations were made for their admission. Eototo, deity of the Bear Clan, and Áholi, deity of the Water Clan, welcomed them at the foot of the mesa, escorted them up to the village, and led them to the Típkyavi [Womb] in the plaza.

Here a sacred well, symbolized by a small hole, had been dug. Once again, as at the beginning of their migration, the two clans sealed the bonds between them. Then in the same ceremony that is still performed every year, Eototo and Áholi went through the rituals, which ended as they poured water into the hole from the water jars on their sacred *mongkos.*[*]

The Side Corn Clan's account of its migrations gives some interesting additions and variations.

According to this, people of the Side Corn Clan were members of the Water Clan when Palátkwapi was destroyed. It was near Globe that the two brothers contested for leadership, which confirms the version given by the informants who related the history of Wénima. The Side Corn places of settlement, after the two groups separated, include:

---

[*]This takes place during the Powamu Ceremony, as described in Part Three. The Water Clan did not have a *mongko* until it arrived in Oraibi, when it first borrowed one from the Tepnyam [Thorny Stick] or Hard Stick Clan.

Máwyavi [Picking Cotton From Pods], north of Nuvátuky'ovi [Snow Top Mountain] or San Francisco Peaks; Pavi'ovi [Wet Hill], the highest part of Black Mesa; Siova [Onion Spring]; and Savútuika [Rock Point Hammered], about eight miles north of Oraibi. After requesting admittance to Oraibi, the Side Corn people lived on the east side of the village at Sikya'wa [Yellow Stone] for two or three years before moving into Oraibi.

Apparently there were many more divisions of this large clan as it kept growing. One of these came about when two groups entered a contest to find out which could bring the most rain. One group called enough rain to fill a deep cistern, and thereafter became known as the Wupávatki [Deep Well or Cistern] Clan. The losing group became the Short Well Clan, finally settling at Walpi. According to the Walpi people, they called on the Deep Well Clan for help during a drought, so both clans were united again on First Mesa and are living today in Hano. The Oraibi version relates that the main Water Clan settled at Awatovi and then moved to Oraibi, where the two groups were united.

8

The Snake and Lizard Clans

The Lizard Clan began its migration northward by following almost the same route taken by the Snake, Spider, Fire, Sun, and Flute Clans as they traveled north to the Back Door of the continent. Turned back by the ice, the Lizard Clan settled in a village by Homowala [Round Top Cape] near St. George, Utah, where lay the ruins of a village left by the Snake Clan. From here they traveled southwest, settling for a time near Needles, California. Here on the cliffs along the river may still be found their inscriptions of the horned toad, *máchakw,* and the lizard, deities of the clan.

The people liked this location so much that they again stopped here after they had traveled westward to the Pacific and back. This time they found evidence that the Fire Clan and the Water Clan also had stopped to work the· fertile bottomlands, but had quarreled, and the Fire Clan had driven the Water Clan away. The story was told by one great figure on the ground, made of rocks (Figure 41). It was the figure of the Fire Clan deity, arms outstretched to show that the Fire Clan had driven the Water Clan away and was barring its return.

After migrating across the continent to the eastern *páso* on the shore of the Atlantic, the Lizard Clan again returned to the rich bottomlands along the Colorado near Parker, Arizona. Here it met the Snake Clan, and for a long time the two clans worked peacefully together, raising corn, beans, cotton, and tobacco.

When the Bow Clan arrived the people knew they were in for trouble, for the Bow Clan always carried evil. It developed when the Bow Clan planted corn on Lizard land, claiming the ground as its own. The Lizard Clan protested, but the Bow Clan called upon its deity, Sáviki. His features were evil. He had a dark face with round eyes and he wore dark clothes. Sáviki counseled war.

The Lizard Clan called on its deity, the horned toad, and the Snake

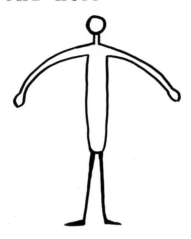

Figure 41. Fire Clan deity

Clan called on its deities, the snakes of the directions, for help. Then they made ready for a battle. First they sent all the old men, women, and children to a new location they had picked: Wukoskave [Wide Valley] along Gila Bend. These people moved out at night, unseen by the Bow Clan. Then at dawn the young men, all armed for battle, moved close to the Bow Clan settlement and waited for the attack with their deities, the horned toad and the snakes.

Soon Sáviki came, leading the Bow Clan warriors, and the battle began, deity against deity, people against people. It was a fierce fight, lasting all day, but at sundown the Bow Clan admitted defeat. In order to disgrace Sáviki, the Lizard and Snake Clans took his bow away from

Figure 42. Bow Clan deity with snake in mouth

him and put a snake in his mouth. So it is today that the deity of the Bow Clan is always pictured with a snake in his mouth, and the bow taken from the Bow Clan is now used by the Snake Clan in its own kiva rituals. The signature of the Bow Clan found at Salapa, on Mesa Verde, shows the snake in his mouth (Figure 42), so this battle must have taken place before the Bow Clan reached Mesa Verde.

After the battle the young warriors of the Lizard and Snake Clans joined their people along Gila Bend. For a long time they lived here, and the ruins of their village, ball court, and race track may still be found. From here they migrated to Chukake [Mud House Village, possibly Casa Grande], then to Homolóvi [Mud Mound], and Tuqueovi [Cliff Top Village]. Going north, they stayed at Masípa [Gray Spring] below present Zuñi. At Canyon De Chelly they found the Asnyam people [the Mustard Clan] already established, so moved on to Mesa Verde.

Once again many clans united, the Fire and Flute Clans calling their settlement Kawéstima [Cold Place]; the Spider Clan, Kokynki [Spider House]; and the Snake and Lizard Clan, Chu'kiva [Snake House]. They all then moved to the cliff called Pavakyki [Swallow House]. After several years the Fire Clan moved directly to Oraivi [Oraibi]. The Snake and Lizard Clans moved to Sunava [Sound of Waterfall] or Grand Falls on the little Colorado before entering Oraibi.

9

The Bow and Arrowshaft Clans

An aura of mystery and evil has forever hovered about the very name of the Bow Clan. Every Hopi knows that the Bow Clan was the ruling clan in the previous Third World and that its wickedness and corruption caused the world to be destroyed.

As we remember, the people left that world secretly just before it was destroyed by water, and made their Emergence to the present Fourth World.* They did not tell the Bow Clan they were leaving or where they were going, because they did not want the Bow Clan to follow them. But long after they arrived and began their migrations over the continent, members of the Bow Clan also landed on the shore of this Fourth World. No one knows why they were not all destroyed or how they managed to get here. One only knows that the power of evil is very great.

When the members of the Bow Clan arrived, they first established themselves at a place called Púpsövi [Seven Caves].** These group caves or villages in which they lived were:

Pamösi	(Water Vapor or Fog)
Wáki	(Place of Escape)
Taiowa	(Supreme Deity or Sun God)
Pávati	(Clear Water)
Hopaqa	(Large Reed)
Wikima	(Being Guided Ahead)
Alósaka	(Deity of the Two Horn Society)

Multiplying and prospering, they began their long migration north-ward to catch up with the other clans. Their route extended up through

---

* As related in Part One.
** Both the Aztecs and the Quiché Mayas have a tradition that they came from seven womb-caverns, caves, or ravines, thence migrating to their historical homelands in Mexico and Yucatán.

the central part of Mexico. Along it they made seven stops, establishing a village at each place, in which they lived several years. These seven villages they named after their first cave-villages at Púpsövi.

The first was Pamösi, the second Wáki, and the third Taiowa, said to have been not far from Mexico City. The fourth was Pávati and the fifth was Hopaqa. Here the chief's wife gave birth to twin girls. One was wrapped in a blanket of woven reeds, *hopaqa,* and the other in a *suongknah,* a covering of smaller reeds. After growing to womanhood, the first twin organized a large group of her people into a new branch of the clan. Because her name was Hówungwa, the clan was called the Hówungwa or Arrowshaft Clan.

Breaking away from the Bow Clan, the Arrowshaft Clan passed two villages abandoned by clans who had preceded them: Chosóvi [Blue Bird Hill] and Paví'ovi [Water on High]. These villages are believed to have been in the vicinity of the present Casas Grandes in Chihuahua. Going east and then north, they followed up the Rio Grande River, passed Mesa Verde, crossed the Colorado, and went far north. They then came back, went to the Pacific, and returned to the three Hopi mesas, some of the people settling at Awatovi and some at Walpi.

During all their migration they were in trouble. For although their leaders knew the rituals and ceremonies, they did not have the *mongkos,* which the Bow Clan had retained. Every time they set up their altar and appealed to their deity, Sáviki [Guardian of the Water Flow], they found that they had no power. And without power they could not get along with the other clans they began to meet. A quarrel always came up, for which they were blamed, and they had to move away.

Meanwhile the Bow Clan moved north from Hopaqa and established its sixth village, Wikima. As the name of the village meant "Being Guided Ahead," the chief sent out four young men to climb a high ridge to the north and wait there for four days for a sign to guide them. On the fourth day the sign came: a tall cloud that built up like a tall pillar and fell, pointing the way to Oraibi. At once the Bow Clan made preparations to move again in this direction.

Once more the people established a village—their seventh and last, named Alósaka after the deity of the clan's powerful Two Horn Society. Its ruins today may be found about twenty miles west of Meteor Crater and about forty-five miles southeast of Flagstaff. After they were settled, the chief sent a messenger to Oraibi, requesting permission to enter.

The village chief of Oraibi, a member of the Bear Clan, sent back word that the Bow Clan could not be permitted in Oraibi, but could settle in any of the other villages that were being built. This was when the Bow Clan tried to destroy the village, as has been previously related.

For many years afterward the Bow Clan remained at Alósaka. Then it moved to the bottom of the cliffs on the south of Oraibi and lived there several years more. Once more permission was asked to settle in Oraibi. For a long time the matter was argued. The Bow Clan was known to have caused evil and trouble wherever it went, both in this world and in the previous one. But also it had great power which could be used to advantage. This power was symbolized by the *mongkos* which the Bow Clan had brought with them from the Third World.

The *mongko* is the supreme symbol of spiritual power and authority. Ritual *mongkos* are held by only three societies, the Two Horn, One Horn, and Flute. Those of the Two Horn Society are most important, for the Two Horns are the only ones who possess full knowledge of the three previous world, and these Two Horn *mongkos* are the ones belonging to the Bow Clan. The long one—nearly four feet long—is the largest known and was used to close the kiva entrance during the Wúwuchim initiation ceremony. Tied to the short one was the shortest ear of corn, the tiny little ear brought by the Bow Clan from the Third World to guarantee everlasting food on this Fourth World.*

These *mongkos* decided the argument. All the people of various clans who had settled at Oraibi needed the Two Horn rituals to complete their ceremonial pattern. So reluctantly they agreed to admit the Bow Clan for permanent settlement. . . .

Here the story of the Bow Clan must end for the time. But, as we will see later, the evil of the Bow Clan persisted to disastrous ends. For just as a bow and arrow are no good separately, it was necessary for the Bow Clan and the Arrowshaft Clan to reunite in order to complete the ritual. But the Arrowshaft Clan was living in Awatovi, which in time came under the domination of the incoming Spaniards and their Christian Church. Hence the destruction of Awatovi and the massacre of its inhabitants by the other Hopi villages was for the purpose of wiping out the foreign Christian religion and bringing the survivors of the Arrowshaft Clan to Oraibi to complete the Two Horn Society ritual of the Bow Clan.**

THE SKUNK AT POTTERY MOUND

Despite the lack of knowledge about the history of the Bow Clan and the aura of evil about it, the Bow Clan was a powerful clan. Traces of it and of the rituals of the Two Horn Society which belong

* Sketched and described in Part Three, Chapter 2.
** Related in Part Four, Chapter 2.

to it are found far off its direct migration route, which has been outlined. One of these is the painting of a skunk (Figure 43) found on the wall of a kiva excavated by the University of New Mexico at Pottery Mound, southwest of Albuquerque, New Mexico.

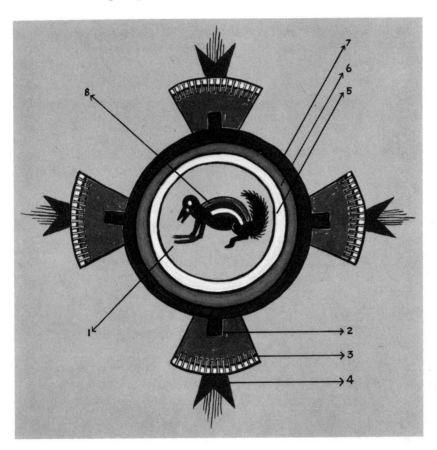

Figure 43. Pottery Mound skunk painting

Two Hopi religious societies use the skunk as a ritual symbol: the Snake Society and the Two Horn Society. The Snake Society, as a signal that its members are holding a ceremony within the kiva, displays a bow to which are tied the skins of a skunk or *kolichiyaw* [carrier of hot embers] and two weasels or *pivane* [tobacco-odor-carrying animal]. The Pottery Mound painting definitely belongs to the Two Horn Society of the Bow Clan.

In the center is pictured a skunk holding in his front paws (1) a *nacha* [wood that opens back and forth]. These tongs or *nacha* are used during the New Fire Ceremony in Wúwuchim, when hot embers are carried in them from the Two Horn kiva to light ceremonial fires in the other three participating kivas, the One Horn, Flute, and Wuchim.*

When this is done there are four fires lighted to the four directions in the four kivas; the fire pits (2) are illustrated by the four small squares in the four directions.

The eagle feathers extending from these four directional fire pits (3) represent the power of the ceremony, as eagle feathers symbolize power.

The four objects at the tips of these eagle feathers (4) represent the rays of the sun, from which fire itself derives.

The outer circle around the skunk and linking the four fire pits (7) is dark red, symbolizing the sun itself and the derivative fires in the four kivas. The orange circle within it (6) symbolizes its germinating heat, the theme of the entire Wúwuchim Ceremony. And the white inner circle (5) symbolizes the pure white heat of the sun.

The skunk himself symbolizes the sun, for his strong scent extends like the sun's rays, which reach out over all the world to give life to all forms of life—plant, animal, and man. This is again symbolized by the marking above the skunk's back, which is called a *tuvottaot* or sun shield —the face of the sun or the Creator, as represented by the complete design itself.

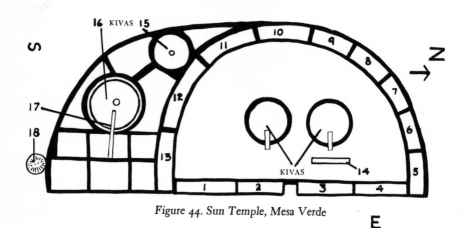

Figure 44. Sun Temple, Mesa Verde

THE SUN TEMPLE, MESA VERDE

All this is structurally recapitulated in the great edifice at Mesa Verde, Colorado, commonly known as the Sun Temple (Figure 44). The ruin stands on top of the lofty mesa overlooking Cliff Palace Canyon

---

* Described in Part Three, Chapter 2.

The "Vernon Image," found near Vernon, Arizona, in 1960 within a large kiva excavated by the Chicago Natural History Museum. The sandstone figure, nine inches high and with its right arm missing, was discovered in an adobe-sealed crypt twelve inches square and twelve inches deep.
(Photos: Chicago Natural History Museum)

Great cave enclosing the ruins of Betatakin, in Arizona.

(Photos: National Park Service)

Closer view of one end of Betatakin ruins.

Ruin of immense D-shaped Pueblo Bonito, Chaco Canyon, New Mexico.
(Photos: New Mexico Department of Development)

A portion of the Pueblo Bonito ruins, showing construction of rooms and kivas.

Ruins of Sun Temple, Mesa Verde, Colorado.
*(Photos: Mesa Verde
National Park)*

Ruins of Spruce Tree House, Mesa Verde, Colorado.

A portion of Aztec Ruins. New Mexico, showing one of fifty-two kivas in the foreground.

(Photo: New Mexico Department of Development)

Fresco picture-writing on wall of Aztec Ruins. The timbers in the roof vigas overhead were cut between 1110 and 1121 A.D.

(Photo: New Mexico State Tourist Bureau)

Aerial view of the Hopi village of Walpi, on the tip of First Mesa. *(Photo: Ed Newcomer)*

Snake Rock in Walpi.

Entrance to Snake Kiva, Walpi.

(Photos: Ed Newcomer)

A portion of the Hopi village of Moencopi.

(Photo: Ed Newcomer)

Ruins of Keet Seel, in Arizona.

(Photo: National Park Service)

and is in an excellent state of preservation, the walls standing nearly six feet high. It was dubbed the "Sun Temple" when it was discovered in 1915, but its purpose and symbolism have never been revealed till now.

Its very shape shows it was a ceremonial building erected for the conduct of ceremonies belonging to the Bow Clan. The immense structure, facing east, has the shape of a bow with a drawn string. The northern half of the building—another bow within the greater bow—comprises a semicircular row of thirteen rooms surrounding an open plaza, within which are two kivas. The one to the north was the kiva of the Two Horn Society and the one to the south that of the One Horn Society.

In front of the Two Horn kiva is a small ledge or platform (14). Here during the ceremony the Two Horn leader sat down to the north, both feet on the platform, holding in his lap his symbol of spiritual authority, the *mongko*. He was followed by the One Horn leader. The feet of both men touched, again forming the symbol of the bow and signifying the unity and authority with which they now recited the complete history of their Creation and their migrations. The One Horn, with his limited knowledge, spoke first, followed by the Two Horn, who traditionally has full knowledge of all four worlds.* It is said there might have been a cotton cord strung between the heads of the two priests, symbolizing the string of the bow formed by their feet and bodies.

The thirteen rooms surrounding the two kivas held the Two Horn initiates being instructed by their godfathers. From these rooms they were dispatched by couples to patrol the area on the night of Ástotokya [Washing of the Hair Ceremony], the initiation night of terror and mystery. The first four rooms in front, forming the string of the bow, were the most important. They symbolized the four worlds and the four kivas participating in the ceremony.

The southern half of the building also contains two kivas. The smaller one with a firepit in the center (15) belonged to the One Horn Society. The larger one was the Two Horn kiva (16). Into this, from underneath an adjoining room which held the Flute Society members, ran a vent (17) known as the Huiksi, the Breath of Life. The surrounding rooms were occupied by members of the Wuchim Society, which traditionally has the largest membership of the four participating societies, is not so secret, and keeps its ritual paraphernalia in such rooms.

The vent ran from the Flute Society chamber because the ceremony is dependent upon the Flute Society, which helps to produce the warmth for germination. Also from the Two Horn kiva, on the night of the New Fire Ceremony, are carried embers to light fires in all the other kivas,

---

* Chapter 2, Part Three, should be read in its entirety for a description of this complete ceremony, which is still carried on within the kiva today.

symbolizing the kindling of life anew. The embers are carried in the tongs called *nacha,* described in the preceding section. The construction of the Huicksi [Breath of Life] shows it to be in the form of a torch which overcomes darkness and evil with its light—the torch carried by the patrolling couples on the mystery-filled night of the Washing of the Hair.

Perhaps the most mysterious detail of construction in the building is the "Sun Dial" at the southeast corner. It is a small stone containing four small indented dots with grooves extending from them. The stone is known as the Tawalaki or Sun Ray Stone. It lies in a direct line with the string of the bow formed by the four chambers in the north section of the building (1–4), and its four dots also symbolize the four worlds and the leaders of the four participating societies, the Two Horn, One Horn, Flute, and Wuchim. The stone was watched carefully in the late afternoon preceding the night of the Washing of the Hair by the leading Two Horn priest. When the rays of the lowering sun struck the grooves so that no shadow was formed, he and his assistant, the Qaletaqa, made their pilgrimage to the shrine at Apónivi to plant a *páho* before the sun went down. As described in Part Three, the same ceremony, Wúwuchim, is still performed; the timing for this rite being established by the striking of the sun's rays at a certain angle on the wall of the Two Horn kiva.

The small platform (14) in front of the Two Horn kiva carries an additional meaning, signifying the *mongko* which is the emblem of authority of the Bow Clan. There seems little doubt that the Sun Temple is the one great monument of the now almost extinct Bow Clan, offering additional proof of Hopi occupancy of Mesa Verde.

10

The Coyote-Swallow Race at Sikyatki

Many centuries ago, when Sikyatki was a prosperous village, a beautiful girl lived at the corner of the plaza. Young men from Awatovi and Walpi as well as those of Sikyatki came to court her. The courting was simple. A boy would come in the evening and talk to her through the little window of the room where she was grinding corn. When she got tired of talking with him and sent him away, another and then another would take his place until she drew a blanket over the window.

Every evening for months this continued until there were only two boys left for whom she would stop grinding corn long enough to talk. Both were Sikyatki boys: one of the Coyote Clan and one of the Swallow Clan. Finally she told the Swallow boy that he must not come to visit her any more, and next morning she went to the Coyote boy's home with the marriage proposal, which was *tosi* [sweet cornmeal]. The boy's mother accepted it, taking the girl into her home to grind corn for the boy's uncles while they wove her wedding garments.

Swallow Boy was jealous and angry at losing her and appealed to the elders of his clan for help. They all began to scheme how they could take the beautiful girl away from Coyote Boy.

On the day of the wedding, the time for the washing of the hair, the leader of the Swallow Clan announced that his clan would not allow the wedding to take place until a contest was held between Swallow Boy and Coyote Boy. The elders of the Coyote Clan were forced to agree to the rules proposed. The contest was to be a race, and life was to be at stake. Immediately the elders of each clan began to prepare their runners for the ordeal. The time for the race was set, and people from all nearby villages came to see it.

On the day of the race all gathered down on the flat. Five parallel lines colored black, blue, red, yellow, and white were marked on the ground. The Coyote Clan grouped at the south end of this multicolored line, sticking into the ground a long knife of obsidian. Another long

obsidian knife was stuck into the ground at the north end by the Swallow
Clan. Swallow Boy and Coyote Boy were called to the line. Each wore a
short kirtle, a feather in his hair showing the society to which he belonged, and a line of *suta* [red paint] drawn across his nose and cheeks.
They were then given their instructions. They were to race eastward to
the Rio Grande River, north to the San Juan, west to the Colorado,
south to the Salt River, northeast to the Rio Grande, and back to the
starting line. The winner, upon reaching the line, was to pick up his
clan's obsidian knife and cut off the head of the loser when he arrived.

The big crowd was noisy now, forming groups behind the two rival
runners and shouting encouragement. Only the beautiful bride-to-be
stood off alone and sad, wondering if Coyote Boy would win and be her
husband or if he would lose and have his head cut off. Soon the Swallow
Clan leader held up his hand, counted four, and the two runners leaped
away.

In a little while Swallow Boy drew ahead of Coyote Boy and disappeared. Coyote Boy did his best, following the footprints of his rival.
Suddenly there were no more tracks to be seen, even though he zigzagged
back and forth trying to pick up the trail. When he reached the river
there were still no tracks to be seen, but there was the clan symbol, which
Swallow Boy had planted to show he had reached there.

Mystified by this strange occurrence and worried because he was so
far behind, Coyote Boy remembered that his elders had told him to sound
his call if he was losing the race. So he climbed a hill and gave the coyote
call as he had been instructed.

Traveling through the mystic air waves, the call reached the Coyote
Clan elders sitting in their kiva at Sikyatki, smoking and praying for
Coyote Boy's success. Right away their hearts were saddened, for they
knew the Swallow Boy was using by magic the swiftness of the swallow.
To make sure, they sent a messenger to the north point of the race. Sure
enough, a swallow soon came, marked the Swallow Clan symbol, and
flew on. After a long time Coyote Boy arrived, still far behind. Immediately the messenger sent back the coyote call to the elders at Sikyatki.

"Well! It is as we thought," the elders said among themselves. "The
Swallow Clan has used its power to turn Swallow Boy into a swallow.
What bird can fly faster? Clearly we are forced to use our own power."

Having the magic power to make rain and hail, they filled their pipes
and began to blow the smoke upward through the roof opening. The
smoke formed big thunderheads that traveled west and south along the
course of the race, and then began to rain upon Swallow Boy. The water
soaked his feathers, and to escape the hail he had to take shelter under
trees.

This slowed his progress so much that Coyote Boy soon caught up with him and passed him. But the heavy storm had made the ground so muddy that he could not run. Before long Swallow Boy passed him again. Now he remembered the cotton string, sinew, and the shell of a dried gourd his elders had given him before the race, with instructions to use them if necessary before he reached the south point. So he placed them on the ground behind him and waited a few minutes. When he turned around he saw prepared for him a large oval-shaped gourd cut in half— a *taweyah* or magic shield by which he could travel through the air.

After crawling into the lower half of the big gourd, Coyote Boy drew the upper half over him. To make them fit tight there was a loop of cotton string at the top and bottom, through which ran a length of sinew. Taking the sinew between his two palms, he spun it one way, and the *taweyah* moved forward. Spinning it the other way, he made the *taweyah* rise into the air. Maneuvering the magic carrier, he soon was able to pass Swallow Boy, who had had to stop under a tree to dry his feathers.

So they raced to the south, to the east, and turned back west again. When it rained, soaking Swallow Boy's feathers, Coyote Boy took the lead. Then Swallow Boy caught up and passed him.

Halfway back to Sikyatki they were stopped by messengers from the Coyote Clan with instructions to shoot Swallow Boy if he was still in the form of a bird. So Swallow Boy had to turn himself back into his own human shape. But Coyote Boy was also instructed to get out of his magic carrier and destroy it. So now they raced together on foot toward the starting line at Sikyatki.

Shoulder to shoulder they ran, straining every muscle. One drew ahead, then the other. Coyote Boy with blurred eyes could see the crowd gathered at the starting line on the flat. He was ahead, but only a step, for he could feel Swallow Boy's hot breath on his shoulder. With his last ounce of strength, and thinking of his beautiful bride-to-be, he hurtled forward to the south end of the line. He had just time to jerk up his clan's long obsidian knife before Swallow Boy stumbled up. Grabbing Swallow Boy by the hair where his feather was tied, Coyote Boy without hesitation cut off his head and gravely handed it to the Swallow Clan elders.

There was a great sadness throughout the village after the race, for the Swallow Clan was a powerful clan and the people feared more trouble. So the Coyote Clan leader told the Swallow Clan leaders, "You have brought this sadness upon us all. It was you who demanded this race and set the rules, who first used your power wrongfully and caused the death of your runner. Now you and all your clan must prepare to leave the village."

Four days later each man in the Coyote Clan dressed in his ceremonial Qaletaqa costume and escorted the Swallow Clan people out of
Sikyatki. The Swallow Clan went eastward and established its first new
village on the east side of Wúpovakavi [Reed Field], near Ganado. From
there it went on eastward again, and it is said the Swallow people went
to live at Kuaua.

The wedding of Coyote Boy and the beautiful girl took place. They
were blessed with long lives and many children, from whom many present
members of the Coyote Clan in Oraibi are descended. For the time for
"closing the door" of Sikyatki soon came; the Coyote Clan abandoned
Sikyatki and moved to Oraibi. It was the last clan to enter Oraibi, completing the religious quorum according to tradition.

The ruin of Sikyatki [Narrow Valley] lies on top of a high foothill
of First Mesa about three miles north of the Gap. Between it and the
rocky wall of the mesa curves the narrow valley which gave the prehistoric
village its name.* Above it stretches an outcrop of dark jagged rock.
Below it in dunes of yellow sand grow patches of corn and peach trees.
Scarcely anything of the ruin is visible today. Drifting sand covers the
fallen walls. The great plaza is overgrown with weeds. Yet the whole
desolate waste is still littered with broken pottery—perhaps the most distinctive pottery found north of Mexico. In no other pottery, ancient or
modern, is found such picture writing: figures of human beings, animals,
birds, reptiles, and insects, drawn with inexhaustible stylistic variations,
symbols, geometric designs, and ornamentations.

In the summer of 1895 J. W. Fewkes and F. W. Hodge of the Bureau
of American Ethnology briefly excavated several rooms. One of their
workers was Lesso, a Hopi from Walpi, who carried back to Nampeyo,
a Hano potter, some of the pottery he unearthed. Nampeyo was entranced
with the artistry of their shapes, softly muted colors, and wealth of design.
She copied and adapted them to her own use, reviving the art of Hopi
pottery in all three villages on First Mesa. The fame of her own work
spread rapidly and widely. She was taken by the Santa Fe Railway to
demonstrate her skill at the Chicago Railway Exhibition, to work for a
year at Grand Canyon under the sponsorship of the Fred Harvey Company, and again back East. Even after she became blind, Nampeyo continued to model pottery, relying on her daughters to do the designing.
Today she is regarded as having been one of the greatest American potters,
and her work is internationally famous.

Lesso was equally fascinated by some of the designs which indicated

---

* According to the Coyote Clan, its founders. The name is most commonly reported as
meaning "Yellow House."

that Sikyatki had been the traditional home of his own Coyote Clan. Disappointed because Fewkes and Hodge had given up their excavating work after a few weeks, he brooded about it for many years. Finally he went to Sivanka [Flower Painting], the oldest member of the Coyote Clan in Oraibi, and obtained permission to dig into a kiva at Sikyatki, thus making sure that no evil effects would result from his digging.

Taking with him to Sikyatki a young man of the Coyote Clan, Lesso located and unearthed a kiva. On the west wall was a mural whose figures are shown in Figure 45.

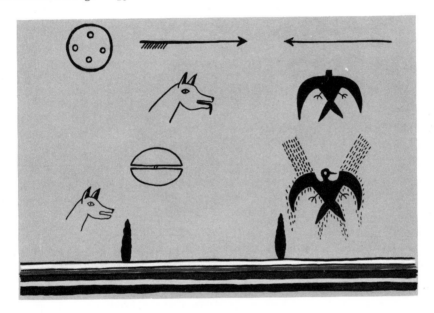

Figure 45. Sikyatki, kiva mural

The five horizontal lines along the base are colored underworld-black, the blue of the water, earth-red, the yellow of Sikyatki's top soil, and the pure white of the sun. Standing on this border are two black obsidian knives. Over the left is drawn the head of a coyote. Over the right is a swallow with V-shaped lines of rain falling upon it and water dripping from its wings and tail. In the center, right, is the figure of the swallow with its head cut off; and to the left is the head of the coyote. The oval with a line through its center represents a *taweyah*, a magic shield upon which people could travel through the air. In the upper left corner Lesso found, partially washed away, the remnant of a circle and three dots. It is shown here complete with four dots inside, representing the four leaders of the Coyote Clan praying for the success of their people. Across the top are two arrow shafts. To the right there was probably another circle containing four dots to show that the elders of the Swallow Clan also were praying for victory, but this was obliterated from the wall of the kiva and is not shown in the sketch.

Lesso carefully drew the figures on a board with charcoal, planted a *páho* at the base of the mural, and sealed up the kiva again. He then returned to Oraibi with the charcoal sketch he had drawn, paying his debt to his religious society and his clan. He had found what he wanted. The kiva mural depicted the Coyote-Swallow race and confirmed tradition that Sikyatki was the legendary home of the Coyote Clan.

11

The Ancient Record

As the migrations began to end, the record of the people's wanderings was left engraved on rocks over the face of all the land. Pictographs and petroglyphs in many different sites bear a striking resemblance. A few of the most common examples are shown in Figure 46.

ORAIBI

CHACO CANYON

GILA BEND

MESA VERDE

SPRINGERVILLE

CHICHÉN ITZA

Figure 46. The migration symbol

In the migration symbols shown, the circles record the number of rounds or *pásos* covered, north, east, south, and west. The one at Oraibi shows the completed four circles, with three points covered on the return. The Chaco Canyon symbol indicates two points covered and that the people are returning, as the second circle moves in the opposite direction. The people at Gila Bend, Arizona, were on their third round when the symbol was inscribed, but stayed some time, as indicated by the connecting line. The clan signature is that of the Snake. The square and the circle both mean the same at Mesa Verde, Colorado. The people came from the south and were of the Badger Clan. The two types are also shown in the Springerville, Arizona, drawing with the symbol of a village. The symbol found at Chichén Itzá indicates that the people covered only one round before returning to the same area and attests Hopi belief that the Mayas were simply aberrant Hopi clans who did not complete their migrations.

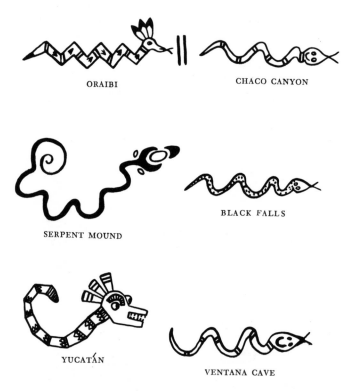

ORAIBI   CHACO CANYON

SERPENT MOUND

BLACK FALLS

YUCATÁN

VENTANA CAVE

Figure 47. The Snake symbol

The many snake carvings found everywhere are signatures of the Snake Clan (Figure 47). They bear many similarities. The vertical lines indicate sections of the snake which are equated with the corresponding sections of man. The three feathers on the head of the Oraibi figure are duplicated by the abstract feathers drawn on the snake found at Uxmal, Yucatán. Both represent the water serpent of the south whose ceremony is still performed in the kivas on First Mesa during Pámuya. The Serpent Mound in Ohio, as previously explained, is said to represent the guardian snake of the east, Tokchi'i.

The Humpbacked Flute Player, Kókopilau, we are already familiar with. Among the drawings pictured in Figure 48, the two lying on their backs are said to indicate that the Flute Clan had settled down for a long time in the areas. The one in Sonora, Mexico, was found in a cave and was ten feet long.

Figure 48. The Humpbacked Flute Player

ORAIBI

CHACO CANYON

GILA BEND

SPRINGERVILLE

VENTANA CAVE

GUATEMALA CITY

PETRIFIED FOREST

Figure 49. The coyote

The coyote figure at Oraibi (Figure 49) illustrates that the Coyote Clan had completed all four rounds of its migration, the tail pointing to the center point meaning that the clan finally had reached its permanent settlement. The Chaco Canyon figure shows that the clan had reached only two *pásos* at that time. The two figures at Gila Bend indicate that the clan had gone in one direction and had then returned. The tongue hanging out of the coyote at Springerville shows that he had been running ahead of the clan to find a place to settle and had turned back. It was a function of the Coyote Clan to perform this duty. In front of the coyote found in Ventana Cave, Arizona, is a four-pointed star—the "hurry star," whose appearance warned the people they must hurry to cover the four directional legs of their migration. At Petrified Forest a man is shown holding the tail of a coyote—in this case called a *poko,* "an animal who does things for you." To some Hopis the coyote figure reported found at Guatemala City indicates the starting place of the migrations.

ORAIBI   CHACO CANYON   OLDHAM COUNTY, TEXAS

MESA VERDE   GILA BEND   SPRINGERVILLE

Figure 50. The religious leaders

Near almost every ruin is found the figure of a man who represents the religious leader of the principal clan which occupied the village. The examples in Figure 50 show their variations and meanings.

The figures at Oraibi and Gila Bend have their right hands upraised, indicating that they are responsible men religiously carrying out their ceremonies to insure bountiful moisture. The two circles around the extended arms of the leader at Chaco Canyon show that he and his people have made two rounds of their migration. The loop over the heads of the figures found in Oldham County, Texas, and at Mesa Verde, Colorado, is known as the *equilni* [burden of weight], for during the migrations valuables or ritual objects were carried on the back of the leader with a tumpline around the head. Hence the *equilni* symbolizes the great responsibility the leader carries. The spider below the figure cut into the lava rocks near Springerville or the ruins of Wénima shows that he was the leader of the Spider Clan. It was here, we remember, that a contest was held between the Spider Clan and Parrot Clan.

THE TWO HORNS

As previously described, the ceremonies conducted by the Two Horn and One Horn Societies and owned by the Bow Clan are still today among the most important in the annual cycle. On the night of the Washing of the Hair during Wúwuchim, a pair of Two Horn members patrol the section of the village around the guarded kiva. The godfather who initiates them follows behind to guard them in turn against temptation or evil.

These Two Horns are the larger figures found at Oraibi and Mesa Verde and carved on a cliff bank of the Colorado River in Utah (Figure 51). The smaller figure to the right is their godfather. The middle figure in the Utah drawing carries an oval-shaped object identified as the *móng-wikoro* [chief's water jar], which is emptied into the small hole known as the Típkyavi [Womb] during the ceremony. The two figures colored with *suta* [red paint] and found in a cave in El Paso County, Texas, are members of the One Horn Society as shown by their single horns. The figure on the right is a member of the Two Horn Society.

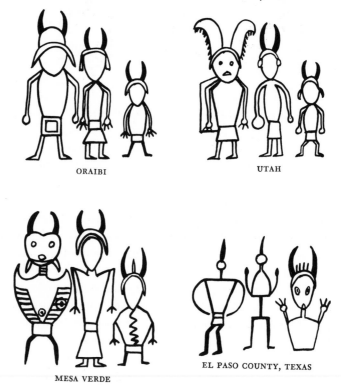

ORAIBI

UTAH

MESA VERDE

EL PASO COUNTY, TEXAS

Figure 51. The Two Horns and One Horns

12

The Founding of Oraibi

The Bear Clan was the first to complete all four legs of its migration to the directional limits of this Fourth World. From the sacred tablets given them, the people recognized the land that was to be theirs stretching between two mighty rivers now known as the Colorado and the Rio Grande. In its center, from a vast upland plain, rose three high mesas, the Hopi mesas of today. Here the people finally settled down to build permanent homes.

The first village built was Shongopovi, located at the bottom of the jutting spur of Second Mesa, on which historical Shongopovi stands today. For a time all went well. Then the younger of two brothers, Machito [Crowded Fingers], discovered that his older brother, Yahoya, was carrying on an affair [*chunta,* cheating] with his wife. That night he put his few belongings and the sacred tablets given to the Bear Clan in a buckskin bag and stole out of the village alone. On the cliff to the west, looking down into the valley between Second and Third Mesa, he carved four lines on the rock, signifying the breach between him and his brother and claiming all the land to the west for himself.

After walking north to Pavátuwi [Spring in the Cliff], he turned west across the wash and came down along the cliffs of Dodocowah [Bodies of Plants that Form a Rock] to Kachina Point. Here at the foot of the cliff he made his first home, carving on the walls the history of his clan. A friendly hawk always perched near him, giving warning of anyone's approach and often bringing him back rabbits for food.

One day a group of hunters from Shongopovi discovered him and invited him back home for a feast. "No. I will never go back there again," answered Machito.

Next morning his older brother, Yahoya, came and shouted, "I hear that you live here and I am come to take you back home." Three times he shouted this, but Machito still did not answer. Then he screamed angrily, "Why do you not speak to me?"

At this Machito answered, "You know I will not go back. You saw the four lines I put down between us. You know that all the land on this side is now mine."

After a long quarrel Yahoya agreed to the boundary, a line running south from Táwaki [Sun House], the point of the mesa, to Hövatöqa [Cut in the Cliff], toward present Winslow.

Several days later Machito's wife came to beg his return. She felt guilty about the wrong she had done him. Also the people of Shongopovi had discovered that Machito had taken all the sacred tablets and that Yahoya had lost his power. In order to save himself from their anger, Yahoya had abandoned his own wife and fled with his sister to the south. Machito sent his wife away; he would not return.

Finally he moved up on top of the cliff and founded the village of Oraibi, which he named after the cliff itself, Oraivi [Rock Place on High], the great rocky spur of Third Mesa.

As one clan after another arrived, it requested permission of Machito to settle in this village on the high rock. Machito was slow to decide. He first asked each clan, "During your migration did you ever use your supernatural power wrongly and for evil purposes, or did you come out of trouble the humble way?"

If the people had used their power wrongly, Machito refused them admittance, telling them they would have to settle in one of the other villages. If the clan had conducted itself properly, he asked, "What is the special power your deity has given you? What is your ritual or ceremony for evoking it? And how will it benefit all of the people here. Will you please demonstrate it to us?"

So each clan erected its altar, conducted its ceremony, and demonstrated the power it possessed to bring rain or snow, control underground streams, prevent cutting winds—whatever it was. The clan was then admitted to permanent settlement, and its ritual or ceremony was fitted into the annual ceremonial cycle to help complete the universal plan.

Machito then got out his sacred tablets, which showed the contours and the divisions of the land, and assigned farming and grazing land around Oraibi to each clan according to its ceremonial importance.

All this was in accordance with the prophecy as written on the tablets given the people at the beginning of their migrations.

The clans entering Oraibi renewed the quarrel with Shongopovi. The two villages now agreed that the village which gained the most population could claim the greater area of land between Second and Third Mesa. Before long Oraibi outgrew Shongopovi, and its people began using the land to the base of Táwaki [Sun House], the point of the mesa southeast of Oraibi.

Shongopovi, however, claimed all the land bounded by Dodocowah, Yangáchaivi [Place Where Chipmunks Run], and Munyá'ovi [Cliff of the Porcupine].

The dispute grew. Oraibi insisted that the reason it was growing so fast was because it held the core of the great ceremony which annually laid out the life-plan for all the people and insured germination and reproduction of all life. This great ceremony was Soyál,* brought by the Bear Clan. Many members of the Bear Clan, descendants of Machito's older brother, were still living in Shongopovi but did not know all the correct Soyál rituals. Moreover, after the two brothers had parted, it was agreed that if either leader lost or forgot any part of Soyál, the other leader would not give it to him.**

Finally the Fire Clan carved out a stone head of its deity, the powerful Másaw, and planted it near the Táwaki cliff between Pa'uuchvi [Spring Closed With Sand] to the south, and Munya'ovi on the north, establishing a boundary line respected by both villages. In this new area now guaranteed to Oraibi, clan holdings were allotted to all the clans which participated in Soyál with the Bear Clan—the Side Corn, Parrot, Rabbit, and Reed Clans.

Many miles away in every direction Oraibi now established shrines or altars marking the farthest limits of the land claimed by the Hopis. These included: Pisísvaiyu, the continuation of the boundary marked by the Colorado to the Pacific; Nuvátuky'ovi [Snowtop Mountains] near Flagstaff; and, farther south, Nuvákweotaqa [Snowbelt], home of Alósaka, the Two Horn deity; Kísiwu to the northeast; and the Zuñi Salt Lake to the south and east.

This, then, was the way it all began many years ago in the middle of this vast continent. All the clans had arrived from their migrations and had settled down in permanent villages. Farming and grazing lands outside were allotted them according to their ceremonial importance. Each contributed its ritual or ceremony, which was fitted into the annual ceremonial cycle, and its power brought rain and snow, controlled the wind, regulated the underground flow of water, prevented flash floods, insured germination and reproduction of all forms of life. Every year the *kachinas* came to help the people, bringing blessings from other stars, worlds, and planets. Grass grew knee-high on the vast plain. Herds of antelope grazed within sight of all villages. Bighorn sheep were numerous on the farther mesas. Game of all kinds was abundant everywhere.

---

* Described in Part Three.

** This is the Oraibi view. It must be stated, however, that the Bear Clan was never as prominent in Shangopovi as in Oraibi; and that Old Oraibi always adhered more closely to the traditional form of Soyál and other ceremonies than any other village; elsewhere omissions and deviations occur.

And this was all as it had been ordained. For this high, barren plateau had no rivers and streams for irrigating corn, squash, beans, tobacco, and cotton; no tropical climate to make people soft and life easy. The people had to depend upon their ceremonies, their prayers, the universal plan of life to which they had been confirmed. They were, in short, living a religious life which controlled every detail of their secular affairs.

But now a great change was imminent. The ice-locked Back Door to the continent far to the north had been opened. New people were beginning to wander down, naked, hungry, and ignorant, menacing these People of Peace. Far to the east another new race had landed on the shore of the continent. And far to the south, still more white strangers were following the trails of Hopi migrations.

The People of Peace were not worried at these reports and signs of change. They got out their sacred tablets again and read what had been prophesied. When they first had landed on this Fourth World, a certain person had been sent east to the rising sun. Upon reaching there, he was to erect a shrine and rest his forehead on the ground once. Then he was to return with the people of the rising sun and they would all become brothers again in fulfillment of the universal plan. If he rested his forehead more than once, it would take much longer, hundreds of years longer, for him to return. This lost white brother's name was Pahána [from *pásu,* salt water]. When he left, a piece of the sacred tablet was broken off and given to him so that when he rejoined his brothers this piece would match the tablet it had been broken from and identify him as their lost brother.

Yes. Pahána, their lost white brother, was on his way to rejoin them. Where would they meet him and when?

Prophecy told them this too. In the custody of the Bear Clan was a stick about six feet long. On the last day of the Soyál ceremony each year, a line was drawn across the stick. Pahána was due to arrive when the last line was drawn on the stick.

The people also knew where to meet the white strangers. Along the trail up the east side of the mesa to Oraibi there were four locations: Sikya'wa [Yellow Stone], Chekuwa [Pointed Rock], Nahoyungvasa [Cross Fields], and Tawtoma [Where the Sunray Goes Over the Line to the Place], just below Oraibi. If the strangers arrived on time, according to prophecy, the people were to meet them at the bottom of the mesa. If they did not arrive at the designated time, the people were to wait five years and receive them at the first location on the trail. If they still did not arrive, they were to wait periods of five years more in turn at each of the other three locations.

13

Commentary: The Hopi Clan

We can see now that the complete pattern formed by the migrations was a great cross whose center, Túwanasavi [Center of the Universe], lay in what is now the Hopi country in the southwestern part of the United States, and whose arms extended to the four directional *pásos* (Figure 52).

Túwanasavi was not the geographic center of North America, but the magnetic or spiritual center formed by the junction of the North-South and the East-West axes along which the Twins sent their vibratory messages and controlled the rotation of the planet. Hence it was called the Center of the Universe.

Three *pásos* for most of the clans were the same: the ice-locked Back Door to the north, the Pacific Ocean to the west, and the Atlantic Ocean to the east. Only seven clans—the Bear, Eagle, Sun, Kachina, Parrot, Flute, and Coyote Clans—migrated through South America to the southern *páso* at its tip. The rest of the some forty clans, having started from somewhere in southern Mexico or Central America, regarded this as their southern *páso,* their migrations thus forming a balanced symbol.

Upon arriving at each *páso* all the leading clans turned right before retracing their routes:

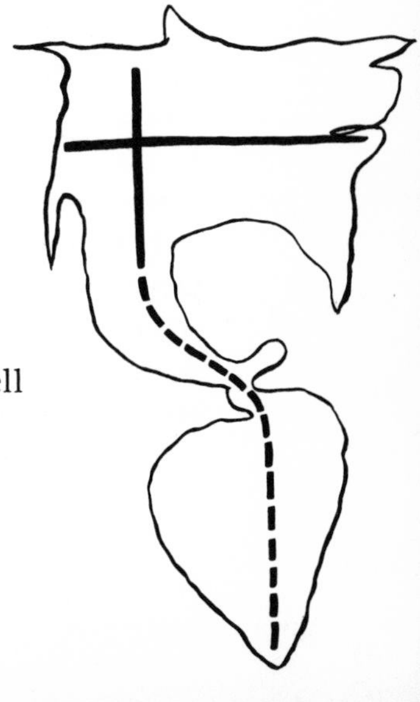

Figure 52. The migration pattern

Bear	Water	Flute
Spider	Kachina	Snake
Fire	Badger	Tobacco
Eagle	Flute	Lance
Parrot	Bow	Deep Well
Coyote	Side Corn	

This transformed the cross into a great swastika rotating counter-clock-wise to indicate the earth. These leading clans, beginning with the Black Bear Clan, were the first to begin the migrations and possessed high knowledge, and in turning right they were claiming the land for their people in accordance with the Creator's plan.

The rest of the clans turned left:

Strap	Millet	Cloud
Mole	Rabbit	Grease Eye Socket
Greasewood	Pumpkin	Black Seed
Bluebird	Short Well	Crane
Sparrow Hawk	Fog	Corn
Crow	Sun	Lizard
Butterfly	Sand	

These minor clans did not have complete ceremonies; they simply greeted the sun in prayer, lighted fires at their shrines for the four ele-ments and directions, and later supported the ceremonies conducted by the leading clans. In turning left they formed a swastika rotating clock-wise with the sun, whose course they were following, symbolizing their faithfulness to the Creator, their Sun Father.

All this is symbolized on the *kachina* rattle given children (see Figure 57).

Behind the minor clans much later came other people who separated and lived apart in other villages now known as follows:

People	Village
Túwi'i [Terrace]	Santo Domingo
Hemis [Mask-Kachina]	Jemez
Chiyáwwipki [Narrow People]	Isleta
Laguna [Buried Homes]	Laguna
Acomi [Rock Height]	Acoma
Ceoh [originally Ceohgonah or "Tried All"]	Zuñi
Pima [Reed Grass]	Southern Arizona near Sacaton
Papago [Mark on Head]	Southern Arizona near Sells

Thus the pattern and the meaning of the migrations were essentially religious, and they are so regarded today. At the conclusion of each major ceremony all the men who have taken part must remain in the kiva for another four days before returning to their families and fields. This retreat is an important part of the ceremony, for on the second day older men begin to relate the history of their clans and their migrations "so that we will always keep them deeply in our hearts. For the telling of our journeys is as much religious as the ceremonies themselves."

HISTORICAL CONJECTURES

The Emergence and the migrations are so beautiful in concept, so profoundly symbolic, one is tempted to accept them wholly as a great allegory of man's evolutionary journey on the Road of Life. Certainly the pure and perfect motherland the Hopis were seeking did not exist on this mortal earth.

It is difficult to reconcile a people having such an enlightened concept of spiritual life with an actual primitive people wandering over a vast and undiscovered continent in prehistoric times. Yet such were the Hopis. Archaeological remains and ancient records attest this.

Just who were these ancestors of today's Hopis? Where in America did they begin their migrations? When?

Finds made throughout America and dated by carbon-14 tests prove that man existed in America at least twenty thousand and possibly thirty thousand years ago. New blood-group studies of living Indians may push this horizon back still more. The purest O groups in the world have been found among Indians. If these Indians are direct descendants of the people of twenty thousand years ago, they may be the oldest known race, which first peopled this continent.

There then followed, in successive, slow waves of migration over the Bering Strait crossing, an influx of Australoid, Negroid, and Mongoloid people extending into comparatively recent times.

Anthropology asserts that the Hopis were members of the Shoshonean branch of the Uto-Aztecan language family of Mongoloids, who migrated to America by way of the Bering Strait crossing, arriving in the Southwest about 700 A.D. Other tribal groups include the Ute, Kiowa, and Tanoan Pueblo in the United States, and the Yaqui, Tarahumara, and Aztec in Mexico. After arriving at this late date, they are said to have adapted themselves to at least five different and previous culture patterns, adding not one independent discovery or invention.*

This is far afield from Hopi tradition, which asserts that the Hopis came much earlier; that they did not enter this continent through the Back Door to the north—via Bering Strait; and that their Place of Emergence was "down below" in the tropical south, somewhere in Middle America.

---

* Harold Sterling Gladwin, *Men Out of Asia* (N.Y.: McGraw-Hill, 1947).

Yet there is an indication that they may have been Mongolian in origin, for each Hopi child is born with the "Mongolian spot" at the base of the spine.* How much earlier could they have come to America?

There is a great body of literature, ever growing from antiquity to the present, asserting that sea crossings were made from Asia to America centuries before the Vikings and Columbus arrived from across the Atlantic. The earliest of these is the most ancient Chinese classic, *Shan Hai King,* compiled about 2250 B.C. It describes a voyage across the "Great Eastern Sea" and a two-thousand-mile journey down the length of the land beyond. Long regarded as a book of myth, it is now asserted to be an accurate geographic description of various landmarks in America, including the "Great Luminous Canyon" now known as Grand Canyon. A second Chinese classic, the *Kuen 327,* written in the fifth century A.D., relates the journey of Hwui, a Buddhist priest, to a far land called Fu-sang. This also is interpreted as an accurately described journey through Mexico and Yucatán.**

Gladwin postulates a sea crossing from Asia to Middle America in 323 B.C., the voyagers becoming the bearded white gods of the Mayas, Toltecs, and Aztecs.*** An older book † postulates a large influx of Mongolians into Mexico in 668 A.D. and 1175 A.D. They were said to have come from a kingdom in Mongolia called Tollan. The region was known as Anahuac [Near the Water], as it was in the vicinity of Lake Baikal and the river Tula. After emigrating across the sea, these Mongolians founded in Mexico a new Tollan and Tula named after the sites in their native land. In time the region came to be called Anahuac also, as it too was "near the water," the great lake at the present site of Mexico City. The people identified themselves as Nahuatlaks, were divided into seven "standards" or divisions, and said they had come from Aztlan.

However insubstantial these countless postulations and conjectures may be considered by scholars, they seem in curious conformity with native myth.

The *Popul Vuh,* the Sacred Book of the Quiché Maya in Yucatán also states that the Maya ancestors originated in seven womb-caves or ravines, left Tulan Pa Civan, and crossed the sea on stones placed in a row—similar to the steppingstones by which the Hopis crossed the Sea.

Tulan, Tollan, or Tula and the seven womb-caverns also figure promi-

---

* According to the doctors at the hospital at the Keams Canyon agency.
** Henriette Mertz, *Pale Ink* (privately printed, 1953).
*** Gladwin, op. cit.
† John Ranking, *Historical Researches on the Conquest of Peru, Mexico, Bogata, Natchez and Talomeco in the Twelfth Century, by the Mongols, Accompanied with Elephants* (London: Longman, Rees, Orme, Brown, and Green, 1827).

nently in Toltec and Aztec legend. Acosta, who arrived in Mexico soon after the Conquest, found that the Aztecs had a full tradition of their seven migrations from seven caves in Aztlán. His findings, published at Seville in 1589, name these successive tribes in the order of their arrival.* Clavigero affirms the tradition, giving a detailed timetable of the migration of the last tribe from Aztán to Tenochitlán, which they founded in 1325 A.D.** The *Codex Vaticanus,* which pictures four previous "worlds," and the *Codex Telleriano-Remensis,* containing a chronology of Aztec history from 1197 to 1592 A.D., both name the seven migrating clans and state that they originated from seven caves in Aztlán.

It seems certain at least that a horde of nomads known as Chichimecs from Aztlán, whatever and wherever it was, migrated into the northern end of the Valley of Mexico and in 856 A.D. founded the resplendent capital of the Toltec empire, Tula, whose ruins have been located fifty-four miles northwest of Mexico City. It lasted until 1168 A.D., when it was destroyed by successive new tribes of barbarians coming from the north, among them the Aztecs. The Toltecs migrated farther south to dominate the "new" empire of the Mayas, whose cultural center was Chichén Itzá. Here the Toltecs became known as the Itzas, and their bearded white god Quetzalcoatl as Kukulcán. The Aztecs meanwhile pushed south to found Tenochtitlán in 1325 A.D. and to establish the far-flung Aztec empire after conquering all neighboring tribes.

But all is still shrouded in the mists of time—the myths, the legends, the postulations and conjectures, the great stone pyramids and temples, and all the great ruins yet undiscovered. All we know is that here in Middle America *** during the first centuries in the Christian era there sprang up, under the impetus of belief in bearded white gods who may or who may not have been voyagers from Asia, the great pre-Columbian civilizations of the closely interlocked Mayas, Toltecs, and Aztecs. Here was the hub of life in the New World, the new Fourth World, with its magnificent stone cities, pyramid-temples, dominating priesthoods, abstract symbolism, and a calendar more accurate than the one we now use—here at the Place of Emergence where the Hopis began their continental migrations.

Without doubt the Hopis were once part of this great complex, whose perimeter was gradually extended northward through Chihuahua to the Four Corners area of the United States. It is no exaggeration to

---

* *Natural and Moral History of the East and West Indies,* London edition, 1604, Grimstone's translation.
** *History of Mexico,* Philadelphia edition, 1817, Cullen's translation.
*** This term, as used by archaeologists, includes Central America and Mexico.

say that among the Hopis of today we find living traces of this great pre-Columbian culture. The myths and traditions of the Aztecs and Hopis are similar in many respects, and modern Hopis still carry on many of the same religious rituals observed by the Aztecs. Moreover, abstract symbols and pictographs carved on Mayan stelae and temple walls have been readily interpreted by our Hopi spokesmen in terms of their own migration legends. It is not the purpose of the present book to encompass this larger field, which is a rich one for further study while the opportunity for comparison still exists.

The Hopis believe that the early Mayas, Toltecs, and Aztecs were aberrant Hopi clans who failed to complete their fourfold migrations, remaining in Middle America to build mighty cities which perished because they failed to perpetuate their ordained religious pattern. This may well be a case of the tail wagging the dog. It is more likely that the people who later called themselves Hopis were a small minority, perhaps a religious cult, who migrated north to the Four Corners area of our own Southwest about 700 A.D.

During the next four centuries, between 700 and 1100 A.D., were built all the great pueblos in the area—on Mesa Verde, in Chaco Canyon, and at Aztec; Wupatki, Betatakin, Keet Seel, and many others. If they were not built by the Hopis, their occupancy by migrating Hopi clans is attested by both clan legends and clan signatures carved on walls and cliffs. Their period of greatest occupancy was roughly from 1000 to 1300 A.D., most of them having been abandoned shortly before and during the Great Drought from 1276 to 1299 A.D.

This period coincides with the establishment of the first Hopi villages on the three Hopi mesas. Although some contemporary Hopis maintain there are three successive ruins below the present village of Oraibi on its rocky mesa top, the earliest date established for it by tree-ring chronology is 1150 A.D., which still makes it the oldest continuously occupied settlement in the United States. Hence it seems probable that the Hopis first settled in their present homeland early in the twelfth century, followed by a host of clans abandoning the surrounding pueblos.

What shape did they give to this new population center in the heart of the northern wilderness? The precedent had been set by the resplendent temple- and pyramid-studded cities of the Mayas, Toltecs, and Aztecs, by Casas Grandes, and by the magnificent complex of Chaco Canyon, which have evoked the admiration of centuries. If we grant the relationship of the Hopis to these ancient city-builders, it seems strange that now, when all the Hopi clans had finally arrived at their preordained place of permanent settlement, they did not pattern it upon these previous great cities. Instead, one sees from the start, the continual growth of many small villages spread over three widely separated mesas and founded by different clans:

Village	Location	Notes
Shongopovi	Second Mesa	Settled by Bear Clan
Oraibi	Third Mesa	Settled by Bear Clan from Shongopovi
Mishongovi	Second Mesa	Settled by Bear Clan from Shongopovi
Shipaulovi	Second Mesa	Settled by Bear Clan from Shongopovi
Walpi	First Mesa	Settled by Fire Clan
Hano	First Mesa	Settled by Tewa-speaking people from the Rio Grande valley
Awatovi	Antelope Mesa	Settled by Bow Clan
Sikyatki	East of First Mesa	Settled by Coyote Clan
Piutki	Second Mesa	Abandoned when people moved to Sandia Pueblo in Rio Grande valley
Machongpi	Third Mesa below Hotevilla	Abandoned when people moved to Cotiti, now Cochiti Pueblo in Rio Grande valley
Kateshum	East of First Mesa	Abandoned when people moved to San Felipe Pueblo in Rio Grande valley
Chemonvasi [Jimson Weed]	Third Mesa	Abandoned when people moved to Jemez Pueblo in Rio Grande valley
Tiquiovi [Pointed Hill]	Eastern edge of Third Mesa	Abandoned when people moved to San Ildefonso, Santa Clara, or San Juan Pueblo in Rio Grande valley
Hotevilla	Third Mesa	Settled by Fire Clan from Oraibi after split of 1906
Bakavi	Third Mesa	Settled by Spider Clan from Hotevilla after split of 1907
Moencopi	Fifty miles west of Third Mesa	Settled by Pumpkin Clan from Oraibi

Why was it that the Hopis did not concentrate in one great cultural center comparable to nearby Chaco Canyon, to Casas Grandes, and to those of the Aztecs, Toltecs, and Mayas to the south? Could they have, if left alone for a few centuries more? Perhaps the scarcity of water throughout all this vast arid plateau was enough to retard the growth of such a center. Yet the curious pattern of continual separation of clans, of founding and abandoning villages, shows that the nature of the people themselves militated against unity and centralization.

Even under more favorable climatic conditions the Hopis could never have consolidated at Oraibi the clans and cultural patterns drawn from the other population centers after the Great Drought. They were an intensely religious people, a confirmed people of peace, with an inherent repulsion against secular control of any kind. And the key to this positive and inherent allergy to unification, organization, and expansion was the clan.

SECULAR ASPECTS

The clan is still the heart of Hopi society. We cannot understand the legends of the migrations or the turbulent history that followed without understanding the meaning and functions of the clan. To it can be ascribed all the virtues of group cohesiveness and loyalty to tradition that mark the individual. Upon it also can be blamed all the evils that still restrict the Hopis within a social mold too narrow and frigid to expand with the ever-widening pattern of modern life.

A clan is comprised of several families, the members of each family being related through matrilineal descent and taking the clan name of the mother. The name and functions of the family are of little importance; it is the clan that counts, determining the standing of the individual in both religious and secular matters.

Ethnology defines a Hopi clan as a totemically named, exogamous, unilateral aggregation of matrilineal kindred. Without attempting to explain this rather imposing definition, let us simply recall what we have observed of a clan during its migration. Each has a name—usually that of a bird, beast, or other living entity. It also has a special guardian spirit, deity, *kachina,* or *wu'ya,* represented by a stone or wood fetish, the *tiponi.* Most of the important clans possess a ritual or complete ceremony whose power benefits all the community. Land allotments are held in the name of the clan.

The principal clans are:

Bear Clan	*Parrot Clan*	*Eagle Clan*	*Badger Clan*
Black Bear	Crow	Sun	Butterfly
Gray Bear	Rabbit	Forehead	Kachina
Strap	Tobacco		
Grease Eye Socket			
Bluebird			
Mole			
Water Coyote			

Spider Clan	Fire Clan	Snake Clan	Water Clan
Gray Flute	Blue Flute	Sand	Deep Well
		Lizard	Short Well
			Side Corn
			Fog
			Cloud

Pumpkin Clan	Bow Clan	Black Seed Clan	Coyote Clan
Crane	Arrowshaft		
Hawk	Greasewood		
	Large Reed		
	Small Reed		

These principal clans are grouped, as shown, in clan-succession groups or phratries. Like the family, the phratry is unimportant compared to the clan. It has no name, holds no property, exercises no secular powers. It simply designates the sequence of clans in carrying out the ceremonial for which the leading clan is primarily responsible.

Even this succession of clans within a phratry is unimportant. The Bear Clan is acknowledged the leading Hopi clan; it lays out the life plan for the year in the great Soyál ceremony, and the Village Chief of Oraibi must be a member of the Bear Clan. But the clans in the phratry of which the Bear Clan is the leader succeed to no power whatever. The power actually passes to the Parrot Clan. For the four most important clans are the Bear, Parrot, Eagle, and Badger, whose chiefs are known as the Nalöönongmomgwit, representing the four directions from which these clans entered Oraibi upon the conclusion of their migrations. The standing of a clan and the relative value of its land holdings, then, is based solely on religious grounds—whether it had successfully completed its migrations to the four directional *pásos,* and the ceremony which it possessed.

The long migrations reveal the inherent weakness in this clan system. The people never viewed themselves as a tribal whole, a Chosen People led by a Moses through the wilderness to the Promised Land. They traveled separately as clans, in different directions, owing primary allegiance to their own guiding spirits. When several clans joined to build and occupy a village, quarrels between them arose, and they separated again. As the people multiplied, more splits occurred within the clan itself, resulting in the formation of a new clan. This indeed is the principal motif of all the migration legends—a quarrel between two brothers in the same clan or between the leaders of two clans, each challenging the power of the other's deity and ceremony with his own, causing another split. We see, then, in the migrations the curious paradox of one people landing on a new continent under one divine injunction to seek one permanent homeland, but succumbing on the way to a constant and ever-growing rivalry between an ever-increasing number of clans and minor deities.

The premise of Hopi life then and now, however, is the ideal of unifying at their permanent homeland, the Center of the Universe, where they are to consolidate the universal pattern of Creation. To this end all clan rivalries and disputes simply served as a weeding-out process to test the people's adherence to this traditional ideal. It is a profound concept, this great universal pattern of Creation to which man must conform in every act of his daily life. And these intertwined legends of a people's migrations comprise a beautiful story, essentially religious. This premise we must accept.

But now, after centuries, their wanderings were over. They had arrived in the Promised Land to weld themselves into a tribal unity, to confront imminent changes with one heart. One would expect that the inherent weaknesses in the clan system would now crop out. This is indeed the bitter story of the historical period that followed the legendary period of the migrations.

The Hopis, however, have never faltered in the belief that their secular pattern of existence must be predicated upon the religious, the universal plan of Creation. They are still faithful to their own premise. Let us, then, observe the great annual cycle of ceremonies which they established at Oraibi—a living monument to a living faith that has outlasted the crumbling ruins of Tenochtitlán and Pueblo Bonito alike.

PART THREE

THE MYSTERY PLAYS:

The Ceremonial Cycle

1

Elemental Symbols

The entire course of the Hopi Road of Life is unfolded every year in an annual cycle of nine great religious ceremonies that dramatize the universal laws of life. No other "folk art" in all America remotely compares with these profound mystery plays. They wheel slowly and majestically through the seasonal cycles, like the constellations which time their courses and imbue their patterns with meaning. Barbarically beautiful, ancient and alien to modern eyes and ears, they take on for us the dimensions of the mystical unreal. Even their names seem derived from an ancient and cryptic mythology known only to the mirroring stars above: Wúwuchim, Soyál, Powamu, Lakón, Owaqlt—words unknown to us, perhaps, but great names for great things, old names, as old as the shape of America itself.

Why these mysteries should seem strange to us now an onlooker cannot say. Their songs and dances form simple rhythmical patterns. The costumes and decorations are even more simple. A deer horn, an eagle feather, a turtle-shell rattle, a twig of spruce and an ear of corn, daubs of mineral paint—no more than these. Have we of this Synthetic Age grown so far away from our earth that we read no meaning in the elements of its mineral, plant, and animal kingdoms? Yet these ceremonies hold a deeper truth than this. For to the Hopi the cornstalk, the talking stones, the great breathing mountains—all are significant and alive, being mere symbols of the spirits which give them form and life. These invisible spiritual forms are in turn but manifestations of the one supreme creative power which imbues them with meaning, which moves them in their earthly orbits and seasonal cycles in unison with the constellations of the midnight sky. And again, their unhurried, stately movements follow the inexorable laws of universal life itself—symbols for symbols, layer upon layer of ritual esotericism, through which man reaches at last the ultimate meaning of his brief existence on this one puny planet among count-

less myriads more. Such are the truths deeply embodied in Hopi ceremonialism, whose complex symbolism and ritualism have long been the
despair of rational observers.

But we do not need to be confused by their seeming strangeness.
By the miracle of their truth they speak intuitively to the heart with the
appeal of the appallingly simple. Something about them, however vague,
seems comfortingly familiar. One takes from them according to his measure, whatever it is. No living being is excluded from the blessings they
invoke—the earth, the seas, the entities of the plant and animal kingdoms,
and man, wherever he exists.

We today can witness on these three lofty mesas the last full moon
of Hopi life, a cultural erasure even as we look. Yet it is no paradox that
from these tawdry villages choked with refuse still springs such profound
beauty. For the persistently obdurate dramatization of the law of laws
alone marks the Hopi Road of Life. These annual cycles of great ceremonials are monuments that leave no petroglyphs to fade into obscurity,
no stones to topple into ruin. They are written, like life, on the vast
palimpsest of the earth and sky, and in the enduring heart of man.

But before they unroll before us, we must understand the meaning
of a few of the elemental symbols common to all ceremonials.

THE KIVA

Most important of all is the underground chamber in which
the rituals are held—the kiva.

Long, long ago, when the people were following their migrations
over the earth, they had no homes save small pits they dug in the earth
and roofed over with brush and mud. Thousands of these rude prehistoric
pit houses are still being discovered throughout all America. Gradually
the migrations of the clans became slower. The people had reached the
ends of the earth and claimed the continent; now they were looking
for places to settle and to grow crops. They built small groups of houses
in and upon high cliffs and out upon the plain, but they still dug pits
for use as storage cists to hold their corn and as burial places for their dead.

One after another the clans united, their small house groups cluster-
ing together and expanding into pueblos or village-sized single dwellings.
The people became farmers, growing corn, squash, beans, and cotton in
the fields outside. The pit houses and storage cists in which they had
stored the corn that gave them life and in which they had buried their
dead now began to be used for performances of the sacred ceremonies by

which the people bridged life and death in an enduring continuity. They became kivas.

As its name signifies, the kiva [world below] was large enough to hold the members of several clans and it abstractly symbolized the tenets of their faith. Cylindrical or rectangular, it was sunk deep, like a womb, into the body of Mother Earth, from which man is born with all that nourishes him. A small hole in the floor symbolically led down into the previous underworld, and the ladder-opening through the roof symbolically led out to the world above. The kiva was the most distinctive structure in all the great centers of prehistoric life in North America, reaching the epitome of structural symbolism in the Great Kiva of the twelfth century.

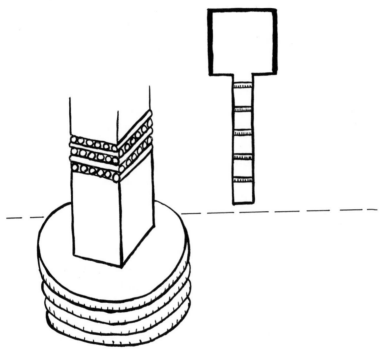

Figure 53. Great Kiva at Aztec

The largest yet completely excavated and reconstructed is the cylindrical Great Kiva at Aztec, New Mexico (Figure 53). It stands in the central plaza of a pueblo now in ruins that was three stories high and contained five hundred rooms. The main altar room is more than forty-eight feet in diameter. Connected with it by a flight of steps to ground level is a small square room at the north. After entering this from outside, one stares down into the great lofty room that still gives forth the ineffable and ineradicable feeling of a strange temple in an antediluvian world which existed long before this continent emerged from timeless time. For it is more than a record of the prehistoric past. It is an architectural symbol of the soul-form of all Creation.

We enter it with a Hopi friend who, though seeing it for the first time, easily reads for us the cryptic meanings of its details of construction. Four great pillars of masonry uphold the lofty ninety-ton roof. The ground has been cleared away to show that each rests on a footing of four huge stone disks which represent the four successive worlds upon which man has led his existence.

One of the columns shows another peculiar feature. Interspersed between the blocks of stone are layers of round cedar poles stacked crosswise. They symbolize the reeds woven crosswise into the rafts upon which the people crossed to the present Fourth World.

Around the high walls are narrow vertical slots or ladderways, as shown in Figure 53. Each contains five rungs of cedar symbolizing the four worlds to which man has climbed and the fifth to which he will climb next. These ladderways widen out at the top into openings into twelve small peripheral chambers built on the outside circular wall of the kiva.* Here, then, is outlined the cosmography of the universe.

On the floor is a raised stone fire altar, and on each side is a large vault or pit walled with stone, whose purpose has never been definitely known. These were used for performances of a magic fire ritual, vestiges of which are still held in modern Hopi villages.**

This great chamber was the altar room, reserved for the priests with authority to conduct the religious ceremonies. In the smaller upper room adjoining it sat the novices being initiated. Such great kivas set the general pattern for the early, circular kivas such as those still in use in the contemporary pueblos along the Rio Grande.

Just when the Hopi kiva was made rectangular in form and set from west to east is not known. Yet only the outward form was changed. The symbolic features inside remained, a strikingly original pattern of profound meaning.

Here, then, is the Hopi kiva of today: sunk in a central plaza, the *kisonvi* [center of the village], where public dances are given at the conclusion of the secret ceremonies held inside; rectangularly set with the directions, the east-west axis formed by the path of the sun running through it lengthwise, and running crosswise the north-south axis of the earth, at whose ends sit Pöqánghoya and Palöngawhoya who keep the

---

* There are fourteen chambers in the reconstructed kiva, two more than indicated in the original ruin.
    ** Fully described in Chapter 11.

planet rotating properly. Sometimes the kiva is widened at one end, forming the same shape as the T-shaped doorways found in all the ancient Hopi ruins, which are again the "hair identifications" of the Hopis (see page 130).

Inside, the floor of the eastern half is raised slightly above the level of the western half. During initiation rites the novices occupy the raised level, the lower level being always reserved for the priests, thus reflecting the different stages of their religious development. The whole architecture of the kiva, like the concepts embodied in its cermonialism, is thus directly opposite to that of the church of European lineage. The Christian church is built above ground, its phallic steeple thrusting into the sky; the kiva is build below ground, a womb of Mother Earth. Inside the Christian church, altar and priests are raised above the level of common worshipers and adorned with the richest vestments; while in the kiva, altar and priests occupy the lowest level, where the priests are always barefoot to show their humility.

In the center of the kiva, on the altar level and directly below the roof opening, is the sunken fire pit in which a fire is lighted in the New Fire Ceremony during Wúwuchim, for life began with fire. Next to it is the small hole in the floor called the *sipápuni*.* Etymologically derived from the two words for "navel" and "path from," the *sipápuni* thus denotes the umbilical cord leading from Mother Earth and symbolizes the path of man's Emergence from the previous underworld. It is usually plugged and covered by a plank which is ritually removed when the Emergence from the underworld is re-enacted. The altar is set in the center of the altar-level floor. In the seating ledge running across the west wall and directly opposite the ladder is the "*kachina* house," referred to as the *kachinki* when talking to the uninitiated, and as the *tuwaki* because it contains the *kachina* masks when they are not embodied by the spirits which give them life. The ladder represents the reed up which man climbed during his Emergence, and through the roof opening are watched the constellations in the sky above, whose movements time all rituals. At other times the opening is closed by a straw thatch called the *núta*, meaning "cover it up," "hold it in place." Here then is the whole structure of the multi-world universe: the *sipápuni* leading down to the Place of Beginning; the sunken fire pit where life began with fire, representing the First World; the altar level, the Second World; the raised level on which the ladder rests, symbolizing the Third World; and the ladder, which serves as another *sipápuni* to the present Fourth World outside and above the kiva.

---

* More commonly known by the Tewa name of *sípapu*.

Built of native stone, as are most Hopi buildings, the central part of the kiva protrudes some four or five feet above the surface of the ground. This is called the *kivaove*, meaning simply "the part above." Many terraced Hopi houses are built the same way. The appearance of these houses and of the visible part of the kivas is distinctively Hopi and have long given rise to many questions about their form.

The Hopis are never without an apt and amusing answer. They simply turn the sketched outline of the structure upside down, add facial marks, and point out that the distinguishing feature of every Hopi man is the traditional hair bangs falling down over his ears (Figure 54).

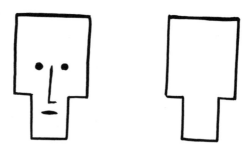

Figure 54. Form of kiva

Of more significance is the fact that this is the outline of the ladder-way entrance in the Great Kiva at Aztec and the shape of the traditional doorways of the Hopis. The name *túoinaka* [stack-up-corn ear jewel], used for the inlaid earrings worn by the Flute Maidens during the Flute Ceremony, refers also to this shape and to the men's hair bangs and is said to prove the Hopi origin of similar doorways found in ruins throughout the Amercan Southwest and northern Mexico.

Hopi kivas are not built in the double system of the Tewa and Keresan pueblos along the Rio Grande, which have two kivas, nor in the sixfold system of the Tanoan group, such as Taos Pueblo, which has one kiva for each of the six directions. There may be any number of kivas in each Hopi pueblo, reflecting not only the population of the village but the important part kivas play in Hopi life. They range from the maximum number of fourteen once in use in Oraibi to the two in use at Shipaulovi. Primarily associated with the clans that build them and conduct their distinctive ceremonies in them, they are used between ceremonials as meeting or lodge rooms. At these times there is a ground-floor entrance for use by aged and infirm members. Throughout the year they are almost constantly in use and reflect the predominantly religious tenor of life that affects even the administration of secular affairs.

In order to be acknowledged as a true Hopi village, each village must have a village chief selected from the Bear Clan. Otherwise it is regarded merely as a settlement with a governor elected by the Tribal Council. The Tribal Council is of course commonly regarded as merely a puppet government of the United States Indian Bureau, set up for administrative purposes. It is not representative of the people, has no real authority, and little interest is taken in it. Such a settlement is Kiakochomovi or New Oraibi, whose governor in 1959 was elected by four votes out of a total of ten votes cast for all candidates. It has three kivas, used only for *kachina* dances, not for ceremonies—like churches not sanctified and without priests.

Bakavi also has three kivas but a governor only. Of the fourteen kivas at Oraibi, the parental home of Hopi ceremonialism, three are still being used by the last fifty residents. Moencopi, fifty miles west, has three kivas. Its village chief is a member of the Side Corn Clan, associated with the Short Cistern Clan, because its guiding *kachina* is Áholi, who, with Eototo, must be personified only by the Bear Clan. Hence Moencopi is a "baby" of Oraibi, which validates all its ceremonies.

Hotevilla, with six kivas and now ceremonially the most important village, was formed in 1906 when Chief Yukioma and his followers left Oraibi, supposedly returning to Betatakin, whence came his Ghost Clan. Hence today a member of the Ghost Clan or the succeeding Fire Clan and Smoldering Wood Clan serves as village chief. Hotevilla still indomitably refuses to cooperate with the Tribal Council.

On Second Mesa the large village of Shongopovi supports five kivas, and its village chief is of the Bear Clan. The smaller villages of Mishongnovi, with three kivas, and Shipaulovi, with two kivas, use the same village chief, a member of the Bear Clan.

On First Mesa all members of the five Bear-succession Clans have now died out. Hence the village chief of Walpi is selected alternately from a new phratry of four clans: the Flute, Snake, Antelope, and Water Snake—accounting for the predominance of their ceremonies on First Mesa. Walpi has five kivas, Sichomovi has two, and Hano one.

The kiva is thus the focal point of Hopi life. It abstractly symbolizes the tenets of the ancient ceremonials performed in it; it functions on the secular level; and it is the underground heart of all that is truly, distinctively Hopi.

THE PÁHO

The preparation of *páhos* is a prime requisite of all ceremonies conducted in the kiva. A *páho* is a prayer-feather made from any kind of feather but usually from the feather of an eagle. Simple as it is, it carries a long tradition.

When the people emerged to the present world they first met a great bird, the eagle, and asked his permission to occupy the land. The eagle put them through several tests, which they passed successfully.* He then granted them his permission, saying, "Any time you want to send a message to our Father Sun, the Creator, you may use my feather. For I am the conqueror of air and master of height. I am the only one who has the power of space above, for I represent the loftiness of the spirit and can delivery your prayers."

From that time on, eagle feathers have been used to carry the people's prayers aloft to their Creator. The simplest *páho* is merely a single "downy" or down feather of an eagle, to which is attached a string of native cotton ** measuring from the wrist to the tip of the middle finger.

One of the most exquisitely made and beautifully symbolic is the male-and-female *páho* (Figure 55). It consists of two red-willow sticks about eight inches long. Both may be painted blue, or the male stick black. The female stick has a facet cut in the upper end, which is painted brown. Tied to the base of the sticks and binding them together is a small sack made of a cornhusk folded to a point—the *nöösioqa* [nourishment], symbolic of the spiritual body. Inside it are cornmeal, representing the physical body; a pinch of corn pollen to symbolize the power of fertility and reproduction; and a drop of honey, the "sweet," the Creator's love. Both *páho* sticks are tied together because the Creator is both male and female; and in mankind both sexes draw together into a single unity for the creative act of reproduction. The cotton string which ties them together is the life cord; for when the cotton blossomed it received its first fertilization from the Sun Father, creating a cord within itself, the bud, to receive the life fluid from the Sun. To the end of this cotton string is tied a downy eagle feather to symbolize the breath of life, the length of cord representing a long life.

The clear blue or turquoise color is called *páskwapi*, and denotes the spiritual qualities inherent in the sky, the waters, and the plant life which clothes mankind. It is secured by Wúwuchim initiates when they make their first pilgrimage to Salt Cave in Grand Canyon, ninety miles west. Coming to this certain place, each initiate kneels, reaches in to plant his prayer feather, and pulls out some of the colored earth.

The brown paint, known as *pávisa*, is also brought back from Grand Canyon. Being the color of the Mother Earth, it is used to represent the face on the facet of the female stick.

---

* Described in Part Two, Chapter 2.
** A distinct species to which botanists have given the name *Gossypium Hopi*.

The base of both sticks below the binding is colored with a black paint, *toho*, secured from outcroppings of decomposed rock and coal. This part of the *páho* is placed in the earth, just as man is rooted in this world until he is planted on another world or planet at a future time.

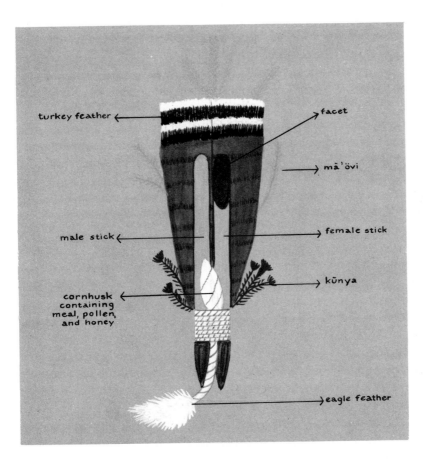

Figure 55. Male-and-female páho

When the *páhos* are thus prepared, a turkey feather and two small twigs are finally fastened to the back. The wild turkey feather signifies the wildness and the mystery of Creation that man has never completely tamed and understood. One of the twigs comes from the *má'övi* [plant where the katydid sits], the rabbit bush or *chamisa*, which symbolizes the heat of summer. The other is from the *kúnya* [water plant], which is used when a person is ill to remove extra water from the body.

Every *páho*, simple or complex, is made with prayerful concentration and ritually smoked over. Then it is carried to a shrine, where it is stuck in a cleft of rocks or hung on a bush and left until the invisible vibrations of the prayer it embodies are slowly absorbed by the forces of life to which it is dedicated.

THE CORN MOTHER

It is inconceivable that any Hopi ceremonial could be conducted without cornmeal, so varied is its use and so significant its meaning. With cornmeal is drawn the Road of Life in the kiva. Paths of cornmeal are marked for approaching *kachinas*. Conversely, roads and trails are blocked to passage of all living creatures by lines of cornmeal on the night of terror and mystery during Wúwuchim. *Kachina* dancers are welcomed with sprinkles of cornmeal. Baskets and plaques of cornmeal are common offerings during all rituals. The rising sun is greeted with cornmeal. Ears of colored corn designate the six directions and are stacked at the base of the chief's altar. To the staff of the Áholi Kachina are tied seven Corn Mothers. A Corn Mother is fastened to the sacred *mongko*—the "law of laws." Corn kernels, stalks, leaves, meal, and pollen are ritually used.

Even less conceivable is Indian life throughout all America without corn. Indigenous to the Western Hemisphere, Indian maize has been the bread of life to Indian America since the beginning of time. So synonymous are they that it is difficult to tell which was created first, land, man, or corn. Certainly maize is so old that modern science has been unable to find any direct evidences as to what wild plant it might have derived from and when its culture began. Corn is the supreme achievement in plant domestication of all time, but its origin remains a botanical mystery.*

The Hopis assert that corn was divinely created for man in the First World. When this world was destroyed and man emerged to the Second World, corn was again given him as the staff of life. When that world was in turn destroyed and man emerged to the Third World, corn was

---

* We cannot overemphasize the importance of corn in the mythology of the New World. According to the *Popul Vuh*, the ancestors of the Quiché Mayas of Guatemala were four perfect men made from maize. The Navajos also hold that the prototypes of man were created from corn. Maize was sacred throughout the New World centuries before the first record of it in a European language was made in Columbus's log for November 6, 1492. Where and when it originated is not known. Borings in deposits which underlie the ancient Aztec capital of Tenochtitlán, now Mexico City, reveal fossil pollen grains of maize, teosinte, and tripsacum, all of which grew long before the beginnings of agriculture anywhere in the Americas. Innumerable varieties of maize deposits have been found near the old Inca capital of Cuzco in the Peruvian Andes. Probably the oldest known remains of maize have been found in deposits in Bat Cave, New Mexico, and in Tularosa Cave, New Mexico, both estimated to be 4500 years old by radiocarbon analysis, according to *Indian Corn in America* by Paul Weatherwax (New York: Macmillan, 1954).

given him once more. By this time mankind had multiplied into many races and the earth was beginning to be contaminated by wickedness as before. Realizing that this world too would have to be destroyed so mankind could make an Emergence to the present Fourth World, the Creator decided to find out how much greed and ignorance had crept into the various races. Accordingly he laid out before them ears of corn of all sizes.

"The time has come for you to make an Emergence to a new world," he told them. "There you will spread out, multiply, and populate the earth. So choose now, according to your wisdom, the corn you will take with you to be your food."

The people made their choices. Some took the large ear, some the long, some the fat. Only the small, short ear was left. This the Hopis took because it was like the original humble ear given them on the First World, and they knew it would never die out.

Growing in small ears on short, stunted stalks in sandy fields and rocky hillsides with only an occasional rain to nourish them, Hopi corn is still an agricultural miracle and a dependable staple that has earned for the Hopis the name of Corn-Eaters among neighboring meat-eating tribes.

The Hopis have never forgotten their choice of the smallest ear.* Every year at harvest time a man goes into his cornfield and selects first the smallest ears on the stalks, saying, "Now you are going home." Singing softly, he carries them home in a basket and gives them to his wife. She, without setting them down, carries them to her storage room, where she stacks them on the floor as a base for all the larger ears in the crop, saying, "Now, seed, you have come home."

There are many reasons for the Hopi veneration of corn. When the earth was first created it was created female, our Mother Earth. Its tutelary deity, Sótuknang, was instructed to create a substance to provide nourishment to mankind. Having no female partner, he gathered the moisture and fertilized the female earth with rain, bringing forth vegetation to supply with food all living creatures crawling upon her breast. Grass thus became as milk to the creatures of the animal kingdom, and corn became the milk for mankind.

Corn, then, unites the two principles of Creation. It is a sacred entity embodying both the male and the female elements. When the plant begins to grow, the leaf curves back to the ground like the arm of a child groping for its mother's breast. As the stalk grows upward in a spiral the first tassel appears, which is male. Then appears an ear of corn, which is female. This point of growth corresponds to the halfway span of a man's life. The

---

* Sowiwa (length of the newborn rabbit).

female element, the ear of corn, is now ready to be fertilized by the male element, the tassel. Then the silk appears and pollen is dropped on the "life line" to mature and season it to its fullest expression. When finally the tassel begins to turn brown and bend downward, male and female have reached their old age and the end of their reproductive power.

The Corn Mother from whom we receive our nourishment is thus an entity like Mother Earth, and so closely are they united that they are virtually synonymous. Because we build its flesh into our own, corn is also our body. Hence when we offer cornmeal with our prayers we are offering a part of our body. But corn is also spirit, for it was divinely created, so we are also offering spiritual thanks to the Creator.

All these concepts are embodied in a perfect ear of corn whose tip ends in four full kernels. This is the Corn Mother saved for rituals. Without her and all that she provides, Hopi life and ceremonialism could not endure.

OTHER CEREMONIAL REQUISITES

With cornmeal and *páhos* there are many other fundamental symbols and observances too numerous to detail here. Their rigid adherence to tradition only illustrates the closely knit and complex web of Hopi ceremonialism.

Every ceremony is announced from a housetop by the Crier Chief, and the announcement is a function of the Reed Clan. No ceremony is complete without ritual smoking. The pipe is used only by the chiefs of the Two Horn, One Horn, Flute, and Wuchim Societies; all others use cigarettes of native tobacco rolled in cornhusks. The preparation of tobacco for both pipe and cigarette is the exclusive function of the Tobacco and Rabbit Clans. The Sand Clan, traditional keepers of the soil, gathers the sand upon which the altars are set up. The final setting up and consecration of the altars concludes the ritual preparations for all major ceremonies. For as the kiva symbolizes both the world and the universe, the altar represents both the village dwelling which man inhabits and the fleshly house wherein his spirit dwells.

The altar, the male-and-female *páho,* the Corn Mother—each of these, it is significant to note, is ritually equated to the body of man, as the feather, cornmeal, and tobacco smoke are representative of his spiritual body, his thought and prayers. These are the foundations of Hopi ceremonialism.

But now it is time to see how dramatically they are used; it is time for the curtain to lift on the annual cycle of the ceremonies themselves.

2

Wúwuchim

There are three phases of dawn: Qöyangnuptu, the purplish dawn-dusk when the shape of man is first outlined; Sikangnuqa, the yellow light of dawn which reveals man's breath; and finally Tálawva, the red sunrise glow in which man stands proudly revealed in the fullness of his creation.

The dawn of each new day and the dawn of each annual cycle endlessly repeat these three phases of all Creation at the dawn of life, the beginning of man's evolutionary journey.

Wúwuchim is the first of the three great winter ceremonies which begin the ceremonial year with the portrayal of the three phases of Creation. The singular form of the word, Wuchim, is etymologically derived from *wu*, to germinate, and *chim,* to manifest, and designates members of the Wuchim religious society. In its plural form Wúwuchim thus denotes a ceremonial supplication by the Wuchim and other participating societies at this first dawn of Creation for the germination of all forms of life on earth—plant, animal, and man.

It takes place during November, Kélmúya, the Initiates' or Hawk Moon, when the days grow short and the earth lies cold and lifeless. The date is determined by lunar observation. On the first day of the new moon, kiva members gather materials for making *páhos* or prayer sticks, which they cut on the second day and ritually pray and smoke over on the third day. The following day the *páhos* are carried to their proper shrines, and the Crier Chief publicly announces the beginning of Wúwuchim from a housetop. The ceremony lasts sixteen days: an eight-day period of preparation and an eight-day period of secret rituals in the kivas, followed by a public dance on the day concluding the ceremony.* It is commonly reported as being a nine-day ceremony in recogni-

---

* In 1959 Wúwuchim was not announced in Shongopovi until November 11, four days after the first-quarter moon, and in Hotevilla on November 15, the first day of the full moon. The reason was that Oaqöl, the women's ceremony ending the previous ceremonial year, was delayed because of an accident, necessitating postponement of Wúwuchim in order to keep it out of the same moon phase.

tion of the important last nine days, but in disregard of the equally important first eight days of preparation.

Wúwuchim is observed at Walpi on First Mesa, at Mishongnovi and Shongopovi on Second Mesa, and at Hotevilla on Third Mesa. From time immemorial Oraibi on Third Mesa has been considered the parental home of Hopi ceremonialism, all the ceremonies being given here in their purest and fullest forms. In the other pueblos, especially on First Mesa, which has been most exposed to white, Tewa, and Navajo influence, the ceremonies have been more or less corrupted. Today Oraibi is almost a deserted ghost town, observing few ceremonials, but its forms are followed most closely in Hotevilla.

THE NEW–FIRE CEREMONY

Four religious societies participate in Wúwuchim: the Alwimi, Two Horn, in the Ál or Horn Kiva; the Kwákwan, One Horn, in the Kwani or Lance Kiva; the Tátawkyam, Flute, in the Taw or Flute Kiva; and the Wuchim in the Wuchim Kiva.

After public announcement of Wúwuchim by the village Crier Chief, the chiefs of the Two Horn, One Horn, and Flute Societies enter their respective kivas for the first eight-day period of preparation and purification, each planting the na'chi on the kiva roof. On the ninth day the Wuchim priests enter their kiva for the second eight-day period. The na'chi [father planted us here] is a standard signifying the kiva's participation in a ceremony. That of the Wuchim Kiva is made of sparrow-hawk feathers tied to a stick with raw cotton, and those for the Flute and Two Horn are of wood shaped with a crook on one end. The One Horn na'chi is not planted overhead but set on the ground below. It is a ball of earth into which are stuck four short sticks representing the reeds by which man made his Emergences from the underworld. In the center is a longer stick symbolic of the reed by which man will emerge to the next world. The dots on all represent snowflakes, moisture.

General direction of all the rituals in Wúwuchim is under the Two Horn Society. The only religious order with the original concept of Creation, it is the most important of all societies participating in Wúwuchim. No one is allowed to enter its kiva. To it all the other societies bring reports of the progress of their preparations for review. Yet the Two Horn Society does not take active part in the rituals of the One Horn, Flute, and Wuchim Kivas, for these orders have knowledge only of this present world, and if anything should go wrong because of their adherence to their limited, earthly laws, the Two Horns are not to be held responsible.

The Two Horn Society's symbol of two horns designates knowledge of, and remembered experiences in, the three previous worlds as well as in this present Fourth World. Their Six Directions altar represents the First World at the time of Creation, with colored sands spread for the four primary directions: yellow for the West, blue for the South, red for the East, and white for the North. An ear of dark mixed corn is laid for the Above, and an ear of sweet corn for the Below. The wooden backdrop of the altar is painted with the corresponding colors of the successive four worlds, and there are symbols of the primary elements: fire, earth, water, and air represented by eagle down.

In front of the altar and dominating all these symbols are placed two elk horns standing nearly six feet high, their many prongs representing all the races of mankind. These two horns are the symbol of the society's deity, Alósaka, who has been given permission to manifest himself by dream or vision.

Prominently placed between these two horns is the *tiponi*. Etymologically derived from the three words for "person," "altar," and "authority," its name denotes a person who has spiritual authority to conduct rites at the altar. A *tiponi* is a fetish of stone or wood belonging to a clan or society. The leader keeps it in his home, where it is blessed with corn-meal and fed with pinches of food each day. It is seldom brought out into the open, being reserved for altar use during rituals. The *tiponi* for the Two Horn altar consists of the wooden figure of a man about twelve inches high with a bow beside him. Members of the society include men of the Bow Clan who are known as Tövúsnyamsinom, Smoldering Wood Partners. These Partners hold knowledge of the Creation.

The supreme symbol of spiritual power and authority is the *mongko*. It gives evidence that each society and the clans comprising it had completed their centuries-long migration. It is the Hopi "law of laws." *Kachina mongkos* are carried during rituals by Eototo and Áholi to show that these most important *kachinas* have power and authority in the spirit world. Ritual *mongkos* are possessed by only three societies, the Two Horn, One Horn, and Flute, each distinctively marked.

The Two Horn *mongko* (Figure 56) is a flat piece of wood whose main body is painted white, representing the faultless body at Creation. One end of the stick is painted blue to symbolize the earth's carpet of vegetation, with two additional blue lines to denote water. The serrated other end of the stick symbolizes the three dominating factors of the Hopis' supreme law: respect, harmony, and love. Attached to it is a small

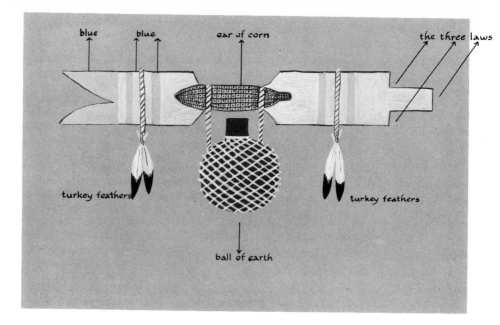

Figure 56. Two Horn mongko

ball of earth in a cotton net, containing a drop of water; they symbolize the earth and the seas of this planet. Tied to it lengthwise is a perfect ear of corn representing man. Strung from it also are turkey feathers. The wild turkey is a part of the wildness of the earth and the everlasting mystery of Creation which man has never quite understood and will never completely dominate and domesticate.

The Two Horn *mongko* is of three sizes. One is only about four inches long, to which is tied the smallest Corn Mother. Another is about sixteen inches long, one of which is carried by every member during the rituals both inside the kiva and outside in the plaza. The third, nearly four feet long, is used to close the kiva entrance during the initiation ceremony.

Empowered by these symbols of supreme spiritual authority, and having concluded the first period of kiva preparations, the Two Horn priests are now ready for their first significant ritual, the New-Fire Ceremony—literally Kokostawis, Building of the Fire. With fire, life begins. So now in this first cold dawn of Creation dramatized by Wúwuchim, a new fire is kindled by flint and native cotton. It is kept going with coal from the countless outcrops nearby, accompanied by prayers to Másaw, deity of the Nadir, of death and the underworld, where coal comes from. Másaw gets his power from the sun to keep burning the fires in the underworld and deep in this earth, which are manifested during the eruption of volcanoes—the new fire thus representing the cosmic power directed from the sun to Másaw, who then projects its germinating warmth to the earth and mankind. The ritual kindling of the fire takes place at dawn before the sun is up. It symbolically begins to warm only the upper crust of the earth. Then, as the sun rises, later rituals represent the germination of seed, the appearance of vegetation, and the maturity of crops at harvest. Brands from the new fire are then carried to light fires in the other three kivas.*

CLOSING OF THE ROADS

Meanwhile, similar preparations have been made in the other three kivas.

The One Horn Society ranks second to the Two Horn. Its deity is Sótuknang, who helped the Creator, Taiowa, to establish the universe, and who is the highest god of this planet. But as its members have had experience only of this Fourth World, their judgment is not as sound as the Two Horns', and they are often too quick to act. The One Horn *mongko* is similar to that of the Two Horn, except that the color of blue is missing because its priests do not have the complete pattern of the law. The *tiponi* planted before the altar is the figure of a woman holding a child. She is Tauzaza [Earth Body Formed by Heat], deity of the Fire Clan.

Also in front of the One Horn altar in the Lance Kiva is planted a six-foot lance with a flint point sharpened for destruction or for correction of world evils. Each of the twenty members carries one as they make the rounds of the village all night in pairs, going faster and faster.

On the altar itself is a small bell of baked clay which further identifies the One Horns as people of this earth only, and gives them warnings of danger to come. The two Hero-Twins sit at the opposite ends of the earth's north-south axis, Pöqánghoya at the north and Palöngawhoya at the south, keeping the earth properly rotating. They give warning of anything wrong on the planet by sending vibrations along the axis to all earth-centers. This small clay bell is a symbol of these earth-centers, receiving and resounding the vibrations. The One Horn priests can hear them, being of this earth, like the clay bell itself, though they cannot receive the intuitional glimpses of their meaning as do the Two Horns.

---

* A similar New-Fire Ceremony was held in Aztec Mexico, a new fire being kindled in the principal *teocalli* or temple at the beginning of each fifty-two-year cycle, and flames being carried from it to other temples and thence to homes.

The other axis of the earth is marked by the east-west path of the sun. The Flute Society in the Flute Kiva helps the sun to establish the seasonal cycle with its songs and the music of its flutes. Hence the flute is its emblem, six flutes being placed before the altar. The deity of the society is Múi'ingwa, the god of germination; and predominant on the altar are feathers of birds from the fruitful South: parrot, macaw, bluebird, cardinal, and hummingbird. The *tiponi* is a wooden figure of a man patterned with flowers. He is Seechgeech, symbolizing the charter of the society. The Flute *mongko* is of wood, shaped like an ancient hoe. It is painted white and carries a crook, cord, and downy eagle feather dangling from it for long life. Its shape of a hoe, used to cut down weeds, is a reminder that on the spiritual level man must cut down the evil grown from the assertion of his own selfish will.

The Wuchim deity is also Múi'ingwa, but its priests have no *mongko*. Wúwuchim takes place symbolically in the dawn of Creation, before the sun appeared, when the earth was lighted only by such reflected and shadowless light as is now given by the northern lights. Hence the first *páhos* or prayer sticks are made for the sun; for the first vegetation, including the primary corn, squash, beans, and tobacco; for the first animals and man; and for the earth itself as it expands under the warmth of the sun.

Now, with the conclusion of all these preparations, comes the Closing of the Roads for the final ceremonies. Four main roads or trails lead into Oraibi from the four directions: Kúiwanva [Place Where Másaw Peeks at the Village] from the west; Ischomo [Coyote Hill] from the south; Sikya'wa [Yellow Rock] from the east; and Botatukyah [Hill Stacked like a Plaque] from the north. Just before sundown of the fifteenth day a One Horn in full ceremonial costume emerges from the kiva and closes each road by drawing four lines across it with sacred cornmeal, sealing the village from any evil power that might come. No man dares to cross these lines, for he would die within four years; and animals and birds which have crossed them have been found dead next morning. Throughout the night One Horns check each closed road. Not until morning, when the ceremony is over, are the roads opened again, and this can be done only by a One Horn priest who cuts the cornmeal lines with his *mongko*.

Only one trail into the village is left open. It is a narrow, tortuous trail that winds southwest along the ridge, past the unexcavated ruins of the ancient village of Pivánhonkyapi, to the westernmost spur and highest point of Third Mesa, Apónivi. Here at this lofty point, in whose sheer cliff-walls eagles nest and on whose summit is a Two Horn shrine, is an invisible archway through which pass spirit people from Grand Canyon— the only beings permitted entrance into the village during the coming midnight ceremony. Even so, a spirit guard is posted there to inspect those who pass.

All families living on the east side of the main plaza set their tables for these spirits, who will come and partake of the spiritual essence of the food prepared for them, and they bury the dishes and the physical husks of the food left next morning. They vacate their homes and spend the night with families living on the west side of the plaza. All doors are closed and the windows hung with blankets. By evening the streets are empty, the village dark and quiet, and all is ready for the night ceremony.

THE NIGHT OF THE WASHING OF THE HAIR

This major ceremony is so sacred and secret that no one talks about it; it is referred to only as Ástotokya, the Night of the Washing of the Hair.

It is held every four years, when there are initiations into one or all of the four societies. All Hopi children before the age of adolescence are initiated into either the Kachina or Powamu Societies. The Wúwuchim initiates are young men, adults, who are now inducted into a higher stage of spiritual training. Also, significantly, they symbolize the first human beings emerging upon this new world at the dawn of Creation. As such, they are considered to be uncontaminated by any human frailty and must be held inviolate from mortal evil. Hence the Closing of the Roads has sealed off the village from all human beings, and the eastern half of the village itself has been vacated by townspeople, isolating the initiates from contact with anyone except the priests and the incoming beneficent spiritual beings.

With this secrecy and in an air of great solemnity they are now conducted by their godfathers to the Hawiovi Kiva. Here they are seated on the raised floor at the eastern end of the kiva, leaving the lower altar level on the western end to be occupied by the priests. The name of the kiva, Hawiovi, means the One-Way Trail. The kiva itself symbolizes the previous underworld, from which they will soon emerge to the present world. There is only one opening, the roof entrance above reached by the ladder—the One-Way Trail. Not until the ceremony is over and they have been ritually confirmed to the pure pattern of Creation will they be allowed to come out. If anyone by chance or evil intent breaks through the closed roads, contaminating them with evil, their fate is sealed. No initiate, or godfather, or priest will be allowed to come out of the kiva alive.

So as soon as they enter the kiva pairs of Two Horns and One Horns begin their night-long patrolling of the dark and empty village streets. Hearing a step or glimpsing a passing shape, they call out loudly, *"Haqumi?* Who are you?"

Immediately the answer comes back, *"Pinú'u,* I am I," * revealing that the accosted is one of the spiritual beings who has come by way of the one open trail. Such visible and audible manifestations are commonly experienced by the One Horn and Two Horn priests on this night, attesting to their high degree of spiritual attainment, and often the apparition immediately fades into a stone wall.

If, however, no answer is received or a human sound is betrayed by the passer-by, the sacred duty of the One Horns is to rush upon him, stab him with their long lances, and dismember his body. Bits of his flesh must then be carried by all the priests in different directions and as far as they can travel that night, and secretly buried. The Two Horns, being of a higher order, are more merciful. They too rush toward the intruder, trying to reach him before the One Horns, to protect him with their *mongkos* until his fate can be ceremonially decided upon.**

All the villagers shut up in their homes are aware of these tragic possibilities as they listen to the resonant clacking of turtle-shell rattles on the legs of the patrolling Two Horns, the sound of the clay bells worn by the One Horns, and the faint calls while the hours drag by. Meanwhile in the other kivas preparations are continuing. A member of the Short Cistern Clan goes from kiva to kiva, carrying a bundle of short sticks painted different colors at one end. Each kiva member pulls out a stick. Those pulling out yellow, blue, or black will represent stars, spirits, and other-world beings. The one who selects the single stick painted red is designated to impersonate Másaw, the deity of the Nadir and underworld. Dressing in their costumes, they get ready to go to Hawiovi Kiva.

It is now nearly midnight. The kiva is dark save for the faintly reflected glow of the fire burning in the fire-pit. In its dim light the initiates massed on the raised level watch a priest ritually remove the plug from the little round hole in the floor of the altar level—the *sipápuni,* the symbolic place of Emergence. Now as the seven Pleiades, symbolic of the seven universes, followed by the three stars in Orion's Belt, rise into his view through the ladder opening above, he recounts to them man's journey on his Road of Life through the successive seven worlds that comprise

---

* In former times a Hopi, upon being asked who he was, answered simply, "I am I"—this being enough to acknowledge his debt of life without pride in his mortal identity. Someone else would identify him by clan.

According to the *Popul Vuh,* the ancient Quiché Maya called themselves "I am I, the people of the Quiché."

** An incident of this kind in past years, involving a Hopi of high rank, establishes this concept on a level of realistic practice. The tragic details are recounted in Part Four.

each of the seven universes. Life on the First World began with fire—symbolized by the one in the fire-pit before them—but the pure pattern of man's existence on it was contaminated by evil. The world was destroyed and man emerged to the Second World. Here the same thing happened. Listening to the happenings during their previous existence in the Third World, the initiates are made to understand that they themselves are symbolically still residents of this Third World, as are all people not yet initiated into their spiritual responsibilities in this stage of existence, even though they occupy physical bodies born of the present Fourth World. This, then, is the reason for the initiation ceremony they are about to experience. It is an enactment of their spiritual Emergence from the Second World through the *sipápuni* before them, into the Third World architecturally symbolized by the kiva in which they are sitting, and thence up the ladder, itself serving as another *sipápuni*, to the great Fourth World which lies outside.

It is midnight by the stars above when the priest finishes his recital and partially covers the fire-pit with a flat rock until only a faint red glow is cast over the altar level below. And now suddenly the men from the other kivas come down the ladder, dimly coming into sight as if emerging from the *sipápuni*. All are ceremonially robed but unmasked, wearing large four-pointed white stars on their foreheads, which almost cover their faces. Másaw appears among them, his face and head painted ash-gray. One by one they file around the three sides of the altar level to stand three deep around the fire-pit and the *sipápuni*. They are the spirits of past and other worlds, and the only sound they make is a low hum and a strange blowing of breath sounding like the winds from outer space. Gradually it rises in pitch and volume.

In the midst of this a lone white-robed figure wearing a large white star quietly enters the kiva and announces, "I am the Beginning and the End." He is Nútungktatoka [First and Last] of the Pikyasya [Side Corn] Clan. After making this single announcement, he leaves the kiva as quietly as he came.

The star-masked figures become noisier, their movements faster. Suddenly, all at once, the flat rock is thrown over the fire-pit, plunging the kiva in darkness to illustrate how wickedness suddenly envelops the world. A yell sounds. Star-spirits, priests, initiates, and godfathers throw off their stars and clothes. Stark naked, in riotous confusion, all leap for the ladder to get out unscathed before the world is destroyed. The rungs of the Hawiovi Kiva ladder are longer than those on any other kiva ladder, extending out on each side of the poles. Yet even so, the first to reach it are often the last to leave; before they can climb up, others leap on and climb over their naked, sweaty bodies.

Finally reaching the roof of the kiva, they are drenched with buckets of water that symbolically wash away all wickedness, and greeted by three men: the Kikmongwi, Father of the People, the village chief, who is of the Bear Clan, traditionally first in precedence; the Cha'ákmongwi, the Crier Chief, who calls out to the people; and Qaletaqa, the Guardian of the People, who is of the Coyote Clan, always last in precedence and designated "to close the doors." When they are all out, the village chief calls down into the dark, empty kiva, telling anyone who may remain there to come out. Naked and wet as infants just born into this new world, the initiates are taken to a nearby home, where the kiva chiefs wash their hair in nine successive bowls of yucca suds. The nine bowls represent the seven successive universes through which they will travel on their evolutionary journey, the domain of Sótuknang who helped to establish them, and the realm of the Creator, Taiowa, who rules over all. The initiates are then taken back to their own kivas by their godfathers.

This Washing of the Hair does not complete their initiation. Late in the spring each initiate is required to make a pilgrimage to the Salt Cave in Grand Canyon, testing his spiritual wings for the first time.* He must then participate in another ceremony held during Powamu the following winter.

CONTROLLING STARS

During the years when there are no initiations, emphasis is given to the prolonged fasting, prayer and concentration, and ritual songs that mark not only the shorter form of Wúwuchim but all ceremonials. There emerge here more clearly the patterns and movements of the stars which guide the chief of the Two Horn Society who directs all Wúwuchim rituals at Hotevilla. His name translated into English means "White Cloud above the Horizon." On the evening of the ninth day just before he entered the kiva he said to us, "If I am right [i.e., if my heart is right] during my duties tomorrow the clouds will gather above me." The next evening, for the first time in many days, the clouds were piling up in a rosy flare at sunset.

At sundown on the fifteenth day he emerged from his kiva retreat for the first time to make a circuit around the village in the proper order

---

* Initiates on First and Second Mesa go to Salt Lake below Zuñi, the initiates on Third Mesa making the more difficult, ninety-mile pilgrimage on foot to Grand Canyon and bringing back a heavy gift of salt for their sponsoring godmothers. The last pilgrimage was made in 1957, and I am told the hardship is so great that few young men now make the trip. Those who do not go always remain young hawk fledglings too spiritually weak to fly.

of directions. It is a long, symbolic journey he makes: not only to the directional shrines just outside the pueblo, but to the shrines far beyond the borders of Arizona which these closer shrines symbolize, and to the important places in the world beyond, west, south, east, and north. By his journey he indicates that he is claiming all this earth for the Creator. At all these points beneficent spirits respond with blessings that extend not only to the Hopis but to all men and to all living creatures on earth.

"Early next morning," he relates, "I, the Two Horn chief, pick up my *mongko* [the law of laws] and my *chóchmingwu* [Corn Mother] and I go to the Wuchim Kiva. I enter in silence, for all the men inside are in deep concentration, all heads bowed, not a face looking up. I stand at the right of the ladder, not stepping down to the lower level. There I remain. It is my time to speak. I have the authority. If there is any movement of heads toward me or around the kiva it is an indication of disrespect to me and our faith.

"My first command is, 'Go now to your homes and bring the food in, and when you have prepared the ceremonial meal sing praises to the food and make a joyous sound with your voice and your feet and your actions.'

"When the meal is finished and the food taken away, my next command is, 'Go out and cut the willows and bring in the eagle plumes with this one thought: that in all your preparations the greatest faith may be carried throughout the world by your harmonious actions. Then you shall watch Our Father the Sun, and when he enters the mid-point of day you shall emerge from your kivas to bless the people of the village with your song and ceremony. Carry the ceremony as far as you can till sundown.' "

So shortly after noon the men begin to emerge from the kivas. It is a warm, sunny day with only a wisp of cloud drifting over Thundering Mesa far out on the plain. With everyone else we stand on a housetop overlooking the sandy streets of the tawdry village, watching the first group coming out from the Chief Kiva: five barefoot Two Horns wearing pure white horns with no markings; four Wuchims wearing the customary kirtle and moccasins but no body markings; also a Wuchim-mana, a man garbed as a woman in a cape to represent the Earth Mother. They walk in two parallel lines closed in front, the drummer in the center wearing a black velvet shirt as a reminder of the black woven *manta* used in former days.

This group is followed by a second group of seven Wuchims and four Flutes who wear two blue horns and a blue marking under the left eye. It in turn is followed by two more groups of eight Wuchims, each wearing on his forehead a star of corn leaves painted blue.

Their song is low and deep and powerful like the voices of their big drums. The vibrations of both are originated by the War Twins sitting at the opposite ends of the world's axis, and they sing to the highest deity, Taiowa, to Sótuknang, deity of this planet, and to Múi'ingwa, deity of germination. Dancing slowly, the four groups successively make four circuits around the village, each one smaller, claiming the earth for the Creator as did the leader of the Two Horns. Their circuit is counterclockwise, being of this earth; that of the sun is clockwise. Stopping in front of the kiva, each group sings a last chorus, slowly moving to right and left in a short arc, leaving a visual pattern of harmony in the deep, soft sand. Then one by one they climb down the ladders of the kivas, planting the *na'chis* in the *nútas*.

The *núta* for all kivas is the same. It is a straw thatch placed over the opening, woven of wild wheat stalks, which in the plant kingdom represent the same mystery of Creation as the wild turkey feathers represent in the animal kingdom.

"So the ceremony is carried on until sundown," continues the chief of the Two Horns, "and the people have been made happy. We could feel this in the kivas. So then it is my duty to go to the Wuchim Kiva again. Entering with the same silence and reverent conduct, I give them my message. 'You have beautifully performed the ceremony during the day. Our people are happy. So if it need be for any of you to take a short rest before the star appears, you may do so.'

"I go back to my kiva. It is the time called *tásupi* [before the sun has pulled down all its light]. Following this period it becomes dark and we of the Two Horns know that the time is at hand for the messages to be brought in. We wait, and suddenly the silence of the darkness is broken by a thump on the roof of the kiva. The man on the upper level climbs up the ladder to greet the messenger who has just announced his presence. The messenger informs him that he has a message for the chief. This request is delivered to me, chief of the Two Horn Kiva, in a whisper. I then put on my moccasins * on the upper level and go up the ladder to meet the messenger, for no one is permitted to enter this kiva, which has the most important function in the universal plan. I carry the *mongko* with me. The messenger is an elder from the Flute Kiva and also carries a *mongko*. Since we both carry the sign of authority, the message may be transmitted.

"The Flute elder tells me that the world must return to its first state of purity, that all plant and animal life as well as all mankind must be cleansed and return to a harmonious life. For the people we have prepared a joyous harvest for the coming year. This is his message. It is then

---

* The Two Horn chief conducts the rituals before the altar barefoot to show his humility.

my turn to bless him for the helpful performance of his kiva. All this is said in a low-voiced whisper.

"Similar messages are delivered by elders from the other kivas. Then an elder of the Two Horn Kiva asks this one, 'At what point are our stars located at this moment?'

"We, the religious leaders, have always before us the celestial patterns which guide and control our rituals. The most important is the sun itself, and when the sun is down we conduct our ceremonies by the stars of night. So now the assistant to this Two Horn chief takes his position a few feet west of the fire circle and surveys the sky through the rooftop opening of the kiva. Our first indication that it is time to prepare our rituals is the appearance of Hotamkam.* Slowly the star moves westward until it reaches the center of the roof opening. The assistant to this one now places himself beside the fire circle and carefully watches the sky. It is only a short space of time before the three stars [in Orion's belt] are now in line [lengthwise] with the kiva opening, the center star directly above the fireplace [midnight]. At this moment we begin our most important ritual according to the pattern first laid down on this planet Earth. Life began with fire. Thus we begin.

"The first two important elders are members of the Tobacco Clan and the Side Corn Clan. They pack tobacco into the pipe and light it from the fireplace for our smoke ceremony. Then we sing seven songs: of the preparation of the world, the germination of life, the appearance of the first vegetation, the planting of the corn, the growing of the corn, the harvest of the corn, and the rain that the Creator sends us for this.

"For our Hopi villages do not lie in the path of the running water as do those of the pueblos along the Rio Grande. Everyone sees that there are no ditches in our fields. It is only by our faith that our fields are watered. By our prayers the rains come from the clouds. And after it rains that insect, Nuvákosio [singing bug], sings in the fields of the generosity of the Creator to those who have had faith in their prayers. But those who are living along the running water will be the first to lose their faith because they do not have to depend on prayer.

"There are seven of these songs, and we must be careful to sing them before the seven stars, Chööchökam [Harmonious Ones, the Stars that Cling Together] ** disappear. By the time the harvest song is finished the Hotomkam [Orion's Belt] is upside down [about 2:30 a.m.]. We then have a moment of rest while one of the elders goes outside to sight Nátupkom [Two Brothers],*** which are soon followed by one large star, Taláwsohu

---

* Identified as the first or highest star in Orion's belt.
** The seven stars of the Pleiades.
*** Castor and Pollux.

[Star Before the Light].* Our last part of the ritual must be completed before the elder who is watching the sky sees the big star appear through the opening overhead. When it appears, this one knows that an elder from the One Horn Kiva is beginning to lay with cornmeal the Road of Life from his kiva to the east, just as the Creator first laid it for all men.

"In the Flute Kiva at the same time begin the three songs called Havivokyaltáwi [Song of the Awakening], Talátawi [Song of the Rising Sun], and Titaptawi [Song of Happiness]. Then it is the people gather outside the kiva. . . ."

One outside can see them massed there in the early dawn-dusk, listening to the low swell of song rising from the kiva; stepping up to take hold of the knee-high ngölakpi [crook] planted in the ground, that they may be granted a long, happy, and healthful life; then making their own life road with cornmeal along the same path laid earlier by the One Horn.

"Now," the chief continues, "another star appears in the southeast, Ponóchona [The One That Sucks From the Belly].** This is the star that controls the life of all beings in the animal kingdom. Its appearance completes the harmonious pattern of the Creator, who ordained that man should live in harmony with all the animals on this world. The singing in the Flute Kiva stops when the sun rises above the horizon. With his manifestation our ceremony is over."

A priest now brings out a blanketful of sand from the altar of the Flute Kiva, which he empties in the plaza, returning it to the earth, just as the afterbirth is buried when the umbilical cord is broken. Before it is carried out, the same amount of dew is found on the sand as will be found on the ground next summer. A few minutes later he comes back out of the kiva with a squash rind filled with water which he carries to the east, thus watering the earth.

The kiva priests then return home for a feast of knukquivi, a stew of lamb and hominy, and the traditional pik'ami, a mush of cornmeal and sprouted wheat. When the oven is opened the vapor from the pik'ami should rise like the soft, fluffy feather of the eagle, as a sign that all the kiva groups have successfully performed their duties.

The chief of the Two Horns further tells us, "If one of our religious orders has not carried out its ceremonies perfectly, there will be a rainbow on the left side of the rising sun. Its colors will not be in the proper order, revealing that one of the kivas has been influenced by evil thoughts. If a rainbow does not appear, we wait until the sun sets that night. Then, if all our rituals have been perfectly carried out, there will be a rainbow

---

* Procyon, the Morning Star.
** Sirius, the Dog Star.

on each side of the sun. Thus we know by the signs of morning and evening how successfully we have performed Wúwuchim, and how successful will be our harvest for the year."

THE PUBLIC DANCE

In Old Oraibi with its fourteen kivas and strict ceremonialism, the public dance on the last day must have been an imposing sight as the painted and helmeted priests filed out through the narrow streets and causeways to sing and dance in the little open plazas, coming in two long parallel lines, open in front and closed in back, an elongated oval sack carrying the world and its deepest meanings. The Two Horns always in front, with the Wuchims following, the drummer in the center with the Chief Crier, the body of One Horns following behind for protection. . . .

This year at Shongopovi the pattern of the dance is much the same. First come four leading Two Horns, wearing two long white horns tipped with blue and marked with blue cloud-terrace symbols at the base; white buckskin robes over their bare bodies; turtle-shell and deer-hoof rattles on each leg; and each carrying a *mongko*. Behind them come thirty-six Wuchims, wearing tufts of parrot feathers and eagle down on top of their heads, with two corn leaves hanging down behind. Their shoulders are painted yellow, and three yellow bands run across back and belly. A red bandoleer passes over the right shoulder from waist to back. They wear the usual Hopi kirtle with a foxskin dangling in back, moccasins, and one vertical mark down each leg. Each has a mark painted under the left eye, as they see only this world. All hold hands to form the *nakwách* symbol of brotherhood. Behind them, also holding hands, come six Flute priests with bodies painted red and blue. They include one Blue Horn priest wearing a helmet of two blue horns, representing Múi'ingwa, their deity. Between the two lines walks the drummer, and on the outside the barefoot asperger with his bowl of water and eagle feather, sprinkling each dancer.

How beautiful and brilliant they are, touched by a strange other-worldliness, as they come dancing slowly and singing deeply through the narrow, dusty streets. It is shortly after noon. The frozen pond behind the village has melted, and naked children are crowding the sunny stone walls. From the high mesa top one can see the dry, tawny desert stretching emptily away to the lofty buttes sixty miles south.

The softly pounding feet, the soughing voices. . . . It is a little mesmeric, as always. But one notices that while all the others dance in beat with the drum, the Two Horns maintain a steady rhythm out of time with the rest. With knowledge of all previous worlds, and not being restricted to the life of this present world, they keep time with an inaudible cosmic pulse impervious to time and place.

After parading around the village, each group returns to its separate kiva, and the cornmeal gatherer goes from house to house for offerings of meal.

They come out four times. There are no tourists, no visitors on this cold November afternoon, only the silent and respectful villagers crowding the rooftops—no one being permitted to witness Wúwuchim from ground level.

When they come out for the fifth time the Two Horns are wearing trousers under their robes, and the Wuchims and Flutes are naked save for breechcloths or shorts. Now comes what is called the Bath Ceremony. It is profanely simple and hilarious—women running out to pour buckets of cold water over all the dancers save the Two Horns, while we onlookers shiver in blankets and coats. This is no squeamish and simulated baptism. The women empty their buckets with lusty drenchings and run back to their water tubs for more, taunting the dancers, being taunted in turn, and winding up in a roughhouse in front of the kivas. All this stems from the traditional taunting byplay between Wuchim men and Máraw women, reminding each other of the danger of contamination by loose indulgence in sexual practices. One hears talk after the ceremony that one of the women inadvertently touched one of the solemn and inviolate Two Horns, arousing fear the ceremony had been profaned. It is a reminder that no one should be allowed to follow the dancers in the plaza.

The Horn priests' circuit of the pueblo at sunset ends the ceremony. All spectators properly retire to higher ground. This conforms to the observance in the kivas, where initiates are confined to the raised portion, leaving the lower altar level to the priests. So in the biting cold the people scramble up ladders to stand shivering on the flat rooftops.

Eventually the Horn priests file out of the kivas—first the One Horns, fifteen of them, in a long white file. Each of them is cloaked in a pure white cape surmounted with a one-horn helmet. They do not dance. They do not sing. There is only the clear, brittle tinkle of the bell which each carries. Striding slowly and silently in the yellow glow of the setting sun, they make a counterclockwise circuit of the village, west, south, east, and north, and return to the kiva.

A few minutes later fifteen Two Horns make the same circuit so as to correct any mistakes made during the whole ceremony by the One Horns. Their helmets carry two horns, and they wear the same white capes. It is later, colder now, and from high above we watch their gray, phantasmal shapes gliding into dusk in a silence accompanied only by the far-off clacking of their turtle-shell rattles. . . .

So concludes the first great ceremony in the annual cycle. The creative fire with which life begins is lighted; the Emergence from the underworld is enacted. Ritual supplication is made for the germination of all forms of life on earth—plant, animal, and man—and the course of its development is laid out.

3

Soyál

At the Winter Solstice comes the second great ceremonial, Soyál, which symbolizes the second phase of Creation at the dawn of life.

Soyál, etymologically derived from *so* [all] and *yal* [year], accepts and confirms the pattern of life development for the coming year. It is one of the most important of all ceremonials, being often referred to as Soyálangwul [Establishing Life Anew for All the World]. No spectacular public dances mark or mar its deep significance. Even its kiva rituals are climaxed by silence, fasting, and prolonged concentration. For now, out of dawn-darkness, germinated life is about to make its appearance. The sun, reaching the southern end of its journey at the Winter Solstice, is ready to return and give strength to budding life. To all this Soyál is dedicated to give aid and direction.

It occurs during December, Kelmuya, the Respected Moon, and is scheduled to take place during Soyala [Time of the Winter Solstice], the period between the first appearance of the first-quarter moon and the last appearance of the last-quarter moon. The determination of its beginning date is tied in with solar observations which determine the time of the Winter Solstice. Beginning with the first day of the new moon, the chiefs of the Sun and Flute Clans make solar observations each sunrise from a house in Oraibi on a high point which gives an unobstructed view of Sun House Mesa across the valley.* Each morning the rising sun casts its shadow a little closer to a designated mark on the west wall. When it reaches the mark, the chiefs are able to determine the exact number of days until the Winter Solstice, when the most important ritual in Soyál is observed. A four-day leeway is allowed, however, according to the belief that the sun may be turned back any day within this period. As with

---

* Traditionally solar observations on Third Mesa are always made at sunrise, looking east. Those on First and Second Mesas are made looking west at sunset until April, and thereafter looking east at sunrise.

Wúwuchim, the preliminary four days of making *páhos,* ritually smoking over them, planting them at shrines, and announcing Soyál are observed. On the day following, Soyál begins. In its full form it lasts twenty days: an eight-day period of purification and preparation, followed by an eight-day period of rituals, and concluding with a rabbit hunt, feast, and blessing rites lasting four days more.*

Customarily announcement of the ceremony comes on the day following Wúwuchim. That afternoon the Soyál Kachina appears, coming from the Kachina Shrine to the east. He is the first *kachina* to appear during the year. Masked in his turquoise helmet and white robe, he wobbles and staggers like a child learning to walk, signifying that new life is being reborn.** Having arrived in the village, he makes four stops: at the home of one who participates in the Powamu ceremony, where he marks four horizontal lines with cornmeal on the outside wall beside the door; at the entrance to the Flute Kiva, where he softly sings a sacred song; in the plaza, where he sings again in a low tone; and finally at the Mong [Chief] Kiva, at whose entrance he plants the four Soyál *páhos* he is carrying, as a sign that the Soyál ceremony is about to begin. The Soyál Chief blesses him, and in return receives cornmeal with a prayer feather from him. The Soyál Kachina then returns to the Kachina Shrine, after stopping at the Powamu Kiva for a last blessing.

The Mastop Kachina appears the following day, a frightening figure in his black mask, his body painted black, with the imprints of human hands in white, a wild animal's pelt worn for a kilt, and his feet covered with wildcat skins. He has come a long, long way. His black helmet mask suggests the interstellar space he has traveled, the three white stars on each side of his head being the three stars in Orion's belt. His actions are still more frightening as he enters the village, grabs a woman from the crowd of onlookers, and goes through the motions of copulation. Perhaps no other *kachina* and his actions have been more shocking to outside observers.

Múi'ingwa is the god of germination of all plant life.*** Mastop is not

---

* The dates for Soyál in 1959 adhered closely to this somewhat confusing manner of reckoning. It was held at Hotevilla between December 7 and December 26, fitting in between the first day of the first-quarter moon on December 6 and the last day of the last-quarter moon on December 28. The Winter Solstice ritual was held promptly on December 22. Shongopovi held only an abbreviated eight-day form from December 17 to December 25.

** Many anthropologists, such as Dr. Frederick J. Dockstader in *The Kachina and the White Man* (Bulletin 35, Cranbrook Institute of Science, 1954), assert the Soyál Kachina acts like a weary old man, walking torpidly as one who has slept too long in the underworld. This erroneous interpretation, say our Hopi spokesmen, negates the meaning of the whole Soyál ceremony.

*** Dr. Harold S. Colton in his book, *Hopi Kachina Dolls* (Albuquerque: University of New Mexico Press, Revised Edition, 1959), asserts that Alósaka is the "germ god" of reproduction of man, animals, and plants.

a deity but a *kachina,* and thus a spirit, who represents the male power of fertility for human beings alone, not for plants and crops. His name signifies, and the symbol for his mouth and nose represents, a gray fly which carries the germ cells of mankind. His black body represents the earth; the ruff of wild grass around his throat, the vegetable kingdom; the wildcat kilt, the animal kingdom; and the white imprint of human hands, the touch of man upon all—the imprint which man will make upon the earth when he is fully created during this phase of beginning life. It is not a gross touch. For these human hands are seer instruments for divination of the life of the body—just as hands are used by a medicine man when he lays them on one's belly, heart, and crown of the head.* But man already has had existence in previous worlds and will have existence in future worlds. So the short black staff painted with white rings which Mastop carries symbolizes the ladder with its rungs up which man climbs during his successive Emergences. Hence one like it is also placed on graves, enabling the deceased to climb to another world.

Mastop's simulated copulation is not promiscuous, as it might appear. It is with married women only, not virgin girls, for copulation is for the express purpose of procreation of man, that he may climb from world to world on his continuing Road of Life. Also, it is said, certain women in the crowd offer themselves as participants in his sexual actions. These are mothers of babies who have died early in infancy "before they had a chance," and the simulated fertilization contains the hope that these mothers will get the same babies back "for another chance."

Running now around the opening of the kiva, Mastop is invited inside for the duration of a song which is sung over four *páhos.* Following the song, four members of the Soyál Society come out, encircle the roof entrance of the kiva four times, and carry the *páhos* to Flute Spring. The Soyál Chief presents the Mastop Kachina with a special *páho,* requesting blessings for the people during the coming year. Mastop then returns westward to his shrine at the bottom of the cliffs.

Soyál is controlled by the Soyál Society, which uses the Chief Kiva and is composed of five clans: the Honnyam [Bear], Pikyasyam [Side Corn], Kyáshyam [Parrot], Tapnyam [Rabbit], and Hopaknyam [Reed]. Four other societies participate: the Two Horn, One Horn, and Flute in their respective kivas, and Powamu in the Hawiovi Kiva. The Bear Clan dominates all these groups. The chief of the Bear Clan is the village chief, Chief of Houses in Oraibi, and head of the Soyál Society, and the Soyál Kachina must be impersonated by a member of the Bear Clan.

Today in Oraibi no Soyál ceremony is held. In Hotevilla there is no

---

* The locations and functions of the vibratory centers of the body described in Part One, Chapter 1.

member of the Bear Clan and hence no Soyál Kachina, but the ceremony is still held because the Soyál Society retains members of the other four clans. In Shongopovi the ceremony is carried out in abbreviated form.

PURIFICATION AND PREPARATION

So, in an air of portentous silence, solemnity, and secrecy, Soyál begins.

The four Soyál *páhos*—each a reed divided into four sections with a sparrow-hawk feather tied to each section—remain on the Chief Kiva four days. On the fifth day the Soyál Chief takes them into the kiva, where he smokes and prays over them four days more. He is alone save for a member of the Sand Clan who comes at night, bringing sand to spread on the floor, representing the whole earth.

Here it is, then, in a dusky kiva—the wide and naked earth at the dawn of Creation. The Soyál Chief feels it; it is solidifying. Now it is time for man to appear and to construct upon it homes and villages. So he plants in the middle of the kiva two poles about four feet apart. On these he fastens crossbars which he decorates with painted wooden flowers. Framework and flowers symbolize the house of the village and the fields around it. Four *mongkos* are leaned against it, for all is done according to the "law of laws," and at the bottom he stacks corn in the same manner as women stack corn in their homes. The corn is blessed, as it represents the food needed for all people during the coming year. In front of it he sets bowls of *ngákuyi* [medicine water] made from bones of fierce animals such as the bear, mountain lion, and wolf, ground and mixed with water. This then is the chief's altar, known as the Chief's House.

Meanwhile preparations are being made in the Flute Kiva. As Soyál lays out the pattern for the entire year, the first *kachinas* appear during Soyál. So also must be enacted their departure in July during the Niman Kachina or Homegoing of the Kachinas. Hence in the Flute Kiva the Niman Kachina dance is given. This is rotated among the four kivas, having been given in the Snake Kiva last year, and being given in the Flute Kiva at Hotevilla this year. A skin painting of Múi'ingwa is taken to the Chief Kiva, where the Soyál Chief hangs it on a frame which is set on the north side of the chief's altar.

On the ninth day the Soyál Chief is joined by other members of his society, including members of the Side Corn, Parrot, Rabbit, and Reed Clans, who help him erect the Soyál altar to the south of the chief's altar. This is of conical shape, about three feet high and made of twigs covered with cotton. Its height and whiteness represent the thickness of snow needed during these winter months to penetrate the ground sufficiently to bring up the seeds which will be planted in the spring. In front of it are planted the four prayer feathers by whose power the plants will grow. And in front of these are placed the fruit and vegetables which they will bear: melons, squash, beans, and gourds.

On the twelfth night the altars are consecrated. All must be ready when the group of seven stars in Pleiades (Chööchökam—the Harmonious Ones, the Stars That Cling Together) is halfway between the eastern horizon and directly above, and the first star in Orion's belt below it is just rising into view through the ladder opening, about ten o'clock. The seven stars in the Pleiades are symbolic of the seven universes, and their positions time the duration of the seven Pavásiya [Creation] songs that consecrate the important chief's altar. As the altar symbolizes the dwelling place of man upon the newly created earth, the seven songs describe and consecrate the seven stages of its construction: laying the foundation; erecting the walls; closing in with beams and roof; plastering with a finishing coat; building the niche [the heart-place]; placing the *kokuiena* [character], the wood sticks on which to hang articles; and finally that which gives life, the fireplace, the warmth of the Creator's spirit. This village dwelling which man inhabits on the newly created earth itself symbolizes in the subtle wording of the songs the fleshly house wherein man's spirit dwells, for the building of the world itself, the home, and man's own physical body follow the same creative process. All songs must be finished when the Pleiades stand halfway between the midnight sky and the western horizon, and the three stars in Orion's belt lie across the roof entrance of the kiva.

As the sun appears, yellowing the eastern horizon, the priests emerge from the kiva. In a slow procession led by the Soyál Chief with Qaletaqa [Guardian] behind him, they walk to the eastern edge of the mesa. Here the Soyál Chief prays to the sun and with cornmeal marks a path to the sun for all his people. Then with the wings of a hawk he brushes each priest in turn, down each side of the body from head to foot, as if spreading upon him the yellow sun-pollen from the horizon which purifies his physical imperfections. Each morning thereafter for three days there is a similar procession. On the second morning the priests go only to the eastern edge of the village; on the third morning they go only to the midpoint of the village; and on the fourth they go only to the plaza.

During the significant last three days, beginning at sunset on the thirteenth night of the ceremony, the Soyál priests take no food until evening, when water and unsalted food are brought them, and sit before the altar in silence and deep concentration, praying for the harmonious unity of all forms of life.

Páhos are made in all kivas on the fifteenth day. The first one is made for the Creator, the next two for the sun and moon. Many others are made for the springs, animals, birds, all things that make man happy. Significant among them are the male-and-female *páhos* similar to those made during Wúwuchim.

At the end of the day all the *páhos* are fastened to the ceiling. The Soyál Chief lights his pipe and blows into one of its three openings. Smoke fills the kiva, purifying all the *páhos,* so that when the people of the village receive them they may breathe from them and receive a long and happy life.

One *páho* is put aside. To it is tied the long blade of a corn leaf with a cotton string painted with honey and pollen and secured to an eagle feather. This *páho* is taken to the Flute Spring.

A path of cornmeal is now drawn in the kiva from west to east, symbolizing the Road of Life for all men, animals, birds, and plants on earth.

Meanwhile, during these sixteen days of purification and preparation, the little planet Earth has been making its diurnal revolutions about its own axis; it has been slowly revolving in its great orbit around the sun; and the constellations have been majestically moving across the skies of night. Now all is ready for one of the two great moments of the year. It is the time of the Winter Solstice, when the sun has reached the southernmost end of its journey and must be turned back on its trail to bring ever-lengthening days of light, warmth, and life for plants, animals, and men. It is time for the rituals that give Soyál its great validity.

THE WINTER SOLSTICE CEREMONIES

By midnight members from all the other kivas have assembled in the Chief Kiva to help the Soyál Chief perform the ceremony dedicated to the sun, the deity of Soyál. The altar is blessed. All participants purify themselves by lightly brushing themselves with water in which has been boiled fresh cedar and then drinking from the bowls of *ngákuyi.*

In the Flute Kiva a man wearing a white skullcap and a white cape, and holding a stone axe and a bow and arrow to represent Pöqánghoya, the War Twin stationed at the north end of the world's axis, finishes dressing another man who represents Múi'ingwa, the god of germination and deity of the Flute Clan. A large star is fastened to his head to indicate how far his spirit has traveled. It is made of white corn leaves, four-pointed and more than two feet from tip to tip, and in the center is the blue circle of the sky. Then he is painted with white dots from his toes, up his legs and breast to his shoulders, and down the arms to his thumbs; the dots are like stars at night. His back is marked in the same manner. A kilt is fastened around his waist, knitted anklets put on his feet, and a turquoise necklace hung round his throat. A staff to whose crook is tied a small ear of corn symbolizing seed and an eagle feather symbolizing power is given him to hold in his left hand, and a white Corn Mother is put in his right hand.

Now, at the moment "when Hotomkam begins to hang down in the sky" [midnight], Múi'ingwa runs to the Chief Kiva. As he jumps down from the ladder his arrival is announced by a loud drum beat. He goes to the north of the ladder on the lower level and makes his first recitation, saying that he has heard a ceremony is being performed and he has come to help the Flute Society fulfill its obligation.

Finishing his recitation, he dances in one direction to the beat of a drum, throwing cornmeal to the Above and Below that the Six-Point Cloud People may send moisture from all directions. Going to another compass point, he tells of the re-establishment of life, and dances again. At the third station he reaffirms the power of the ceremony and again dances. After jumping to the fourth station at the sound of a drum beat, he dances once more and then hands his crook to the Soyál Chief, saying, "May Mother Earth bless all your people and all life throughout the world, and may all seed come back for renewal."

The Soyál Chief then escorts into the kiva a hawk maiden dressed in ceremonial robes, her freshly washed hair hanging loose around her shoulders. She is taken to the north side and seated on a specially woven plaque filled with seeds and *páhos*. Here, like a setting hen, she squats during the rest of the ceremony. Then she is taken back to the Parrot Clan home by the leader of the Soyál Society.

The girl is commonly known as the hawk maiden because young men initiates are called *kékelt* [fledgling hawks], but she is always of the Parrot Clan. This clan, as we know, is the symbolic Mother of the Hopis, and in this ritual she is symbolically carrying out the female function in reproduction by hatching the seeds and *páhos* in the plaque. The seeds are of all kinds, and the *páhos* include the short male-and-female *páhos* which represent people yet to be born. When she leaves, the *páhos* are placed in a sacred niche underneath the ladder on the right-hand side. The plaque of seeds is set on the floor in the middle of the kiva. After the ceremony clan members in proper sequence—the Bear, Tobacco, Corn, and finally the Coyote—pick up the seeds in their right hands to carry home, to sprinkle some of the corn kernels over the stacks of corn in the storehouses, and planting many of the *páhos* in the beams of the house. Hence from these germinated seeds hatched by the traditional

Mother grow the plants and the people in this symbolic re-creation of all life throughout the world.

The presence of this hawk maiden, whose function in this important ritual has always been shrouded in secrecy, is a lingering reminder of ancient times when human sacrifice was made. A young virgin girl was sacrificed usually every four years, this being the duration of the power derived from the sacrifice. She was usually of the chief's family, and thus few young girls reached marriageable age in his family. In later times actual physical sacrifice of the girl was not made. Instead, the name of the girl selected for spiritual sacrifice was whispered to a special *páho,* and she died within four years. Such a sacrifice—physical, spiritual, or symbolic—illuminates one of the great hidden meanings of Soyál. For this is the Winter Solstice, the time for the rebirth of all life. But life must be paid for with life; the germinated seed must give up its identity as a seed that a new form may rise from it; the earth itself must periodically die to insure rebirth.

The Soyál Chief now takes down from the north wall of the kiva, where it has been hanging, the symbol of the sun. It is a buckskin shield about a foot in diameter. The lower half is painted blue, the upper right quadrant is red, and the upper left quadrant is yellow. As it represents the face of the Sun, eyes are marked in black and the mouth is a triangle painted black. A black strip outlined in white runs down from the middle of the forehead, another crosses nose and cheeks, and there are tiny white dots in the background. The whole face is edged with long human hair stained red to symbolize the rays of the sun, and eagle feathers radiate from the outer circumference of the shield like the aura of power from the Creator. For while the sun is himself a deity, the chief of our solar system, his is but the face through which looks the omnipotent Creator, Taiowa, who stands behind.*

Having taken the shield from the Soyál Chief, Múi'ingwa jumps in front of the fire-pit to the beat of the drum and begins to dance and to spin the sun shield, dancing rapidly toward each of the four directions at each of the four directional points in turn, whirling the sun with a fast spinning motion toward each of the four directions at each of the stations—all to the mounting swell of song. The dancing increases in tempo. The sun shield spins faster. The song grows louder. All minds and hearts are now bent in harmony upon one single purpose: to help the sun turn back on his trail.

All these dances, songs, and spinning of the sun are timed by the changing positions of the three stars, Hotomkam, overhead. Now is the

---

* Dr. Harold S. Colton in his book, *Hopi Kachina Dolls, op. cit.,* defines the Supreme Creator, Taiowa, as a "handsome little fellow," a "minor god of ornaments."

time this must be done, before the sun rises and takes up his journey. Nothing can be allowed to go wrong; not a directional step in the dance, not a line in a song can be omitted; no evil thought can be allowed to cross the minds of those in deep concentration. So the Two Horns and the One Horn priests watch and listen intently. The Two Horn priests have final authority. If they say that the dancing, recitation, and song are not in perfect order, the One Horn priests agree at once. For they have derived their authority from the Fire Clan's order of the law, closely allied with that of the sun, and if anything goes wrong they are endangered themselves. Nor are the Two Horn and One Horn priests alone in this careful watchfulness; they have detected the manifestations of spiritual beings who also come to insure the harmonious right action of the ceremony. . . .

Finally, suddenly, it is done. The stars overhead proclaim it. The great turn of the Winter Solstice has been made.

BLESSING RITES

At the conclusion of the ceremony members of the other kivas file out, carrying the painting of Múi'ingwa back to the Flute Kiva. Two plaques of *páhos* are blessed with cornmeal, pollen, and honey. One is taken to the shrine of Másaw, guardian of the people and god of the underworld. The other one is carried to the shrine of the sun on Táwaki [Sun House] Mesa to the east. They must be deposited before dawn, requiring a long and difficult run by the messenger. In case of a storm, he deposits the *páhos* in a special shrine just below Oraibi. All the other *páhos* made on the fifteenth day are now distributed to the homes in the village.

It is now about 4:30 a.m. in Shongopovi—Christmas morning, as the abbreviated Soyál here is off schedule this year—and we are waiting in a home near the Kwan Kiva. Everyone in the family is up in the single big room—grandmother, mother, two little girls, and a baby—when the members of the kivas begin to arrive. Rain has been falling all night, and the messengers, one at a time, come in dressed in muddy boots and overcoats, but each wearing a garland of feathers around his sopping head.

For each family there is one of the exquisitely made male-and-female *páhos.* Then come the single prayer feathers with a length of cotton string tied to the quill—a feather apiece for each member of the family and its guests. When the messenger clumps out, the mother ties the feather to a long red-willow branch. For an hour it goes on. The prayer sticks hold between thirty and forty feathers—prayers for the sun, the fields and orchards, the springs, health, love, homes, and the animals. Now at dawn the people take the prayer sticks to a shrine at the edge of the mesa, plant them firmly, and draw a cornmeal path from them to the east. This year there is no dawn. The rain has stopped, and a thick mist hangs over the mesa. Through it people poke eerily with flashlights to find the shrine hidden in the cliffs. For four dawns the people must revisit the shrine to renew their prayers. Then the feathers may be taken home and hung in the house, on the stunted peach trees, the animals, the truck.

Meanwhile the priests in the Chief's Kiva are breaking their fast with special food—*piki*, the thin wafer bread, but not folded into rolls as usual, representing the flat surface of the land; a bowl of beans; and a plaque of white cornmeal mush symbolizing the runoff from the hills to the fields where the corn is planted in the spring.

About noon the Ahööla Kachina and the Ahööla-mana make their appearance, going from house to house. On the outside wall Ahööla makes four horizontal marks with cornmeal. The woman of the house comes out, sprinkles him with cornmeal, and takes out a few seeds from the *mana*'s basket. This of course is the same function prescribed earlier for the Soyál Kachina in other villages. The two then go to the Kwan Kiva roof entrance and stop, Ahööla facing the *mana*, who is dressed like a woman in an *atu'u*, a beautiful cape of white with a wide red border. One sees his helmet mask clearer now. On the left side of his great black-and-white upcurving nose his face is painted yellow, and on the right side turquoise, the whole mask being thickly tufted with long eagle feathers. Holding out his staff for support, he bends his right knee and goes through rhythmic kneeling motions. Then he rises and utters a strange loud call which brings out the kiva chief. For a moment there is conversation between them, formally opening the kiva to the *kachinas* for the year. Ahaliya, representing the "uncle" of the *kachinas*, substitutes here in Shongopovi for the Quaquakleum Kachinas.

On the sixteenth day one sees in Hotevilla the more correct closing ritual. By afternoon when the Qoaquakleum come out, it is bitterly cold. There are fourteen of them, wrapped in overcoats, but each wearing a mask with a green line, representing a cornstalk, drawn from the mouth upward over the nose and over each eye. Each cheek is painted green and marked with bird tracks. Hawk feathers stick out from the head like ears, and rabbit skins are worn around the neck in a thick ruff. Rabbit skins are wrapped around the feet, and a turtle-shell rattle is worn below the knee of the right leg. All these symbolize the animal kingdom. In the left hand is carried a stick around which is twisted the skin of a rabbit; in the right is the customary rattle.

As they stop in a long line to dance, four Kókoyemsim [Mudheads] stand behind them, wearing masks of buckskin colored to give the appearance of reddish mud heads knobbed and hairless, and with grotesquely distorted eyes and mouths. They symbolize the early stage of mankind upon its first Emergence to this world, muttering incoherently, as men had not yet learned to talk—just like the Zuñis, it is said, when the Hopis met them upon their Emergence and gave them food. Hence Zuñi also has Kókoyemsin.

The purpose of these spirit people and the Qoaquakleum with them is to entertain the people and distribute gifts to the children. So despite the freezing cold they dance quickly at four places, hurry through a little horseplay, and give watermelons, sweet corn that has been baked in a pit, and their rabbit sticks to children.

As the dance ends, the Soyál Chief takes to the Powamu Kiva the four *páhos* that the Soyál had brought to the Chief Kiva at the beginning of Soyál. The Powamu Chief takes them to the edge of the village and gives them to the Qoaquakleum. They in turn carry them back into the village, planting one on each of the kivas that will participate in Powamu, the next ceremonial. Four days later the Powamu Chief takes the *páho* which has been planted in the *núta* overhead down into his kiva, signifying that he now takes over the religious authority. Thus, just as Soyál was closely tied to the preceding Wúwuchim, so is it tied to the coming Powamu that there may be no break in the ceremonial portrayal of developing life.

For three days now there is a rabbit hunt, and on the fourth day the rabbits are cooked for the concluding feast. All the Soyál priests, still wearing their ceremonial kilts, carry a bowl of rabbit stew to the home of the designated Soyál-mana, who takes it inside. The women now come out and throw water on the Soyál men that snow and rain may come to bless the crops. *Somíviki*—sweet blue cornmeal cooked with ashes and tied into little packets of corn husks with yucca fiber—is then distributed to the people as final assurance of a happy and bountiful year.

Who can doubt that it will be?

For now at last comes the snow, a prolonged heavy white fall that blankets the tiny sandy fields, the sparse fruit trees clinging to the rocky hillsides, the desolate wilderness stretching unbroken to the far horizon—all the brown, barren earth of a people whose lives are dependent upon their prayerful knowledge of the source of all blessings and the means by which they can be evoked.

4

The Kachina Night Dances

The first two ceremonials portraying the first two phases of Creation are over. The earth has been solidified. Life has been germinated and is ready to make its first appearance. The first of the *kachinas* have come to help its growth. So now during the month of the Pámuya moon a series of night dances are given in the kivas by the host of *kachinas* who follow.

The *kachinas* are popularly believed to live on top of the San Francisco peaks to the west. Every winter they come to the Hopi villages during Soyál and Powamu, returning home after Niman Kachina in midsummer. Actually they come from much farther away, a long, long way—from neighboring stars, constellations too distant to be visible, from mysterious spirit worlds.

To understand the *kachina* we must learn a little bit more of Hopi cosmography and cosmology. The planet earth is the fourth physically manifested world we have lived upon. There have been three previous ones, and there will be three more. It has its own sun, moon, and satellites, forming a little solar system of its own. A glance into the midnight sky is sufficient to show us how puny and insignificant are our attempts to span the little distance to our moon by space-rockets and such mechanical contraptions. For beyond our own little universe we see extending into illimitable space the great constellations which form six more universes or solar systems marking our Road of Life.

Man starts out pure on each new world upon his Emergence. That world becomes corrupted with evil and is destroyed, and man makes another Emergence to the next. It is a long, slow road along which mankind plods interminably. But an individual who obeys the law of laws and conforms to the pure and perfect pattern laid down by the Creator becomes a *kachina* when he dies and goes immediately to the next universe without having to plod through all the intermediate worlds or stages of existence. From there, traveling through the vast wastes of interstellar space, he comes back periodically with *kachinas* of other forms of life to help mankind continue its evolutionary journey. Beyond these seven universes, each a great stage of development, lie two more beyond man's reach. The eighth is the realm of Sótuknang, who helped to create and still helps to maintain the other systems; and the ninth is the indefinable, incomprehensible domain of the one divine Creator of all.*

The *kachinas,* then, are the inner forms, the spiritual components of the outer physical forms of life, which may be invoked to manifest their benign powers so that man may be enabled to continue his never-ending journey. They are the invisible forces of life—not gods, but rather intermediaries, messengers. Hence their chief function is to bring rain, insuring the abundance of crops and the continuation of life.

All this is concretely symbolized by the markings on the rattle given to children before their initiation (Figure 57).

Figure 57. Kachina rattle

The flat round face of the gourd represents the earth. The circle inside symbolizes the sun, whose radiating rays give it warmth and life. The swastika symbol may show clockwise rotation with the sun, or counterclockwise to indicate the earth. The stick thrust through the

---

* "There are other worlds than this one of ours. There is an infinity of worlds. And Spirit, which is God, inhabits the infinity, even down to its minutest member. The Will of God is within each of His creatures in His infinitude of worlds."

For uttering this similar heresy, Giordano Bruno in Rome was imprisoned for eight years and burned at the stake in 1600 by the Papal Inquisition.

gourd for a handle symbolizes the north-south axis of the earth, at whose ends sit the Hero Twins, Pöqánghoya and Palöngawhoya, who keep the planet rotating. The markings shown on the side represent the constellations in the Milky Way. Both Twins constantly send out echoing vibrations along the earth's axis. These constitute the real source of the noise of the rattle, which re-echoes their vibrations as either a signal or a warning. Children after their initiation into the Kachina or Powamu Societies are given plain rattles similar to those the *kachinas* use.

This cosmological concept is embodied in the pattern of the *kachina* dances and in the structure of the *kachina* songs performed outdoors during Niman Kachina.* Both reflect the great dramatic struggle going on within the ceremony. This the real *kachinas* know; it is the cosmic battle that has persisted throughout Hopi mythology.

Hence *kachinas* are properly not deities. As their name denotes (*ka*, respect, and *china*, spirit), they are respected spirits: spirits of the dead; spirits of mineral, plant, bird, animal, and human entities, of clouds, other planets, stars that have not yet appeared in our sky; spirits of all the invisible forces of life. Dr. J. W. Fewkes, in his classic first study of Hopi *kachinas* a half-century ago, identified about 220. Estimates by later statistical anthropologists range up to 335. This enumeration of *kachinas* is akin to measuring how many angels can be accommodated on the head of a pin. A star burns out; another is born. The effect of one life force wanes, that of another replaces it. So with *kachinas*. They appear and disappear with the ebb and flow of time, like life itself, and they are as legion as its infinite forms.

During the six months they are here on earth the *kachinas* manifest themselves in physical form. So the masked men who impersonate them are also *kachinas,* losing their personal identities and being imbued with the spirits of the beings they represent. During their impersonations they must be above reproach: remaining continent, refraining from contact with whites, avoiding quarrels, having only pure thoughts. If one stumbles or falls while dancing, this not only betrays his immoderation but may nullify the ceremony and may even bring drought. The masks of the chief *kachinas* themselves are invested with spiritual powers, and the right to wear them is hereditary. Each is ceremonially fed and carefully preserved; and when its owner dies it is buried, with the understanding that its supernatural power must be returned whence it came.

Children are given small figures carved of soft cottonwood roots, correctly painted and costumed to represent the masked impersonators. These "dolls" are also called *kachinas* but are not invested with power;

---

* Detailed explanation given in Part Three, Chapter 6.

they serve only to help familiarize children with the masks and names of the real *kachinas,* as every Hopi child upon reaching the age of six to eight years must be initiated into either the Kachina or Powamu Society.

Simple as is the meaning of the *kachina,* everything about it is stylistic and complex, and it has exerted a powerful influence throughout all the pueblos in the Southwest. There are no *kachinas* in the Rio Grande pueblos, but in many of their unmasked dances one often detects the distinct *kachina* stylizations. Zuñi is the only other pueblo which has *kachinas;* these, say the Hopis, were given them by the Hopis who preceded them during the Emergence. The origin of Hopi *kachinas* lies far back in the prehistoric past. The Kókopilau Kachina sings a song in a language so ancient that not a word of it is understood by the modern Hopis, who know only that *kachinas* accompanied them throughout their migrations. Indeed, they assert that *kachinas* came up with them during their Emergence from the womb of Mother Earth. Típkyavi, meaning "womb," is the name given a place at the base of the San Francisco peaks, the last site where the Hopis lived before settling in their present villages and still the last stopping place of the *kachinas* on their way home from Niman Kachina; it is also represented on Third Mesa by a *kisonvi* in Oraibi.

All these academic considerations, however, are invalidated by the basic truths and meaning of the *kachina.* It is distinctively Hopi. In its conception the Hopis have created a form for the everlasting formless; a living symbol unique in the world for that universal and multifold spirit which embodies all living matter; which speaks to us, as only the spirit can speak, through the intuitive perception of our own faith in the one enduring mystery of life. One cannot doubt its veracity when in a kiva we hear the strange falsetto yell announcing a presence above, feel the stamp on the roof demanding admittance, and see coming down the ladder a spirit whose manifested form has never been glimpsed among the figures of this mortal world.

THE SOCIAL HOYA DANCES

The dances held during the Pámuya [Moisture] Moon between Soyál and Powamu are not solely *kachina* nor are they held only at night. They include preliminary social dances that take place outside in the *kisonvi* during the day as well.

Oraibi on a cold January night is a fitting place for them to begin. It is ten o'clock, and in spectral moonlight the snowy plain below stretches out like an unbroken icy sea. Up on this jutting reef the village lies dark and lifeless, row upon row of deserted buildings, crumbling walls, fallen roofs, and weedy plazas, an archaeological ruin through whose shadows prowl ghosts with flashlights, converging for rendezvous in the last three remaining kivas.

Inside the decrepit, water-stained Sakwlenvi Kiva the dying life of Oraibi flickers with a last glow. An old wood stove has been set over the fire-pit, its rusty stovepipe stuck up through the ladder opening. Beside it squats the aging kiva chief, feeding it sticks of piñon. The room is crowded with the last villagers—old men with deep-sunk eyes, slumped on the seating ledge around the altar level; blanketed women with babies and rachitic children, packed on the raise. All waiting with silent expectancy. For what? Apparently for a resurgence of life. It comes with several carloads of Hopis from Shongopovi on Second Mesa.

Finally they enter the kiva: ten dancers with a drummer and a chorus of some twenty men. Four of the dancers are men whose faces are un-masked and painted, wearing on heads and shoulders great buffalo hoods with upcurving horns. They are accompanied by four beautifully garbed women and followed by two small boys dressed from heads to toes as coyotes. They dance for a half-hour to the beat of the drum and the resonant singing of the chorus.

Following this Buffalo Dance another group comes in to give the White Buffalo Dance. The chorus of singers with their drummer is larger, but there are only four dancers: two men whose faces and bodies are painted white and who carry white lightning frames; and two small ten-year-old girls shrouded in white capes and wearing their hair done up in the squash-blossom whorls formerly worn by all unmarried Hopi maidens. The dancing is exquisite. Periodically it stops. The White Buffalo bend down, arms to floor as if serving as forelegs, and carry the little girls piggy-back. Then again the dancing resumes.

Buffalo bring snow, which provides good hunting as well as moisture, so all Buffalo Dances traditionally invoke consent from the game for the sacrifice of their lives. These dances have no other significance; it is the dancing itself that counts.

The next group consists of two couples accompanied by a chorus of fourteen. A titter of amusement ripples through the kiva. All are dressed to the teeth in Spanish Colonial costumes: *charro* and *china poblana* correct to every detail, flaring mustaches, straw sombreros, ten-cent-store paper roses in hair, tiny guitars, guns carried jauntily on the left shoulders. But they dance as Hopis dance—except that periodically they march around with the stiff posture of American GIs. The whole thing is so unbelievably ironic and delicately done that full appreciation comes slowly and lasts long—a fitting commentary by a dying culture on one already dead.

A few nights later in Shongopovi a group of nearly forty men and boys from Oraibi present another take-off, on Apaches, realistically dressed in tattered clothes and carrying rifles. But accompanying them as side dancers are two men brilliantly bedecked as fictional Hiawathas, and two women as Pocahontas, wearing the beaded headbands with red feathers typical of the "Indian Princess" fiction of several decades ago.

They are followed by some fifty men from Hotevilla doing a take-off on Paiutes, realistically dressed except for gaudily painted conical dunce caps tipped with bunches of hawk feathers.

Both these groups dance outside the next day on an icy plaza covered with fresh sand to prevent them from slipping. Two days later they dance again in the plaza of Hotevilla, followed by a third group dressed up as Navajos. One of the chorus prominently displays on his bare back the lettering: "Paul Jones, No Good, Tribal Chairman."

In the thin winter sunlight these dances are colorful enough. The dancers shout derisively, jostle one another, shoot off cap pistols and blank cartridges, ostensibly providing a little fun in the dead of winter. Yet bystanders feel much concern because they are so out of keeping with the religious pattern of life being set up by the winter ceremonials. Their mock warlike antics, it is said, presage an outbreak of war somewhere in the world.

Still the groups visit back and forth. From Michongnovi come two men eagle dancers, two small girl butterfly dancers with huge butterflies pinned to their backs, and three singers with small drums accompanying them. In Shipaulovi are more Buffalo Dancers, without real hoods but wearing masks of black wool spotted with tufts of cotton.

All these visiting groups are known as Hoya [Fly off Nest], and each group must return home for its final performance before stopping for the season. Such unmasked dances, given in Rio Grande style with a drummer and a chorus, are social dances held only for pure entertainment. They are simply a prelude to the *kachina* night dances that follow.

THE KACHINA NIGHT DANCES

These begin this year [1959] in Hotevilla. It is early, scarcely seven o'clock. Everyone has eaten and is crowding into one of the six kivas. Here in the Flute Kiva the air of expectancy is keyed with wonder. One sees it in the faces of the children upturned to the ladder opening.

And now at last the stylized pattern of the *kachina* dances takes shape: a curious falsetto yell and the shake of a rattle above, followed by a stamp on the roof. The old kiva chief calls up an invitation. Then down the ladder the *kachinas* come, and take positions in a long line extending around the three walls of the altar level. How strange, horrible, and wonderful they are!—twenty black-masked figures with long red tongues hanging down over coarse black beards; bodies painted black, with yellow shoulders and arms; each wearing a *kachina* kilt, Hopi sash, and foxskin hanging down behind; a ruff of spruce around the throat, and twigs of spruce stuck in waist and arm bands. They are the Chá'kwana, very old, who come from the tropical South. The kiva chief sprinkles each with sacred meal, lays a path for them. Then the leader, always in the center, gives the cue. The right arms raise slightly, the rattles shake. The right feet come down with a powerful stamp. The song begins. And the turtle-shell rattles tied under the right knees mark the beat. All figures are exactly alike and act in unison with a perfect synchronization of song, motion, and sound.

One group replaces another. Still they keep coming, to different kivas, to different villages, night after night. Some are simple and benign, as the Catori, commonly known as "seed carriers" from the bags of seeds which they distribute, or the familiar Corn Dance Kachinas. Still other groups are complex in organization, like the Knayaya [Swaying Heads], who wear masks painted turquoise on the left side and yellow on the right, with blue tubular snouts. Two leaders act as side dancers: Tócha, the Humming Bird, with a pale violet head and a long, sharp yellow beak; and Avachhoya, the Spotted Corn Kachina, painted with mixed corn of all directions. Also accompanying them are two little Cloud Maidens with faces painted white and hair built into whorls of white cotton. Sometimes women *kachinas* accompany a group, like the four Hemis Kachin-manas with blue faces and dressed in their women's capes, who come in with the Koa Kachinas [High Pillared Clouds] to kneel with their grinding sticks and plaques to rasp out the sound of distant thunder. Still again there may be a group of mixed *kachinas* of all kinds, as if to show how inexhaustible are the variations in their masks and meanings. A beautiful group of Quiquikivi come in, whose masks are pink, with black cloud terraces marking the eyes, green squash-blossom ears, and toothed snouts, all righly ornamented with jewelry. Such richly costumed *kachinas* are always called "proud" *kachinas*, yet they are always comparatively new ones. The old ones, more restrainedly beautiful, are subtly distinguished as *kuwan kachinas*. It is difficult to tell the groups apart, they are all so beautiful, with a strange other-worldliness and inexhaustible variations. Nor can one tell the individual figures apart. All are dressed exactly alike and their perfect synchronization creates an effect of the line as a whole rather than of the units composing it—a row of figures endlessly repeated by a set of mirrors. It is always mesmeric.

But one cannot ignore the songs. One sung by the Long Hair Kachinas one night in Hotevilla illustrates how beautiful and meaningful they are. The song describes how, eight days previously, a Hopi leader had gone to every kiva leader with instructions to plant a prayer feather at all the directional shrines and to send up prayer smoke requesting the *kachinas* to visit their people. These *kachinas,* the Long Hairs, had received the leaders' message through the scent of their prayer smoke. Arriving at the shrines, they had found the prayer feathers and traced the leaders' spiritual footprints here to this kiva. Now they were here to answer the prayer, to manifest themselves before the gathered people, and to bring them happiness.

"In the summertime we will come again," they sang. "We will come as clouds from the west, the south, the east, and the north to bless the Hopi people and to water their fields and crops. Then the Hopis will see their corn plants majestically growing. They will be so happy they will joyfully sing praises to the spiritual beings who brought moisture. At the edge of the cornfield a bird will sing with them in the oneness of their happiness. So they will sing together in tune with the universal power, in harmony with the one Creator of all things. And the bird song, and the people's song, and the song of life will become one."

Now, in the harsh white light of the overhead lamp, one awakes to a new group of twenty, still more horrible and strangely beautiful. From their great black heads, yellow on top, protrude upcurving horns, bulging eyes rimmed in white, and long-toothed snouts. A white star is painted on the left cheeks and a white crescent moon on the right. Each wears a ruff of spruce around the throat. Their bodies, bare to the waist, are painted black with yellow shoulders and forearms and white hands; and a red bandoleer is worn over the right shoulder. Each wears a buckskin kilt secured by a Hopi sash, blue moccasins, and a turtle-shell rattle tied below the right knee. A bunch of parrot feathers is tied to the top of the head; a fan of eagle feathers projects back of the head. He carries a gourd rattle in the right hand, a twig of spruce and a bow and arrow in the left. These are Ahótes, the Restless Ones, ever restless to warn and punish. Even as they come down the ladder one by one, they utter their low eerie moans and move restlessly about, spirits of planets from the depths of space. Suddenly the dance begins.

Everything about Ahóte breathes power: the powerful magic of his grotesque mask, the powerful stamp, the deep soughing voice, the metallic rattle, the accompanying drum whose beat is itself supposed to have a strange power. One is swept away by it all in a queer, momentary illusion. One feels oneself to be a passenger on a steam locomotive, feeling the powerful beat of the pistons below him, hearing the soughing of the forest he is rushing through, and vaguely wondering where he is going. Then suddenly he realizes he is a passenger in a human body instead, the piston thrusts being the beat of his heart, and the soughing of wind in the forest the sound in his ears when he is alone and all is still about him. But still he wonders vaguely where he is going. . . .

Such momentary illusions projected so powerfully on the unconscious by the grotesque imagery of these strange and indescribable figures must certainly be the supreme achievement of the *kachinas* and the secret of their unbreakable hold upon the imagination of their people. Spirits temporarily embodied in flesh themselves, they remind us all of our own brief roles on this transient earth. So they keep coming—a swelling host of *kachinas,* the spirits of mineral, plant, bird, animal, and human entities, of clouds and stars and all the invisible forces of life.

Then suddenly the dances stop and the earth grows still. The voice of the Crier Chief is heard calling to the Cloud People of the Directions: "People of the West, hear my call and come! People of the South, hear my call and come! People of the East, hear my call and come! People of the North, hear my call and come!"

Then he calls to the people of the village: "You people of the village! The chief of the Powamu Society now begins his prayers and concentration in his kiva. He wants all the people of the village to be of the humblest nature for sixteen days. Beat no drum. Make no loud noises. Do not raise your voices against each other. He wishes you to speak in low voices during this time."

Pámuya, the time of *kachina* night dances in the kivas, is over. The new moon of Powámúya has appeared, and it is time for the great ceremonial symbolizing the last phase of creation at the dawn of life.

5

Powamu

To recapitulate the three phases of Creation, Wúwuchim laid out the pattern of life development for the coming year, Soyál accepted it, and Powamu now purifies it. This is the etymological meaning of its name, "purification."

The functions of the Powamu ceremony itself are far more complex. In the last phase of Creation, which it portrays, life manifests itself in its full physical forms. All the spiritual counterparts of these have arrived as *kachinas* to sanctify their growth. Hence every Hopi child before reaching adolescence must be initiated into either the Kachina or Powamu Societies. Concluded also is the final initiation of young men who were initiated into Wúwuchim the preceding year and who by now have made their first pilgrimage to the Salt Cave in Grand Canyon. As Powamu purifies the life pattern for the whole year, it is necessary also to prepare now the *páhos* for, and to give in preliminary form, each of the ceremonials to follow throughout the year. Powamu is the first of two major ceremonies connected with the *kachina* cult, and is so important that every kiva chief must be a member of the Powamu Society.

The date for Powamu is determined by lunar observation. Following the first day of the new moon there is the usual preliminary period for preparing *páhos* and announcing the ceremony. The Powamu Chief then begins his kiva retreat, planting the *na'chi* on top to signify the ceremony has begun. There are eight days of preparation, followed by eight days of ritual, making sixteen days for the complete ceremony.* Every village holds Powamu except Moencopi, still allied with Oraibi. The two principal societies participating are the Powamu Society and the Kachina

---

* In 1960 Hotevilla announced Powamu on January 29, one day after the new moon, and concluded it sixteen days later, on February 13. Villages on First and Second Mesa observed only twelve-day ceremonies, beginning at different times in each village.

Society. Controlling clans in order of succession are the Badger, Kachina, Parrot, and Tobacco Clans.

PLANTING OF THE BEANS

The first important ritual is the planting of beans in the kivas during the first four days. Upon receiving the *páhos* from the Powamu Chief, each kiva chief selects a member to whom he gives a prayer feather with instructions to gather the soil in which the beans are to be planted. All these men must secure permission from the Sand Clan, which has been the keeper of the soil from the beginning of time. Then, having gone to the designated spot, the men plant their *páhos* with the prayer that the beans planted in this soil will grow quickly and well as an omen of an abundant harvest. After gathering the soil, they return to their kivas and fill numerous earthen pots and trays in which they plant the beans.

Day and night the stoves are kept stoked with wood, and the beans are carefully watered, ritually smoked over, and sprinkled with sacred meal. Under this forced growth the young plants begin to appear about the eighth day—a wonderfully green-leafed growth in the dead of winter, symbolizing the first complete physical form of life to appear in this last phase of Creation.

Beans are chosen for this important role simply because they can be grown and matured so fast, and all of the plant can be eaten. Of the four sacred plants—corn, squash, beans, and tobacco—corn, of course, is the most important; no ritual can be held without cornmeal. Hence corn is planted at the same time the beans are planted, but only a few special sprouts, only by the chief of all *kachinas*, Eototo, and Áholi, who always accompanies him, and only for one brief and highly significant ritual.

As the hundreds of bean plants begin to sprout, unmasked Powamu *kachinas*, wearing on their heads their distinctive squash-blossom flowers made of cornhusks begin to visit the kivas, dancing to help their children, the bean plants, to grow. As each enters the kiva, a *kachina-mana* makes fun of or praises him, causing him to review his past actions. This "confession" or "purification" also helps the bean plants to grow. Meanwhile other members of the Powamu Society compose the songs to be sung during the ceremonies and complete the Powamu altar.

The altar is set on the west side of the kiva on a layer of the same sand in which the beans are planted. Upon the sand the Powamu Chief and his assistant, accompanied by ritual songs, prepare a sand-painting with colored sands of the Angwushahai'í Kachina [Mother of the Whipper Kachinas], flanked on each side by the two Hu' [Whipper] Kachinas. The altar, made of wood and painted earth-brown, is decorated with *páhos*. Propped against it is an oak rod about four feet long, crooked for longevity at top, and with several Corn Mothers tied to the bottom. When all is ready for the ceremonies to begin, the Powamu Chief carries it to the Ahl Kiva, where the Kachina initiations are to be held.

INITIATION OF CHILDREN

Every Hopi child upon reaching the age of six to eight years must be initiated into either the Powamu Society or the Kachina Society. The parents and the godfather selected to sponsor each child choose the society into which he is initiated. The Powamu is the more important. The initiate is not whipped; and as a member he becomes a "Father of the Kachinas," guiding them around the village and sprinkling them with cornmeal. Hence the boys selected for this society are the more serious and interested in religious functions.

When there are only a few children to be initiated they are taken separately to their fathers' kivas for a simple initiation rite known as Polatkwua [Red Hawk], as the novices are commonly called *kékelt*, young hawks not yet ready to fly. Usually initiations are held every four years, at which time the full ceremony is held. Kacha Hónaw [White Bear] was initiated into the Powamu Society at Oraibi in 1914, and describes the rites:

"At sundown on the eleventh day my godfather came to our house and tied a prayer feather to the top of my head, showing that I was to be initiated into Powamu. Then he took me to the Marau Kiva, where I was seated with twelve other small boys on the north side of the lower level. He went to the raise with the other godfathers. We boys had to sit with our feet raised to the seating ledge, our knees under our chins, because we were *kékelt*, too young to fly. About midnight we heard noises on top of the kiva. The kiva chief called up, '*Yung-ai!* Come in! You are welcome!'

"Then the *kachinas* came in. They were Powamu *kachinas*, men and women, but without masks. Each man's face was painted white with a red circle on each cheek, and his long hair hung down to his shoulders. His body was painted yellow on the left side, with chest, shoulder, forearm, and hand painted blue. On the right side his chest and shoulder were blue, his forearm and hand yellow. The rest of his body was earth-red, with a narrow line running from the breast, to mean rain. A red bandoleer passed over his right shoulder and was fastened to the Hopi sash around his waist to keep up the ceremonial kilt. Flowers of cornhusks were tied to his hair, and on top a bunch of eagle feathers known as *nakwa* [mark of identification].

"The Powamu maidens each wore the women's black *manta*, over which was draped the white cape. Her hair was done up in squash-blossom whorls, and on her forehead she wore a squash-blossom made out of corn-husks painted either white or yellow. All the maidens carried spruce branches, which they held over their faces so we would not recognize them. I didn't find out until later that all these Powamu maidens were men dressed as women.

"Having come down the ladder, the men lined up in front of us on the north side and the women on the south side. Then they danced and sang, one pair at a time coming together to hold each other's arms and dance down the center toward the fire-pit, then separating again. Groups from other kivas came in to dance. Between dances we were allowed to stretch our legs, but we were glad when it was all over and we were permitted to go to sleep with our godfathers in the kiva.

"Next morning we went to school as usual, still wearing the little feathers stuck to our hair with piñon pitch, but we had to go into the kiva again at sundown. For two more nights the same ceremony was repeated. The evening of the fourth day—Píktotokya [Piki-Making Day]—we were taken to the Ahl Kiva for Kachinyungta, the Kachina Society ritual.

"There were a lot of us, boys and girls, the boys on the north side of the lower floor, the girls on the south side. We were all stripped naked, holding blankets around us. Those of us being initiated into the Powamu Society wore the little feather in our hair, showing that we were not to be whipped. From the ceiling hung many kinds of feathers—eagle, hawk, owl, crow, and buzzard. On the floor west of the fire-pit I saw a large willow hoop to which were tied the same kind of feathers.

"We did not have long to wait. The Powamu Chief came in, wearing a white cape and carrying a long rod with a crook on top and several Corn Mothers [*Chóchmingure*] tied to the bottom. Standing between the fire-pit and the hoop, the Kachina Chief sang to us of the world we left behind. The story told of one wicked woman who corrupted most of that world, boasting that she would take so many turquoise necklaces from men for her favors she could wind them around a ladder from her kiva so long it reached to the end of the pole.

"At the end of the song each boy or girl in turn was led out and made to step inside the large hoop or ring of feathers. The Powamu Chief and the Kachina Chief moved the ring up and down over his body from head to foot four times. When he stepped out of the ring, several

Kókoyemsim [Mudheads] came out from behind our godfathers on the upper level and made a circle around him. Carrying Corn Mothers in each hand, they moved them from his feet to his head four times, making him grow. All this had to be done quickly, I learned later, for if it had not been finished when the whippers arrived the Powamu and Kachina Chiefs would also have been whipped.

"Just as the Mudheads were running back behind our godparents, I heard a dreadful noise on top of the kiva. I knew the moment had come. The two Hu' whippers and their mother Angwushahai'i had arrived. Circling the ladder entrance four times, they were lashing the ladder poles and the straw *núta* in what seemed an uncontrollable fury. We all trembled with fear, though my godfather had told me I was not to be whipped.

"They came down into the kiva without invitation. Angwushahai'i first, carrying the *na'chi* and many yucca whips. Her helmet mask was turquoise, her face formed of an inverted triangle and a rectangle in black outlined in white with white dots for eyes, and a large black crow wing tied to each side. She wore a black *manta* dress and white wedding sash, over which was flung a bride's blanket.*

"The two Hu' whippers behind her were terrifying. Their bodies were naked save for red horsehair kilts, and painted black with white dots except for forearms and lower legs painted white. From their black masks stuck out horns, bulging eyes, huge mouths with bared teeth, and long black-and-white-striped horsehair beards. In both hands they carried long yucca whips.

"The whipping started immediately. A sponsor led out a boy to the middle of the floor, and one of the whippers struck him four times. Then a girl was led out and whipped. The two Hu' *kachinas* took turns with the flogging, and when their whips became worn out the Whipper Mother handed them others. You can be whipped once across the back, once across the bottom, the thighs, and the calves, or you can take all four in the same place. They aren't easy lashes. I could see the blood running on one boy who had always been disrespectful to his elders, and I was glad I had been polite. But sometimes a godfather will get sorry after a blow or two and take the rest of the lashes. It was a noisy ordeal, the Whipper Mother encouraging the whippers to strike harder, the godfathers and godmothers yelling about favoritism, the children screaming loud with fear and even louder when their turn came, and all the yells and noises of the *kachinas*. Finally it was over. The Kachina Chief said, 'I am the Father of all of you, yet as a father I have failed to protect you as my

---

* She is generally confused with Angwúsnasomtaqa, the Crow Mother, who is dressed and masked the same except for her face-marking of two inverted triangles.

children, and it makes me sad to see this happen to you.' He warned us never to tell anyone what we had seen, or the *kachinas* will punish us even harder.

"That night I went home and stayed with my godfather. Before the sun came up I was awakened by my godfather's mother, who removed the feather from my hair and washed my head in yucca suds. Then she held a Corn Mother to my chest, and passing it up and down toward my head said, 'From this day forth your name will be *Sikyátavo* [Yellow Rabbit].' I was named this because my godfather belonged to the Rabbit Clan, but the name didn't stick like the one I have now." *

THE BEAN DANCE

This same dawn—on the fifteenth day, Totokya [Day Before Dance]—Angwúsnasomtaqa, the Crow Mother Kachina, appears at Po'ki [Dog] Shrine near the village and begins singing. She is a beautiful and majestic figure. Two large crow wings stick out from the sides of her blue mask, which is tufted with breath-feathers and carries as face markings two inverted black triangles. Over her black loomed dress secured at the waist with a long fringed white wedding belt, she wears a beautifully embroidered bride's blanket, knee-high white bridal moccasins of buckskin, and a ruff of spruce around her throat.

Angwúsnasomtaqa, a tutelary deity of the Kachina Clan, is the sister of Chowílawu, deity of the Badger Clan, which directs Powamu, and lives with him at Kísiwu [Spring in the Shadows], forty miles north. At sunrise of the twentieth day after her marriage to another *kachina*, her brother, according to custom, was bringing her back in her wedding clothes from the home of the groom's parents at Típkyavi, at the base of the San Francisco peaks, to her own family home. At this moment she received the urgent call from the Hopi people requesting her assistance at the Powamu ceremony. The Crow Mother could not fail to heed their call and came immediately, without waiting to change her clothes. That is why she appears at dawn in her wedding clothes. But just the same, underneath the bean sprouts, the spruce, and the corn which she carries in her plaque are strips of bayonet yucca which she will use if things do not go right.

---

* The initiation of children at Hotevilla on February 10, 1960, adhered to the same pattern. Initiates comprised forty-one small boys and girls and one adult. There was blood on the adult's legs when he came out of the kiva, attesting to a severe whipping. The Hu' whippers symbolize storm and snow; and by odd coincidence a gusty snow squall blew up during the whipping ceremony inside the kiva—expressly to lash the waiting parents and spectators outside also, it was said.

Finishing a verse of her song, the Crow Mother comes to the edge of the village and sings another verse, then moves into the *kisonvi* to sing again, and finally to the Powamu Kiva. Her song tells the Kachina Clan migration story. She ends it with a long sigh, "Hu huh hu huh uh uh uhah," meaning that she has traveled a long way and is very tired.

The Powamu Chief comes out, takes the plaque from her, and blesses her with a prayer feather. She then starts home to her shrine while the Powamu Chief takes the plaque into the kiva to place in front of his *pongnya* [altar].

Meanwhile in all the kivas the bean plants have been cut and tied into small bundles with yucca. Now as the sun rises the *kachinas* deliver them to all homes in the village with presents for the children: a *kachina* doll and a plaque tied with a bean plant for each girl; and for each boy a pair of moccasins, a painted lightning stick or bow, a *tatachpi* [painted ball], and a *kachina* rattle also for those who have not yet been initiated.

Just as the Crow Mother leaves the Powamu Kiva to return home, two other important *kachinas* come out from the One Horn Kiva to the east. In the lead is Eototo, chief of all the *kachinas* and always impersonated by a member of the Bear Clan. His round, bare mask of white buckskin is painted only with three black dots for eyes and mouth, and embellished on top only with three sparrow-hawk feathers. He wears a ruff of foxskin, a buckskin jacket, a plain white cotton cape and a rope of black yarn all draped over the right shoulder, and the usual *kachina* kilt and Hopi sash. Black yarn is tied also to his wrists and knees. His hands are painted white with wave lines; in his right he carries a bag of cornmeal, in his left the supreme authority, the *mongko*. This one is carved with a cross in front and a split in the back. On it are tied with yucca a Corn Mother, a bundle of new corn plants, and a small water jar. The corn sprouts have been grown in the kiva by Eototo and Áholi, who planted them when the beans were planted by the other *kachinas*, and they are the only two who carry corn in the Powamu ceremony. The water in the jar has been taken from Flute Spring and specially blessed for this occasion.

Áholi always accompanies Eototo, walking a step behind. He is the chief *kachina* of the Side Corn Clan and wears one of the most unusual of all *kachina* masks. It consists of a tall conical or funnel-shaped head-mask with shoulder cape fastened in front and hanging down to his knees behind. Both are made of buckskin splotched with variegated colors. Sticking up from the point of the mask is a tuft of brilliant red horsehair and macaw feathers. The eyes are two thin slits, the mouth a small inverted triangle. Painted on the back of the cape is a strange winged figure with a human head. His body is bare to the waist, with two blue lines running down the right breast and two yellow lines down the left breast. Forearms are turquoise, hands white with wave lines. In his left hand he also carries the distinctive *mongko,* and in his right hand a staff with seven small white Corn Mothers tied to the top.

Their first stop is on the south side of the Snake Kiva. Eototo with cornmeal draws a horizontal line running north and south, and on top of this three short vertical lines running west and east. Aholi steps up and plants the foot of his staff in the middle of the center line. Rotating the staff in a circle from right to left, he begins to sing:

> A—ho—liiiiiiiiiiiiiiiii
> A—ho—liiiiiiiiiiiiiiiii
> Holi—holi—ho—liiiiiiiiiii. . . .

After finishing his call, Aholi turns completely around once to the left, stamping his right foot and the butt of his staff upon the ground seven times, once for each of the seven successive worlds in this universe. The same ceremony is repeated on the south side of the Marau Kiva, in the *kisonvi* between the Powamu and Maraw Kivas, in the plaza southwest of the village, at the house of the village chief, on the north side of the Mong Kiva, and at the house of Aholi's clan, the Side Corn Clan. These seven stops symbolize the seven universes, each with its seven successive worlds, comprising the total of forty-nine stages of man's development along his Road of Life.* The ceremony thus designates that all universes and worlds, or stages of existence are embraced within the one kingdom of the Creator who rules over all; and in accord with the prime meaning of Powamu, it purifies the whole pattern of man's existence.

To complete their rituals, Eototo and Aholi go to the Típkyavi [Womb], the open plaza in front of the Snake Kiva, and stop in front of the *sipápuni,* the small hole representing the place of Emergence from the underworld. Eototo with cornmeal successively marks lines from it to the west, south, east, and north. Both Eototo and Aholi then pour a little water into the *sipápuni* from the water jars on their *mongkos,* thus purifying as well man's routes of Emergence between all his successive stages of evolutionary existence. They then go to the Powamu Kiva, where the Powamu Chief blesses them by blowing smoke from his pipe over them, and return to the One Horn Kiva.

These two additional stops, symbolizing the exclusive domains of

---

* Occult teachings common to northern India and Tibet similarly assert that there are seven worlds or seven degrees of *Maya* within the *Sangsara,* or phenomenal universe, constituted as seven globes of a planetary chain. On each globe there are seven rounds of evolution, making the forty-nine (seven times seven) stations of active existence for the human species as the fetus passes through every form of organic structure from amoeba to man. Similarly, at death man's principle of consciousness passes through forty-nine After-Death or *Bardo* stages of psychic existence anterior to its re-emergence in gross matter.

Sótuknang and the Creator himself, make the total of nine kingdoms created and ruled by the omnipotent Creator of all.

That evening at sunset the Powamu initiates are once more taken to the Maraw Kiva to witness the last rituals of Powamu. Again they are stationed on the altar level, facing a beautiful sand painting of the Whipper *kachinas* and their mother, laid on the floor west of the firepit. About midnight a far, faint call is heard outside the kiva. Immediately the men who have been singing scramble up the ladder to bring in the Chowílawu Kachina.

Chowílawu [Join Together] is one of the most important of all *kachinas*. This moment, at midnight, is the only time throughout the year that he appears, and he is never represented. Chowílawu lives at the shrine of Kísiwu [Spring in the Shadows], some forty miles to the north. Here he hears the first call for him. He hears the second call at Siova [Onion Spring], fifteen miles away; the third on Cha'aktuika [Crier's Point], two miles away; and the fourth on top of the kiva. The men from inside the kiva have hardly scrambled up the ladder before Chowílawu arrives; that is how fast he travels. Chowílawu has a strange power called *tamöchpölö* [muscle pulling back of knee]. Hence during his swift journey all Hopis hearing the calls stretch out their legs and keep them straight to avoid having their muscles draw up behind their knees and lock; several Hopi men are lame because they failed to do this.

Chowílawu slides down the ladder into the kiva so fast that he hardly seems to touch its rounds. His dark face is splotched with white spots. Naked except for a breechcloth, his body is painted gray. Around his waist is a belt of small pieces of petrified wood highly polished, which make a tinkling sound like icicles hitting together. He jumps immediately upon the sand painting, and the men on the raise begin to sing for him. As the song progresses he moves over the sand painting, jumping up and down, until the sand painting is completely destroyed at the conclusion of his song. He then leaves the kiva as quickly as he came, the same four calls being made upon his return home.

When he leaves, the Powamu Kachinas perform the Bean Dance until sunrise. As the *kachinas* are unmasked, all initiates know by now that the *kachinas* are merely men who impersonate them, and have full knowledge of the meaning of Powamu and their responsibility toward their people.

PÁCHAVU

This same day—the sixteenth, known as Tíkive [Day of the Dance]—the Páchavu ceremony is held when adult men have been initiated into Wúwuchim the preceding year. Its name, Páchavu [plant life carried on plaque], describes the ceremony perfectly.

Beans for this ceremony have been planted four days earlier than the others so the plants will grow longer and be almost ready to blossom when they are cut. Preparations are made in the morning, when all initiates into the four Wúwuchim societies and women belonging to the families of the chiefs of the participating kivas assemble at the Kachinki [Kachina House] on the southern edge of the mesa. The men dress in the masks of different *kachinas,* and the women in the costumes of *kachina-manas* or Bean Maidens. Into large plaques wooden rods about eighteen inches high are stuck upright with mud. Sweet cornmeal, baked and molded into the shape of beans, is tied upon the rods and entwined with the new bean plants.

Early in the afternoon a long procession forms, headed by the village chief, and followed by the Crier Chief, Qaletaqa the Guardian, Eototo and Áholi, and alternating *kachinas* and Bean Maidens carrying the large plaques, with a large group of Mong [Chief] Kachinas bringing up the rear and singing. Slowly the procession approaches the village from the south. The large plaques with their gorgeous displays of bean plants are heavy, and no Bean Maiden is allowed to set one down. When one grows tired, she stops. The *kachina* in front of her turns around, places his hands underneath hers to support the weight while she rests. Then again the procession takes up its slow march to the constant singing of the Mong Kachinas.

Shortly before, at high noon, a frightening figure with several war gods has first appeared on Pumpkin Seed Point across the valley. She is Héhewúti, the Warrior Mother. On her black mask are painted two great yellow eyes with black pupils, a rectangular mouth edged with red and showing her bared teeth. From it protrudes her long red tongue. Her hair is done up in a whorl on one side and hangs full length on the other side. She wears a black loomed dress secured at the waist with a long fringed sash, over which is draped a black cape of the same material. Over her shoulder is hung a buckskin quiver full of arrows. In her left hand she carries a bow, in her right a rattle.

Héhewúti is very old and once lived far to the south in the mysterious red village known as Palátkwapi. On the morning when it was attacked and destroyed by enemies, Héhewúti was just putting up her hair. That is why her hair is done up on a whorl on one side but still hangs loose on the other. Immediately she threw on her clothes, which is why she looks so untidy, and grabbed up her bow and quiver to help defend the city. She acted like a man, so her moccasins are fringed like a man's. Standing on Pumpkin Seed Point, she sings four verses of a song which echoes the cries of her people in their distress.*

Still singing, she approaches the village, stopping at shrine after shrine to pick up still more *kachinas:* at Hótoto [Warrior Spirit Who Sings], where she picks up the two warrior *kachinas* Havajo and Hánia, named for the two who killed the Catholic priest at Oraibi with a flint knife during the Pueblo Revolt of 1680; at Sumáviktukya'ovi [Rocks Like Beeswax], picking up the Suhumsomtaka Kachina; at another shrine, where she is joined by Palákwaio, the Red Hawk Kachina; at Kúiwanva [Place Appearing over Horizon], and at Koritvi [Holes in Sandstone]. Finally, after entering the village, they proceed to kiva after kiva, encircling each one four times and gathering still more *kachinas* from each, all stopping at last in front of the One Horn Kiva.

Their song reaches a crest of volume and intensity as the Bean Maiden procession now also moves into the plaza. Here now is the final grand assembly of the host of *kachinas* who have come from their otherworld homes. It is said that in Old Oraibi there used to be nearly three hundred *kachinas,* each one masked and costumed differently, uttering his own unique cry, executing his own individual step or dance. . . .

Still today in Shongopovi ** Páchavu is a scene of indescribable beauty. All afternoon the gathering crowd of visitors waits in the plaza, only to be periodically chased indoors by a Whipper *kachina,* who lashes even a window if he sees a face peeking out. One waits and sweats in a crowded room, then goes out again into the cold. Finally they come into the *kisonvi* in a long procession of breath-taking beauty. One is never prepared for the profuse electric-green growths of bean sprouts borne by the Bean Maidens, from which protrude the brilliant scarlet beans molded from cornmeal—huge bunches nearly two feet high, so heavy that they must be set down often on cornmeal swastikas marked on the ground for them by the Kachina Fathers. Behind them, at each pause, the seventeen initiates, dressed in pure white, lie down to rest the burdens of bean sprouts carried on their heads. And behind them the *kachinas,* some 125 of them this year.

For an hour or more they fill the plaza, dancing in a great circle, singing, uttering their strange cries, breaking into their own peculiar

---

* The Side Corn Clan came from Palátkwapi when it was destroyed, according to the informant Otto Pentewa; his brother, Masawistewa [Wind Spreading over Earth], who was head of the Powamu ceremony; and another informant, Koyawesima [Gray Low Cloud]. Pentewa some years ago was informed by several Jehovah's Witness missionaries that while they were stationed in Central America they heard the natives sing the same song now being sung by Héhewúti.

** February 19, 1961.

steps and postures. The sun lowers. And now, in its glowing effulgence, it is the feathers one notices, tossing from the masks. A forest of sunlit feathers shaking and rippling in the wind . . .

Suddenly it is over. A Kachina Father yells out for all mothers to cover the eyes of their uninitiated children. A *kachina* yanks off his mask, and they all disappear into their kivas. The bean plants, having been blessed, are taken to shrines and carried home to the following feast.

Páchavu is held only once every four years or more. In 1962 in Shongopovi, when Páchavu was not held, four pairs of *kachinas* delivered the bean plants and children's presents to all homes: yellow Qoaquakleum, blue Qoaquakleum, Koala, and Home Kachinas. They were proceeded by a single Chochap [Ashes] Kachina, painted black and gray, known as the "Purifier." As he passed by, every villager dropped a pinch of meal on the ground and spat, ostensibly to clear out all impurities from his body.

Neither First Mesa nor Second Mesa has a Chowílawu and a Warrior Mother. Hence their place is taken at midnight by two Qoaquakleum Kachinas dressed in long buckskin robes and yellow masks with black markings, including the imprints of bird feet on each cheek, and a quail mounted on top the head, who enter the kiva and relate a detailed two-hour story of their journey from Kisiwu.

The people on First Mesa always have been disgruntled because Chowílawu does not visit them. Many years ago they decided to find out if he was as powerful as he was said to be, and a group of them closed the entrance to Kisiwu with heavy timbers. That night they camped not far away. The shrine is nearly forty miles north, yet at midnight, when the first call was made for Chowílawu, the Walpi people heard the voices as clearly as if they were camped outside Oraibi. Hardly had the call died away when they heard a tremendous explosion at the entrance to the spring. Frightened and trembling, they waited until dawn, then rushed to Kisiwu. What a terrible sight confronted them! The great timbers they had cut and braced against the opening had been thrown fifty feet away, and the dry timber jammed between them was a mass of splinters. Since then the Walpi people have never doubted the power of Chowílawu. . . .

THE MONSTER KACHINAS

The coming of the So'yoko Kachinas climaxes Powamu for all children on First and Second Mesas. One sees them make their rounds at Sichomovi during the morning. Disobedient children have been warned by their parents that these monsters will come and eat them if they do not behave. The appearance of these "Monsters" or "Scare" Kachinas justifies the warnings. Their leader is So'yo'kwúti. She wears a black mask with a red and white mouth stretching from ear to ear, a black-and-white-striped beard falling to her waist, and long disheveled black hair spotted with cotton falling over her glaring yellow eyes. Wearing a black robe, she carries a long crook with which to catch her victims and a huge meat cleaver with which to dismember them.

Natá'aska is even more terrifying. From his white mask protrudes a watermelon-size gourd snout which opens and closes to reveal its sharp teeth and red interior, bulging black eyes, upcurving horns, and a fan of eagle feathers. Around his shoulders he wears a white buckskin cape and a sheepskin dyed red; in his hands he carries a saw. Others in the group are Tahahum, the "uncle" of the So'yoko; Heheah [Crooked Mouth], dressed in animal skins; Hahewuhti, with a mop of white hair; Héhewúti; and a *kachina-mana*.*

Stopping at a house, they call out with low rumbling noises, scraping their saws against the walls. Then they go inside the house and demand the disobedient child. The mother protests, offering a present of food if the So'yoko will go away. The So'yoko refuse the offer three times, calling out louder, banging their saws against the wall, jumping around and posturing, and finally grabbing and carrying the screaming child out the door. At last the desperate mother offers enough food to satisfy the monsters—a quarter of lamb, a bag of flour, a box of staples—who then release the child and go to the next house.

The spectacle at Sichomovi is a disagreeable sight: the screaming children being dragged out of doorways, the avid greed for groceries, the grim faces of bystanders—the whole scene in this squalid village seems to reflect the cultural dissolution which is almost complete on First Mesa.

On Second Mesa at Shongopovi there is still some charm in the procedure. The group includes the So'yoko Talker, whose role was evident. Approaching a house, he called for the child and recited to him several specific examples of his disobedience. The child was then allowed to offer tribute—a mouse or two strung on a stick. This was kindly refused as insufficient. He was then undressed, led outside, and cold water was poured on him as he was admonished to be always obedient to his parents. The mother then offered presents of simple food, a stack of *piki* or basket of meal.

Third Mesa traditionally abhors even this as detrimental to the pure pattern of Creation being established during Powamu, and prohibits the

* The appellations *wuti* and *mana* both designate female *kachinas*, the former connoting those of ancient times.

appearance of the Sosoyok during the Powamuya moon. The Sosoyok's breath brings cold besides, hence they should not appear until early spring.

Powamu, however, seems great and flexible enough to withstand all deviations. In 1960 the ceremony in some form spanned the period from the appearance of the new moon on January 28 until February 21. Old Oraibi even managed a Bean Dance with the assistance of *kachina* dancers from Moencopi; and New Oraibi, with no ceremonialism to back it up and no authority granted it by religious leaders, insisted on putting on a *kachina* dance of its own.

Powamu is finally concluded with four days during which the priests purify themselves in the kivas and carry out the sand to bury carefully in the ground. A feast is prepared for the godparents of initiated children by their parents, which includes four bowls containing flat *piki* heaped with corn mush, representing the earth and the spring run-off of melting snow. On the last dawn a long procession files out to the edge of the mesa to pray: the village chief, the Crier, the Guardian, and all members of the kivas, followed by people of the village.

Silently, in prayerful concentration, they watch Qöyangnuptu, the first phase of dawn when the purplish dawn-dusk first outlines the shape of man. Slowly the horizon grows yellow with pollen in Sikangnuqa, the second phase of dawn which reveals man's breath of life. Priests and people scrape the pollen off the horizon with cupped hands, swallow it, and breathe deeply the breath of life. And now in the red sunrise glow of Tálawva, the third and the last phase of dawn, they stand proudly revealed in the fullness of their creation. The lifting sun reminds them always to face life with its full, beaming countenance; and as it changes to the pure white light of day, they spread it over their bodies with out-spread hands. . . .

It is over, all over at last, this great three-act drama of all Creation. There is no mistaking its meaning. In Wúwuchim, the first phase, man made his Emergence to this new world, the first fire was lit, and life was germinated. In the second phase, Soyál, man's dwelling place was erected on the solidified earth, the sun was redirected on its course to give warmth and strength to germinated life, and the first *kachinas* arrived to consecrate its growth. With Powamu, in the third phase, plant life made its first appearance, mankind, as children, was initiated by the host of *kachinas,* and the entire Road of Life throughout all worlds was purified. So man stands now, fully formed and informed, in the proudness of his pure Creation.

In this great ecological pattern no aspect of life has been ignored.

It is a web of relationships that includes not only all the societies of man, but all the sub-orders of the plant and animal kingdoms, the super-orders of spiritual beings, and the living entities of the earth and the stars above. None of them is alone and free to act independently. They are all inter-related in a web of correlative obligations and must function harmoni-ously for the perpetuation and progression of all on that one cosmic Road of Life. Wúwuchim, Soyál, and Powamu, whatever their separate mean-ings and individual functions, and despite their inexhaustibly intricate and confusing rituals, are supremely dramatic interpretations of a creative plan whose power supersedes that of the limited human will.

6

The Road of Life

The three closely linked winter ceremonies just described are the cornerstone of all Hopi ceremonialism. Every significant motif of Hopi religion is expressed in one or another of their inexhaustibly complex and esoteric rituals. To understand better the Hopi conception of life and death, the structure of the universe, of time itself, we must look more closely at their explicit and implicit meanings.

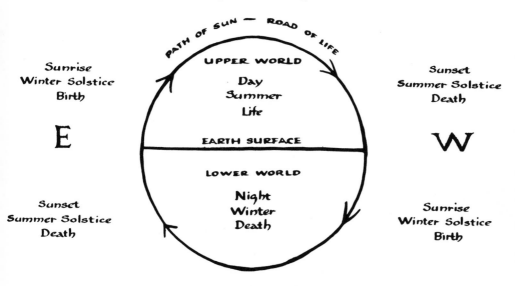

Figure 58. The Road of Life

It is no coincidence that the path of the sun and mankind's Road of Life are virtually synonymous. As shown in Figure 58, they both describe the perfect rounded whole with the same clockwise circuit about the dual division of space and time.

Each morning at sunrise the sun emerges from his sun-house in the east, travels in a circular path above the surface of the earth, and descends into his sun-house in the west at sunset. During the night the sun completes his circular journey, traveling west to east through the underworld. Day and night are thus reversed in the upper and lower worlds, the sun rising in the lower world as it sets in the upper world and setting in the lower as it rises again in the upper world.

This same diurnal reversal takes place during the annual shifts of the seasons. Each year at the time of the Winter Solstice, December 21, the sun leaves his winter house and travels to his summer house, where he arrives at the time of the Summer Solstice, June 21. During this period the upper world experiences increasingly longer days for planting and growing crops, which the Hopis regard as summer.* Then again he returns to his winter house, the period of his journey, from June 21 to December 21, being considered as winter in the upper world. So again conditions are reversed in the underworld, which experiences winter while the surface world enjoys summer, and summer during the winter period above.

Fundamental to this concept of the year's duality is the premise that life in the underworld duplicates life in the upper world. Whatever takes place during a certain month above also takes place during the corresponding month below. Hence the supremely important four ritual "Powamu Months" occur twice in the Hopi calendar—during the winter, when the yearly plan for life is set up with ritual and prayer, and during the summer, when the winter's prayers are harvested: **

Kelemuya	November	June
Kamuya	December	July
Pámuya	January	August
Powamuya	February	September

Thus the Powamu ceremony is held during the same month in both the upper and lower worlds—during February in the upper world and in the lower world during September. Also, because corresponding ceremonies in both worlds are held simultaneously, with the seasons reversed, their rituals are observed twice annually. Hence, during Soyál in the winter above, the *páhos* are made and preliminary rituals are conducted for the Niman Kachina ceremonies which will be held during the summer, for these ceremonies are currently being held in the world below.

---

* Astronomically we regard summer as the period from the Summer Solstice, June 21, to the autumnal equinox, September 22.

** A perfect balance of summer and winter months is impossible, for the thirteen lunar months cannot be equally divided between the two solar periods between the solstices. Hence the slack is taken up by the inclusion of the extra calendar month in the relatively unimportant fall.

NOTE

THIS SECTION contains photographs from a collection of hundreds of negatives made in the first decade of the century by the Reverend H. R. Voth, who established the Mennonite Mission Church in Old Oraibi. Photographic plates of that time were wholly inadequate for action pictures and for scenes in dim light, such as the interiors of the kivas; nevertheless Voth patiently amassed his voluminous picture record of the Hopis and their ceremonials as he saw them fifty years ago. Though photographs from his negatives are of poor quality by present-day standards, they often have a remarkable sense of the authenticity which Voth strove to capture, as well as great historical interest. Voth is believed to be the only person ever to have made photographs inside the kivas. Photography, even of public ceremonies in the open plaza, was prohibited soon afterward. Through the courtesy of Mrs. Martha Voth Dyck and of the Bethel Historical Library in North Newton, Kansas, where the collection now is, a few of the Voth photographs are here published for the first time. Others appear in the picture section facing page 286.

Two Horn priests, Oraibi
(Photo: H. R. Voth)

One Horn kiva, Oraibi, showing four plaques filled with cornmeal, in which are planted *páhos*. At the end of the ceremony the cornmeal is used to make a path for all mankind.

(Photos: H. R. Voth)

Soyál priests carrying cornmeal to Flute Spring. Tawákwaptiwa is in the lead.

Soyál altar, Oraibi, showing figures representing the twin War Gods, fetish, *páhos*, sand pile, flowers, and stack of corn to be blessed for germination. *(Photo: H. R. Voth)*

Parrot Clan maiden sitting on
plaque of seeds during Soyál ritual.

Warrior Mother Kachina appearing at the
Pachávu ceremony. *(Photos: H. R. Voth)*

Flute chief carrying *páho*
and cornmeal to Flute Spring.

(Photos: H. R. Voth)

Blue Flute altar, Mishongnovi.

Antelope priests entering plaza after circling the village four times to claim the earth for the Creator. *(Photos: H. R. Voth)*

Antelope altar in Antelope kiva.

Snake priests in plaza, ready to begin the Snake Dance.
(Photos: H. R. Voth)

Priests at prayer in front of Snake altar, Mishongnovi. In the foreground are a sand paint-ing, and *páhos* in small mud-earth containers representing vibrations of the earth and the snakes' close relationship to the earth and moisture.

Women's Basket Dance, Oraibi.

(Photos: H. R. Voth)

Altar of the Márawu women's society. The figures on each side represent mothers and their children to come, and the male-and-female *tiponi* symbolizes the powers of reproduction.

During these preliminary observances the priests below are ritually informed that the priests above are also carrying on simultaneous rites. Conversely, in summer, when the Hopi priests above are conducting the formal ceremonies with their public dances, they are assured that the priests below are cooperating with synchronous, minor rites.

It is consistent with this that the *kachinas* are present on earth during the first six months of the year, appearing in time for the Winter Solstice ceremony during Soyál, and returning home to the lower and other worlds after Niman Kachina, which is held just after the Summer Solstice.

Day and night, summer and winter, rhythmically alternating in the upper and lower worlds—these are the dual phases of time marked by the sun on its daily and yearly path through the dual divisions of space as it describes the circular form of the perfect rounded whole of life. But man's total existence is also circumscribed by the pure pattern of Creation and is led in both stages of one great cycle. In this unbroken continuity, he lives in the upper world from birth to death in one stage of existence and from death to birth in the lower world.

The path of the sun thus coincides with the Road of Life. Like the sun emerging from his sun-house in the east, which serves as a *sipápuni* leading from the underworld, the newly born also emerge to this earth from the underworld through the *sipápuni* [navel, path from]. Their birth too is associated with the east and the sun. For twenty days after birth every newborn child is kept in darkness. Then at dawn he is carried to the east and held up to the rising sun, the mother saying, "This is your child."

Also like the sun, man travels west at death to re-enter the *sipápuni* and return to the world below. Here he is reborn, like a baby, to live another stage of existence in the same great cycle. As previously pointed out, there may be two deviations from this slow and ceaseless course of mankind on its evolutionary Road of Life. If a man adheres rigidly to the ritually pure pattern in this stage of existence, he is released at death from plodding through the remaining three worlds of this universe and goes directly to the next multiworld universe as a *kachina*. On the other hand, if he is evil and becomes a witch or sorcerer, his return to the underworld is painfully slow. He progresses at the rate of but one step a year, being allowed only one drop of water and one kernel of corn to sustain him.

East, then, is associated with the rising sun, with the birth of day, of the calendar year, of life. West is associated with death and the setting sun. Hence the kiva is set facing east and west. Novices are always seated on the raise to the east, as they are being reborn by ritual initiation; the lower altar level lies to the west, as it holds the *sipápuni,* fire-pit, and altar which function in the ritualism of death and rebirth. The circular course of the path of the sun and the Road of Life is clockwise, but, contrary to expectation, it is represented laterally on the floor of the kiva by a line of cornmeal running west to east, toward the rising sun, which ever heralds the beginning of another new cycle.

Life and death, then, are considered not as two separate stages completing mankind's temporal and post-earthly existence, but as complementary phases in an ever-recurring cycle; a continuity that remains unbroken until mankind passes through the seven successive worlds of each of the seven successive universes, completing at last the forty-nine stages of his complete existence. This is explicit in Hopi ritualism and symbolism. But the idea of personal reincarnation is no more explicitly expressed by the average Hopi than the idea of personal religiousness, importance, honor, and gain. These are eschewed by the Hopi traditionalist, who refuses to seek honor and high office, avoids manifesting exceptional talent and ability, and seeks to show humility on all occasions. There are no Hopi priests, properly speaking, to expound any religious beliefs whatever. Every adult Hopi man participates during the year in at least one major ceremony, after which he returns to work in his fields, wearing no vestige of priestly garb and carrying no aura of sanctity.

This absence of a formal priesthood aloof from the rest of society, and of a religion separated from the daily functions of ordinary life, shows how deeply the tenets of Hopi ceremonialism are embodied in every Hopi and how closely temporal life conforms to ritual belief. For Hopi ceremonialism is not concerned with expounding the means by which the individual can save his soul from eternal damnation at death. It simply presents the cosmic pattern through which all forms of life move to their appointed ends. The Hopi seeks no short cut on the Road of Life. He is content to move slowly and in unison with all around him in this pattern into which he has been inducted at birth.

THE ANCIENT LADDER DANCE

With the end of the three winter ceremonies, life seems to follow the pattern they have set. The cold has been exorcised, the snow begins to melt. When the mesas seem likely to dissolve into mud, the wind begins to blow; the earth is obscured by one monstrous cloud of stinging dust and sand. Then it begins to rain.

To these horrors of fickle weather the Hopis give gentle names that label the months during which they plow their sandy fields, erect windbreakers, and plant their crops: March—Isumúya [Whispering Noises of

Breezes]; April—Kwiyamúya [windbreaker]; and May—Úimúya [planting moon].

Spring apparently leaves no time for major ceremonies, and there are none. But the season is marked by many dances. Chief of these are the *ankti* [Repeat] dances, which repeat the *kachina* night dances held in the kivas before Powamu.

Among them is the dance of Pálulukang, the Water Serpent— although in 1958 it was prematurely given at Sichomovi during the last night of Powamu. Actually it is not a dance but the manipulation of puppet serpents, a male, female, and two "children," whose heads, protruding from a screen, are made to sway by hidden manipulators.

With better weather come *kachina* dances outside in the *kisonvi* or plaza. Featured are "racing *kachinas*," who race with children, always losing in order to present the winners with small gifts.

In former days there were many other races: kick-ball races and four-day races around the valley. None of these dances and races are entirely devoid of ritual meaning, but they lack the significance of the great ceremonies that take place in the winter, summer, and fall. One wonders why spring alone is without a major ceremony, and one seeks in Hopi tradition to discover if there ever has been one.

The evidences of what may have been an important ceremony, or at least the strangest ritual north of Mexico, lie on the high ridge leading to the westernmost spur and highest point of Third Mesa. It is accessible only by foot; one climbs through a thick growth of juniper to the top of the high barren ridge, then climbs down to a bare level flanked by huge cliffs that drop sheerly to the valley floor below. Cliff walls and boulders are covered with petroglyphs. The floor of the clearing is littered with fragments of broken pottery. A few shallow holes show where Hopi boys have dug for whole pots; they reveal the corner walls of buried rooms, the ashes in an ancient fireplace, a tiny blackened corncob. This is the site of the unexcavated ruins of Pivánhonkyapi.

Etymologically derived from *pivan* [tobacco], *hon* [spring], and *kapi* [village], its name denotes that it was once "The Village By the Spring Where Tobacco Grows." No one knows how long ago it existed, but legends tell why it was abandoned. According to tradition, something had gone wrong during its most important ceremony, and all the priests were gathered in the kiva to talk about it. Suddenly the roof fell in, killing all the members of the kiva; their skeletons with all their turquoise jewelry are supposed to be still buried there. The calamity was a clear omen to the people of the village. They packed up and resumed their migration, finally settling near Mono Lake, California, where a few of their descendants still live today.

To the east of the site of the ancient village the clearing pinches out to a narrow, rocky ledge running along the sheer edge of the 150-foot cliff. In it are four holes spaced well apart and chipped deep into the solid rock. They are round and nearly a foot in diameter—just large and deep enough to hold securely the trunks of four spruce trees. Here each spring was enacted Sáqtiva, the Ladder Dance.

According to tradition, the two poles to the east were stripped of branches and bark, but slightly protruding lengths of several limbs were left, upon which a man could climb to the top. These were known as *sak* [ladder], as they made the high pole a virtual ladder; and this word, combined with the word *tíva* [dance], thus named the mysterious Sáqtiva. At the top of each of these two poles was securely fastened a crossbar. The two poles to the west were stripped completely smooth. Crossbars were fastened to their tops, and somehow attached to these were long buckskin thongs or ropes wound round the poles.

At the edge of the wall behind these two poles and at the foot of the two other poles stood waiting four performers. They were virginal young men selected for their skill and daring, their naked bodies painted as for death, and wearing hawk and eagle feathers in their hair. On the wall overlooking the ledge behind them stood a chorus of old men, a drummer, and a flute-player. Behind them were massed the people of the village.

The ceremony began with song: the chorus of old men accompanied by the drummer and flutist. At its conclusion the two performers to the east began climbing the tall poles; they stood precariously upright and faced each other when they reached the crossbars on top. Then at a given signal they jumped forward, passed each other in mid-air, and grabbed the opposite crossbar to swing out over the edge of the precipice. At the same instant each of the two performers crouching at the edge of the wall leaped forward to one of the two poles to the west, grabbed the thong secured to the crossbar on top; and swung out in a wide arc over the floor of the valley far below, flying free as an eagle as the thong unwound around the pole. This was a "jump of death," for a miscalculation or any faltering of strength or skill would hurtle him to the rocks below, to that death for which he had been ritually painted.

Present-day Hopis know even less of the meaning of this strange and extinct Ladder Dance than of its exact procedure and mechanics. There has never been any ceremony in this country comparable to it. But in Mexico there has existed from prehistoric times a ceremony so parallel to it that a comparison must be made here. Even the name of it is strikingly familiar—Los Voladores, The Flying Pole Dance.

For centuries it was performed by the Aztecs. Still today it is given by the Huastecas of San Luis Potosí, the Otomís of Pahatlan, Hidalgo, and by the Totonacs, who stage it before the thousand-year-old pyramid-temple of Tajín near Papantla, Vera Cruz. Their preparations and performances of the ceremony follow the same general pattern. The single tree used for *el volador,* the "flying pole," is ritually cut and firmly planted in the ground. A small revolving platform is fitted to the top, and four ropes are wound round the pole from top to bottom. A musician with a drum and a flute climbs to the platform on top, followed by four men known as the *voladores* or fliers. While the musician plays, the fliers tie the ends of the ropes about them. Then they throw themselves into space and fly like birds around the pole as the ropes unwind.

Simple as it is, the performance is a complex ritual whose symbolism would not seem unfamiliar to the Hopis.

Like Sáqtiva, Los Voladores is performed in the spring; by the Totonacs during Corpus Christi. The men who select the tree first dance around it, asking its permission to cut it down. After the first few blows the tree is given a drink of *tepache* so it won't feel pain. Stripped of branches and bark, the pole either is carried home without letting it touch ground or is sprinkled with brandy whenever a stop is made for rest. This sacrifice of a living tree for ritual use adheres to the same pattern still observed in Taos, New Mexico, when men cut the tree for the annual pole climb on San Geronimo Day. So too do the Hopis first ask permission of any plant before cutting it for ceremonial use; moreover, they do not gather the first plant from which permission is obtained, but go on to the second.

Before planting the "flying pole" both the Otomís and Totonacs place a live chicken or offerings of food in the hole prepared for it; the food gives it strength to support the fliers, and the accompanying blessings beseech it not to claim the life of one.

The four Huastecan fliers are dressed to represent *gavilanes* or hawks. Hence the ceremony is often called La Danza de Los Gavilanes, the Dance of the Hawks. The Totonac performers, known as *tocotines,* are said to be "dressed as eagles dedicated to the sun" in red jackets and trousers, with bunches of eagle feathers stuck in their pointed hats. The four performers of the Sáqtiva also wore eagle or hawk feathers in their hair; and the word *kékelt* or "young hawks" is still used to designate young Hopi initiates into the four principal religious societies.

The musician, who is also the captain of the four *voladores,* ascends to the small platform on top of the "flying pole" and plays on his drum and flute. He first faces east, playing his simple melody seven times. Then he successively faces south, west, and north, playing seven times more to each of these directions, after which he makes seven quick turns on the platform. All these observances are familiar in Hopi ceremonialism: the four directions observed in the clockwise movement of the sun; the seven songs and turns, one each for the seven universes; the beats of the drum resounding the pulse beats sent through the world axis by the Hero Twins stationed at each end; and the important flute itself, whose music in spring helps to bring up all growing plant life.

With the end of the music, the *voladores* fling themselves into space with piercing shrieks—four sacred birds flying with the four winds to the four sacred directions. Traditionally each makes thirteen revolutions around the pole, their total flights symbolizing the four epochs of thirteen years each which made up the ancient Aztec time cycle of fifty-two years.

A still more significant parallel between Los Voladores and Sáqtiva is the sublimation of sex so that the generative power of the fliers may be transferred to the power of the ritual. The Totonacs always select a tree "farthest away from where women live." The four fliers are always selected from young unmarried men who have no sweethearts. They are required to observe rigid continence and to promise to fly for seven successive years.

According to Hopi tradition it was this sex taboo that led to the tragic ending of the last Sáqtiva ceremony and the abandonment of the ancient village of Pivanhonkapi. The four Ladder Dancers were also young virginal men who had no sweethearts. One of them was particularly stubborn in refusing the overtures of a young woman who desired his love. Angry at being rebuffed, she stole out to the high ledge one night before Sáqtiva and secretly cut halfway through one of the high spruce poles so that it would break and plunge him to death on the rocks below.

Fortunately Másaw, god of the underworld, detected the break and healed it. Next night the girl cut through the second pole. Again Másaw mended it with his power. This happened a third time. Indomitably the girl cut the fourth pole on the night before Sáqtiva, and on the day of the ceremony the pole broke, plunging the young man to his death.

The tragedy obviously posed many questions: why Másaw had not interceded the fourth time; whether the young man had secretly desired the girl, interjecting an element of impure thought in the ceremony; and what the failure of the ceremony portended. Hence all the priests gathered in the kiva to discuss these questions, which were suddenly answered when the roof fell in, killing them. This second tragedy left the people of Pivanhonkapi no doubts of ill omen, and they immediately abandoned the village. . . .

Scarce as are the shreds of evidence of Sáqtiva left to tradition, the symbolism of Los Voladores is cryptic enough; its exact meaning is forgotten by the modern Huastecas, Otomis, and Totonacs who still perform it. Yet the ancient Aztec and Hopi performances seem connected not only by their parallel rites but by the possibly ancient relationship of the people themselves. Undoubtedly both Los Voladores and Sáqtiva point back to an ancient ceremony embodying all the elements of a rite of spring: the sacrifice of a living tree and the proffered sacrifice of a living man to help insure the continuity of life at the crucial season of spring planting.

7

Niman Kachina

There come now three major summer ceremonies that continue the cycle begun with the three great Creation ceremonies of the winter.

They begin at the time of the Summer Solstice with Kachin-nima, which means simply the going home of the *kachinas*, the ceremony being commonly known by the singular form, Niman Kachina, or simply the Home Dance. Since the Winter Solstice the *kachinas* have been on this earth, helping to establish the Creation pattern for the year. Now life is in full flower and the first fruits are coming in; their work is done. But, with the reversal of seasons above and below, it is the Winter Solstice in the lower world, and to it and their other-world homes the *kachinas* must return for the balance of the year. So with Niman Kachina they make their ceremonial departure.

The deeper meaning of the ceremony is acknowledgment of the manifestation of the four powerful forces appealed to during Soyál and Powamu: the power of germination, of heat, of moisture, and of the magnetic forces of the air. It is the harvesting of the winter's prayers and planning, the result of the symbolic, sacred corn planted by Eototo and Áholi during Powamu.

The ceremony is held in the second Kelmuya month of the year, July, *páhos* and preliminary preparations for it having been made in the first Kelmuya month, December. In Old Oraibi it was customary at that time for the chief of the kiva wishing to hold the ceremony to request permission first from the village chief, always a member of the Bear Clan, and then from the Badger Clan, which is custodian of the sacred spruce. It is understood that permission to hold the ceremony during the coming summer entails taking over full responsibility for the village for the duration of the ceremony. So, upon being granted permission, the kiva chief and his sub-leader enter the kiva in the winter to smoke and make *páhos* for four days. On the fourth day the *páhos* are planted in the shrines, and the members remain in the kiva for four days more for prayer and concentration.

Today the ceremony is still controlled by the Badger Clan but is performed by different kivas in rotation each year,* though only by members who participated in Soyál and Powamu the preceding winter. When the ceremony is over, the kiva chief returns to the village chief and after a smoke ceremony says formally, "I now place all our children back into your hands." The village chief replies, "I thank you for the happiness you have brought to our village, I thank you, my child." For even though the kiva chief who had performed the ceremony is older than the village chief, he is still a child to the ceremonial father of the village.

GATHERING OF THE EAGLES

Early in the spring the next important preparation is made: the gathering of eagles to be sacrificed at conclusion of the ceremony. Each clan has established claim to its own eagle-hunting ground. The Bear Clan claims all the Grand Canyon area and the ridge extending from Lee's Ferry to Moencopi. The Parrot Clan claim ranges from the Little Colorado to Flagstaff. That of the Side Corn Clan runs north from Oraibi on the east side of the cliffs to Onion Spring. Each has its own and does not encroach on another's territory. The nests have long been spotted in the sides of the cliffs. Here the hunters plant *páhos* expressing their prayers that the eagles will come willingly to the village and live happily until their spirits are released after the ceremony. The hunters then lower themselves on ropes from the tops of the cliffs or climb up by precarious ledges to remove from the nests the birds too young to fly. The eaglets are brought back with great honor and tied by the feet to eagle platforms built on the rooftops of the homes of clan members. Here they are fed daily and treated respectfully while they grow to maturity by summer. It is said that there were as many as twenty-five eagles each year at Old Oraibi, every clan bringing back an eagle even though it did not actively participate in the ceremony. In 1961 at Shongopovi there were seventeen.

Slowly the days lengthen; the eagles put on feathers; the corn sprouts poke through the sandy soil. Late in May or early in June, about twenty days before the Summer Solstice, when the rising sun strikes Owátuiqa [Rock Point] north of Third Mesa, the sun is asked to continue north to Táwaki [Summer Sun-House]. This is very important, as the last stage of its journey and its increased warmth is necessary to mature the crops fully,

---

* At Hotevilla: Snake Kiva, 1959; Flute Kiva, 1960; Hawiovi Kiva, 1961; Antelope Kiva, 1962.

so *páhos* made during Soyál are planted at the Táwaki shrine. Two days before the sun reaches this northernmost end of its journey at Táwaki on June 21, the Summer Solstice, Niman Kachina is announced. The following day the ceremony begins; it lasts sixteen days. In any event, it must be over before July 15, for any delay means that the corn will not mature early enough.*

On the evening of the first day the men enter the kiva. Each is welcomed by the chief and reminded that he is now responsible for the welfare of the village. A smoke ceremony is held, and the first songs composed for Niman Kachina are sung. They may be composed and offered for use by any or all members. By the fifth night all songs have been presented. The chief of the kiva then selects those to be used, arranging them to be sung in chronological order during the last dance-day, making sure that the words of each song fit the time of day. From then on until the night before the Home Dance the men practice these songs nightly.

With this immuration of men in the kiva to pray, concentrate, and practice their songs, Niman Kachina begins.

THE PILGRIMAGE FOR SPRUCE

The sacred spruce is all-important. Branches and twigs of it are worn by all *kachinas*. In some winter *kachina* dances twigs of pine may be substituted when distance and snow do not permit the gathering of spruce, but spruce is mandatory for Niman Kachina. Even Indians from the Rio Grande pueblos come to pluck twigs from the departing *kachinas* to plant in their fields at home. For spruce has the magnetic power to bring in the clouds and moisture. Some day, it is said, the white man will find out that the spruce has the most powerful magnetic force of all trees. The pilgrimage for spruce is thus one of the most important rituals of Niman Kachina.

On the thirteenth day *páhos* are made, including the special male-and-female *páhos,* and delivered to the three men selected to make the pilgrimage. It is a long trip fraught with spiritual danger. Hence the

---

* 1960 is a disastrous example. According to traditional pattern, Niman is announced June 19, two days before the Summer Solstice, begins June 20, and ends July 6. This year the ceremony ended at Mishongnovi on July 9, but not until July 23 at Shongopovi and Hotevilla, and July 24 at Walpi. The reason was lack of coordination at the time of planting *páhos* for Rock Point, the Powamu Chief of Hotevilla delaying until July 8. Hence there had been no rain since May 11, the corn was small and stunted in growth, and it was feared it would not mature at all. Other deviations illustrate the crucial laxity in the ceremonial observances this year. A Long-haired Kachina Dance was given at Hotevilla, and a Whipper Kachina Dance at Bakavi, instead of the Home Dance; and no spruce trees were used in the ceremony at Shongopovi. To most Hopi traditionalists this shocking disregard of the meaning of the ceremony augured a disastrous year.

leader, the "message-carrier," is usually accompanied by two men on guard against any evil manifestation that might hinder or delay their trip.

Kísiwu [Spring in the Shadows] lies some forty miles northeast in a long, desolate, and remote canyon of Black Mesa. The spring itself is in a cave at the top of a high rocky ridge spotted with pine and spruce. Water oozes out of the walls and ground, forming a deep pool.* The dampness of the overhanging roof is an indication of how much moisture will come during the year, and only one man at a time enters the cave, for it looks different to each man according to his nature. The round trip takes three days by foot—as the men must travel—during which they must forgo salt.

Climbing up the steep, rocky trail, the men stop some distance from the cave and take off their moccasins and headbands. Then, barefoot and bareheaded, the leader makes his ceremonial approach. He gives four loud calls at proper intervals, sprinkling cornmeal at each stop. In front of the cave he prays. Then he enters and carefully plants his *páhos* on a ledge above the spring in prescribed order and positions. The order and position governing the planting of the prayer-feathers determine in what direction, how far, and with what power their prayers will carry: west as far as the Pacific Ocean, whence the Bear Clan migrated to claim all the land to Oraibi; south by the Parrot Clan to South America; east by the Eagle Clan to the Atlantic; as far as the land of ice to the north by the Badger Clan; and here around this spring where the Badger Clan lived before going to Oraibi. Each of the other two men then delivers his "message," the *páhos*, and they retire some distance away to smoke ceremonially before making camp for the night.

Next morning they go to a spruce tree, and the leader says to the tree, "Salavi, we have come to get your leaves to use for our clothes, so come with us." After blessing the tree and leaving a *páho* there, the men go to other spruce trees and pick their green branches—without having touched the first. They then return to Kísiwu Spring to ascertain how the prayers of their people have been received.

From the moment they enter the cave they feel the presence of the spirit people evoked by their *páhos*. The condition of the *páhos* themselves is an eloquent answer. Some are still standing straight and firm, their color dulled, indicating they have drawn moisture. For these the leader will be thankful. But other carefully planted *páhos* will be disarranged, knocked down and scattered in all directions, showing that the men in the kiva who made them were impure of thought. Then it is incumbent upon the leader, when he returns to the kiva, to identify these *páhos* so that the clan members who made them can concentrate more

---

* The front of the cave is now walled with stone in order to prevent Navajo sheep from drinking at the sacred pool—another desecration of Hopi shrines by encroaching Navajos.

deeply and pray that their weaknesses will not bring hard times to their people. Many other manifestations of good or evil have been seen by men making this pilgrimage.

Mindful of what they have witnessed, the men then select the two spruce trees for the Home Dance. John Lansa, Badger Clan, Oraibi, who has made the trip twelve times, describes the procedure:

"We pick out a good-sized one about two and a half feet high, one with needles which show it is the male tree. We then look around carefully for another which has the female needles. Picking them up gently after they are cut, we put our arms around them and take them to our bosoms, for we know that we are bringing their *kachina* spirits into our village, and the *kachinas* who participate in the ceremony are the spirits who bring rain. For you must know that the spruce tree has a magnetic power upon which the clouds rest. Salavi [the spruce] is the *chochokpi* [throne] for the clouds. That is what we say. For the spruce tree's branches swing outward and upward, and these arms are *chochokpi*, the throne where the clouds rest. When we take the branches of the spruce we are *höhöqya* [harvesting], just as we will harvest our corn which will grow from the rain the clouds bring. It is the spirits of the spruce, the clouds, and the rain who give this life to us, you understand. So we offer our prayers again to the male and female branches, and we invite all the spirits to our village to take part in the ceremony.

"With the trees and branches bundled on our backs we then head for home, ever watchful during our journey that we and the spirits accompanying us do not fall into the trail of evil. Arriving at the kiva, I, the leader, referring to the spirits accompanying us, say to the kiva chief, 'We have come.' His answer is, 'Enter our kiva. Come in gently. You are all welcome.' The bundles of spruce are placed to the north of the fire-pit, sprinkled with cornmeal, then blessed with smoke which the Powamu chief and the Kachina father blow upon them. In this way the spirits are welcomed to Oraibi."

Two days before the Home Dance all the *kachina* masks are painted. Next day the feathers are tied upon them, and that evening all the masks and costumes are placed in position on the seating ledge in the kiva. That night at midnight all the men, dressed in costume but without their masks, plant the two spruce trees in the *kisonvi* or plaza. The ritual is conducted by the leaders of the Powamu and Kachina Societies. Helping them is an ordained woman of the Badger Clan.

It will be remembered that during the midnight ceremony of Soyál the preceding winter a woman of the Bear Clan, the Soyál-mana, participated and sat on the seeds before the altar. Also during the Toktaita [awake all night] preceding Powamu, a Powamu-mana stayed in the kiva all night, praying, concentrating, and affirming the Powamu Chief's prayer for all the children to come into the world. Hence the Powamu-mana now participates in the midnight planting of the spruce, which represent the children which have come.

The male spruce is first planted to the right of the *pohoki*—the shrine in the *kisonvi* "where the *kachinas* are close to listen"—and then the female tree to the left. *Páhos* are planted at the bases of both trees, and a cornmeal line is drawn to the east from the *pohoki*. Prayer feathers are also left along the cornmeal trail to welcome the sun, our Father, when he rises next morning to bless the ceremony and the village.

From this time on until the conclusion of the Home Dance the men deny themselves water, humbling themselves so that the cloud spirits will bring rain. If it should rain between midnight and noon, however, they may drink.

Páhos are now carried to the Salapa shrine, a symbol of the original Salapa [Spruce Spring] located in front of Spruce Tree House on Mesa Verde, where the Badger Clan lived before coming to Oraibi.* Just before dawn the men carry their masks and costumes to another shrine outside the village called Kowáwaimave [Where the *Kachinas* and the People Live Together in Harmony] to pray, smoke, and dress.** Here at dawn they dance and sing. Then at sunrise the long line of *kachinas* starts for the village. It is the beginning of the inexpressibly beautiful Home Dance.

THE HOME DANCE

Over and over through the years one sees it, and it is never less beautiful: the still, flocculent dawn; the wonder and the mystery in the eyes of the villagers crowding the housetops; and, down below, the two spruce, male and female, standing in the empty plaza. Nothing breaks the silence save the great, proud bird tethered by one leg to his platform nearby. No living being has soared alone so high as this lord of the air. None is so proud—too proud to pick at the leash that tethers him. He simply flaps his great wings to soar aloft, only to be jerked down once more. One knows now again that this great proud eagle must die. And one knows why.

For suddenly, as the shafts of the sun are loosed from the horizon,

---

*The story of this spring, the tall spruce, and the name of Spruce Tree House itself, which is one of the legends that indicate the occupancy of prehistoric Mesa Verde cliff-dwellings by Hopi clans, is related in Part Two.

** The original Kowáwaimave is said to be located in Central America, where the Emergence to the Fourth World was made.

the *kachinas* come in single file through the narrow streets into the plaza, the Powamu Chief, unmasked, wearing a single eagle feather and an embroidered kilt, leading the Kachina Father and his assistant, both members of the Powamu Society, wearing plain kilts, then some thirty *hemis kachinas* and eight or more *kachina-manas.* "Hemis" means simply "far-away," the far realms from which these *kachinas* have come and to which they are soon to return. Their bodies are painted black with white *nakwách* symbols on the breast and back. Spruce branches hang from the belts of their kirtles, and twigs are stuck in their blue arm bands. In the right hand each carries a rattle; black yarn is tied to the wrist. In the left hand each carries a twig of spruce and a downy feather. Deer-hoof and turtle-shell rattles are worn on the right leg, a strap of bells on the left. What holds attention is the distinctive headdress. Surmounting a ruff of spruce around the throat, the face mask is painted yellow on the left side, blue on the right; and above this rises a blue cloud-terrace *tablita* or tiara tufted with heads of wild wheat and downy eagle feathers, and topped by two eagle-tail and two parrot feathers symbolizing the *kask-nuna,* the parrot's power of warmth. Just above the face a red rainbow arches over a field of white on which is painted a frog or butterfly.

The eight *kachina-manas* are no less striking. Each wears a bright orange face mask and the hair whorls ceremonially worn by unmarried Hopi maidens; a black *manta,* a red and white blanket, and white deer-skin boots. Each carries a pumpkin shell, notched stick, and the scapula bone of a sheep or deer, with which to make their own musical accompaniment.

After entering the plaza, they stand silently, the *kachinas* in a long line, the *kachina-manas* behind them. The Powamu Chief sprinkles each with cornmeal from a sack worn on his breast. The Kachina Father encourages them with talk. Then suddenly the leader of the *kachinas,* standing in the middle of the line, shakes his rattle. The powerful legs lift and stamp; the low, strong voices break into song—a day-long dance and song, beautiful and compelling, but with infinite variations in which are found its deepest meanings.

The pattern of the dance embodies the familiar cosmological concept. The dancers first enter the plaza in a single file from the east and line up on the north side, facing west. As they dance, the end of the line slowly curves west and south, but is broken before a circle is formed, just as the pure pattern of life was broken and the First World destroyed. The dancers then move to the west side, the line curves to the south, and is broken as was the pattern of life in the Second World. Moving to the south side and curving east, the dancers repeat the procedure at this third position representing the Third World. There is no fourth position, for life is still in progress on this Fourth World and it remains to be seen whether it will adhere to the perfect pattern or be broken again.

The same cosmology is again reflected in the structure of the song. It is divided into five sections. The first two are known as the bottom part of the structure, the second two as the upper part, and the fifth section also as the bottom. The first section corresponds to the First World's perfect pattern of Creation, so great emphasis is given it. The Kachina Father encourages the *kachinas* to sing louder and dance harder in order to uplift the thoughts of the people to this perfect First World. Villagers themselves come forward to bless the *kachinas* with pinches of cornmeal so that in time they may again experience full unison with the Creator. The second section recounts how man had to emerge to the Second World because of his disregard for the laws. The third section reminds its listeners of the Emergence to and destruction of the Third World, which is again full of rival rulers, strife, and war. Now in the fourth section the song wells louder from the broad breasts, and the dancing feet stamp more powerfully. And in the fifth section of the song, mankind too is at the "bottom." Hence the *kachinas,* who are struggling to maintain this Fourth World in proper balance, work hard to lift up the performance and the thoughts of the people watching it.

The cosmological pattern is also suggested by the three appearances of the dancers during the day: at sunrise, midmorning, and after the noon recess, when they dance until sunset. As they file in at sunrise they bring armloads of gifts for the children, which they heap in the plaza. That afternoon they distribute the gifts to the children: the first corn from the fields, the cattails, rolls of red, white, and blue *piki,* bows and arrows, plaques, and *kachina* dolls for the children who have not yet been initiated into the rituals. And here again the symbolic marking of the bows is significant.

When a boy is still too young to be initiated he is given a toy bow marked with segments of different colors. The middle section is white, representing the perfect pattern of the First World. On each side are a segment painted blue, symbolizing the Second World; a yellow segment symbolizing the Third World; and a red segment, extending to the tips of the bow, symbolizing the Fourth World. Black dots on these color markings represent the life experience of mankind on the successive worlds, and the boy is told that the red means blood which will be shed if man does not learn to live peacefully with his fellows. To those boys who have been initiated the *kachinas* give a second bow which is uncolored, telling them that they now know right from wrong and it is up to them to choose their way; that they should strive to help make this Fourth World perfect as it was in the beginning.

How wonderful it is, despite the blazing sun and the acrid dust whipping across the swept plaza, to see a sweating *kachina* search out a shrinking child with a gift. "For when you are a child," says an old man, "you believe that these are spirits come from far away. And these are blessed gifts and you never want anything to happen to them, and all day long you feel that wonderful things will come to you now and in the future." But still the great proud bird overhead flaps his wings to soar away and is jerked back down again, and one knows that his time draws ever closer.

At sunrise, when the *kachinas* first enter the plaza, they are accompanied by the Powamu Chief and eight Powamu-manas. The Powamu Chief and the Kachina Father each carries water in a small bowl and a pipe which has been lighted in the kiva. Each dancing *kachina* they sprinkle with water, using an eagle feather, and blow upon him a puff of smoke. The Powamu Chief then takes the ear of corn which the *kachina* leader is holding and carries it back to the kiva. At the same time the eight Powamu-manas take an ear of corn from each of the dancing *kachina-manas* to carry back to the kiva, where the corn is laid out near the fire-pit and blessed. These ears of corn are the same ears that were purified and stacked at the Soyál altar during the winter Soyál ceremony the preceding winter. Throughout the rest of the day, until the last dance at sunset, the Powamu Chief and the Powamu-manas remain in the kiva to pray and concentrate.*

And now shortly before sunset they come out again. It is the last dance, the farewell dance of the departing *kachinas,* and the village is packed with people. It is also the first dance the year's brides are permitted to attend; attired in their wedding robes, they stand demurely in the crowd. The *kachina-manas* kneel; each places one end of her notched stick on the pumpkin shell which serves as a resonator, and begins stroking with the scapula. The rattles shake. The song and dance begin with renewed vigor. Once again the *kachinas* are sprinkled with water and cornmeal. Then the leader of the Powamu-manas passes slowly along the line of the *kachinas* and with an almost imperceptible motion raises her arm beneath her red and white cape in front of each *kachina*. It is a significant movement seldom observed. For underneath her arm, and concealed by her cape is a *pahosvi*, a "spiritual crown" made of wood, round in form, painted and decorated. By lifting it up and down in front of each *kachina,* the Powamu-mana now makes the same motion made with a hoop in front of each child initiated into Powamu the preceding winter, signifying purification of his Road of Life.

---

* Hotevilla still observes this Oraibi custom. At other villages they may come out at noon also.

The Kachina Father then delivers his farewell to the *kachinas:* "Now it is time that you go home. Take with you our humble prayer, not only for our people and people everywhere, but for all the animal kingdom, the birds and insects, and the growing things that make our world a green carpet. Take our message to the four corners of the world, that all life may receive renewal by having moisture. I am happy that I have done my small part in caring for you this day. May you go on your way with happy hearts and grateful thoughts."

The leader of the *kachinas* shakes his rattle, showing that the Kachina Father's message is accepted and will be delivered.

Now it is over. Villagers and Indians from other pueblos come up to pluck twigs of spruce from the *kachinas* to carry home and plant in their own fields. The crowd parts. And in the setting sun the *kachinas* file silently out of the plaza and through the narrow streets of the village. No man follows them. Only for a moment their unearthly shapes are outlined in the sunset glow at the top of the cliffs before they descend to the Kachina House on the ledge below. Then suddenly, like the spirit that imbues all life for its time, they vanish from the sight of man.

SACRIFICE OF THE EAGLES

The two spruce trees also symbolically return home. After the last dance the Kachina Father carries them from the *pahoki* to the Típkyavi [womb]—like children being taken back to Kísiwu after having witnessed the ceremony.

At Kachinki, the Kachina House shrine on the cliff edge, the Powamu Chief is waiting for the *kachinas.* As each of them arrives he scrapes the paint from under his left eye into a small bowl and buries the scrapings in the ground. Symbolically this leaves the man with only a half-vision of the pattern of Creation. He is warned that if with his incomplete knowledge he uses his *kachina* power it may destroy someone, and he is advised to search for full vision and knowledge. The men then remove their masks and costumes and wash the paint off their bodies, becoming mere members of their worldly community again. Four men are excepted from this eye-scraping: the leaders of the Bear Clan, Badger Clan, Parrot Clan, and Eagle Clan. They wait until dark, then remove their masks and carry them back to the Powamu Kiva.

Next morning at sunrise the concluding ritual is held at the kiva. The leaders of the four principal clans, Nalöönangmomwit [the four leading chiefs], who carry out the important religious ceremonies from midwinter to midsummer, take their positions. Eototo Kachina, who represents the Bear Clan and village chief, stands at the west, as the Bear Clan migrated from the west. The Parrot Clan leader stands in the south, as his clan came from this direction. If he has a sister, she stands beside him; if he does not, he wears the ceremonial red and white cape of the women and thus represents the female polarity. In the east, whence came his clan, stands the leader of the Eagle Clan. And at the north stands the Badger Clan leader to signify the direction whence came the Badger Clan. The kiva symbolizes the body of the universe; hence this placement illustrates the various Emergences and routes of migration taken by the people coming to this land. But the ritual also symbolizes the spiritual uplift of man.

For Eototo at the west holds a thorny branch called *kevepsi* [with abundance], the plant which is said to have been brought here from the previous Third World. Small balls of cornmeal containing no salt are stuck to the thorns, and prayer feathers are tied to the stem. As he watches the kiva entrance, a sprinkle of water is thrown out toward him, and a hand reaches forth. Eototo stands still, and the hand is withdrawn. Three times this occurs. When the hand comes out for the fourth time, Eototo places in it the thorny branch.

The hand is that of the Powamu Chief inside the kiva. After receiving the branch, he swings it in a circle above his head, while walking around the kiva four times. This indicates the raising of man's consciousness to its highest level. The procedure is repeated for each of the other clan leaders. When it is finished, the Powamu Chief comes out of the kiva with the branches in his arm and blows smoke to each of the four directions. Then he leads the four men to the Kachina House and scrapes their masks below the left eye. This completes the *tangave* [religious plan act] and the Powamu Chief's responsibility to the village chief.

At the same time the great proud birds waiting on their platforms are "sent home" with the *kachinas*. No blood is shed during their sacrifice. The clan leaders ascend to the housetop platforms, wrap a blanket around the head of each, and snuff out its life as gently as possible. When it is brought inside the house, the eagle is laid down with its head to the west, and beside it are laid cornmeal and a prayer feather. If it is a male, a small bow with arrows is placed at its head; a *kachina* doll and a small plaque especially made by the woman of the house, if the eagle is a female. When the body becomes cold, the clan leader pulls out the first feather, *piphö* [perfect rounded feather], whose special use is for offering a prayer to the sun. Other feathers, including the down, are now plucked for future use. The body is then carried to the eagle burying ground west of the village. It is buried, head to the west, with cornmeal, *piki*, tobacco, and prayer feathers. Stones are piled over its head, and into them is stuck a stick symbolic of the ladder by which its spirit will ascend on the fourth day to that high realm whose invisible powers ever aid man on his long Road of Life.

For it was this great proud bird who first welcomed mankind to this Fourth World and gave them his feathers for *páhos*—the feathers which still carry our prayerful messages aloft to other planets and stars where life exists, and which in turn demand of us the good thoughts that keep our own planet in order. If the eagle carries in its feathers the greatest magnetic power of the bird kingdom, as the spruce carries in its needles the strongest magnetic power in the plant kingdom, it is appropriate that both take their way home during Niman Kachina with the *kachinas* who imbue the forms of mankind with spirit.

8

The Flute Ceremony

No Hopi ritual is as simple and mystifying to the casual visitor as that portion of the Flute ceremony he is allowed to witness. It is simply a procession winding up the mesa and into the village, headed by two small girls who periodically toss little rings upon cornmeal lines painted on the ground. In the plaza the people sing to the music of a flute, then silently disperse. That is all. Yet this simple ceremony embodies in song and symbolism the whole pattern of man's Emergence to the present world.

The Flute ceremony is held every other year, alternating with the Snake-Antelope ceremony and occurring in mid-August.* It begins three days after the sun rises between the rounded hill to the north and the second terrace to the south of the cliffs known as Munyá'ovi [The Porcupine], lying east of Oraibi. This position signifies that the sun has reached Táwaki, its summer house at the northernmost point of its journey at the Summer Solstice, and is journeying southward again.

At this time corn, squash, melons, and beans are hardening. Hence one of the purposes of the Flute and the Snake-Antelope ceremonies is to help mature the crops and to bring the last summer rains so that the flooded washes will deposit *chivókya* [new soil] in which the people can put in a second planting of corn. This will not mature before winter, but it will give the people a "second taste." If the Snake Society one year fails to bring a last burst of heavy rain, it is obvious that its leaders were not of good hearts and the people are warned to conserve their harvest until the next year. Then, when it is the turn of the Flute Society, its leaders redouble their efforts. If they too fail, it shows that they also have not followed the precepts. The failure of either or both ceremonies does not reflect upon the village chief, for neither the Flute, Antelope, nor Snake Clan was permitted to settle in Oraibi until it had demonstrated the effectiveness of its ceremonials when properly given.

---

* Mishongnovi, August 20, and Walpi, August 30, 1960.

The first responsibility of the Flute Society, then, is to help mature the crops by bringing the last summer rains and warming the earth by singing the songs that evoke heat, supplemented by the power of feathers taken from tropical birds. The second and most dramatic purpose is to enact mankind's Emergence to this present Fourth World. From this derives the origin and composition of the Flute Society.

ORIGIN OF THE GRAY FLUTE AND BLUE FLUTE SOCIETIES

When the Third World was destroyed by water, mankind emerged to the Fourth World by crossing the water in reed rafts to the shore of this continent. The place of Emergence was in the warm country to the south, believed to have been Central America.* The people then separated into various groups to begin their migrations over the continent.**

Those going north under the guidance of Spider Woman included members of the Spider Clan, the Ghost Clan—sometimes known as the Fire Clan—the Sun Clan, Blue Flute Clan (another segment comprising the Gray Flute Clan separating and going east), and Snake Clan. After traveling as far as they could go, they attempted to melt the arctic ice cap by evoking the powers given them: the Sun Clan using the power of the sun, the Fire Clan the inner heat of the earth, and the Blue Flute Clan playing the flute, singing the songs, and using the feathers of tropical birds, which evoke heat. Four times they tried and failed, so they turned back south again.

Turning east, the Blue Flute Clan met the minor Gray Flute Clan and recounted their experiences. They were reminded that they had failed because their efforts were not in accord with the Creator's plans, and that they had done wrong in using their supernatural power before coming to the right place. The Gray Flute Clan accordingly assumed leadership of the two clans. After migrating to Oraibi and demonstrating their powers, both clans were accepted, but ever since then the Gray Flute Clan has been predominant over the Blue Flute Clan.

Like the Snake-Antelope Societies, the Gray and Blue Flute Societies conduct ceremonies apart: the former in separate kivas, the Blue Flute in its kivas, and the Gray Flute in its leader's home on the east side of the plaza next to the Sun Clan leader's home; but they combine on the last day, when the ceremony is held outside.

---

* See Part One: "The Creation Myth."
** See Part Two: "The Migrations."

RITUAL PREPARATIONS

Preliminaries begin in winter, when both societies participate in Soyál, which establishes the life plan for the year. They prepare the *ngákuyi* [medicine water], containing water from Flute Spring, honey, pollen, and *rúpi* [mineral which creates heat]. The Flute chief sprinkles this water with an eagle feather on all the corn and seeds on the Soyál altar. Assisted by the Two Horn and One Horn chiefs, he also sprinkles with it the sand on the floor, which represents the earth needing water for crops. Hence, when summer comes, the Flute Societies carry out this plan in actuality.

Two days before announcement of the summer ceremony the Gray Flute and Blue Flute make *páhos*. The following day the *páhos* are smoked over and concentrated upon. That night *páhos* are taken to the Gray Flute home and blessed. Then they are taken to Muyíovatki, southwest of Oraibi. Other *páhos* are planted at Sun House, east of the village.

The Flute ceremony lasts sixteen days. During the first eight days of preparation the altars are set up, and each day the Blue Flute chief goes to the Gray Flute home to smoke and pray. The wooden backdrop of the Blue Flute altar is carved into panels of cloud-terrace symbols on each side, with streaks of jagged blue lightning across the top. In front of it are placed three wooden or stone figures representing the Flute deity and his male and female aspects. To the left are a water jar and four ears of colored corn laid in their proper directions. Near the center are wooden birds carved to represent parrots, and other fetishes representing tropical birds made out of cornmeal which has been crystallized. To the right are two wooden fans or paddles, and two small rings made of reeds wrapped in cornhusks and painted blue. The flute used in the ceremony is a large reed with a hornlike pumpkin rind cut in the shape of a squash blossom, painted with flower colors, and carrying a *páho* attached. The flute signifies completion of *tuwksi* [the full circle of life], when the rinds of pumpkin and squash become fully hardened.

The altar in the kiva-like cellar of the Gray Flute home is much the same. The backdrop is narrower and higher, and gray is the predominant color of its lightning sticks. It is set on a sand painting whose symbols represent the earth, clouds, and lightning, surrounded on four sides by corn of the directional colors. In front of it are placed jars of water from Flute Spring, symbolic of the water from which the people emerged. Here stands the *típoni* of both societies. It is made of *pá'ama* [large bamboo reed] wrapped with cotton yarn, to which are tied the wing feathers of an eagle.

Here on the ninth day are initiated new members of both the Blue

Flute and Gray Flute Societies. The last four days before the ceremony and the four days after it comprise Nánapwala, the period during which the chiefs pray and concentrate, going without salt.

ENACTMENT OF THE EMERGENCE

At noon of the sixteenth and last day both the Gray Flute and Blue Flute Societies gather at Flute Spring to enact the Emergence. This name-place comprises two sites and four pools: Mumurva, where the spring or well of Potkivi is; another well for watering stock; the spring of Lanungva called Muyiovatki [Múi'ingwa, God of Germination, and vatki, well]; and Flute Spring itself, about two miles farther south on the sandy plain.

Tuvéngyamsi [Land Beautiful With Flowers] remembers how beautiful, how exciting it was on a hot summer day when she was a young girl in Oraibi. The men and women, unmasked but wearing headdresses of parrot, macaw, and cardinal feathers, stood in a circle around the terraced, muddy well of Muyíovatki, the Gray Flute in front, the Blue Flute singing behind. Lomáhongva [Beautiful Clouds Standing Up], the Gray Flute leader, wearing only a breechcloth, went into the spring and straddled a small reed raft which he began to paddle around with a blue wooden paddle. Wuwuchpi [the sprayer] the paddle was called because when the chorus described the blessings the people had received he splashed up water to the four directions. Listening to the song and watching him, you knew just how it happened—the rising water destroying the Third World, the people paddling on reed rafts from one stepping-stone, one island, to the next, then finally making their Emergence on the low, hot shore of this new Fourth World. And when the song described their hardships, the leader scooped up a bowl of dark mud, clambered out of the spring, and painted everybody's chins with mud from ear to ear. Then you really knew that a long time ago your ancestors had participated in the Emergence, and you were proud you were participating in this ceremony which had preserved it in memory for countless years.

When it was over, the Blue Flute went off, singing, to Flute Spring, the Gray Flute remaining to start the races. The leader started running to Oraibi, carrying one of the small rings and a water jar. At a signal from the Blue Flute Qaletaqa [Guard], the men ran after him. The fastest would catch up with him and take the ring and water. The ring he carried to Flute Spring, into which he threw it after circling the spring four times. The water jar he then carried to Oraibi.

Started by the Gray Flute Qaletaqa, women ran the second race, their long hair flying loose, their white capes streaming behind. This time there was no water jar. But the winning woman took the little blue ring from the leader and also threw it into Flute Spring after circling it four times. Then she received a green ring to carry to the Gray Flute home in Oraibi. Both races symbolized the carrying of water from the ocean crossed during the Emergence.

The Gray Flute people now went to Flute Spring to join the Blue Flute people. Then they formed a long procession to go to Oraibi. The older women who could not keep up followed behind, stopping at the little orchards to pick fruit, which they would throw to the people watching on the cliffs. *"Ah-ah-hah-hi-ah-hi! Ah-ah-hah-hi-ah-hi!"* they would call with a happy feeling.

This is the Flute Song, remembers Tuvéngyamsi, that the women sang. It starts each stanza with *We we lo lo,* which is just like a humming sound in a lullaby, meaning nothing; and there is a verse for every color of corn.

> *We we lo lo*
> *Ah yum tu wa*
> *Na sa vu eh*
> *Sa qua ma na*
> *Kuh yea va*
> *Nah tuk se na.*

> We we lo lo,
> There at the center of the universe
> Blue Corn Girl came up,
> Growing and maturing beautifully.

That is the way it goes, and anyone who knows this song can go into his field and put his arms around the corn plant, and when he sings this song he is entertaining his child, the corn plant. . . .

By this time it was sunset, and the procession was entering the village.

THE CEREMONY AT MISHONGNOVI

Sixty years later at Mishongnovi it is still much the same.*

Dramatically perched on the end of a high spur of Second Mesa, the tawdry village for once is cleaned up for the occasion. The trails have

---

*The Emergence ceremony is still held by the Flute Society of Walpi at Tawapa [Sun Spring]; of Mishongnovi at Lénvatki Spring; and of Shongopovi at Shongopovi [Reed Spring]. There are no races, the processions to the villages forming immediately after the paddling ceremony.

been cleared. The plaza has been swept of refuse. Even a few benches have been set out for household guests. Rooftops and cliff edge are crowded with villagers and tourists baking all afternoon in the blazing sun. Then toward sunset there sounds a sudden shout.

From the edge of the cliff you can see them coming up from the plain below—from Lénvatki Spring that lies beyond: two groups of about twenty-five men and women each, the Gray Flute in front, the Blue Flute behind. All are barefoot and bareheaded, wearing tufts of tropical bird feathers in their hair, and cloaked in red-banded white blankets. Twice they stop as they slowly cross the wide ledge in front of the trading post, where a lane has been cleared for them between parked cars and horses and wagons, but one cannot tell exactly what they are doing. Then slowly they climb up the trail into the village.

You can see now that each one is marked with a strip of mud running from ear to ear across the chin. Each group is headed by a leader; behind him come two young girls, each carrying a slender black three-foot-long rod on which is strung a small reed ring wrapped in cornhusks painted black (instead of blue as at Old Oraibi); and between them a small nine-year-old boy. The two Flute Maidens wear in each ear a *túoinaka* [stack-up-corn ear jewel], an inlaid earring symbolizing a stack of corn replenished each year. The boy is dressed in a breechcloth; a downy feather is tied to his loose hair with a cotton string; and in his left hand he carries a small water jar. Behind each group walks a Qaletaqa. He is dressed in buckskin, and his face is painted with brown *suta* hematite. He carries a quiver on his back, bow and arrow slung over his left shoulder, and a bull-roarer in his right hand.

Singing softly to the music of a flute, the Gray Flute group stops again at the entrance to the plaza. The leader stoops and, with cornmeal from a bag, draws upon the ground a cloud-terrace symbol (instead of the parallel lines drawn in the Oraibi ceremony). The two Flute Maidens thrust forward their rods and deftly toss their rings upon the symbol, indicating how the people's reed rafts, which they symbolize, landed at one island after another during their Emergence. The Flute Maidens then pick up the rings by their rods again, being careful not to touch them by hand, and the group moves forward into the plaza to repeat the performance. Behind them the Blue Flute group follows suit; there is a total of four performances for each group before they stop in the center of the plaza.

The small reed ring *pangwöla* [water shell or ring], as stated before, symbolizes the reed rafts used during the Emergence. It has still more esoteric significance, for it also symbolizes the "stepping-stones" or islands at which the people stopped as they crossed the water to this new Fourth

World. These islands were the mountain summits of the previous Third World, from which they were escaping or emerging; and immediately they had safely arrived on the shore of this continent, these stepping-stones were also submerged so that all the land mass of the Third World with its vestiges of a past civilization, even the steppingstones from it, would remain hidden from sight. Hence the Flute Maidens cannot touch the rings by hand and must handle them only with their rods, because the knowledge is secret and sacred to the Hopis. The rod is also sacred and is deeply concentrated upon during the whole Flute Ceremony, for it symbolizes a magic wand—the embodiment of the Hopis' esoteric, ritual knowledge of a previous existence. Other profane races and peoples ignore this knowledge, even its existence, and hence do not know who the Hopis are or the origin of mankind. But one day there will come another catastrophic change heralding another cycle, and these stepping-stones will emerge again to view, revealing the Hopis' esoterically pre-served knowledge of man's arising—the touch of the magic wand in the hand of the Creator.

In Old Oraibi the Flute procession always stopped at the *sipápuni*, the small hole representing the place of Emergence, in the plaza in front of the Snake Kiva. This is a very significant spot. Here during Powamu, it will be remembered, the two most sacred *kachinas*, Eototo and Áholi, symbolically designated the seven successive worlds in this universe and poured water into the *sipápuni* to purify man's routes of Emergence between all these stages of evolutionary existence. Here also during the summer Snake-Antelope Ceremony a sounding board is laid over the hole for the Snake priests to stomp upon as they approach the *kisi* or green shelter holding the snakes. So here again the Flute priests poured water into the small hole.

Today at Mishongnovi the two groups, the Gray Flute in front and the Blue Flute behind, stop in front of a similar *kisi* [shade house] of green cottonwood branches whose entrance is closed by a strip of dirty canvas. The Gray Flute leader goes inside, soon followed by the young boy carrying the water jar. For perhaps a half-hour they remain praying inside. The leader makes offerings of cornmeal on the altar. The water-carrier empties his jar of water in the *sipápuni*, which is then sealed up with mud. Then the Blue Flute leader and his water-carrier go inside.

Meanwhile the two groups outside continue singing the story of the Emergence to the music of the flutes. The song is divided into four sec-tions, each representing and relating a movement from one island to another. At each change of section the Qaletaqa swings his bull-roarer.

The sun dips below the horizon. The shadows reach across the plaza. The waiting tourists and villagers on the housetops shiver a little in a sudden breeze. Still the thin voice of the flute and the soft, restrained song of the chorus go on. It is all so curiously dignified and impressively simple, with nothing happening at all! Yet none of the packed crowd leaves. One shivers a little again. Is it possible that this profoundly simple and yet complex symbolism, this unending and untranslated song, still carry a wordless meaning to the patient crowd?

Abruptly it is over. The two men come out of the *kisi*, the song ends, and the two groups file silently out of the darkening plaza.

That night the ceremony is finished in the Gray Flute home with the customary *pavasio* songs. They begin about midnight when the Milky Way, now arching north and south, looms directly overhead, and end when Chuchukam comes up over the same point on the cliffs of Munyá'ovi where the rising sun marked the beginning of the ceremony.

9

The Snake-Antelope Ceremony

Commonly known by its most spectacular ritual, Chu'tiva [*chu'a,* snake; *tiva,* dance], the Snake-Antelope ceremony has gained worldwide fame as a public spectacle. Indians dancing with live rattlesnakes in their mouths!—a "loathsome practice" the United States Indian Bureau once threatened to stop. Still it goes on year after year, and from the four corners of the earth people come to see it. Undoubtedly it is both fascinating and repulsive. Certainly it is the least understood of all Hopi ceremonies. Embodying two dances, two races, and rituals in two kivas, the full ceremony has been more meticulously reported in detail by professional observers than has any other. Yet its deepest meaning lies hidden within a dark and primeval mystery perhaps unfathomable now even to its modern participants.

The Snake-Antelope ceremony, as stated in the preceding chapter, alternates with the Flute ceremony and is held every other year. Like the latter's, its beginning date is determined by observation of the sun rising over the Munyá'ovi cliffs; it lasts sixteen days; and its immediate purpose is to bring rain for the final maturity of the crops. The Snake Dance itself is given on the sixteenth day.*

The well-reported details of preparation include those common to all ceremonies: the announcement, planting of the standards on both the Antelope and Snake Kivas, ritual smoking, making of *páhos,* immuration of society members, and setting up of the altars. The Antelope Society is the more important; its functions precede those of the Snake; and to its kiva the Snake chiefs go each morning and evening to smoke and pray. The Snake altar is set up at night, contrary to usual custom. It is very simple, featuring the images of two Snake Maidens. The Antelope altar is more elaborate. It is set on a sand painting about four feet square, bordered with lines of directional colors, and at each corner is a "cloud

* Hotevilla and Shipaulovi, August 21; and Shongopovi, August 27, 1960.

mountain," a small cone of sand in which is stuck a hawk feather. On it are placed a Corn Mother and four ears of corn pointing to the four directions, and several bowls of water from Flute Spring. The backdrop of the altar, representing a house, is decorated with buzzard feathers. Against it is stood the *tiponi*, about two feet high, made of eagle-wing feathers and with downies tied to the tips, and wrapped with red buckskin thongs. The whole altar complex represents the world as it was formed by earth, air, water, plant life, and mankind; and each step of its construction is accompanied by songs that describe the formation of the world and its occupation, and by purification with the sacred water. The songs are secret, no outside person being allowed to hear them. Upon completion of the altar on the eleventh day the Antelope members go without salt for four days. The next day, the twelfth, the Snake members begin their most important preparation—their four-day gathering of snakes.

GATHERING THE SNAKES

White Bear's maternal grandfather, Koahwyma [Animal Skin Reflecting the Sun] of Oraibi, brings out several little-known facts in relating his own experience. As a young man, a member of the Badger Clan, he became seriously ill. The medicine man whom he called could not help him, advising him that he could be cured only by the power of the Snake Society. Koahwyma asked a man named Siyowma [One Who Carries a Flower] to be his godfather and to intercede for him. The Snake Society, upon being consulted, agreed to help Koahwyma if he would join it and participate in its rituals for four years. He agreed, and with the medicine from the Snake Society and help from his own medicine man he began to improve. By spring he was well and strong, able to work in his fields.

That summer upon returning to his home he found on the path a snake sack and a snake whip, and knew it was a signal for him to go to the Snake Kiva and participate in the rituals according to his agreement.

"There was fear within me," he related. "I could not understand what only those born into the Snake Clan understand: why do our people perform a ceremony with snakes that other men fear, and call them their brothers? But my grandmother prepared food for me to take to the kiva with the snake sack and snake whip, and I walked up the trail to Oraibi on trembling legs. It was getting dark and no one was near the kiva, for according to custom a line of cornmeal had been drawn around the kiva which no one could cross except a member of the Snake Society. Then

I saw the *na'chi* hanging on the kiva ladder. It was made of long hair dyed red to symbolize the rays of the sun, and with it hung the skin of a *kolichíyaw* [skunk]. Fear paralyzed me. Then something said to me, 'You are alive and walking on the good earth,' and I realized I would not have recovered from my sickness if I had not given my life to the Snake Society for four years and promised to help with their rituals. So I said back to that which had spoken to me, 'Yes, I did promise and I am here.' At that moment strength came back to my legs. I stepped across the cornmeal line and entered the kiva.''

Koahwyma as a Tuwálanmomo [Watchful Bee] was welcomed and seated on the raise during the preliminary rituals. Next morning he went out with all the members to gather snakes. The snake hunt lasts four days: first to the west, to the south, to the east, and finally to the north. There were a number of initiates. Each carried a water jar, a sack of cornmeal, and a *kwáwicki* of two buzzard feathers tied together. These wing feathers of the buzzard, Koahwyma was told by his godfather, have gray spots underneath which possess a strange odor and the power to soften the anger of a snake, when they are waved over its head. The snakes are not actually afraid or angry at man; they only coil to strike "when they see what is in man's mind and heart." One, then, must be of good heart and not afraid. He must never try to pick up a coiled snake. He must wave the snake whip over him until he uncoils.

Koahwyma was afraid of finding a rattlesnake or sidewinder, which are poisonous, and hoped to find a bull snake or gopher snake. But he learned that every godfather prayed in his heart that on the first day of the hunt his initiate should first pick up a rattler rather than a bull snake. This was because a bull snake was far more dangerous, being able to suck the life out of a man's body without striking.

There was a sudden call across the desert. A track had been seen and Koahwyma was called to gather his first snake. They hurried up to follow the track of a large racer into the hole of a field mouse. This was fortunate, for the snake had eaten the mouse, and when he was dug out he was too heavy to run. Koahwyma, however, was instructed to be careful not to hurt him, his brother. So he blessed the snake with cornmeal, with the sun, and with the earth, and then picked him up. When the snake began to fight, Koahwyma held him behind the head with his left hand, spat in the palm of his right hand, and began to brush the snake full length. The snake soon hung limp as a length of rope. Everybody was happy at Koahwyma's luck with his first *pókoi'ta* [pet]. That day the hunting party returned home with about twelve snakes, and when the four-day hunt was over there were about sixty snakes, which meant a long and successful dance and a good crop at harvest.

Every night in the kiva Koahwyma remained seated on the raise. Early in the evening the Snake chiefs left to smoke and concentrate in the Antelope Kiva, where the deepest and most sacred part of the ceremony was conducted. It seemed a long time before they returned. Koahwyma could look up through the ladder opening and see the Milky Way stretching north and south across it. Mostly he sat looking at the large jars on the lower, altar floor. Their tops were covered with buckskin punched with holes to let in air. In them were the snakes. Every day they were given pollen for food—usually corn pollen, sacred in all ceremonials, and containing life itself, talásiva [flower-producing life from sun]. Then about midnight the chiefs returned. It was the time for pavásio [deepest concentration], for blessing and entertaining the snakes.

"First sand was spread on the altar floor," continued Koahwyma, "then my godfather showed me how to smooth it out nice with part of a weaving set. This was so we could see the tracks in the sand and know which way a snake was moving. All members of the society seated themselves in a circle around it, each sitting cross-legged and touching the next man's knee. Then one of the men untied the buckskin tops of the jars and let all the snakes loose on the sand. At the same time the singing began, soft and low.

"There were all kinds of snakes: rattlesnakes, big bull snakes, racers, sidewinders, gopher snakes—about sixty all tangled on the floor. The singing stirred them. They moved in one direction, then another, looking over all the men in the circle. The men never moved. They just kept singing with a kind expression on their faces. The snakes began to roll on the sand, taking their bath. Then a big yellow rattler moved slowly toward an old man singing with his eyes closed, climbed up his crossed leg, coiled in front of his breechcloth and went to sleep. Pretty soon this old man had five or six snakes crawling over his body, raising their heads to look at his closed eyes and peaceful face, then going to sleep. It showed they had found their friend, looking within the heart of this one upon whose body they chose to rest. That is the way snakes show who are good and kind men with pure hearts, for some members of the society had one snake on their laps and some didn't have any. So I sang carefully and tried to keep my heart and thoughts pure till dawn, when the singing stopped and the snakes were put back into their jars. Then some of us went out to the spring to bathe ourselves, and others were given special duties to perform before we ate our morning meal." *

---

* Contrary to popular belief the fangs of the snakes are not extracted nor are their sacs of venom emptied. Many instances have been recorded when men have been bitten without any effects whatever. One precaution is taken, however. A concoction named chu'knga [snake medicine] is given to all Snake members, who drink a little and rub their hands with it

THE MYSTIC MARRIAGE

Meanwhile the same four-night *pavásio* of sacred songs and the *nánapwala* [purifying from within] is carried on in the Antelope Kiva. Its concluding ritual begins before midnight of the eleventh day of the ceremony when the Snake chief brings in a young girl, the Snake Maiden, who is the living counterpart of the two wooden images, the *chu'manas*, on the altar in the Snake Kiva.

She is a virgin who has been initiated into the Snake women's society. The upper half of her forehead, her chin, and her throat are painted white with *tuma* [white clay]. The rest of her face is painted black with *nánanha*, a substance taken from a diseased ear of corn. Over her woven black dress, the customary *manta*, she wears a Snake dancer's kirtle and a woman's white and red cape. Her hair is loose and to it is tied a small eagle down feather. A necklace of turquoise and shell is hung around her neck. She carries an earthen jar containing prayer sticks and corn, melon, squash, and bean vines.

The Snake Maiden and the Snake chief are met by the Antelope chief with a young man, the Antelope Youth, who carries a *típoni* and a snake. His hair is also loose, with a small downy feather tied in front, and he wears a white ceremonial kirtle. His face and body are painted ash-gray with *páskwapi* [decayed clay] taken from the edge of a spring and not from under the water. His chin is painted white with *tuma*, and with the same white clay zigzag lines are drawn on his body, arms, and legs.

The Snake Maiden is seated on the south side and the Antelope Youth on the north side of the altar level. Between the fire-pit and the altar is set an earthen bowl containing soapy water made from yucca roots. In front of the altar is placed a woven plaque full of many kinds of seeds. Girl and boy are now brought to the bowl by their chiefs, and a wedding ceremony is performed according to Hopi custom. The Snake Maiden's hair is washed in the milky seminal fluid of the yucca root by the Snake chief, and the Antelope Youth's by the Antelope chief. The two chiefs exchange places to wash the hair again, then twist it together while it is

---

before going out on the snake hunt. If a member is bitten in the kiva while entertaining the snakes, he rubs a little of it on the wound and continues singing. *Chu'knga* is made from the leaves of the large male and the small female plant called *hohoyawnga* [stinkbug plant]; to which are added the root of *chu'si* [snake flower] and leaves of the plant *chu'öqwpi* [snake vertebrae]; all being boiled in water which has been blessed.

In Old Oraibi *povolsi* [butterfly plant] was taken before the dance. Added to the medicine water, it was called *lugupna*. *Kungyna* was also chewed during the gathering of the snakes. *Kunya* [water plant] and *wiqupi* [fatty-looking plant] were added to the emetic.

still wet to symbolize the union. The couple is then conducted to the seating ledge on the north side, the girl being seated upon the plaque of seeds which has been brought by the Antelope chief. The seeds signify food for the birds of the air, the animals of the earth, and man.

It is now midnight and the *pavásio* begins—the period of concentration and the singing of the songs. It lasts until the stars in Orion's belt are hanging above the western horizon. Snake Maiden and Antelope Youth remain seated together until it is finished, being careful not to fall asleep. Then they are blessed and the girl is taken home by her godmother, the boy by his godfather.

The obvious meaning of the ritual is the union of the two societies which jointly carry out the Snake-Antelope ceremony. But as the immediate purpose of the ceremony, like that of the Flute, is to bring rain for the final maturity of the crops, the marriage also signifies the fruition of all life. The snake is a symbol of the mother earth from which all life is born. The antelope, because it usually bears two offspring, symbolizes for the Hopis fruitful reproduction and increase in population. Hence the union of the two is symbolic of creation, the reproduction of life.

Looked at more closely, it has a still deeper meaning. For as the bodies of man and the world are similar in structure, the deep bowels of the earth in which the snake makes its home are equated with the lowest of man's vibratory centers, which controls his generative organs.* The antelope, conversely, is associated with the highest center in man, for its horn is located at the top or crown of the head, the *kópavi*, which in man is the place of coming in and going out of life, the "open door" through which he spiritually communicates with his Creator.** The two then symbolize the opposite polarities of man's lifeline, the gross or physical and the psychical or spiritual which supersedes and controls the functions of the former, just as the Antelope Society supersedes and controls all functions of the Snake Society. Their mystic marriage is thus a fusing of man's dual forces within the body of their common ceremonial for the one constructive purpose of creation.

If this meaning is true we may look for its development throughout the later public rituals, remembering that the Antelopes always first posit the purposeful end, the Snakes following to show the means.

---

* Similarly in Hindu mysticism the goddess Kundalini, personified as the feminine aspect of the universal force latent in man, is envisioned as a sleeping serpent coiled within the lowest center, the *muladhara cakra*, corresponding to the *sacral plexus* and *plexus pelvis*, which stand for the whole realm of reproductive forces.

** Hindu mysticism also uses the horn to symbolize the outgrowth of the highest psychical brain center, and the horned antelope pictured on Buddhist temples is emblematic of the peace of mind attained through divine consciousness.

THE RACES

The Antelope Race is held on the morning of the fifteenth day, and the Snake Race on the morning of the sixteenth. The two races are substantially alike, members of both societies participating in each.

This year, 1960, we see them at Hotevilla. The sun is just coming up. House roofs and cliff top are crowded with people, most of them huddled in thin cotton blankets against the thin wind of dawn sweeping up from the desert below. Directly below in the curve of the cliff lies the spring which gives Hotevilla its name. The spring gushes out of a small cavern, now enlarged, which formerly scraped a man's back as he stooped to gather water. Hence the name of Hotevilla from *hote* [back] and *villa* [scratch]. Below the spring the steep side of the mesa is neatly terraced for tiny fields, which give way to larger fields planted between great dunes of encroaching sand. Beyond, far to the west, stretches the empty desert, now yellowing under the rising sun.

For a while there is no more to see. Gradually in the paling shadow of the cliffs one distinguishes at the curve of the trail below a group of Snake and Antelope priests patiently waiting, the Snakes painted dark brown, the Antelopes ash-gray. Farther away more dim and diminutive men emerge on the trail, carrying green cornstalks, squash, and melon vines. Then an old Hopi nearby points to the horizon with his chin. "They comin'."

A friend has a pair of binoculars. They are less sharp than the old man's eyes, but one distinguishes out on the sunlit desert a moving spot and then another. The racers are coming in.

The starting point is about four miles out. Here an Antelope, a Snake, and a Qaletaqa draw with cornmeal a line running east, encourage and bless all the runners. This talk by the starters is called Mónglavaiti [Priest Talk]. The starter then waves his *pahómoki* [cornmeal sack], and the race begins. It is not exciting at all, for the wait is long. But gradually, one at a time or in small groups, the racers appear over the dunes or between the trees.

Meanwhile an Antelope priest stationed about two miles out is jogging along in front of the runners. He is an old man who can't run very fast. His hair is flowing loose, he wears only a breechcloth, and he is carrying a bunch of prayer sticks and a small jar of water blessed in the kiva. With him is another Qaletaqa to protect the blessed water. Suddenly the leading runner sprints up. The old priest hands him the *pahos* and water jar. "Thank you and bless you, my son. Carry this on to our home." Then the runner heads for the foot of the cliffs. He keeps looking back; for if another runner can catch up with him, he must in turn hand over the *páhos* and water jar and bless his successor.

A tremor of excitement ripples through the crowd. The other runners are trying hard, urged on by the men along the trail waving their cornstalks and vines, and loudly encouraged by the Snakes and Antelopes waiting at the foot of the cliffs. It is no use. The runner is a young boy of perhaps sixteen, said to be the fastest runner in the village, and none can catch him. Reaching the foot of the mesa, he begins clambering up the steep, rocky trail, urged on by the Snake and Antelope Qaletaqas whirling their *tovókinpi* [rolling thunder] or bull-roarers—sticks whirled on strings to simulate the roaring sound of low thunder.

He reaches the kiva before the rest of the runners begin panting up the mesa, accompanied by all the Snakes and Antelopes and the men carrying cornstalks and squash vines. Often a tired runner, his body streaked with sweat, stops to rest his bruised bare feet. There are ribald calls from the crowd on top, jokes and laughter. The warm August sun is up; everybody is in good humor. When all reach the top of the mesa the fun begins: everybody—women and children, even a scattering of tourists—rushes to grab a stalk or vine, a leaf, a tendril, to carry home.

In the midst of the excitement the winning runner, having been blessed in the kiva, slips quietly back down the trail to plant his prayer sticks and jar of water in his family's fields out on the sandy plain.

The races are this simple—deceptively simple, for they are also rituals in a long and involved ceremony, bearing their share of its progressively developed meaning. Just what do they symbolize beneath their charming and colorful aspect on a sunny August morning?

The mystic marriage of Snake Maiden and Antelope Youth stated the purpose and end: the union of man's two life forces, the physical embodied in the lowest center at the base of the spine and the spiritual residing in the psychical center at the crown of the head. But what is the path between them, and how can they be made to fuse?

The channel, as explained by Eastern mysticism, is the main median nerve, known as the *sushumna*, extending through the center of the spinal column. Around it, crossing to the right and left at intervals, are two other psychic nerve channels coiled like snakes, forming the symbol of the caduceus of Mercury. That on the left, Ida, is regarded as "feminine," being the conduit of the negative lunar current; Pingala, on the right, as "masculine" and the conduit of the positive solar current of universal energy residual in man. Up these subtle channels flow and fuse the life forces of man when aroused.

The analogy presented by the Snake-Antelope races is at once apparent. The long racetrack, a mere trail ascending from far out on the desert to the kiva on the crown of the cliff, is the median nerve. It is crossed and recrossed at intervals where prayer sticks are planted and other priests are stationed. These mark the successive centers vitalized by the ascending life force when it is called up. It has two aspects: the feminine or lunar force symbolized by the dark-brown Snakes, and the masculine or solar force symbolized by the ash-gray Antelopes. The full ceremony began when the Antelope chief planted his *na'chi* on the kiva. For it is he, representing the masculine power of the divine, who takes precedence over the feminine and sanctions the awakening and loosing of its power. Throughout the whole ceremony it is always the Antelope which takes precedence over the Snake, and day after day the Snake chief dutifully presents himself at the kiva of the Antelope chief—the lower self before the higher. So in the races the Antelope Race comes first—not with snakes, but with the fruits of the later transmutation, the green cornstalks, squash, bean, and melon vines.

If the mystic marriage of Snake Maiden and Antelope Youth expressed the purpose and end of the ceremony, the Antelope and Snake Races symbolize the means. They lay out in simple, beautiful and strikingly original imagery the pattern of a wholly subjective concept that, if it is not original with the Hopis, is still as ancient as their own prehistoric rites. With the end of the races it is time now for the actual, climactic union.

THE DANCES

The Antelope Dance is given at sunset on the day of the sunrise Antelope Race, and the Snake Dance follows the Snake Race on the next day. The two dances, like the two races, are similar, save that the familiar squash, melon, and bean vines are used in the Antelope Dance, the snakes being danced with only in the concluding Snake Dance. There are few spectators for the former, some Hopis even referring to it as *nátwanta*, a "practice dance." Yet, as in all the preceding rituals, it has its purpose and sets the pattern for the Snake Dance to follow. Running Antelopes make the sound of thunder whose vibration stimulates the clouds to come out of their shrines. Hence the Antelope Dance first draws the clouds. The bull snake has the power to suck out life and rain from the clouds. So on the following day the Snake Dance brings rain.

The focal point at Oraibi was the always significant *típkyavi* [womb], the plaza in front of the Snake Kiva containing the *sipápuni*, the small hole representing the place of Emergence from the underworld. Into this during Powamu, it will be remembered, the *kachinas* Eototo and Áholi poured water from the jars on their *mongkos* to purify man's routes of Emergence from all his successive stages of evolutionary existence. Here in Hotevilla and in other villages a similar small *sipápuni* is dug in the open plaza. Over this is laid a cottonwood plank to serve as a sounding board or resonator, the *pochta*. Behind it is constructed the *kisi* [shade house], a bower of green cottonwood branches over whose opening is hung a blanket or strip of canvas. Into this, early in the afternoon of the sixteenth day, the great day of the celebrated Snake Dance, are carried all the snakes from the kiva.

Already the crowd is arriving for the spectacle—dudes from guest ranches, boys and girls from summer camps and schools, tourists from the world over, government Indian Bureau agents, Pueblo Indians from the Rio Grande, lots of Zuñis, and hordes of Navajos, everybody swarming the sandy little plaza of Hotevilla, fighting for places on the flat Hopi roofs, jamming terraces and doorways. All are broiling and perspiring under the blinding sun and sultry clouds gathering on the horizon, patiently waiting, hour after hour, to see Indians dance with live snakes in their mouths.

Meanwhile in the kivas the participants are getting ready. The Snake members paint most of their bodies with a composition of *suta* [red mineral] and *yalaha* [deep red mineral]. A large oval over breasts and shoulders is painted white with *tuma* [white clay]. White is also used for a strip covering the upper part of the forehead and the front of the throat. The rest of the face is blackened with *monha*. Each member wears a reddish-brown kirtle, carrying in black the design of a snake, and brown fringed moccasins. On both are sewn seashells.

In contrast the Antelope members paint themselves ash-gray with white zigzag lines running up from their breasts to the shoulders and down the arms to the fingers, and down the front of the legs to their big toes. The rattle which each will carry is a gourd covered with the skin of the testicle of an antelope. Each wears a white kirtle and embroidered sash. As a final touch the chin is outlined by a white line from ear to ear.

By now it is after four o'clock and the crowd massed in the plaza is getting restless. A wind has come up, whipping clouds of sand and dust over the rooftops. A little girl strays to the *kisi* and starts to go inside. One shudders to think of her toddling into that mass of writhing snakes, but no one shouts warning; perhaps no one realizes what is inside. Very casually an old Hopi walks up, takes her by the hand, and leads her away.

Meanwhile something more important is happening. We are watching it from a rooftop, White Bear and I, where we are squeezed in a mass of Navajos. The broiling August sun has disappeared and the wind is driving a flock of somber black storm clouds northward along the horizon. Other Hopis are watching too with looks of anxiety on their placid faces. It has been a summer of drought and despair. Niman Kachina brought no rain; for some reason the ceremony was improperly performed in some villages; in others another dance was substituted for the Home Dance. Nor did the Flute ceremony bring rain. The corn is stunted in the fields. Old Chief Tawákwaptiwa died in April, and a successor is not yet appointed. An undercurrent of strife and evil runs through all the villages. This Snake-Antelope ceremony is the last hope, and it always brings rain. So, above as below, the sky reflects this battle between good and evil. And while the crowd, now shivering with cold, becomes restless with the long wait, the Hopis patiently watch the increasing tempo of the battle.

There comes a driving blast of sparse raindrops, each hard and cold as a pellet of ice. White Bear patiently squeezes out from the packed rows of Navajos, climbs down the ladder, and goes to the car. Down in a narrow street one can see him listening to a group of older Hopis. All are looking upward. The black storm clouds are being driven northward past the village. The rain does not come. Instead, the sky gets blacker, the air colder. White Bear returns with a coat to wrap around my thin shirt. The Navajos begin to smell, so closely we are packed together. Still we sit wordlessly, watching the storm clouds turn west across the desert.

Then suddenly they file into the plaza—two rows of twelve men each, like a pair of prayer sticks for each of the six directions, the Antelopes ash-gray and white, the Snakes reddish-brown and black. The appearance of the Snake chief strikes the keynote of the somber scene. There is something neolithic about his heavy, powerful build, his long arms, his loose black hair hanging to his massive shoulders. At the end of the line trudges a small boy. Silently they encircle the plaza four times—a strange silence accentuated by the slight rattle of gourds and seashells. As each passes in front of the *kisi* he bends forward and with the right foot stomps powerfully upon the *pochta*, the sounding board over the *sipápuni*. In the thick, somber silence the dull, resonant stamp sounds like a faint rumble from underground, echoed a moment later, like thunder from the distant storm clouds.

This is the supreme moment of mystery in the Snake Dance, the thaumaturgical climax of the whole Snake-Antelope ceremony. Never elsewhere does one hear such a sound, so deep and powerful it is. It assures those below that those above are dutifully carrying on the ceremony. It awakens the vibratory centers deep within the earth to resound along the world axis the same vibration. And to the four corners it carries to the long-lost white brother the message that he is not forgotten and that he must come. There is no mistaking its esoteric summons. For this is the mandatory call to the creative life force known elsewhere as Kundalini, latently coiled like a serpent in the lowest centers of the dual bodies of earth and man, to awaken and ascend to the throne of her Lord for the final consummation of their mystic marriage.

The power does come up. You can see it in the Antelopes standing now in one long line extending from the *kisi*. They are swaying slightly to the left and right like snakes, singing softly and shaking their antelope-testicle-skin-covered gourds as the power makes its slow ascent. Then their bodies straighten, their voices rise.

The Snake chief at the same moment stoops in front of the *kisi*, then straightens up with a snake in his mouth. He holds it gently but firmly between his teeth, just below the head. With his left hand he holds the upper part of the snake's body level with his chest, and with the right hand the lower length of the snake level with his waist. This is said to be the proper manner of handling a snake during the dance. Immediately a second Snake priest steps up with a *kwáwiki* or feathered snake whip in his right hand, with which to stroke the snake. He is commonly known as the guide, for his duty is to conduct the dancer in a circle around the plaza. As they move away from the *kisi* another dancer and his guide pause to pick out a snake, and so on, until even the small boy at the end is dancing with a snake in his mouth for the first time. It is a large rattle-snake, its flat birdlike head flattened against his cheek. All show the same easy familiarity with the snakes as they had with the squash vines the day before.

After dancing around the plaza the dancer removes the snake from his mouth and places it gently on the ground. Then he and his guide stop at the *kisi* for another snake. A third man, the snake-gatherer, now approaches the loose snake. It has coiled and is ready to strike. The gatherer watches it carefully, making no move until it uncoils and begins to wriggle quickly across the plaza. Then he dexterously picks it up, holds it aloft to show that it has not escaped into the crowd, and hands it to one of the Antelopes singing in the long line. The Antelope, smoothing its undulating body with his right hand, continues singing.

So it goes on in a kind of mesmeric enchantment in the darkening afternoon. There is nothing exciting about these men dancing with snakes in their mouths—only a queer dignity that reveals how deeply they are immersed in the mystery, and a strange sense of power that seems to envelope them. The seashells with their slight, odd sound are calling to their mother water to come and replenish the earth. The song of the Antelopes is describing the clouds coming from the four directions, describing the rain falling. All the Hopis know that if it does not rain during the Home Dance of Niman Kachina rain will come with the Snake

Dance. For this is the consummation of the union of the two universal polarities, the release of that mystic rain which recharges all the psychic centers of the body and renews the whole stream of life in man and earth alike.

It is dusk now. The battle between the elements is over, and the sky is covered by low-hanging clouds. Out of them fall a few drops of rain. It is enough. The last of the snakes has been danced with and a group of women are making a circle of cornmeal beside the *kisi*. All the Antelopes bring their armloads of snakes to deposit within the circle. Then quickly the Snake members grab up as many snakes as they can carry and take them out on the desert, some each to the west, the south, the east, the north. Here they are blessed again and released to carry to the four corners of the earth the message of the renewal of all life, as it is known that snakes migrate back and forth across the land.

When the men come back each drinks a bowl of strong emetic called *nanáyö'ya*.* The men then stand on the edge of the cliff to retch. Otherwise their bellies would swell up with the power like clouds and burst. The women help them clean off the paint on their bodies, after which they return to the kiva for purification.

The Snake-Antelope ceremony is the last major ceremony in the annual cycle which began with Wúwuchim, Soyál, and Powamu and carried through Niman Kachina and the Flute ceremony. It is a great ceremony and a subtle one. For if the first three symbolize the three phases of Creation and the next two carry through in some manner the evolutionary progress on the Road of Life, the Snake-Antelope ceremony cuts through the past to the ever-living now, and its stage is not the externalized universe but the subjective cosmos of man's own psyche. Whatever its meanings, and they are many to many students, it shows how the interplay of universal forces within man can be controlled and made manifest in the physical world. That this is accomplished within the framework of what is commonly regarded as a primitive and animistic rite is a great achievement.

---

* The principal ingredient is the leaf of the plant *tikus musli*, identified as *Gila Aggregate*, to which are added the roots of the plants *casung* or *sue grappi*, the *Curotia Lenta*, and *hohayungua*, the *Pislostrophe Spareiflore*.

10

Lakón, Márawu, and Owaȼlt

The annual ceremonial cycle ends in the fall with three ceremonies performed by the women's societies. The Lakón Society is the most important; its ceremony is performed first and sets the general pattern for Márawu and Owaȼlt. Lakón is an ancient word having no meaning; it is said to be the name of the woman who first conducted the ceremony.

Preliminary rituals are held at corn-planting time in late May and early June, when four women members of the society, accompanied by one man, the Lakón *mongwi* [chief], enter the kiva for eight days. Lakón is controlled by the Butterfly and Badger Clans, so all members belong to one of these clans. No altar is set up. Prayer feathers are made, smoked over, and set next to the fire-pit by the *mongwi*. This is the reason for his presence, as only a man can accomplish this function. Among them is placed the society's *mongko*. The chief and the four women spend the eight days fasting, praying, and singing the *pavásio* songs. From then until fall they try to keep their thoughts in harmony with the meaning of the sacred songs.

The concluding eight days of the ceremony occur at corn-harvesting time in late September and early October. The exact time is set by the sun rising over Achámali [Where Two Rocks Lean on One Another], a point between Oraibi and Hotevilla. On this day all members enter the kiva. For four days they pray and sing, eating no salt or meat. On the evening of the fifth day the initiates who have been seated on the raise are allowed to come down to the altar level and join their elders.

The first important ritual takes place on the seventh day, Totokya [Day before the Dance]. That night the Lakón Chief, the only man participating in the ceremony, waits outside the kiva to watch the sky. He wears only a kirtle, being bareheaded and barefooted to show his humility. When Chööchökam [the Pleiades] rise, he enters the kiva, where all the women are singing. After walking up to the altar set on a sand painting which symbolizes fertility and growth, he picks up its most important part, a long wooden fertility stick. At its lower end ears of corn are painted, and from these a zigzag streak of lightning runs up to the top, forming the shape of a cloud. Holding this in both hands, he walks to the ladder opening and lifts the stick the full length of his arms four times to signify that all mankind will attain spiritual height and be blessed with all needs for their physical being.

All the women now form a circle, taking up lightning sticks, cloud sticks, *páhos,* corn, and all parts of the altar, until nothing remains but the sand painting on the floor. They too lift these in an upward and outward movement four times. They then replace all the articles on the sand painting in their original form of an altar, concluding the ritual. Chööchökam is now descending to the western horizon; daybreak is near.

The wife of the Lakón Chief gives to each member a handful of cornmeal and three prayer feathers. Following her out of the kiva in a long line, the initiates at the end, the women take the trail along the top of the mesa. It is still dark when they stop at the first shrine, Hanányaha [Loose Sand Around Badger Hole], to pray and leave cornmeal. Again they stop at a shrine and at the race track of the Twins, praying and leaving cornmeal at each.

By this time it is dawn, giving enough light to follow the narrow trail twisting down the face of the cliff among tumbled boulders. At the bottom they form a circle around a huge black volcanic boulder out of whose flat top protrudes a complex of small brown nodules surrounded by curious whorls. Underneath the boulder is the Lakón shrine. Into it the chief places his *típoni* and *páhos.* While he smokes over them the women sing again the *pavásio* song. The initiates are now told that if they want to be adept at weaving plaques and baskets, an art in which the women of Third Mesa excel, they must leave offerings of cornmeal in the shrine and then prayerfully rub both their hands in circular movements over the circular whorls on the big boulder. The nodules surrounded by circular whorls also symbolize the embryo within the fetal membranes of the mother's womb, and are commonly known as the "perfect carriage." Hence the virgin Lakón maidens rub hands over the whorls to express also their desires for impregnation and motherhood.

Leaving the shrine they return up the steep trail to Kúiwanva [Coming Over the Ridge], where they sing the Morning Song as the sun comes up. They then file back to the kiva to prepare for the public ceremony.*

Four Lakón maidens are chosen to perform within the circle of

---

* Shongopovi, September 17; Mishongnovi, September 25, 1960.

women and are carefully dressed for their parts. Their faces and feet are moistened with water, then a dry yellow powder of ground sunflower petals is patted on. A headdress, symbolic of a cloud and made of the feathers of an eagle and tropical birds, is put on each with the traditional ceremonial dress and cape. Each is given four ears of corn made into *mátu'uvés* [used also in a boy's game], an eagle feather being stuck in one end of the ear and a stick into the other. The corn is colored according to the cardinal directions: the Maiden of the West holding the four yellow *mátu'uvés*, the Maiden of the South holding the four blue *mátu'uvés*, she of the East the red ears, and she of the North the white corn.

The Lakón women are already out in the plaza, singing in a large circle, when the chief leads out the four maidens. On the ground in front of them he stoops and draws with cornmeal a cloud design, in the center of which he places a *páchayanpi* [water sifter], a small ring made out of cornhusks. The four maidens in turn throw their *mátu'uvés* at the cloud design, aiming at the ring—first the yellow corn, then the blue, the red, and finally the white. When all have thrown their corn, they march up to the design and wait until the chief gives each of them back her own corn. This is repeated four times.

The chief now leads the maidens inside the circle of singing women and around it once, leaving the maiden with the yellow *mátu'uvés* at the west point of the circle, the one with the blue at the south, the one with the red at the east, and the one with the white at the north. He then gives the *páchayanpi*, the cornhusk ring, to the maiden at the west. She rolls it across the circle to the east and swiftly throws her corn at it. The chief retrieves the ring and hands it to each of the other maidens in directional sequence, who do likewise, completing the circle. He then takes all the *mátu'uvés* and the *páchayanpi* back to the kiva.

Throwing the corn at the ring is symbolic of man's four-world journey, the corn representing his provision of food while traveling from one world to another. The use of the cornhusk ring, the cloud design, and the corn by these Lakón maidens is comparable to that of the ring, rod, and design used by the Flute Maidens in the Flute Ceremony.

The four Lakón maidens, still standing at their directional points within the circle of women, sing with them until a new section of song begins. Then the Maiden of the West steps inside the circle, takes out a gift of a plaque or basket from her cape, and makes an up-and-down movement with her arms. Dancing toward the east, she pretends to throw the gift toward the east. Then, after walking quickly back to her position in the west, she tosses the gift over the heads of the women in the circle to the spectators in the west. This performance is repeated by each of the other three maidens in directional sequence.

The performance has two apparently contradictory meanings. The Maiden of the West, dancing toward the east, symbolizes a yellow cloud gathering in the west and moving east; she is followed by a blue cloud from the north, and so on, all coming to bless the people with a good harvest. But to receive their gifts of moisture the people must be of good hearts and strong faith, else the gifts will be withheld. Hence the maidens' first pretense of throwing out their gifts is a reminder that we are on this earth only temporarily, and that unless we keep our faith and adhere to the plan of the Creator we will be moved, as we have been in the past, to still another world.

The Lakón Society is said to possess the power to heal *ka'aichokti* [skin trouble] through the use of a certain plant. Since the Lakón belongs to the Badger Clan, and the badger is the animal that knows all plants, the clan members know how to prepare the right medicine for this disease. The plant is called *katoki*. It is dried, powdered, and added to water. The healer puts it in her mouth, blows the vapor on the affected skin of the patient, and then sucks out the disease.

MÁRAWU

Márawu [Leg Decoration], commonly shortened to Maraw, may be given any time after Lakón. It usually occurs during the period known as Eusaumuya, in September and October, after *tuwksi* [maturity], when melons mature and corn begins to dry at the edges.* It belongs to the Sand Clan, and in Old Oraibi there was a separate Maraw Kiva for it.

The ceremony follows the same general procedure as that of Lakón, with eight days of preliminary rituals in the spring followed by eight days in the fall. The first four days of the fall ceremony are spent in the kiva by the four leaders, who pray, make *páhos*, and go without salt. Two are men—one the chief or *mongwi*, usually a brother or uncle of the woman leader, and the other a male Qaletaqa or Guard. The other two are women—the chief of the society and a female Qaletaqa. On the fifth day the other members of the society enter the kiva, and on the night of the seventh day begins the main ritual before the altar.

The floor of the altar is made of sand specially blessed, as Mazawuh belongs to the Sand Clan, keepers of the soil. Across its back edge are set a number of wooden figures and symbols. The one on the left is the Márawu *típoni*, carved and painted with the face markings of a Márawu woman; that on the right, slightly smaller, is the Márawu-mana. In front

* In 1960 it was held at Walpi on October 3, at Shipaulovi on October 23, and at Shongopovi on October 30.

of each of these are planted small figures representing the Qaletaqa-manas. All four symbolize the love and reproductive qualities of the female sex. Between them in a row from left to right are planted wooden sticks with a cloud symbol painted at the top and a raindrop or a corn symbol at the base, the rest of the stick being painted blue. These represent the Cloud Houses of the directions. Alternating with these stand wing-feathers of eagles. Laid on the sand are four ears of corn: the yellow corn to the west, the blue to the south, the red to the east, and the white to the north. In their center is set a bowl of water which has been blessed.

The ritual on the seventh night is a brief recapitulation of the creation of the world in a series of songs—creation of the earth, vegetation, animals, and man. The *mongwi* sits at the left side of the altar, facing the women members of the society. At each step of world creation he blesses the world at that stage. When the last song describes how man was put upon the earth, dawn is showing through the ladder opening, and at sunrise the ritual in the kiva is concluded.

At this time the village chief and the Crier Chief enter the kiva and announce, "I want all of you to come out of this kiva. We must all come to the light." The village chief then takes hold of the Crier Chief's left hand with his right hand. The Crier Chief takes the hand of the Márawu man leader, who in turn grasps the Márawu woman leader's hand, and so on down the line of all the women members. Forming a long chain, they climb up the ladder and out of the kiva. As they are holding hands and unable to touch the ladder except with their feet, their Emergence is slow and difficult—and this is what their action symbolizes, mankind's Emergence to this Fourth World under the spiritual guidance of the *kikmongwi*, chief of all the people.

After filing out of the kiva, they go to the east to greet the rising sun. When the morning meal is over all return to the kiva to prepare for their public appearance in the plaza. At this time all the women wash their hair, that of initiates being washed by their godmothers. Three young virgins, the Márawu Maidens, are selected. One is Cha'tima [the Caller], who is to sing more loudly than the others, directing the changes of the songs. The mature members dress themselves in the handwoven black *manta*, over which they drape the *atu'u*, the ceremonial cape of white and red. For their first appearance in the morning they carry cornstalks with the ears attached. For subsequent appearances they substitute wooden sticks painted with cloud and corn symbols, which were made at the time they were initiated and are kept in the family thereafter.

The Qaletaqas then dress and paint the two Marawu Maidens. Each wears a *tü'ihi,* part of a decorated wedding dress, which falls below the hips, and a kirtle that reaches to the knees. On her head are fastened four upright sticks painted blue and joined together with eagle feathers at the top. Down feathers are bunched at the back of her head. Each cheek is painted with a brown stripe running down from the eye. Both legs are painted black with the peculiar markings that give Márawu its name. Two circles, like garters, are drawn: one just above the knee and another high on the thigh. From these, four vertical stripes, front, back, and sides, are marked down the legs. These markings carry on the sex symbolism first expressed in Lakón, when the virginal Lakón maidens rubbed hands over the circular whorls on the Lakón shrine, expressive of their desire for impregnation and motherhood. The Márawu leg markings symbolize with their vertical stripes the beginning of menstrual periods, and call the attention of males to the girls' sexual attractiveness. Embroidered anklets represent again the colors of sunlight.

Cha'tima, the Caller, also wears eagle feathers in her hair and the same face markings. In her left hand she carries a long rod. Tied to its top are two eagle tail-feathers and a long streamer of horsehair dyed red to symbolize the power of the sun's rays, and around its center is wrapped a narrow band of fringed buckskin. On her right wrist is fastened a glossy fox pelt that hangs down to her ankles, representing the sexual power of the animal kingdom, which is expressed only at rutting periods, and thus cautioning against sexual indulgence.

The woman leader, carrying the Márawu *tiponi*, then leads all members out of the kiva into the plaza, where they form a circle, leaving an opening to the east. They are followed by Qaletaqa, leading the Márawu Maidens. Four times he stops to draw three lines of cornmeal on the ground in front of them. The maidens first throw on these lines the small hoop or ring each is carrying, the *pátuchaya*, made of cattails and without cornhusk wrappings. Then they throw at these their feathered sticks. As they are now led inside the circle of singing women, each maiden is given a bowl of water and a bowl of sweet cornmeal, which she kneads into two rolls of dough, the *qömi* [food rolled]. One Márawu Maiden goes to the west and then to the south, throwing a roll each time over the circle of women to the men waiting outside, who try to grab it. The other goes to the east and then the north, doing the same thing. The throwing of the food is an offering and an invitation to the clouds of the four directions to come with moisture. It has also another, sexual meaning. For the virginal maiden prayed while kneading the dough that the right man would get it, and the man successful in catching it is supposed to be attracted to the girl. He takes it home to be blessed, knowing his corn will be increased next year.

Meanwhile the older women in the circle continue singing and dancing with their cornstalks, and throwing gifts of food to the spectators.

This is repeated at intervals all day. After the first morning appearance, when they return to the kiva to rest, they leave the cornstalks on the ground. The watching villagers carry the stalks home and place them on top of their stacks of corn ears, knowing that as the corn has been blessed by the Márawu women they will be protected from sickness.

Márawu has the power to cure *pamistuhya* [vapor fever] or rhemuatic fever. Patients obtain from Márawu women the plant *hovakpi*, which they boil and drink, and also steam themselves with its vapor.

Throughout the last four days of the ceremony Márawu women make fun of men members of the Wúchim Society, mocking them with accusations of sexual misbehavior—just as Wúchim men taunt Márawu women during their own ceremony, which soon follows.

OWAQLT

Owaqlt [Melons on Vine] is the last and least important of the women's ceremonies. The word is often interpreted as "Rocks in the Field" because ripe melons and squash look like rocks in the field, and the ceremony is commonly referred to as the "Basket Dance." It belongs to the Parrot Clan and may be given any time between the Márawu and Wúwuchim ceremonies.* Its altar, kiva rituals, and public dance differ little from those of Márawu. Its maidens wear a horn on the right side of the head and a squash blossom on the left; and their faces and feet are painted yellow. The women also throw baskets instead of food to the bystanders.

Nowadays plaques and baskets are difficult to make and expensive, so gifts of packaged groceries are thrown out. The dance at Moencopi in 1959 illustrated how corrupted all Hopi ceremonies will be in time, due to the influx of Navajos and whites. The plaza was so crowded with Navajos waiting for the distribution of gifts that the dance itself was curtailed to get rid of them. When the groceries were thrown out the plaza looked like a football field during a rush for the goal posts—a riot of rushing Navajos, kicking and squirming, emerging with bloody faces, clothes half torn off, clutching empty boxes of Post Toasties.

These three women's ceremonies concluding the ceremonial year must be over before Wúwuchim, which begins another annual cycle. It is late October. The harvest is over, and from its bounty food is given freely. This aspect of the women's ceremonies may have still another meaning. For now the ground is hardening, the days are growing shorter, and

---

* Shongopovi, October 29, and Shipaulovi, October 31, 1960.

preparations must be made for the coming year. It is time to make ready for germination of life anew. Hence the accent on sexual symbolism, woman being the receptacle and carrier for the seed of mankind.

The whole meaning of Lakón, Márawu and Owaq̈lt is perfectly expressed in one carving on a great rock in the desert near Oraibi. It is the lewd figure of a Maraw Maiden wearing her distinctive headdress and leg markings, legs outspread, her huge vulva exposed, ready for copulation and fertilization.

Thus ends the ceremonial year. In the annual cycle there are nine major ceremonies corresponding to the nine universes of Creation. They themselves symbolize the successive stages of planetary creation. Beginning with Wúwuchim, Soyál, and Powamu, which portray the germination and establishment of all life, they carry through its development in Niman Kachina, the Flute and Snake-Antelope ceremonies, and conclude with Lakón, Márawu, and Owaq̈lt, symbolizing its maturity and fruition. The ceremonies of the women's societies, representing the preparation for germination again, bridge the gap between the concluding cycle and the new one to follow.

All these phases of Creation are endlessly repeated each year in annual cycles of germination, growth, and harvest. So the ceremonies also plan, confirm, and help carry through the agricultural cycle upon which all life depends.

And yet again Creation is reaffirmed with the dawn of each new day, and the ceremonies reaffirm with endless repetition a persistent faith in the multifold meaning of the Emergence—of birth, death, and rebirth.

As dramatic portrayals, these mystery plays have few equals in depth and scope. But we must also admit here the obverse and negative side of this great ceremonial structure—an extinct ceremony deteriorated into a witchcraft which is corroding valid religious beliefs.

11

The Ya Ya Ceremony

Of all the unique and symbolic features of the reconstructed Great Kiva at Aztec, New Mexico,* the two large pits in the center of the main altar room have aroused the most curiosity. They are rectangular in shape, more than eight feet long, three feet wide, and three feet deep, walled with stone. What these stone boxes, vaults, or pits were used for in the twelfth century when the Great Kiva was built has never been accurately known.

Yet there was no mystery about them to the Hopi who explained to us the symbolism of the Great Kiva. They were used for a magic fire ceremony called the Ya Ya, a vestige of which is still given in modern Hopi villages and which is the basis of current witchcraft beliefs and practices. His legend of its origin links the Hopis closely with the pre-historic inhabitants of Aztec, Chaco Canyon, and other ancient ruins.

ORIGIN LEGEND

Many centuries ago, before the people settled in Oraibi as their permanent home, one of the migrating clans was living to the north-east, near Canyon de Chelly. Famine had come upon them, and they had to go out and gather the wild grain called *nööna* [covered up]. A young girl about fifteen who went out searching always visited the home of an old couple nearby. One evening, just as she was about to go into their house, she overheard the old man telling his wife he had found a *nöönkoa* [large patch] of ripe *nööna* to the north and would gather it in a few days. So, without going in, she stole home and told her own parents that she was going to gather this wild grain. They gave her a jar

---

* See Chapter 1.

of water and a little *háhálviki* [cornmeal wrapped in cornhusks, flattened, and cooked between two flat stones], and she started out at midnight.

Next day she came to the edge of a high mesa and looked down into the valley upon the patch of ripened grain. Immediately she climbed down to pluck it. Putting a sheaf of it in her cape, she beat it with a stick. Then she cleaned out the chaff. Soon there was a big pile of grain. Darkness was coming, so she built a fire and ate her small supply of cornmeal bread. Fear suddenly overtook her. She could hear something coming closer and closer. It was a strange and powerful-looking man who came up, saying, "Do not be afraid of me. I feel sad for your people. That is why I came."

He threw upon the coals a piece of meat he had brought, waited for it to cook, and shared it with her. Then she shared with him the bed of soft branches she had made for herself.

Next morning she hurried home with her grain to tell her parents about meeting this strange man, and assured them she had had no sexual relations with him. They knew this was true. But before long the girl had a child, a boy. Since the boy had no paternal grandparents, his mother's father washed his hair and gave him the name of Siliómomo,* as his clan was Sawungwa [Yucca Fruit Plant]. Also, as there were no aunts to wash the baby during the first twenty days, his mother's mother had to do this.

Siliómomo grew up fast, developing skill with the bow and arrow. One day he went hunting to the same place where his mother had met the strange man. He chased a cottontail rabbit into a hole between two rocks. Twisting a stick into the rabbit's fur, he kept trying to pull out the animal. Suddenly a strange and powerful-looking man came up to him and said, "I will help you!" The man lifted the big rock, reached down, and pulled out the cottontail. When the boy had tied the rabbit's neck and feet together so he could sling it around his neck, the man said, "I am your father and I have come to get you. I know what has been said about you, so I will show you who we are."

After they had traveled through the *salápqölu* [forest of spruce] they came to a kiva. The man stamped his foot on the roof. Siliómomo knew then that he was a person of importance. For only when one of authority brings someone important does he stamp, making a vibration which spirit people recognize. "Climb on my back. We will enter together," said the man.

Many people were in the kiva, both men and women. "You are welcome! You are welcome!" they told the boy. The women took his

---

* His connection with the animal kingdom is implied, despite his plant-kingdom name. For *siliómomo* means the sound of a yucca pod when shaken, the same sound made by a gourd rattle covered with the skin of the testicles of an antelope.

rabbit, even though it was a dusty little rabbit, blessed it, and put it beside the fire-pit. Then they set out food before him. There were all kinds of food and lots of it, even though the outside world was suffering from lack of food, and Siliómomo ate his fill.

Then his father carried him on his back to another kiva, stamped on the roof, and they were welcomed as before. This kiva was much larger than the first one, and on the walls hung the skins of many different animals—rabbit, deer, antelope, mountain sheep, and many others, both male and female. One by one the people in the kiva showed Siliómomo which skin belonged to each of them. "Now look!" said a man. He wrapped a deerskin around him and immediately became a deer. A woman wrapped a rabbitskin around her, becoming a rabbit. One at a time they did this until they were all animals. Then they changed themselves back into people by taking off their skins. Siliómomo's father was the antelope. Changing himself back into a man, he said to the boy, "There now! You have seen the mystery. You know who we are. We are the animal people, and from the animal kingdom we receive the great power of the Ya Ya."

After taking the boy back to the place he had killed his rabbit, the father killed a deer. He dressed it, wrapped the skin back around the carcass, and put it on the boy's back. It was too heavy for the boy to carry. But the man put his hands upon it, and with the magic power the deer became light as a rabbit. "Now you may carry it home," he said. Siliómomo did so and presented it to his grandparents, who cut it up for *nyöqwivi* [stew of meat and corn]. They invited everyone for a feast, and all were happy.

As he grew into a young man, Siliómomo decided to make a religion of the Ya Ya, based upon the power of the animal kingdom. For at this time his people performed only the Snake ceremony. So he replastered the kiva and found some friends to join him. When it was getting time to perform the Ya Ya ceremony, they all went out toward the forest where Siliómomo had met his father. There they camped four days and nights, singing songs and making prayer sticks in the forest. Just before dawn the call of a coyote was heard in camp, and then the call of a crow. Siliómomo said, "Our prayer is answered. In the future when our people go hunting for any large animal and hear the call of the coyote or crow, they will know their prayer is answered." This is still understood today.

So the hunt was successful, many different animals being killed. At the end of the fourth day Siliómomo took his prayer sticks to the kiva his father had showed him, the one consecrated to the animal kingdom. Then the party returned to the kiva in their village to perform the Ya Ya ceremony.

All the spirit people came to help them, showing their strange powers.

They were not *kachinas;* they were spirit people who belonged to the animal kingdom. Their magic and power was great. They would throw a man into the air over the kiva opening and let him fall in, and he would climb out unhurt. They would put corn in the depression of a large rock, one man holding over it a pole about twelve feet long and about eight inches in diameter. Then, keeping time to the song the other men were singing, this one man would work the pole up and down as if it had no weight until the corn was ground into fine meal. And finally they dug a big pit, lined it with stones, and built a fire in it. When the coals were red and deep, some men would walk barefooted across them. Others would dive naked into the coals, roll around in the fire, and come out without a burn on their bodies.

This is how the first Ya Ya ceremony was performed long ago at Siliómomo's home village near Canyon de Chelly.

HOW IT WAS DEVELOPED AND BROUGHT TO WALPI

After a time the migrating people settled down for many years, building a large village they called Chípiya [Home of the Bighorn Sheep]. Within it they constructed a huge kiva known to them as the Pavásio [Climax of Creation] Kiva. The chief of the village belonged to the Fog Clan [Pamösnyam], and one of the most important ceremonies he conducted in the great kiva was the Ya Ya ceremony.*

By this time the Ya Ya was a fully established ceremony of great power. Its chief deity was Somaíkoli. The call of the Ya Ya ceremony, from which the ceremony derived its name, was *"Yah-hi-hi! Yah-hi-hi!"* It was made by the man who announced the appearance of the deity when the ceremony was performed. Somaíkoli himself made only one sound, *"Huh Huh,"* as if he were blowing his breath like an animal. The great power of Ya Ya was invoked from the animal kingdom, Tuvósi [Animals with Horns].

On the fourth night before the main ceremony the initiates selected their godfathers in a curious ritual. Just before midnight the older members of the society put on the horned heads and skins of the animals they represented, and took their stations in the main altar room in front of the narrow ladder-like slits leading to the openings above.** The fire was then

---

* The remains of this village are now known as Aztec Ruins at Aztec, New Mexico, its celebrated Great Kiva being the largest reconstructed kiva to date. Details of its construction are given in Chapter 1.

** See Chapter 1 for a more detailed description.

extinguished so that the kiva was in total darkness. One by one the new initiates were brought in, each having been instructed to select his godfather by feeling the fur on his chest and the vibrations from his heart.

Slowly the initiate groped his way to the first station to the northeast, where stood Pangwú [Bighorn Sheep]; then to the next station, where Cha'risa [Elk] was standing; and so on around the kiva to the stations of Chöövio [Antelope], Sowi'ngwa [Black-Tail Deer], Masíchuvio [Gray Deer], Cochuschuvio [White-Tail Deer], and all the others. At each he would stop, feel the texture of the hair on the chest, and lay his hand over the heart. Suddenly he would feel a magic attraction holding him close to one of them and knew that this was his rightful godfather and the animal with which he had an affinity.

The fire was then relighted and in its light the initiates saw the animals and godfathers they had intuitively selected. All initiates were then conducted to the raised portion of the kiva, from which they watched the older members perform the magic fire ceremony in the two large pits during the following three nights. On the fifth day the ceremony was given in the pit in the plaza outside, before all the people, the initiates taking part. When the chorus of singers began their song, the performers would walk barefoot across the red-hot coals. Then they would jump naked into the fire-pit, roll around, and come out without a burn.* They were followed by other groups of performers who did more feats of magic.

After many years the Fog Clan again resumed its migration, taking the Ya Ya with it. The people traveled south for four days to another village, believed to have been in Chaco Canyon. Here they stayed for several years. Then they continued south to build a small village whose ruins will someday be found near Nuvatuky'ovi [Snowcap Mountain]. When the stars guiding them moved, they went northwest. After coming to the bank of a large river, they gave a four-day ceremony. On the first day they planted a *salavi* [spruce tree], a *hekwpa* [oak], *tovósi* [smooth wood], a wild berry bush, and a small plant for use as prayer sticks. By the fourth day these had grown and matured. All the Ya Ya animals then appeared, assuring the people they would accompany them wherever they went if a Game Mother of spiritual birth were provided them. So the Fog Clan leader molded sweet cornmeal into the small figure of a woman,

---

* The art of walking barefoot on hot coals is still practiced in India and other countries of the Far East, and has even been seen on television. It is known as an example of "Leindenfrost's Phenomenon," the explanation being that, as a drop of water loosed on top of a red-hot stove does not boil away because of a cushion of vapor that forms beneath it, similarly a bare foot is not burned because of the protective cushion formed by the moisture in the skin, whereas a shod foot would catch fire immediately.

folded his white cape around it, and sang his *pavásio* songs over it all
night. Next morning he unfolded the cape to reveal a baby girl.

The animals were pleased and for the concluding ritual that night
took their positions as they had in the Great Kiva at Chípiya. About midnight a fog came in so thick the people could not see one another. "This
is a sign that your ceremony has been perfect," said the leader of the
animals. "From now on your movements will be secret. Your protecting
star will be Ponóchona [Sucks From the Belly],* the star that you must
ask to increase the animal kingdom on earth. Now you must go. Our
Mother will go first and we will follow."

This took place where there is plenty of turquoise under the bed of
the river, said to be the San Juan River west of Shiprock.

So the people moved on through the fog, the little Game Mother
first, then the animal spirits in line, headed by the bighorn sheep, followed
by the people—all singing as they traveled.

For a long time they stayed with the people of another small village.
Animals were plentiful; everybody was happy hunting them. But the
people of that village were disrespectful of the animal kingdom. So the
leader of the animal spirits said to the leader of the Fog Clan, "These
people are rousing hatred against us. We must depart. Hereafter these
people must hunt a long time for their food. Now you must go too."

So the people traveled on to Nawáivösu [Two Cliffs Pointing toward
Each Other], near Cross Canyon west of Ganado. Learning that they were
so close, the village chief of Walpi sent Rohona [Three-legged Coyote] to
them with this message, "Our land around here is drying up, so come on,
settle with us and help us. We will give you the land south of where
Ponóchona rises, north to the halfway point where the sun stops at the
end of his journey."

The Fog Clan people were happy that they were so close to the end
of their long migration and welcome at Walpi. But on the way they stayed
four years at Masíptanga [Place of Wild Gourds], now a ruin near Jedito.
Before leaving here they gave another great Ya Ya ceremony to which all
the animals returned. When it was over, the procession to Walpi started.
First was the Three-legged Coyote, dressed in his ceremonial robes, who
had been sent to conduct them over a cornmeal path he had laid. Then
in proper order came the Bighorn Sheep, the Elk, the Antelope, and all
the Deer, beautiful and majestic. Behind them came the Game Mother
and the people, the leaders still dressed in their ceremonial costumes.
Overnight they stayed at Mauchovi [Forehead of Bighorn Sheep]—the
point on the first bend out of Keams Canyon.

---

* Sirius, the Dog Star.

The fog was lifting. It was sprinkling. Walpi was waiting to welcome them. So they came to Walpi and settled across the Gap on the north side with the Sun Clan.

HOW THE CEREMONY WAS PROFANED

For many years the Ya Ya was performed at Walpi, special *páhos* being made for Chípiya and the other villages where it had been formerly given. All its powers were used for the good of the people. Among these was the power of the magic eye, which enabled members of the Ya Ya Society to see in the dark and to see long distances away, as animals can. Many Walpi people believed this was derived from the power of evil, especially when many members of the society began to be afflicted with a disease of the eyes. So the Ya Ya Society members were banished from Walpi.

They went to Oraibi on Third Mesa, where they continued to practice the magic fire ceremony and the power of the magic eye. One day they sent out four men to intercept a villager carrying water from Flute Spring back to his house. The men, as directed, emptied the gourd jar of water, split it open, and revealed on the inside the painting of the frog which they had seen with the magic eye of the Ya Ya.

There was another long-distance feat they achieved. They asked for a bowl of the white clay wash with which some people were painting the wall of their house. Then they put their hands in the bowl and made the motions of painting a wall with the wash. Several people laughed, for there was no wall in front of them. But the Ya Ya members quietly pointed across the desert to a cliff ten miles away. It was painted with the white wash.

So many were the tricks they performed, there was no telling what they would do next. Soon the practitioners or medicine men began to exercise the Ya Ya powers for their own selfish and often evil purposes, and people began to be afraid of them. Then again they were afflicted with the disease of the eyes, and were asked to leave Oraibi. It is said they took all the fetishes representing their animals to seal up in a cave in the cliffs west of Oraibi. Here the fetishes still remain.

Members of the society, however, returned to Walpi, where they occasionally still gave a vestige of the Ya Ya ceremony. There is still a fire-pit on First Mesa, and a Ya Ya was performed there in 1927. Another performance was given in Mishongnovi in 1932.

"It was during my father's lifetime that the Ya Ya was stopped at Oraibi," relates Otto Pentiwa. "At Mishongnovi I saw Masákwaptiwa do one of the magic acts while the men and women were singing—tapping a long heavy pole up and down in a depression in a rock as if it were light as a feather. Soon afterward they got hold of another member of the society, took off some of his costume, and began swinging him up and down above the opening of the kiva. But they did not throw him inside. They had lost the power.

"Maybe it was about the time when the Ya Ya lost its power that the Antelope Society was formed. For Siliómomo, whose father was the antelope, had learned the secret and power of the animal people; and when Ya Ya lost out, the Antelope Society took the power, formed a new ritual, and joined the Snake Society to give the Snake-Antelope ceremony, which is very powerful and is still being performed. For no strange reason do the Antelope Society people use for their rattle a gourd covered with the skin of the testicle from the antelope. That is the way it goes. When you receive a wonderful power and use it for evil you lose the power. You have to use it for good to keep it."

Despite this, a vestige of the Ya Ya ceremony called a Somaíkoli was given at Walpi during the fall of 1961. It was in the form of a public dance, no magical tricks being attempted.

WITCHCRAFT

If the Ya Ya ceremony is finally and formally extinct, it is only because its beliefs and practices have gone underground, spreading throughout all Hopi villages in widely prevalent forms of witchcraft.

Túhikya [Healing Others] is the common name for a medicine man. *Pósi* [Eye], however, is the very respectful name for a medicine man who uses the eye of the animal kingdom, which can see in the dark. These two names derive from *tuvósi* [the animal kingdom], from which came the power of Ya Ya. Hence the name for a witch or sorcerer is *powáqa* [eye, walking, doing], as he uses the magical eye of the animal kingdom for evil purposes.

All *powáqa* are of course Two Hearts, having their own human hearts and animal hearts. They gain new members by witching others or kidnaping sleeping children. These they fly with at night, in the dark of the moon, to Pálangwu [Red Rock Place], a great cliff near the mouth of Canyon de Chelly where the first Ya Ya Ceremony was anciently performed. This place-name derives of course from the word *pangwú* for the bighorn sheep, leader of the animal kingdom. Here in a great kiva inside the rock is the rendezvous of *powáqa* from all over the world. New members are initiated into the evil order during a ceremony like the original Ya Ya. Jumping through a hoop, each is turned into an animal.

Powáqa bring misfortune and evil to others, destroying crops, bringing winds, driving away snow and rain, and shooting ants, insects, hairs, bones, and glass into their victims, causing death. There are four classes of *powáqa*, depending upon their degree of competence.

Members of the first class, the least accomplished, can compensate for the evil they do by giving away the fruits of their harvest to non-relations every four years. The second class, more effective and more evil, can compensate by giving away its ceremonial costumes and valuable turquoise jewelry. The third may also stay out of hell by giving away to non-relations every four years twice as much property of value, blankets and buckskins. If these three classes of *powáqa* do not atone for the evil they do, their penalty is severe. An ordinary man at death re-enters the *sipápuni* and returns to the underworld, from which he is reborn to the next world to continue his Road of Life. A witch or sorcerer, however, returns to the underworld at the rate of only one step a year, being allowed only one drop of water and one kernel of corn to sustain him.

Members of the fourth class of *powáqa,* the most evil of all, live on the lives of others and must pay off in life. They must cause the deaths of their own relatives in order to prolong their own lives, the death of a girl giving them four years of life, and that of a boy two years. When these *powáqa* die they go straight to Tupqölu [Earth Hole Full of Fire— Hell]. Here they remain, suffering, until all the seven worlds are completed and the Creator claims all life throughout the universe.

Nevertheless witchcraft is spreading amongst all Hopis at an alarming rate. There are *powáqa* of both sexes—witches and sorcerers—in all clans, in almost every family. A Hopi does not know which of his neighbors, which of his own brothers and sisters, is a *powáqa* bent on taking his life. Ridden by fear, he adds to his normal humility as a Hopi a cringing, obsequious manner, and suppresses all natural desires to show his talents, assume ritual responsibilities, and ameliorate his poverty. These results of witchcraft, as we shall see in another section, are prime causes in the breaking down of Hopi ceremonialism and social structure.

There has never been a religion, a mysticism, without its negative side. So we have among the Hopis a profound religious structure of nine great ceremonies and one extinct ceremony that embodies all the fears and faults of a people whose innate mysticism is being perverted into witchcraft. Both stem from the same valid source—a myth of divine creation and a legend of continental migrations that stem back into the remote prehistoric past.

PART FOUR

THE HISTORY:

The Lost White Brother

1

The Coming of the Castillas

The coming of the Hopis' lost white brother, Pahána, like the return of the Mayas' bearded white god, Kukulcan, the Toltecan and Aztecan Quetzalcoatl, was a myth so common throughout all pre-Columbian America that we can regard it as arising from a concept rooted in the unconscious. Whatever its symbolic meaning, the event was long hailed by prophecy.

The return of Quetzalcoatl to the Aztecs in Mexico was set by prophecy for the year of his name, CE ACATL. In that year, 1519, he came in the person of Hernán Cortés and his Spanish *conquistadores*. Welcomed as Quetzalcoatl to the court of Moctezuma in Tenochtitlán, Cortés betrayed the emperor's hospitality and laid siege to the Aztec capital. By 1533 it was all over: Cortés with a handful of men had conquered the Aztec Empire and won all Mexico for the crown of Spain.

Seven years later preparations were complete to extend the conquest to the unknown wilderness to the north. In February 1540 Francisco Vásquez de Coronado with a resplendent company of mounted gentlemen and foot-soldiers marched north to the fabled seven golden cities of Cibola, the adobe villages of present Zuñi. After looting and raping in these, Coronado dispatched Pedro de Tovar with seventeen horsemen, a few foot-soldiers, and a Franciscan friar named Juan de Padilla to the so-called province of Tusayan, a hundred miles farther north, which was said to contain seven more villages.

The Hopis in these villages had long anticipated the coming of their lost white brother, Pahána. Every year in Oraibi, on the last day of Soyál, a line was drawn across the six-foot-long stick kept in the custody of the Bear Clan to mark the time for his arrival. The Hopis knew where to meet him: at the bottom of Third Mesa if he was on time, or along the trail at Sikya'wa [Yellow Rock], Chokuwa [Pointed Rock], Nahoyungvasa [Cross Fields], or Tawtoma just below Oraibi, if he was five, ten, fifteen, or twenty years late. Now the stick was filled with markings; Pahána was twenty years late. But he came in the person of the Spaniard Pedro de Tovar, the first white man to be seen by the Hopis.*

Just where the Spaniards and Hopis first met is uncertain. It is believed most probable now that it was below Awatovi on Antelope Mesa. Castañeda, chronicler of the Coronado expedition, relates that the Spaniards arrived after dark and camped at the foot of the mesa. Discovering them next morning, the Hopis came down from their village on top and drew a line of sacred cornmeal across the trail. The Spaniards did not understand its symbolic meaning, nor did they waste time in parley. They spurred their horses forward. One of the Hopis struck a horse on the bridle. Whereupon Padilla, the priest who prided himself upon having been a soldier in his youth, cried out, "Why are we here?" Sounding their battle cry of "Santiago!" the soldiers charged the Hopis with lance and sword, driving them up into Awatovi. Shortly thereafter Tovar received the submission of all the Hopis, who offered presents of cotton cloth, corn, dressed skins, piñon nuts, and turquoise.

Hopi tradition supplements this account by relating that Tovar and his men were conducted to Oraibi. They were met by all the clan chiefs at Tawtoma, as prescribed by prophecy, where four lines of sacred meal were drawn. The Bear Clan leader stepped up to the barrier and extended his hand, palm up, to the leader of the white men. If he was indeed the true Pahána, the Hopis knew he would extend his own hand, palm down, and clasp the Bear Clan leader's hand to form the *nakwách,* the ancient symbol of brotherhood. Tovar instead curtly commanded one of his men to drop a gift into the Bear chief's hand, believing that the Indian wanted a present of some kind. Instantly all the Hopi chiefs knew that Pahána had forgotten the ancient agreement made between their peoples at the time of their separation.

Nevertheless the Spaniards were escorted up to Oraibi, fed and quartered, and the agreement explained to them. It was understood that when the two were finally reconciled, each would correct the other's laws and faults; they would live side by side and share in common all the riches of the land and join their faiths in one religion that would establish the truth of life in a spirit of universal brotherhood. The Spaniards did not understand, and, having found no gold, they soon departed.

The Hopis knew then that Tovar was not the true Pahána and that they could expect trouble. Forever thereafter they referred to these gentlemen of Castile as the Castillas, as *kachada,* white man, or as *dodagee,* the dictator.

Spanish conquest and settlement of all New Mexico followed slowly

---

* By odd coincidence the due date of Pahána's arrival among the Hopis corresponds to that of Quetzalcoatl's arrival among the Aztecs.

but remorselessly, bringing the trouble expected by the Hopis to their remote province of Tusayan. In 1583 the expedition of Antonio de Espejo passed through the area on its way to the west, looking for gold and silver. Again the Hopis welcomed the Castillas, casting cornmeal on the ground for their horses to walk upon, feeding and lodging the men. Upon Espejo's departure he was given four Hopi guides and, as he reports, "4000 mantles of cotton both white and painted, and a great quantity of handkerchiefs purled and stitched"—probably ceremonial blankets and dance kilts.

In November 1598 Juan de Oñate arrived with a great company and received the formal submission of the Hopi villages to the King of Spain.

Missionary efforts to convert the Hopis began in 1629 with the arrival of ten soldiers and three Franciscan friars: Padre Francisco Porras, Andrés Gutiérrez, and Cristóbal de la Concepción. San Bernardino Mission was built at Awatovi, and many Hopis were converted. Four years later Padre Porras was poisoned at Awatovi, but the work continued. By 1674, with the arrival of Padre Figueroa and Augustín de Santa María, the San Miguel Mission at Oraibi, with a *visita* at Walpi, and the San Bartolomé Mission at Shongopovi, with a *visita* at Mishongnovi, had been established.

The hated mission at Oraibi is still referred to as the "slave church." The huge logs used as its roof beams had to be dragged by Hopis from the hills around Kísiwu, forty miles northeast, or from the San Francisco mountains, nearly a hundred miles south. Still today the Hopis point out the great ruts scraped into the soft sandstone of the mesa top by the ends of the heavy logs as they were dragged into place. Enforced labor not only built the church but supplied all the needs of the priests. Tradition recalls that one *padre* would not drink water from any of the springs around Oraibi; he demanded that a runner bring his water from White Sand Spring near Moencopi, fifty miles away. The *padres'* illicit relations with young Hopi girls were common in all villages, and the punishment given Hopis for sacrilege and insubordination added to the growing resentment. It is recorded that at Oraibi in 1655, when Friar Salvador de Guerra caught a Hopi in "an act of idolatry," he thrashed the Hopi in the presence of the whole village till he was bathed in blood, and then poured over him burning turpentine.

Under these strict measures the Hopis adopted Christianity. But with the cessation of their ceremonials the rains stopped. Soon, according to tradition, the crops failed and famine spread over the land. Many Hopis migrated to the villages along the Rio Grande. In despair, those remaining secretly conducted their midsummer ceremony, the Niman Kachina, among the cliffs. Four days later the rains began again, proving to the Hopis that their own ceremonies brought rain and that the Christian religion of the Castillas was not good for them. Slowly they gathered strength to revolt.

The time was ripe. Throughout all New Mexico every other tribe and village was planning to rebel against its ruthless subjugation. The leader of this vast, concerted uprising was Popé, a Tewa Indian of San Juan Pueblo on the Rio Grande, who made as his headquarters the always obdurate pueblo of Taos. Knotted cords were sent to each village indicating August 13, 1680, as the day to strike. The secret leaked out, and Popé struck at once—on August 10. Every pueblo revolted; the Indians killed nearly five hundred Spaniards, including twenty-one missionaries at their altars, tore down churches, destroyed government and church records, sacked Santa Fe, and drove the surviving Spaniards back to Mexico.

The Hopis in Oraibi describe in meticulous detail their part in this historic Pueblo Revolt. In making plans to kill the *padres* and the soldiers guarding them, the clans met in secret and designated the Badger Clan as their leader. The Badger Clan, being related to the Kachina Clan, would dress in *kachina* masks and costumes so that its members would not be recognizable in case any Castilla should escape. The two strongest Hopis wore the masks of the Warrior Kachina. One of them was named Haneeya [Name of the Song He Sang], and the other was called Chavayo after the knife he carried.

At dawn the call of a screech owl signaled the attack. Led by the *kachinas,* all clans rushed to the church and the priests' quarters. Chavayo killed the soldier guarding the entrance. Then the fighting began, some Hopis forcing their way inside to kill the Castilla soldiers, and others battering holes through the roof to reach the room of the priests. It was Haneeya who finally dropped inside to kill the priests with his flint knife.

There is little documentary evidence of the Hopi revolt, but the deaths of four friars have been established: those of Padre José de Figueroa at Awatovi, Padre José de Trujillo at Shongopovi, and Padre José de Espeleta and Padre Augustín de Santa María of Oraibi and Walpi, who were reported to have been thrown over the cliffs at Oraibi. The Hopis assert that the bodies of the two priests killed at Oraibi were carried to the bottom of the cliffs and buried under an avalanche, and all their vestments hidden in the rocks. The large church bell, the chalices and small bells were sealed in a cave with the swords and armor of the soldiers. The spears or lances of the soldiers were given to the One Horn Society to use during the performance of the Wúwuchim ceremony.* Then the

---

* It is said that Homer Naquahoniwa, a One Horn priest of Oraibi, now has in his custody four of these lances, which he loans to the One Horns of Hotevilla to carry during Wúwuchim.

church was completely obliterated; every stone was carried away, and the huge beams were utilized in the kivas. Only the sheep and cattle were spared, being divided among the people—marking the beginning of Hopi stock raising and weaving with wool instead of cotton.

The Pueblo Revolt of 1680, then, completely ejected for a time all the hated Castillas. The true Pahána, the symbol of all America's deep-rooted need and vision of the universal brotherhood of man, was yet to come.

ARRIVAL OF THE HEAD–POUNDERS

Shortly before or after the coming of the Castillas a strange tribe of barbarians began to trickle into the Hopi villages. Today they are known as Navajos, an Athabascan people who had entered this continent through the Back Door to the north. To the Hopis they became known as the Tavasuh, derived from Tusavuhta [tu—person, savuhta—to pound], because they killed a captured enemy by pounding his head with a rock or stone ax.

At first only one stranger came, hungry and without weapons, his long hair uncombed, clothed only in the skin of a wild animal. Then little bands of men, women, and children came, all dressed the same way, all hungry and homeless. The Hopis were good to these barbarians. They fed and sheltered them. They taught them to work in the fields, to weave baskets, and to spin cotton. The Tavasuh would not learn to make pottery, however, because they would not eat any food that was boiled in a pot, only food that was cooked over an open fire. They were sharp observers, and, although they were not allowed to participate in any ceremonies, they learned what went on and began to copy some of the simple rituals such as páho-making. Their two outstanding characteristics were that they had no legends to tell the Hopis during the winter story-telling period, and that they never stopped eating until everything was gone. The Tavasuh called the Hopis the Corn Eaters.

Pretty soon large bands of Tavasuh came every year at harvest time, camping above Kuymahwah [Face Painting White Rock], on the Hotevilla Spring trail. Two other tribes began to visit the Hopis about this time—the Paiutes and the Conena [from Yavaconeni, the "Far Away People"]. The Conena, now known as the Supais, Yavapais, and Havasupais, always brought things to trade for corn: beautifully tanned deerskins, a food called sahu which was made from bulbs of the yucca plant, and horn dippers greatly treasured by all Hopi women. These dippers were made from the horns of the bighorn sheep so numerous in the

Grand Canyon area where the Conena lived. The horns were first boiled, then steamed to softness in a fire-pit covered with wet sand. They were then pounded and molded into the shape of large dippers. The Paiutes were poorer, more lazy, and less friendly, but they wove large, strong baskets to trade for corn and beans.

The Conena and Paiutes always left when harvesting and trading were over, but the Tavasuh stayed until everything was gone. Soon the Tavasuh began to steal corn from the stalks, then piles of corn drying in the sun. It became necessary for the Hopis to guard their fields and homes day and night. Bad feeling grew up between the Hopis and the Tavasuh. This changed to war when the Tavasuh burned Hopi cornfields and killed some Hopi men, which happened soon after the Castillas were driven out of Oraibi.

One day the Crier Chief awakened the village with a war cry. A large war party of Tavasuh was massed in the valley. The campfires spread from Savatuk [Pound Rock Point] to Kalava [Sparrow Hawk Spring]. Immediately all the sheep were driven into the village, the streets were posted with guards, and the men were called to arm themselves for battle next morning. Each man was provided with a club or bow and arrows, and two or three stout buckskins to wear as armor.

At dawn they sallied forth. Obeying the chief's order, they did not draw their bows but waited for the Tavasuh to shoot the first arrow and so take the blood of battle upon themselves. Till noon they waited, but nothing happened. Years later a Tavasuh revealed why his people had not attacked the Hopis. They had a vision of two tall men dressed in white and armed with shield and spear who marched back and forth in front of the Hopis to guard them.

Shortly after noon a strange thing happened. A woman with a spear burst out of the ranks of the Tavasuh, calling them cowards and men with faint hearts and demanding that they follow her. Two Tavasuh warriors, carrying shields to protect her, advanced to the Hopi line. Knowing this meant the start of battle, the Hopi chief gave the word to attack. Whereupon a Hopi threw his throwing-stick with a wide, rolling motion. The stick flipped over the shield of one of the warriors, struck the man on the head, and killed him. The battle then began.

It was a terrible fight, but by sundown the Tavasuh had been driven back to Botatukaovi and thence to Coiled Basket Cliff. The hero was Chiya [Being Sifted], a Hopi warrior of the Sand Clan, a young man at the height of his strength and courage who could run all day without getting tired. Many stories are told of his bravery as he leaped out from behind rocks to kill one Tavasuh after another. That night the Hopis returned to Oraibi, bringing those wounded by clubs and arrows. Next morning they went out to see the bodies of the dead. They were a terrible sight, so terrible that Chiya had bad dreams night after night and had to be given ceremonial help before he was finally cured of them.

This victory stopped for a time the depredations of the Tavasuh, but the Hopis were left with a great sadness. They were a People of Peace who did not believe in war, yet they had been forced into killing both the Tavasuh and the Castillas in order to protect their homes and their religion. This was an omen of more trouble to come. And it came from both the Tavasuh and the Castillas, who soon returned to destroy forever the deep inward peace of the Hopis.

2

The Destruction of Awatovi

For twelve years after the Pueblo Revolt of 1680 all the province of New Mexico enjoyed independence from Spanish rule. Then came the wave of the Reconquest with Don Diego de Vargas riding on its crest.

The resubjugation of the rebellious territory was far from being impelled by pride and patriotism. De Vargas had gained attention of the crown as *justica mayor* of the mining camp of Tlalpujohua. After being placed in charge of the royal supply of quicksilver, he was recommended to the viceroy. Conde de Galve promptly granted De Vargas the governorship of the deserted province and sent him a letter which read in part: "I understand that within the rebellious area of New Mexico lies a province called Moqui,* and that twelve leagues from it in the direction of the Rio Grande is situated one of the most important of its ranges from which are extracted the minerals or vermilion-colored soil used by the Indians to daub themselves." ** De Vargas was requested to investigate thoroughly this soft and butter-like substance, which was believed to be a high-grade ore of quicksilver. The viceroy did not have to state that a royal decree already had been issued to him, advising that "without bringing about the subjection of New Mexico first, it was vain to discuss the advantages which might accrue from developing the quicksilver mines." De Vargas was well aware of the advantages to the new governor who should find these rich deposits of quicksilver. He promptly outfitted an expedition at his own expense and set forth.

Within a few months after his arrival, De Vargas was able to report on November 30, 1692, the subjection of seventy-three pueblos, although he had found no trace of the mercuric ores. His method of reconquest was simple. He promised forgiveness and gifts of sheep, cattle, and horses

---

* The origin of the name Moqui, as the Hopi were first called, is related in Part Two, Chapter 7.

** The colored clay used by Indians in this vicinity as body paint was discovered nearly three centuries later to be uranium ore. The discovery, credited to Paddy Martinez, a Navajo, stimulated the uranium boom in northwest New Mexico.

to all pueblos that would resubmit to Spanish rule. When he marched to the province of the "Moquis," he apparently had no difficulty in securing the resubmission of Awatovi, Walpi, Shongopovi, and Mishongnovi on these terms. There is no Spanish record that he entered Oraibi, which he may have found too hostile.

The Hopis of Oraibi, however, assert that De Vargas did enter the village, offering gifts in return for its resubmission. The chiefs obdurately refused allegiance to the Castillas and their "slave church" again, affirming their belief in their own religion and traditional way of life. "Take your gifts to the other villages east of us. Let them accept them or not. We speak for ourselves. This we say." Still today the village takes pride in the fact that it did not submit to Spanish rule.

So the Castillas drove away their sheep, cattle, and horses, which were accepted by Awatovi, Walpi, Shongopovi, and Mishongnovi. Oraibi, however, still prospered from their acceptance, many of its inhabitants trading for stock. Increasing rapidly under the prayers and *páhos* made for them, herds were soon grazing as far as the Little Colorado, Koyunkpa [Turkey Spring], Shumavi [Noise of the River], and Wacasva [Cow Spring] north of Moencopi. Here at Cow Spring was erected a shrine, a stone carved in the shape of Mother Cow, to bless the cattle and to mark the northern boundary of Hopi grazing land.

With this peaceful prelude there burst the terrible calamity which seared the Hopis with an ineradicable guilt they were to bear forever.

AWATOVI

Early in the spring of 1700 Padre Juan Garaycoechea visited Awatovi and persuaded seventy-three Hopis to be baptized. This effort to re-establish Christianity aroused resentment in the other Hopi villages. Slow to anger, they waited until the *padre* returned to Zuñi. Then in October they sent the chief of Oraibi with a delegation of twenty men to Santa Fe to ask for religious toleration. Governor Cubero rejected their plea. The Hopis then requested that the *padres* should not be sent to live with them permanently, but should visit one village each year for six years. This request was also refused. With the return of the unsuccessful delegation, the hatred of the Hopis for the "slave church" burst into flame.

Awatovi was an important village, reported at that time to have nearly eight hundred inhabitants. Its name, as we have previously noted, meant the "Place of the Bow," as it had been founded by the ceremonially powerful Bow Clan before it moved to Oraibi. However, its sister clan,

Figure 59. Religious leader, Awatovi

the Arrowshaft Clan, still resided in Awatovi. This posed a ceremonial problem. For just as a bow and arrow are no good separately, it was necessary for the Bow and Arrowshaft Clans to reunite in order to complete the ritual of the Two Horn Society. Other important clans residing in Awatovi included the Badger, Eagle, Parrot, and Tobacco. The nuclei of these clans had been accepted into Oraibi to complete the religious quorum. Yet mural paintings on the walls of the kiva at Awatovi reveal that other members of these clans still lived in Awatovi, carrying out their rituals in unison with the ceremonies being performed in Oraibi.

Figure 59 is an important religious leader, as shown by the feather on his head, the band painted across his chest, and the brown-dyed feather worn beside his ear. His costume, markings, and necklace are similar to those of the figures found in kiva murals at Kuaua and Pottery Mound, indicating their occupation by Hopi clans.

Figure 60. Arrowshaft Clan deity

Figure 60 symbolizes the deity of the Arrowshaft Clan who delivers the *páhos* to the highest being, the Creator. His black color shows that this powerful spiritual being travels to regions beyond man's knowledge. Two lightning symbols worn on the kilt hanging on his side show that he is related to both the Bow and Arrowshaft Clans in Awatovi and Oraibi. He has just received the *páhos,* which he is holding in both hands. They are made from the wing feathers of a sparrow hawk, representing its swiftness and power when used during the important Wúwuchim ceremony.

Figure 61. Corn mural

The corn mural shown in Figure 61 forms what is called the "House" in Hopi ritual. In Oraibi the corn was gathered from each home at the time of Soyál, blessed by the chief in the Chief Kiva, and then stacked, one ear on top of another, under the altar known as the Altar House. The murals had been done away with in Oraibi, being replaced by sand paintings under the altar during the Wúwuchim, Soyál, and Powamu ceremonies. At Awatovi, as this mural shows, the mural painting was still used as a backdrop for the ceremony. The eleven ears of corn represented the eleven Awatovi clans participating. The earth-brown color below them symbolized the warm earth, and the black indicated the depth of moisture necessary for the growth of corn. The paintings on each side represent the staff of the leader conducting the rituals.

The eleven ears of corn are of all colors, representing the directions: yellow, blue, white, and red. The one ear marked with cross-hatching indicates that it is a Mother, the most perfect of all ears, the mark # symbolizing the perfect pattern of life. The ceremony at Awatovi thus was directed toward the establishment of the perfect plan of Creation among its inhabitants—which was now menaced by the introduction of the foreign Christian church.

Figure 62. Eagle Clan symbols

Figure 62 indicates the importance of the Eagle Clan at Awatovi. The stylized figure of the eagle to the left has its head missing, destroyed by weather. It holds in its claws the present world and the world to come, both immersed in the forces of water symbolized by the band below. To the left is the sun symbol still painted on *kachina* rattles; underneath is the skunk (see previous description of Pottery Mound); and to the right is the sun symbol divided into the four directional colors. To the right of the eagle is a corn jar containing seeds of corn, and above it is a squash also containing seeds.

Hence the conversion of Awatovi to the foreign Christian church and the abandonment of its ceremonies was a menace that threatened the whole pattern of Hopi ceremonialism. It came at a crucial time, for there had been some ill feeling between Awatovi and Oraibi as a result of ceremonial races between the two villages. To add to the dissension there was apparently a growing rivalry between two leaders in Awatovi: the chief Tapolou [Arch in Rainbow Formed by Reflection of the Sun], a member of the Sun Clan, and a man named Sachvantewa [One Who Paints the Earth Green]. Tapolou had repeatedly warned his people not to encourage the advent of the foreign religion. When they refused to heed him Tapolou went secretly to the chief of Oraibi, accused his people of betraying their faith in their traditional religion, and asked that they all be killed.

It was now late October or early November, just before the time for Wúwuchim, the first of the great ceremonies beginning the annual cycle. It was inconceivable that this symbolic portrayal of the first phase of Creation, establishing the pattern of life for the year, be polluted and nullified by Awatovi's participation in Christian rites. Time was short; drastic action had to be taken at once. Accordingly a secret meeting of the chiefs of all other villages was called: Oraibi, Walpi, Shongopovi, and Mishongnovi. Here it was decided that Awatovi should be destroyed. The attack was planned for the first night of Wúwuchim, when all the men of Awatovi would be meeting in the kiva.

Accordingly large bands of men from all these villages met at a spring not far from Awatovi on the designated night. Each man was armed with weapons, a cedar-bark torch, and a bundle of greasewood. Shortly before dawn they marched silently up to the top of the mesa. Long before, the Castillas had built along the east side of the village a wall whose only opening was a stout wooden door. Tapolou was waiting. He opened the door to the armed attackers, who quickly ran through the streets and converged at the kiva where the men were assembled.

The attackers immediately drew up the ladder, trapping the occupants of the kiva inside, and began shooting arrows down through the roof opening. In countless fire-pits throughout the village fires had been maintained throughout the night for cooking food for the feast next day. From these, other bands of assailants lighted their torches and ran through the streets, setting fire to the village. Reaching the kiva, they cast down inside bundles of burning greasewood. Awatovi was famous for the red peppers grown in the terraced gardens of the mesa. It was now late fall, and every house was hung with strings of peppers drying in the sun. These the attackers tore down, crushed in their hands, and flung down into the burning kiva also.

When all the helpless men trapped in the burning kiva were killed, the attackers ran through the streets of the village, murdering other men, boys, women, and children. By dawn the massacre was almost complete. The survivors were dragged to the sand hills below Mishongnovi. Here many of them were tortured, dismembered, and left to die at the spot now known as Maschomo [Death Mound]. The remaining few women and girls were then divided among the villages of Oraibi, Walpi, Shongopovi, and Mishongnovi.*

The women and girls spared were those who had not been baptized and who were versed in their own rituals, knowing their own clan songs

---

* Reported by J. W. Fewkes, 17th Annual Smithsonian Report, 1898, from the version given by the village chief of Walpi. Other versions relate that the distribution of survivors was made at Walpi.

and prayers or possessing their *tiponis*. Several members of the Bow, Badger, Sun, Tobacco, and Rabbit Clans were brought to Oraibi, thus perpetuating some Awatovi rituals and strengthening these clan units in Oraibi.

The long-pent-up fury of the Hopis was still not spent. The following day they returned to smoking Awatovi, tore down house walls, smashed pottery bowls, broke grinding stones and weaving sets—destroyed every article used by the massacred inhabitants. By nightfall the destruction of Awatovi was complete. It was an empty, smoking ruin abandoned to the elements and left to be buried by drifting sand.* What became of Tapolou is not recorded. According to Oraibi tradition he went to live in one of the pueblos along the Rio Grande.

The almost complete obliteration of Awatovi was for the purpose of rooting out forever the growing influence of the foreign Christian "slave church" and preserving unchanged traditional Hopi ceremonialism. That purpose was achieved. For more than a century the Hopis in their isolated province successfully resisted the re-establishment of mission churches and all attempts to convert them.

One of the most famous Franciscan missionaries to court martyrdom later was Fray Francisco Garcés. In 1775 he made his way alone from the Colorado River to the Hopi mesas. Visiting the Havasupais, he was the first white man to see the Grand Canyon from the west, possibly from the site of El Tovar. Thence, jogging alone on his mule, he finally reached Oraibi on the evening of July 2. All the following day the weary *padre* tried to make friends. No Hopi would listen to him or even sell him corn. Again that night he camped in the street. Next morning four chiefs came up and sternly demanded that he leave. Garcés sadly packed his mule. "Having arranged my things," he reported, "I mounted on her back, showing by my smiling face how much I appreciated their pueblo and their fashions." To make sure that he left their country, a crowd of villagers escorted him out of Oraibi. It was July 4, 1776, and the Hopis were declaring their own independence.

Late that November the equally famous Franciscan, Fray Silvestre Vélez de Escalante and his party passed through the region on their way to Santa Fe. At Oraibi they were given food but also ordered to leave at once.

---

* J. W. Fewkes, who excavated it in 1892, reports finding evidence of wholesale slaughter near the outbuildings of the church, in the kivas, and throughout the whole eastern section of the village. "The earth was literally filled with bones, evidently hastily placed there or left where the dead fell. These bodies were not buried with pious care. . . . Many of the skulls were broken, some pierced with sharp implements. . . . I was deterred from further excavation at that place [one of the chambers where many died] by the horror of my workmen at the desecration of the chamber."

Still today, nearly two centuries later, there is no Roman Catholic church in the villages of Second and Third Mesa, although the Hopis have permitted the entrance of other Christian missionaries and churches.*

The terrible tragedy of Awatovi, however, must be measured in other terms—by its effect upon the Hopis themselves. Their complete destruction of one of their own villages, and their ruthless massacre of their own people for betraying a human tolerance toward a new faith, was an act of religious bigotry that equaled if it did not surpass the cruelty of the hated Christian "slave church" itself. For the Hopis were a People of Peace, dedicated since their Emergence to a universal plan of Creation which ever sought to maintain in unbroken harmony the lives of every entity—mineral, plant, animal, and man. Now, in one act of unrestrained hate and violence, they had committed a fratricidal crime of mass murder that nullified their own faith and stamped forever an ineradicable guilt upon the heart of every Hopi. It revealed for the first time a hidden and immeasurable chasm between Hopi religious perfectionism and its attainment in human terms. Never again could the Hopis justify their supreme religious idealism as a faith more workable than others. Awatovi revealed also a schizophrenic rift that was to keep widening. The principal motif of all the migration legends, as we have seen, was a quarrel between two brothers in the same clan or between the leaders of two clans, resulting in a split, a separation, or the formation of a new clan. These were minor breaches that did not impede the unification of all the clans at their final, ordained place of settlement. But now for the first time we see with the destruction of Awatovi a major split among inhabitants of whole villages, a rent in the web of Hopi brotherhood. It was a definitive expression of the Hopi theme of intertribal schisms that was to be restated years later in the disastrous Oraibi split of 1906 and in the following split at Hotevilla, both impelled by religious differences. The ruin of Awatovi is the first great monument to the tragic defeat of the Hopi spirit of universal brotherhood by the frailties of the flesh.

INTERREGNUM

With the coming of the Tavasuh and the Castillas early in historical times Hopi life began to change. One village after another was moved from its original location to the top of the mesa, where it could be better protected from attack by the Navajos and the Spaniards.

---

* The Catholic church on First Mesa, and the Baptist, Mormon, Holy Gospel, and non-denominational churches, are said to be results of the influence of the Tewa people in Hano.

Walpi was moved from the lowest terrace on the northern and western sides of First Mesa to the summit of its western spur. Shongopovi, built on a ridge of foothills to the east and near the spring, moved to its present site on top of Second Mesa. Mishongnovi moved to the mesa top from its ancient site not far from Corn Rock below. Only Oraibi remained, on the lofty summit of Third Mesa.

There came also a new influx of Tewa or Tanoan people from the Rio Grande villages, fleeing the wrath of the Spaniards. They were given permission to settle on top of First Mesa in return for guarding the trail up through the Gap. Their village is now known as Hano, and their descendants still speak their original language, as well as Hopi.

With the Spaniards had come the horse, and with horses the Navajos now rose swiftly into prominence. The record of Coronado's expedition made no mention of the Navajos; it is probable that none were seen. But by 1776 the region was marked on Escalante's map as the "Provincia de Navajoo." And in the report of the commander-general of the Interior Provinces of New Spain, drawn in 1785, he carefully recorded that "the Navajo nation has 700 families more or less with four or five persons to each one in its five divisions of San Matheo, Zebolleta or Cañon, Chusca, Hozo, Chelli, with its thousand men of arms; that their possessions consist of 500 tame horses; 600 mares with their corresponding stallions and young; about 700 black ewes, 40 cows also with their bulls and calves, all looked after with the greatest care and diligence for their increase."

With horses the semi-nomadic Navajos could move swiftly and widely. Superb horsemen, they raided not only the villages of the sedentary Hopis but other Indian villages and Spanish settlements on the Rio Grande. Soon they were running off sheep, cattle, and still more horses from the outskirts of the royal villa of Santa Fe itself. At no time did the Spaniards feel equal to the task of "surrounding them and pressing upon them from all sides at once" although "there existed an almost constant condition of warfare with that powerful tribe." The Navajos in turn boasted that they let the Spaniards live on only because of their "usefulness as shepherds to the tribe." Their taunt was not exaggerated. Wild and unrestrained, proud and arrogant, the Navajos were making themselves masters of the vast desert wilderness surrounding the small Hopi villages on their lofty mesas.

Still for a century after the Spanish reconquest the Hopis enjoyed an interregnum comparatively free from foreign domination.

Time and again companies of mounted Spaniards pursued bands of marauding Navajos. Those captured were taken back to Santa Fe and sold as slaves to work on the haciendas throughout the region. Often these companies entered the Hopi villages, causing more trouble. One instance, which illustrates the life of that time, is related in detail by several living Hopi spokesmen who heard it from the lips of the participants. It happened in 1832, when preparations were being made for Soyál.

Seaknoya's uncle, a young boy then, and Tuvengyamsi's grandmother, Naquamuysee [Prayer Feathers Flown Bright], who was a small girl, both remembered that it was about four or five days before Soyál when the Castilla soldiers rode into Oraibi. All the Hopi men were in the kivas making *páhos,* and the women were busy making *piki* for the feast. The Castillas made camp near the earth dam, where they could water their horses, and were given food by the Hopis.

Then, on that terrible morning, the Castillas rode into the Snake plaza. They blew their brass horn. Then they began to run through the streets after children, firing their *eamunkinpi* [guns] at the men who ran out of the kivas. Seaknoya's uncle saw Hoyentewa [One Who Inspects Traps] shot while he was trying to protect his son, and watched a Tewa or Taos warrior with the Castillas scalp Wuhwuhpa [Long Ear of Corn]. Naquamuysee watched a Castilla soldier grab a little boy named Lomaesva. At the same time his father rushed out of a kiva and threw a blanket around the boy to protect him. While the two men were fighting for possession of the boy, a second Spaniard came up and shot his gun. The boy and his father fell to the ground and blood began to run out. But in a little while Lomaesva crawled out from under the blanket alive. His father lay there; he was dead.

A little girl named Kaeuhamana [Corn Girl] was sitting on a housetop with her sister Neseehongneum [One Who Carries a Flower on the Day of the Ceremony], both wrapped in a blue blanket, when a soldier captured her. She was about seven years old. A little boy about the same age, Masavehma [Butterfly Wings Painted], was captured too. Altogether there were fourteen children captured, and with them was the young wife of Wickvaya [One Who Brings]. Two Castillas were killed during the fight. The Hopis later buried them in a dry wash east of Oraibi and drove stock over the graves.

The Castillas then drove off the Hopi sheep and with the fourteen captured children marched back to Santa Fe. All during the trip the soldiers raped the young wife of Wickvaya. Masavehma remembered that Corn Girl, being so little, was tied on a horse so she wouldn't fall off. But the horse ran away. The rope came loose. And Corn Girl fell and was kicked so hard that the horse's hoof left its print under her chin.

In Santa Fe all the children were sold as slaves to different families. Masavehma was bought by a Spanish couple, loaded in that thing with two wheels, and carried to their home far away at La Junta [Colorado?]. He was lucky. The Spanish couple had no children. They gave him the name of Tomás, dressed him in warm clothes, fed him good food, and treated him like their son. The work he liked to do was to gather the eggs laid by their many *kowakas* [chickens], and to drive the *molas* [mules] to pasture. In a little while he forgot his homesickness and liked it all right.

Meanwhile, in Oraibi, Wickvaya was wild with anger and determined to get his young wife back. So he packed *piki* and *tosi* in a bag which he made out of her wedding dress, and started out on foot alone. He went to Ceohhe [Zuñi], and from there to Cheyawepa [Isleta], where he met a man who spoke Spanish. This man went with him to see the Spanish captain in the governor's palace in Santa Fe. There it was explained to him that the children captured by his soldiers were Hopis, not enemy Navajos. The captain was sick in bed, but this made him so angry that he jumped out of bed, called all his soldiers, and sent for all the captured children and the people who had bought them. Wickvaya waited and waited until his young wife was brought into the crowded room. Seeing him, his wife was so ashamed at that which had been done to her that she covered her head with her blanket, and it was more shame and sadness for Wickvaya to see her shame.

Masavehma was finally brought in by his new parents. All were closely questioned by the captain. Finding that the boy had not been mistreated, he released the Spanish couple. They hugged Masavehma and went home weeping without him. Then he, with all the other captured children, was taken to witness the punishment meted out to their captors. Some were stood up in front of a grave they had dug, and shot. Others were dragged to death by wild horses. Still others had iron balls with sharp spikes tied to their feet, so that as they walked the spikes dug into their feet. At the same time each was forced to keep throwing another spiked iron ball secured to a chain over his shoulder, the spikes digging into his back at every throw. All this was witnessed by the Hopi children so that they could tell their people how the wicked soldiers had been punished for mistaking the peaceful Hopis for marauding Navajos.

The captured children were then escorted safely home. Ahpa, a medicine man from Walpi who lived in Oraibi, was one of the Hopis who helped bring them back. He often told how he carried Corn Girl on his back. Years later Masavehma married Corn Girl, and this was one of the stories they always told.

All this happened in 1832, which is said to be the last time the Castillas came to Oraibi.

But now a new breed of white men began to appear.

3

Arrival of the Americans

The forerunners of these new white men were trappers: Mountain Men such as Old Bill Williams, who threw in with the Hopis for some time during 1827; Joe Meek, a member of the Rocky Mountain Fur Company party which passed through the Hopi villages in 1834; a dozen —a hundred others. They were followed by a growing stream of explorers, surveyors, agents, missionaries, and settlers that never ceased.

Unlike the Tavasuh, who came from the north, and the Castillas, who came from the south, these new arrivals came from the east—the Atlantic *páso*. They were white men, but not the true Pahána still expected by the Hopis. They were Americans, whose westward march of empire soon brought them to the Hopi mesas. The means by which they swiftly expanded their new nation were far different from the spearthrusts of conquest achieved by the Spaniards with their bold *entradas*. They simply bought the land from whatever foreign rival claimed it, then took legal possession of it. The land was resold to private enterprises which could develop its natural resources, and thrown open to settlers who soon petitioned for admittance as a new state in the confederation of the United States of America. The primary sanctity of property rights was the economic, political, and philosophical basis of the new nation—the premise that was to challenge the Hopis' immemorial religious rights to their ancient homeland granted them by Másaw, its spiritual guardian.

The background events that made possible this economic conquest occurred far beyond the limits of the land itself. In 1803 the United States acquired the Louisiana Purchase from France—which had extorted it from Spain—almost doubling the size of the nation. It consisted of some 909,000 square miles bought pig-in-a-poke for about two and a half cents an acre. This was followed by the acquisition of more territory ceded by Spain in 1819 as its domination of the New World began to wane.

In 1822 Mexico won its independence. But its ownership of the vast province of New Mexico was threatened that same year when William Becknell, a Missouri trader, arrived in Santa Fe with a wagon train of merchandise. Two years later the spring caravan brought in $30,000 worth of goods, returning with $190,000 worth of furs, gold, and silver. By 1844 the value of merchandise carried had increased to $450,000. With this diversion of trade from the new republic of Mexico by way of the old Chihuahua Trail, to the new republic of the United States by way of the new Santa Fe Trail, a change in the ownership of the vast wilderness was indicated—a change to be effected not by the sword and cross, but by the dollar, the greatest weapon for conquest and colonization ever known.

On May 13, 1846, President Polk announced the existence of a state of war between Mexico and the United States. Immediately a secret agent, James Magoffin, was sent to the governors of the Mexican provinces of New Mexico, California, and Chihuahua with ample credit to entertain and an "unlimited capacity for drinking wine and making friends." He was followed by General Stephen W. Kearny, commanding the Army of the West, who entered Santa Fe on August 18. He was cordially received by Governor Vigil and given a salute of thirteen guns. The American flag was raised over the *palacio,* the people were absolved from allegiance to Mexico, and the area was proclaimed a territory of the United States. Not a shot had been fired.

Mexico, however, did not accede to this bloodless conquest until the following year when an American expedition under General Winfield Scott marched from Vera Cruz to Mexico City. The matter was concluded on February 2, 1848, with the signing of the Treaty of Guadalupe Hidalgo by the two republics. By its terms Mexico ceded to the United States, in return for $15,000,000, all the territory north of the Rio Grande by way of the Gila River to the Pacific Ocean, including what are now the states of New Mexico, Arizona, Utah, Nevada, and California.

Shortly afterward, on September 9, 1850, the great portion of this huge wilderness area extending on the west to California was created the Territory of New Mexico. The Hopis now found themselves under the jurisdiction of a third foreign nation, the United States.

Less than a month later the Hopis sent a delegation to the first Indian agent at Santa Fe to ascertain the attitude of the new government toward them. This visit threw into immediate relief the whole, still continuing problem of the Hopis vis-à-vis the national government of the United States.

THE LETTERS OF JAMES S. CALHOUN

Early in 1849 an unusual and dedicated man, James S. Calhoun, had been persuaded by the United States Commissioner of Indian Affairs to go to Santa Fe in the capacity of the first Indian agent in that important and troublesome area. Shortly after he arrived, the Territory of New Mexico was created, and on January 9, 1851, Calhoun was appointed by President Fillmore as its first governor. Hence, from his first letter to the commissioner, dated July 29, 1849, to his last one on April 6, 1852, his bulky correspondence, so little known and appreciated now, constitutes an important and intimate record of the first years of our sovereignty over this newly acquired vast wilderness.*

From the very start Calhoun was sympathetic to the Hopis and apprehensive of the marauding Navajos. As a basis he accepted Charles Bent's report: "The Moquis are neighbors of the Navajos and live in permanent villages, cultivate grain and fruits, and raise all varieties of stock. They were formerly a very numerous tribe in the possession of large stocks and herds but have been reduced in numbers and possessions by their more warlike neighbors and enemies, the Navajos. The Moquis are an intelligent and industrious people, their manufactures are the same as those of the Navajos. They number about 350 families or about 2450 souls."

In his first letter, July 29, 1849, Calhoun estimated the Navajos at from 1000 to 2000 families or from 7000 to 14,000 souls, who had no villages but roamed over the country, having 10,000 head of horses, mules, and asses, 500,000 sheep, and 3000 head of horned cattle.

By October 13, the date of his eighth letter, he had ascertained that "there were seven pueblos of Moquis, six having a language of their own and different from all the others, and one the language of the six." He reported them to be "decidedly pacific in character, opposed to all wars, quite honest, and very industrious. It is said, in years gone by, these Indians abandoned a village because its soil had been stained with the blood of a human being"—evidently referring to the bloody massacre and abandonment of Awatovi.

Calhoun, then, was undoubtedly most receptive to the Hopi delegation sent him within a month after the creation of the Territory of New Mexico. In his letter number 82, sent to the Commissioner of Indian Affairs on October 12, 1850, he reports the meeting:

The seven Moqui Pueblos sent to me a deputation who presented themselves on the 6th day of this month. Their object, as announced, was

---

* *The Official Correspondence of James S. Calhoun.* Washington: Bureau of Indian Affairs, Government Printing Office, 1915.

to ascertain the purposes and views of the government of the United States towards them. They complained bitterly of the depredations of the Navajos.

The deputation consisted of the Cacique of *all* the Pueblos, and a *chief* of the largest Pueblo, accompanied by two who were not officials. From what I could learn from the Cacique, I came to the conclusion that each of the seven Pueblos was an independent Republic, having confederated for mutual protection. One of the popular errors of the day is, there are but five of these Pueblos remaining; another is, that one of the Pueblos speak a different language from the other six.

I understood the Cacique to say, the seven spoke the same language, but the Pueblo in which he resided, Tanoquevi, spoke also the language of the Pueblo of Santo Domingo—hence the error first mentioned.

These Pueblos may be, all, visited in one day. They are supposed to be located about due West from Sante Fe, and from three to four days travel, Northwest, from Zuni. The following was given to me as the names of their Pueblos:

1. Oriva
2. Somonpovi
3. Juparavi
4. Mansana
5. Opquive
6. Chemovi
7. Tanoquevi

I understood, further, they regarded as a small Pueblo, Zuni, as compared with Oriva. The other Pueblos were very much like Zuni and Santo Domingo. They supposed Oriva could turn out one thousand warriors. I desired, and believed it to be important to visit these Indians, and would have done so if Colonel Munroe had not, in reply to my application for an escort, replied that he could not furnish me one at this time. They left me apparently highly gratified at the reception and presents given to them. These Indians ought to be visited at an early day.

This was a most significant report, for it is apparently the record of the first official meeting between representatives of the Hopis and of the United States Government. It brings out two principal points: that the Hopis were evidently satisfied with the purposes and views of the new government toward them, and that they relied upon the government to protect them from marauding Navajos.

This attitude of the Hopis was far different from that of the Zuñis. The Navajos had just made another attack upon Zuñi, despite the fact that United States Dragoons were in sight. The Zuñis protested, claiming that they could muster 597 warriors but had only 42 muskets because the United States Government would not issue them arms to defend themselves. Whereupon 50 old muskets were sent to Zuñi. The Hopis, who asserted that their village of Oriva (Oraibi) could turn out 1000 warriors, made no such request for arms and evidently from the start left it to the new government to defend them.

Another interesting point is Calhoun's correct conclusion that each of the Hopi villages constituted an independent "republic"—bearing out the lack of unity that had always existed.

Apparently Calhoun never did get the opportunity to visit the Hopi villages. Not only did his appointment as governor multiply the work and problems thrust upon him, but he could not obtain from the dragoons an armed escort. Nevertheless, shortly after becoming governor, he issued on March 18, 1851, a proclamation asking all able-bodied male citizens of the territory to enlist in a volunteer corps to pursue and attack hostile Indians plundering the settlements. The same proclamation was sent to the cacique, the governors, and the principals of all pueblos, requesting them to abstain from all friendly intercourse with Navajos and to make war on them if they came into the neighborhood.

His continuing attempts to stop the depredations of the Navajos against the peaceful Hopis and other pueblos and settlements were the main concern of the overworked and ailing first governor of New Mexico. His last letter, on April 6, 1852, begged the government once more to send assistance against these hostile Indians. He sat up in his sickbed to sign his name.

Steadily ailing and knowing that he would soon die, Calhoun ordered his coffin made. Then at last he was granted leave to return to his home back East. He never got there. A brief report in William Walker's *Journal* under the date of July 2, 1852, records his untimely end: "The corpse of Governor Calhoun who died on the road from Santa Fe to Kansas was bro't in for burial. He is to be buried with Masonic Honors. What train bro't the remains in is yet unknown."

THE HOPI VIEW

The Hopi version of the first official meeting between the Hopi Nation and the United States is far different. The current belief, attested to by spokesmen from villages on all three mesas, is that the Treaty of Guadalupe Hidalgo was signed by Spain, Mexico, the United States, and the Hopi Nation. Three Hopi representatives were called to Santa Fe in 1848 for this purpose.

By the terms of the treaty it was agreed that: 1. The United States must respect the religious and land rights of the Hopis and defend the Hopi province at all times. 2. The United States [*sic*] and any party and tribe which trespassed on the Hopi province should be punished by death. 3. If the United States at any time took, divided, or sold any part of the land which the Hopis claimed by religious rights, it agreed to be punished by an unseen power—by the Creator.

In answer to the question whether the treaty was signed or thumb-marked by the Hopi representatives, it was explained that the treaty was sealed by words which were sacred bonds and by ceremonial smoking, which was a signature put into the ether with smoke.

"Any material paper or document agreement could be burned or destroyed or stolen, but a promise or a signature by smoking is a sacred oath and honor between men on this earth and the Creator or Great Spirit to whom the Hopis made their promise. . . . About the destruction. The warning was given to the United States by the Hopis that if it, as a power and spiritual nation, disregarded this promise of the cere-monial signature of the smoking, then the destruction will fall on this nation because of the disobedience to the Creator's promise in the begin-ning. Since Spain has experienced defeat from Mexico and is no longer a power in the Western Hemisphere, and now Mexico being defeated by the United States, so if the United States continues to have no respect and disregards the ceremonial smoking promise of honesty of 'word of bond' between men, then this country is worshiping a false God. And justice will come for sure. So on this basis the Hopi holds the title to this land superior to the United States with all the written documents." *

If these terms of the Treaty of Guadalupe Hidalgo and the place and details of its signing cannot be substantiated by official record, it is quite possible that the meeting to which the Hopis refer was their meeting with Calhoun in Santa Fe.

In any case the significant point is not whether the Hopis were a signatory party to the Treaty of Guadalupe Hidalgo, but the difference between the viewpoints of the Hopi Nation and the United States re-garding the primary issue of land ownership.

The United States, having acquired by monetary purchase and inter-national treaty all the territory embracing Hopi land, was prepared to exercise its sovereignty solely on the basis of its property rights.

To the Hopis, land tenure was basically religious. Promised to them at their Emergence, claimed by them after their migrations, and defined on their sacred tablets, the land held by them extended from the Colorado River on the west to the Rio Grande on the east, and from the northern mountain forests to the southern deserts. The outer boundaries had been sealed by blood, a young Hopi boy and girl having been sacrificed on top

---

* White Bear. He adds: "There is knowledge among my people that there are papers which at the appointed time will be revealed."

of the highest mountain near the source of the Colorado River. Some of their blood was poured into the river to circle the western boundary, and some of it was carried in a jar and poured into the source of the Rio Grande to circle the eastern boundary.* Shrines had been erected on all these boundaries, west, south, east, and north; shrines symbolizing these were erected closer to the Hopi villages; and every year at the time of Wúwuchim a ceremonial circuit was made to reclaim the land in the name of the Creator. Long before the coming of any other tribe or any white men, Hopi ruins, broken pottery, and pictographs and petroglyphs further attested to the Hopis' immemorial title to their land.

This inherent title had not been disputed by Spain, which had first claimed sovereignty over the territory. For all its cruelties and injustices to the Indians, Spain recognized the rights of all pueblos to their land by providing land grants to each. The code of laws of Emperor Charles V made at Cigales on March 21, 1551, and afterward re-adopted by King Philip II, provided sites for all pueblos, with water privileges, lands and mountains, entrances and exits, farming lands, and a common *ejido* of a league in extent where Indians could keep herds without mixing them with those of the Spaniards. This was confirmed by the Royal Council of the Indies in its royal edict of June 4, 1687.

Mexico, upon gaining its independence from Spain and taking over the northern province of New Mexico, confirmed these titles to the communally owned pueblo land grants.

What was the position now taken by the United States upon its annexation of the territory? It also confirmed the pueblos' titles to their lands by the Treaty of Guadalupe Hidalgo, which provided for the protection of the rights of the inhabitants of the ceded country to their property, including the claims of pueblos or towns.

But hardly before the ink was dry its good intentions were nullified by happenings almost too swift to be recorded. Gold had been discovered in California. The whole country was moving westward; sixty thousand people passed through the Territory of New Mexico in 1851. Within two years a feasible route for a transcontinental railroad was being sought to accommodate the westward flow. By 1861 subdivision of the new territory already had begun, its western portion being created the Territory of Arizona, a northern portion being made the Territory of Colorado, and still another portion becoming the Mormon State of Deseret, then the Territory of Utah. Hurry! Hurry! Build up these territories as proper states of the Union. There were fortunes to be dug out of the hills, more

---

* This young boy and girl who were sacrificed are still symbolized by the male-and-female *páhos* made for use during the Soyál ceremony.

fortunes to be made out of sheep, cattle, timber, land. People were pouring in, gold prospectors and timber cruisers, cattle barons and cattle rustlers, land grabbers, surveyors, politicians, squatters, homesteaders, settlers. It was a tide that could not be stopped—certainly not by a few tribes of native Indians who stood in the way of a materialistic people who could never comprehend the religious tenets of the peaceful Hopis.

4

Westward March of Empire

The deeply rooted racial prejudice of the Anglo-white Americans against the Red Indians, virtually a national psychosis, is one of the strangest and most terrifying phenomena in all history. It has no parallel throughout the Western Hemisphere. The hot-blooded Spanish and Portuguese freebooters had achieved the conquests of Mexico, Central America, and South America in the name of the crown and the cross. Yet for all their cruelties they had no racial prejudice. From the start they intermarried lawfully with subjected Indians, creating a new race, the *mestizo*. In Canada and the United States the French also mixed blood with the Indians, and the Germans everywhere allied themselves as colonists with the native peoples.

The Anglo-Protestants were the direct antithesis of these other Euro-Americans. Cold-blooded, deeply inhibited, and bound by their Puritan traditions, they began a program of complete extermination of all Indians almost from the day they landed on Plymouth Rock.

The precedent was set by a Pequot massacre shortly after the *Mayflower* arrived. Of this Cotton Mather wrote proudly, "The woods were almost cleared of those pernicious creatures, to make room for a better growth." A century and a half later Benjamin Franklin echoed this opinion when he wrote of "the design of Providence to extirpate those savages in order to make room for the cultivators of the earth." Still later, in Lincoln's boyhood, the "natural and kindly fraternization of the Frenchmen with the Indians was a cause of wonder to the Americans. This friendly intercourse between them, and their occasional intermarriages, seemed little short of monstrous to the ferocious exclusiveness of the Anglo-Saxon." * This horror of miscegenation and the self-righteous slaughtering of Indians were the banners under which the new conquerors marched westward through the Alleghenies, across the Great Plains, and over the Rockies.

As early as 1641, New Netherlands began offering bounties for Indian

---

* Cary McWilliams. *Brothers under the Skin.* 1943.

scalps. The practice was adopted in 1704 by Connecticut, and then by Massachusetts, where the Reverend Solomon Stoddard of Northampton urged settlers to hunt Indians with dogs as they did bears. Virginia and Pennsylvania followed suit, the latter in 1764 offering rewards for scalps of Indian bucks, squaws, and boys under ten years of age.

In 1814 a fifty-dollar reward for Indian scalps was proclaimed by the Territory of Indiana. In Colorado, legislation was offered placing bounties for the "destruction of Indians and skunks." By 1876, in Deadwood, Dakota Territory, the price of scalps had jumped to two hundred dollars. In Oregon a bounty was placed on Indians and coyotes. Indians were trailed with hounds, their springs poisoned. Women were clubbed to death, and children had their brains knocked out against trees to save the expense of lead and powder.

Massacres of entire tribes and villages, such as that of Sand Creek, Colorado, in 1864, were not uncommon. Here a village of Cheyennes and Arapahoes were asleep in their lodges when the Reverend J. M. Chivington, a minister of the Methodist Church and a presiding elder in Denver, rode up with a troop of volunteers. "Kill and scalp all Indians, big and little," he ordered, "since nits make lice." Without warning, every Indian was killed—75 men, 225 old people, women, and children. Scalps were then taken to Denver and exhibited on the stage of a theater.

Wholesale removal of whole tribes from reservations granted them by solemn treaties was in order whenever their land was found to be valuable. The Cherokee Nation was the largest of the Iroquois tribes; its people had invented an alphabet and had written a constitution, establishing a legislature, a judiciary, and executive branch. In 1794, in accordance with a treaty made with the United States, the Cherokees were confined to seven million acres of mountain country in Georgia, North Carolina, and Tennessee. In 1828 gold was discovered on their land. The Georgia legislature passed an act confiscating all Cherokee lands, declaring all laws of the Cherokee Nation to be null and void, and forbidding Indians to testify in court against whites. The confiscated lands were distributed by lottery to whites.

The case of the Cherokee Nation came up before the Supreme Court. The Chief Justice rendered his decision, upholding the Cherokees' rights to their land. Retorted President Jackson, "John Marshall has rendered his decision; now let him enforce it."

What was enforced was a fictional treaty whereby the Cherokees agreed to give up their remaining seven million acres for $4,500,000 to be deposited to their credit in the United States treasury. General Winfield Scott with seven thousand troops then enforced their removal west of the Mississippi.

Of the fourteen to seventeen thousand Cherokees who started on the "Trail of Tears," some four thousand died on the way. The financial costs of their removal were promptly charged against the funds credited to them. And when it was over, President Van Buren in December 1838 proudly informed Congress, "The measures by Congress at its last session have had the happiest effects. . . . The Cherokees have emigrated without any apparent reluctance."

The legality of this procedure was upheld again on the seven-million-acre Sioux Reservation in the Black Hills of Dakota. To this land the Sioux Nation had been granted "absolute and undisturbed" possession by a solemn United States treaty ratified by the Senate in 1868. But when in 1874 gold was found in the region, General Custer was sent with United States troops to protect white prospectors. After the massacre of his troops the full force of the Army was summoned to eject the Sioux and throw the reservation open to whites. The United States Court of Claims subsequently upheld the legality of the procedure.

Commissioner of Indian Affairs Francis C. Walker gave voice to public sentiment when in 1871 he stated that he would prefer to see the Indians exterminated rather than an amalgamation of the two races, asserting, "When dealing with savage men, as with savage beasts, no question of national honor can arise. Whether to fight, to run away, or to employ a ruse, is solely a question of expediency."

So mile by mile westward, and year by year through the "Century of Dishonor," the United States pursued on all levels its policy of virtual extermination of Indians, accompanied by a folk saying that served as a national motto: "The only good Indian is a dead Indian." A racial prejudice that became an *idée fixe,* a national psychosis sanctioning the wanton killing of Indians, is still the theme of America's only truly indigenous morality play—the cowboy-Indian movie thriller.

This, then, was a great motif of the westward expansion of an Anglo-white nation whose existence and growth was predicated upon the primary sanctity of property rights. In the shadow cast by the death of a race, the tragedy of a continent, we can discern the justified fears of the peaceful, religious Hopis that the approaching Americans were not their long-lost brothers the white Pahánas.

THE LONG WALK

The blow of conquest fell on the Tavasuh, the marauding Navajos, rather than on the remote and isolated Hopis north of the main transcontinental route west along the thirty-fifth parallel.

Despite American occupancy of the new territory, the Navajos had continued their perpetual raiding. Between 1847 and 1851 they were officially reported to have stolen 453,293 sheep, 12,887 mules, 7,050 horses, and 31,581 cattle. The inevitable could be postponed no longer. Elaborate plans were made for a decisive Navajo campaign to begin July 1, 1863. Brigadier General James H. Carleton, commander of the Headquarters Department of New Mexico, and Colonel Christopher Carson, the famous guide and Mountain Man, were selected to direct it. So many private citizens joined the hunt that it was necessary for the governor to call them off by proclamation.

By summer all was ready. The Navajos were given until July 20 to surrender themselves and join surviving Mescalero Apaches at Fort Sumner. After that date every Navajo then living was to be killed or made prisoner.

The hunt began. Carson advanced slowly, destroying patches of corn, running in sheep and horses, relentlessly tracking down every family, every individual, with his Indian scouts. He fought no battles, stormed no cliffs. He could afford to be patient; winter was coming.

The deep snows came. There was no corn in the desert fields. The Navajos could not gather piñons on the lower hills. They could not hunt game; tracking was too easy. They could not light fires to keep warm. On January 6, 1864, Carson, with unfailing instinct, led some four hundred men to the Navajos' last stronghold, the spectacular Canyon de Chelly. Here he destroyed some two thousand peach trees, depriving the Navajos of even the bark for food, and closed the trap. Huddling in icy caves, the Navajos faced starvation, death, or capture. Their surrender marked the defeat of the proud, arrogant people. One after another, small, destitute, and starving bands straggled out.

On March 6, 1864, their "Long Walk" began: 2400 people, with thirty wagons loaded with the aged and maimed, trudging over another "Trail of Tears" to captivity in the Bosque Redondo, 180 miles southeast of Santa Fe. Still they kept coming: 3500 more in April, wise old men, proud young warriors, women and children, trudging past crowds of their jeering conquerors. And still more—a total of 8491 Navajos, all that were left save a few scattered groups hiding like animals in the Grand Canyon and the unexplored basin of the lower San Juan River.

The Long Walk was over. They were Navajo Israelites held in bondage in a Mescalero Egypt. How long, O Lord, how long?

Bosque Redondo, with Fort Sumner in its center, was part of a military reservation forty miles square, occupying the bottomlands of a bend in the Pecos River. The land had belonged to the Mescalero Apaches, and the 400 imprisoned survivors still regarded it as their own. Confined

on it with them, the 8491 Navajos felt like interlopers, even in imprisonment.

The bickering tribes were set to work planting two thousand acres
to wheat and corn and digging thirty miles of irrigation ditches. The
Navajos, nomads for centuries, had never bent back to the hoe. Every crop
planted in three years was a failure. Nor could the Navajos accustom
themselves to wheat flour, their staple ration. The alkaline water sickened
them. Wood was scarce; they shivered in flimsy shelters of canvas and
brush. Finally they gave in to hopeless despair.

Their captors were in a worse mess. The first year it had cost $700,000
to maintain the Navajos. The cost for the second year had been reduced
to $500,000, and for the third year to $300,000. At an average cost of about
12 cents per head a day, this seemed the bare minimum. The remaining
7200 Navajos were being issued each day only a pound apiece of corn
and beef with a pinch of salt.

A special committee from Congress then decided the Navajos would
have to be removed. Lieutenant General William Tecumseh Sherman,
who had made the famous march to the sea through Georgia, and Colonel
S. F. Tappan, peace commissioner, were selected to supervise their removal. It was decided on June 11, 1868, after debating all the sites where
they might be taken, to return them to a small part of their own homeland
that was as far out of the way of the whites and their future wants as
possible—5500 square miles of almost uninhabitable desert, located in the
very center of the wilderness hinterland of the United States.

The bondage was over. A week later the Navajos started home:
"7,111 Navajo Indians, viz: 2,157 under 12 years of age, 2,693 women,
2,060 men, and 201 age and sex unknown."

By terms of the treaty they were issued fourteen thousand sheep and
one thousand goats—an average of two animals per person—and promised
a small clothing allowance, seed and farm implements, and schools,
promises that were never kept. On this sandy wind-swept desert, without
rain for twenty-five months at a time, where water holes were often fifty
miles apart, and with only two sheep apiece, they were confidently expected to die out soon without embarrassment to the remote public.

What did it matter? The Navajos strode off into their wilderness with
their two animals apiece, destitute, without horses and wagons, camping
equipment, cooking utensils, tools, guns, adequate clothing, matches.

They were home—but only to fall in bondage to the docile Hopis
whom they had long persecuted.

THE SACRED BUNDLES

The defeat and capture of the hated Tavasuh, their hereditary enemies, seemed to the Hopis a manifestation of divine justice. It bore out too the reliance they had first placed upon the government of the United States to protect their province from all trespassing. But events conspired to give the lives and future of the Tavasuh into the keeping of the Hopis.

According to present Hopi belief, the Tavasuh or Navajos were still imprisoned by the white men at that terrible place known as Pasquel (Fort Sumner or Bosque Redondo) when they sent medicine men to implore the Hopis to have them released from imprisonment. The Hopis reminded them that their people, the Tavasuh, were the biggest liars, thieves, and murderers ever seen, a people no one could trust. Once they were back they would again start lying, stealing Hopi corn and peaches, killing Hopis, and encroaching on Hopi land. For four nights they talked at Walpi, the medicine men assuring the Hopis that once the Tavasuh got back home they would forever respect Hopi beliefs, possessions, and land. As a guarantee of their solemn promise, the medicine men gave to the Hopis two sacred bundles wrapped in buckskin. Whereupon the Hopis persuaded the white men to release the Navajos from imprisonment and permit them to return home.*

Another interesting version of this meeting relates that the Navajo medicine men were still reluctant to part with their two sacred bundles, knowing that they were giving their people's lives into the keeping of the Hopis. Hence on the fourth night they offered to play a game with the Hopis. If the Hopis could guess what the two bundles contained and tell which was which, the Hopis could retain the bundles. But if the Hopis failed, the Navajos could keep the sacred bundles, giving only their word. The Hopi leaders agreed.

The two sacred bundles were laid out before them. The Hopi leaders lit their pipes, smoked, and thought long and carefully. Without doubt the sacred bundles contained Navajo *tiponis* or fetishes, male and female. According to Hopi tradition, Hopi male-and-female *páhos* were

---

* There is no indication that the Hopis were influential in securing the release of the Navajos from Bosque Redondo. As described in the preceding section, they were released upon the determination of a special committee from Congress. By a treaty made with them, they were returned to a specific "small part of their old country," a reservation of 5500 square miles, rather than being set free to roam at will over Hopi land again.

However, as definite boundaries of Navajo and Hopi land had not yet been agreed upon, Hopi fears of Navajo encroachment were justified. Hence it is quite probable that this meeting of Hopi and Navajo leaders took place after the Navajos returned home, when they were weak and needed help from the Hopis. That the Hopis gave it in return for the Navajos' sacred bundles was entirely in keeping with the character of these People of Peace.

always arranged the same way: the male *páho* was always placed on the right, facing away from one or facing the sun, and the female *páho* was always placed on the left. The Hopi leaders knew that the Navajo medicine men knew this.

But still they smoked and thought some more before making their choice. For the Navajos were always tricky and they might have switched the bundles, believing that the Hopis could not go against tradition.

It was a difficult decision to make. The lives and futures of two nations depended upon it. So they kept smoking and thinking, and the Navajo medicine men kept waiting.

Finally the Hopi leader spoke. "In the bundle on the right is the female, and in the bundle to the left is the male."

For a moment there was silence. Then the Navajo medicine men bowed their heads in the firelight and wept. "You are right," one said. "We switched the bundles, hoping that you would guess wrong. But your power was greater than ours."

"Now we will go and leave them with you," said the other. "If our people ever go back on our word never to steal or trespass on Hopi land, show them these sacred bundles to remind them of the power you have over their lives and future."

When the Navajos had gone, the Hopi leaders carefully unwrapped the sacred bundles, which contained, as they knew, the most sacred Navajo *tiponis*. One, the male, was about eighteen inches long and four inches wide. Inside were a feather and a cotton cord, a *páho* symbolizing animal life. Around this on the outside were eagle feathers wrapped with cotton cord down to four inches from the bottom. In the center was tied the long, soft plume of an eagle. This *tiponi* symbolized the animal kingdom, the life of all animals. Since the Navajos were a nomadic tribe, and not farmers, they depended upon animals for their food—the wild game they shot, and their sheep. Hence this *tiponi* meant the very life of the Navajos, for if the animals died or vanished they themselves would perish. The Hopis, then, were holding in their hands the food of the Navajo tribe.

The other *tiponi*, the female, was about the same size and wrapped in buckskin the same way. But inside it was a long ear of yellow corn turned white with age. Protruding from it was a long eagle plume, the tallest of the soft feathers. Around it were smaller eagle feathers and fluffies wrapped with cotton cord. This was the most important *tiponi*, the one that Navajos called their Grandmother, for it controlled the germination of life, the life of all Navajos. In holding this, the Hopis were holding in their hands the entire Navajo tribe itself.

Let the Tavasuh lie, steal, and trespass on Hopi land again, and the Hopis had only to show them the male *tiponi* as a warning that they could take away their food, and the female *tiponi* as a warning that they could take away their very lives. In their hands they held the sacred hostages of the Navajo Nation.

For almost a century the Hopis kept the two sacred bundles in the home of the Snake Clan at Walpi. Then they were given to two religious leaders to hold in custody: one to Pahona [Beaver], the Village Crier, and one to Taylor of the Reed Clan, a Qaletaqa, because in Walpi the Qaletaqas are always members of the Reed Clan.*

During this century the unbelievable, the miraculous, happened. The hardy 7111 Navajo survivors of the Long Walk returned to their homeland wilderness and swiftly multiplied to 20,000, to 60,000, to 80,000, becoming the largest Indian tribe left in the United States. They wove the wool from great flocks of sheep into Navajo blankets that became a household necessity throughout the whole Southwest and an art famous throughout the world. With silver and turquoise they fashioned jewelry as famous and incomparable. And finally, with the discovery of coal, oil, and uranium in their barren wilderness, they became wealthy and powerful enough to fight for their native rights with modern legal procedures.

During this miraculous growth they ignored the promises given with their sacred bundles to the Hopis in their still small and poverty-stricken villages. Year by year they kept encroaching more on Hopi land, until they finally claimed a large part of it as their own by right of previous occupancy.

Time and again the Hopis considered showing the Navajos their sacred bundles as a warning. Then they decided it was not yet time. As late as 1960, when a court hearing on the land question was held at Prescott, Arizona, Taylor and Pahona resolved to carry the two Navajo *tiponis* there as evidence. They then decided they had better take only one. Then, as Taylor reports, "Something happened, and we were told not to show it, because it was not the right time. So naturally we all came home."

This was the Hopi way, never to rush things, always to wait until the proper time. Perhaps it will come, they say, before the Navajos take all their land and ruin the Hopis forever and run the government itself— when the Hopis will show them that they still hold the Navajos in the hollow of their hand.

---

* Taylor, who gave us this description, still retains custody of the *tiponi* given him.

5

The Betrayal of Lololma

The never-ceasing encroachment of the Navajos and the ever-growing restrictions of the whites were the two mill-wheels that now began to grind down the Hopis' strength and morale, despite their obdurate resistance.

The first Indian agent sent to the Hopis was J. H. Flemming, who established himself in a small cabin at Pakeova [Trout Spring], about fifty miles north of Oraibi. Another early arrival was Thomas V. Keam, a former government interpreter who established a trading post at Ponsekya, now known as Keams Canyon, about ten miles east of First Mesa. Within a few years this latter site was chosen as the location for the agency headquarters.

Both men were well liked by the Hopis and made attempts to stop the depredations of the Navajos, but as the closest military establishment was Fort Wingate at Honoupa [Bear Spring], little could be done. Eventually steps were taken to establish a formal reservation for the Hopis.

On February 23, 1880, E. S. Merritt wrote the Commission of Indian Affairs:

> Allow me to state for the information of the Government that I have in my possession a long letter from the Hon. Comsr. of Ind. Affairs regarding the segregation from the public domain of a Reservation for the Moquis Pueblo Indians, and also, as to whether they would consent to removal to the Little Colorado River, etc.
>
> . . . I most emphatically state that they could not be induced to change their location, and cannot be removed except by force.
>
> They are entirely self supporting in their present locality, and have been so since time immemorial, as reported by Don Cabeza de Vaca centuries ago. They are more frugal and industrious than the Mexicans, have less vices, and more wealth and better land generally, than the same number of Mexicans.

Semoengva, a Hopi man, aged 104.
(Photo: Ed Newcomer)

The H. R. Voth photographs are from the half-century-old collection of glass negatives described in the picture section opposite page 190.

Chief Lololma, head of the "Friendly" faction.   *(Photo: H. R. Voth)*

Chief Lololma's wife, mending a sifter basket.   *(Photo: H. R. Voth)*

Wikvaya, former Márawu priest and first Christian to be baptized by the Reverend Mr. Voth. Wikvaya's wife, as a young girl, was carried by the Spaniards into slavery in Santa Fe, New Mexico. *(Photo: H. R. Voth)*

Hopi children
(Photo: H. R. Voth)

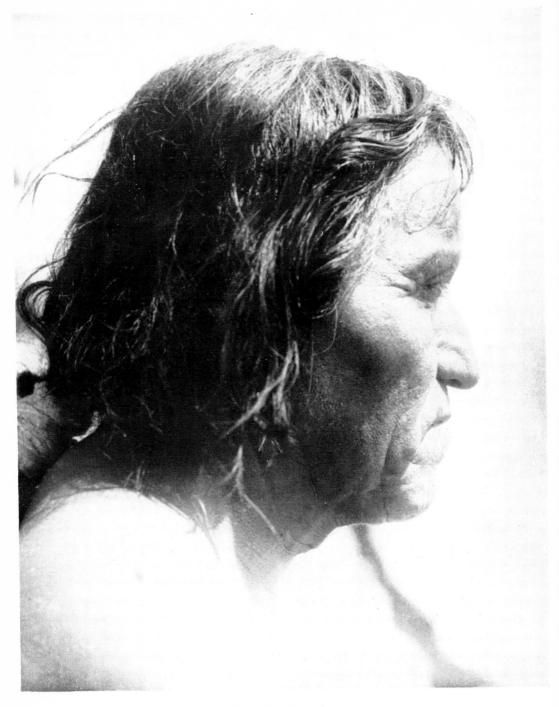

Chief Tawákwaptiwa.
(Photo: Ed Newcomer)

Chief Tawákwaptiwa's wife.
(Photo: H. R. Voth)

John Lansa, Badger Clan, Oraibi, one of the spokesmen.

Awatovi mural detail, which corresponds to the drawing on pages x and 265.

Awatovi mural detail, showing the badger.
(Photos: Museum of Northern Arizona)

They, the Moquis, absolutely require Reservation and action should not be delayed. A piece of land 6 or 8 miles long and 3 or 4 miles wide in the form of a parallelogram, with the Mesa and Eagle Villlage in or near the center, is all which is required. Also a Timber Reservation of 6 or 8 square miles—at a distance of about 10 miles, as there is no timber for fuel or building nearer. . . .

From the Moquis Pueblo Agency, Flemming then wrote the Commissioner on December 4, 1882:

Your telegram of Nov. 27, 1882 directing me to "Describe boundaries for Reservation that will include Moqui villages & agency, & large enough to meet all needful purposes and no larger, and to forward by mail immediately" is at hand, & I cheerfully submit the same, prefacing the following remarks.

. . . In addition to the difficulties that have arisen from want of a Reservation with which you are familiar, I may add that the Moquis are constantly annoyed by the encroachments of the Navajos, who frequently take possession of their springs, & even drive their flocks over the growing crops of the Moquis. Indeed their situation has been rendered most trying from this cause, & I have been able to *limit* the evils only by appealing to the Navajos through their chiefs, maintaining the rights of the Moquis. With a Reservation I can protect them in their rights—have hopes of advancing them in civilization. Being by nature a quiet & peaceful tribe, they have been too easily imposed upon & have suffered many losses.

The following are the lines I would suggest, after carefully consulting such maps as I can command, in connection with my knowledge of the prescribed territory.

Make the N. E. corner the intersection of 36°–30′ with the 110° meridian, running thence west to 111°—thence south to 35°–30′—thence east to 110°—thence north to place of beginning.

These boundaries are the most simple that can be given to comply with the directions of your telegram & I believe that such Reservation will meet the requirements of this people, without infringing upon the rights of others, at the same time protecting the rights of the Moquis. . . .

Hence by an Executive Order of 1882 a Hopi Reservation of 3863 square miles was established within the vast Navajo Reservation. It was much smaller than the area claimed by the Hopis as the nucleus of their land. This area, whose center was Oraibi, extended to the Colorado River on the west and an equal distance to the east, north to a point just below the junction of the Colorado and the San Juan, and south to the San Francisco or Snow Cap Mountains—an area which today includes the towns of Holbrook and Winslow, and through which runs the Santa Fe Railway line and Highway 66. But with the smaller area the Hopis were forced to be content.

Flemming and a small body of Hopis, carrying little American flags, accompanied the surveyors to mark the boundaries. Yestewa, of the Rabbit Clan in Oraibi, carried one little flag from the southwest corner northward to Cow Spring, passing east of Moencopi; then turned east to a point just north of Kísiwu [Spring in the Shadow]. From here a Hopi from Walpi, carrying another little flag, turned south to Indian Springs. Quevaho, a Hopi from Second Mesa, then carried another little flag and an eagle *páho* of the Coyote Clan to the starting point. The flags were then presented to the Hopis as tokens of the government's honesty and integrity.

Five years later, in 1887, the first school was opened in Keams Canyon. Considerable difficulty in securing children for it was encountered. Whereupon Thomas V. Keam wrote the commissioner on January 13, 1890, suggesting that several Hopi chiefs be given a trip to Washington to establish better relations:

> During my stay in Washington last summer, I talked with you in reference to a promise made some of the principal chiefs of the Moqui Indians. This way; that they should visit Washington and talk with their Great Chief on matters of importance to them.
>
> . . . One of the principal objects of this visit is, they tell me, to settle the matter of yearly encroachments by Navajo herds on the land and waters close to their villages. They also desire to see how the white man lives, and how he makes different articles of clothing, implements, etc. they have seen here.
>
> As none of this tribe has ever been east of Albuquerque, New Mexico, I believe it would result in great good. Being one of the most remote from civilization, and rarely leaving their homes, they have not the least idea of this great country and its people. It would also have a beneficial effect on the school, which for some cause, the attendance is less now than at any time since its establishment. I have asked them why they do not send more children, when they express dislike for the Superintendent and his wife but fail to give me the reason. The Oraibis have not sent a child yet, and say when asked, "The Government does not protect us against the encroachments of the Navajos."
>
> . . . Should you favor this visit, I would suggest the following head men of the Moquis: "Shimo," "Anowita," "Polacca," "Loloami," and "Honani." These are the rulers and leading men from different villages, and represent the whole tribe.

This was followed by another letter, a month later, in which Keam wrote that only three boys were attending school and that one of the chiefs had informed him no more would come. There now followed a series of letters and telegrams between Commissioner O. I. Morgan and

Agent C. E. Vandever, who agreed that the Hopi chiefs should make the trip only if they would guarantee to fill the school with children not only throughout the balance of the fiscal year but during 1891. To this the Hopis assented, and on June 16, 1890, the five chiefs, accompanied by Vandever, left for Washington.

THE HOSTILES VS. THE FRIENDLIES

According to Hopi memory, four chiefs made the trip to Washington: Lololma, Bear Clan, Oraibi; Honani, Strap and Parrot Clans, Shongopovi; Semo, Bear Clan, Walpi; and Polacca, Side Corn Clan, Hano. Of these, Lololma, being of the Bear Clan and village chief of Oraibi, was the undisputed leader and virtual spokesman for all the Hopi people.

It was common knowledge before he was born that he was to be a boy, was ordained to become chief, and was to be named Choyla [Burn It All Up]. Upon being initiated, however, he was renamed Lololma [Many Beautiful Colors], referring to the wing colors of a butterfly, as his sponsoring godmother was a member of the Butterfly Clan.

A sincere and devout man, Lololma took with him one or more of the sacred tablets in the custody of the Bear Clan.* None of the government people in Washington could read their spiritual meanings, but they convinced him that the government would protect the Hopi Reservation against Navajo depredations by punishing all trespassers. He in turn agreed to cooperate with the government in all respects for the benefit of his people.

Upon returning home he immediately advised all his chiefs and elders of the rapport that had been established. As evidence of his own faith he took his own son and nephew to school. He also encouraged many families to move out of their villages to remote springs and warm sheltered valleys where they could look after their flocks and herds. He himself moved to Flute Spring, a few miles out of Oraibi.

Opposition developed. A large group accused Lololma and his followers of being too friendly to the government and too progressive. They insisted that all Hopis, like themselves, adhere to their own traditional way of life and ignore government promises that would never be kept. There thus developed two factions—the so-called Hostiles or Traditionals and the Friendlies or Progressives—that were to split the entire Hopi nation.

---

*Sketched and described in Part Two, Chapter 1.

The leader of the Hostiles was Lomahokenna [Being Set Up Good], head of the Spider Clan and the chief of the Blue Flute ceremony. He was supported by Yukioma [Nearly Complete or Almost Done] * of the Fire Clan, whose son, Qöchhongva of the Sun Clan, was married to Lomahokenna's niece. The two factions thus opposed the Bear Clan to the Spider Clan and the Fire or Ghost Clan—between whom relations always had been strained. For the Bear Clan was traditionally the keeper of all the land around Oraibi, and it had never allotted land holdings to the Spider Clan. The breach, then, followed the old pattern of clan rivalries established during the migrations.

The first trouble occurred soon after Lololma's return from Washington. In the summer of 1891, when threats were made on both sides, troops were called in; Lololma and men from both factions were taken to Fort Wingate and jailed.

The Hostiles, now contemptuously sure that the government would not keep its promises to Lololma, proposed a test, to which Lololma agreed. The young man chosen to risk his life was Lololma's own nephew, Tuvayesva [Butterfly Resting]. Dressed in his finest clothes and loaded with silver and turquoise jewelry, he was sent on a trading trip to Talestima [Blue Canyon].

"He will never come back," asserted the Hostiles. "The Navajos will kill him."

It was as they said. Three days later Tuvayesva's burro returned. Lololma and a large party retraced its trail ten miles north of the Hotevilla spring to Untema [Sound of Thunder]. Here they found Tuvayesva's body, despoiled of clothes and jewelry, with his head smashed by a rock—undoubtedly by a Tavasuh [Head-Pounder].

The agency was notified at once and requested to advise Washington that a Hopi on his own reservation had been murdered by a Navajo. Led by a special agent, a large group took up the trail of the murderer. He was eventually traced to the Shiprock area, captured, and jailed. Days dragged by without a trial. Finally the agency offered to turn the Navajo over to the Hopis for punishment.

Lololma refused, insisting that the government punish him, according to the agreement made with the Hopis in Washington.

The quandary in which the agent now found himself was obvious. Squeezed between the Hopis, the Navajos, and Washington, which expected him to solve his own problems, he did nothing. Then, conveniently, the Navajo was allowed to escape.

The Hostiles laughed with bitterness and contempt. "What did we

---

* Referring to corn fields almost completely planted, as his godmother belonged to the Corn Clan.

tell you?" they said tauntingly to Lololma. "The government will not keep any of the promises made to you in Washington. It will never protect us from the Tavasuh. You were a donkey to believe it."

Lololma hung his head in shame and wept for the death of his nephew. He had been a big man among his people. Now he had lost face, and he had lost all faith in the government. It was the tragic turning point in his life. But, having committed himself, he now tolerated the encroachment of a foreign religion.

The first Christian sect to gain a foothold among the Hopis was the Mormons, who had settled near Moencopi. Here they persuaded a man of the Pumpkin Clan named Tuvi * and his wife to adopt their religion—the first Hopis to join the Mormon Church. After a visit to Salt Lake City, Tuvi brought back many gifts, including a children's doll, which the Hopis called a *mormonhoya*, the name still used for dolls. Years later the small settlement near Moencopi was named Tuba City after him.

The Hopis liked the Mormons, but Lololma did not allow them to establish a mission church in Oraibi because they practiced polygamy, as did the Tavasuh. So while he was in Washington he had interviewed the leaders of several other sects to determine whose church he would admit. The Mennonites were accepted because, like the Hopis, they did not believe in war. In making this decision Lololma was guided by prophecy. The introduction of the Catholic "slave church" of the Castillas had been credited to or blamed upon the Badger Clan; and the second religion, Mormonism, had been accepted by the Pumpkin Clan. This third religion, however, was sponsored by the leading Bear Clan, and much was expected of it, when the first missionaries arrived in 1893.

In 1901 the Mennonite Mission Church was built on top of Third Mesa near Oraibi itself: a large and imposing edifice whose gaunt spire still sticks up from the now crumbling ruin.** Its presiding head was the immortal H. R. Voth, to whom the Hopis gave the name of Kihakaumta [One Who Digs among Old Ruins]. The Reverend Mr. Voth was a psychological puzzle, an enigmatic paradox to Hopis and whites alike. Nominally a Christian zealot consecrated to the task of winning savage converts to his church, he seems to have devoted his whole efforts to ferreting out the secrets of Hopi ceremonialism. He would boldly enter a kiva during the progress of a ceremony, only to be thrown out bodily—whereupon, just as determinedly, he would force his way back in. A sharp observer and a meticulous worker, he recorded in detail everything he saw and heard, even measuring the sizes of Hopi altars,

---

* *Tuvi* is the name of a children's game played with a small ring made out of a pumpkin rind.
** It was struck by lightning and destroyed in 1942.

sand paintings, and ritual objects. Although Voth was never told the esoteric meaning of the rituals, his exoteric descriptions comprise the first and best ethnological studies of Third Mesa ceremonialism. Published by the Field Columbian Museum in Chicago, they rank with the classic ethnological studies made on First Mesa by the pioneer Alexander M. Stephen, who was politely squeezing his way into Walpi kivas during the same decade.

Yet the results of Voth's achievement were disastrous to the Hopis and far-reaching. A white man and the leader of a new church, he not only cracked the centuries-old secrecy that had enveloped Hopi religious ceremonialism; he profanely exposed to public view their most sacred beliefs and customs, their very altars and ritual objects, now displayed in the Natural History Museum in Chicago. And, in rending the religious fabric, he also helped to destroy the social fabric of Hopi life.

Lololma had gone too far now to turn back. Having encouraged his people to move off the mesa, he permitted without protest the construction of white men's homes with windows and tin roofs for families who wanted to live the white man's way and put their children in school. Most of these were built by Mr. Stubler, whom the Hopis called Kivahana [Home Built White Man]. A little settlement of about twenty-five families grew up at the foot of the mesa at Kiakochomovi [Place of Ruined Village], now known as New Oraibi.

Soon there were a school and a trading post run by Lorenzo Hubbell. Then a Hopi named Koyaneinewa [Gray Dawn in Early Morning] was appointed policeman by the agency. When he began to take his duties too seriously, Lololma spoke to him disrespectfully. Whereupon Koyaneinewa hauled him off to jail at Keams Canyon.

Lololma's shame grew deeper. Opposition of the Hostiles kept increasing. They refused to send their children to school. The schoolteacher or principal, a man named Kampmayer, whom the Hopis called Kepma, resorted to chasing the children through the streets of Oraibi, firing a gun over their heads to stop them. Parents began to hide their children. Then Negro troops were ordered by the agency to ferret them out and punish the stubborn parents. So in 1894 the troops captured nineteen Hostiles, who were imprisoned for eight months.

Then in 1898 a smallpox epidemic broke out and reduced the Hopis to a scant population of 1832. Troops were rushed in to cremate the bodies and to quarantine Oraibi, the only village to escape. Meanwhile another movement was under way by which Lololma was to be betrayed by whites, shamed by his own people still more, and tested by the prophecy of the Hopis' sacred tablets.

6

A Test of Prophecy

The new movement was the government's attempt to break up and allot the land in contradiction to the religious tenure prescribed by the sacred tablets.

THE ALLOTMENT SYSTEM

The allotment system was conceived by Senator Henry L. Dawes of Massachusetts during a visit to the Cherokees' new home in Oklahoma. He reported:

> The head chief told us that there was not a family in that whole nation that had not a home of its own. There was not a pauper in that nation, and the nation did not owe a dollar. . . . Yet the defect of the system was apparent. They have got as far as they can go, because they own their land in common. . . . *There is no selfishness, which is at the bottom of civilization.* Till this people will consent to give up their lands, and divide them among their citizens so that each can own the land he cultivates, they will not make much more progress.

Wherefore in 1890 the "Dawes Act" or "General Allotment Act" was passed. Briefly, it provided that instead of communal, tribal ownership of reservations, every Indian was to be allotted a piece of reservation land under a fee simple title. Indians were not expected to increase; therefore the "surplus" was to be purchased by the government for $1.25 an acre and thrown open for settlement.

So effective was this system that Indian-owned land swiftly dwindled from 138 million to 52 million acres, 86 million acres having been stolen by white settlers, land sharks, lawyers and politicians, and 60 million acres more of the "surplus." To aid Indian progress further, children were forcibly taken from their parents and sent away to white boarding schools. Their hair was cut; they were forbidden to speak their own language, to wear their own clothes, and to maintain their own customs. They were given English names and compelled to undergo religious training by designated Christian sects. The erosion of Indian lands was accompanied by further reduction of the Indians themselves until by 1923 there remained scarcely 220,000 Indians in the United States.

Three years after the General Allotment Act was signed into law steps were taken to enforce it on the Hopi Reservation, despite the question whether it was legally applicable to the Hopis. In a long letter to the Commissioner of Indian Affairs, W. Hallett Phillips of Washington, D. C., wrote on November 5, 1893:

> For many years I have been deeply interested in the Mokis of Arizona. . . . I have only recently ascertained that allotments are being made of their lands. The matter to which I wish to call your attention, is whether the allotment law is applicable to these people, and in this connection I particularly direct you to the decision of the Supreme Court of the United States in the case of the United States against Joseph, reported in the United States Supreme Court reports, 614. . . .
>
> Mr. Justice Miller says in his opinion they hold their land in common and in this respect they resemble the Shakers and other communistic societies in this country and cannot for that reason be classed with the Indian tribes to which the general laws of the government are directed. The decision continues:
>
> "Turning our attention to the tenure by which these communities hold the land we find it wholly different from that of the Indian tribes to whom the Act of Congress applies. The United States have not recognized in these latter any other than a passing title, with the right of use until by treaty or otherwise that right is extinguished, and the ultimate title has always held to be in the United States, with no right in the Indians to transfer it or even their possession without consent of the government. The Pueblo Indians, on the contrary, hold their lands by right *superior to that of the United States*. Their title dates back to grants made by the government of Spain before the Mexican Revolution. A title which was fully recognized by the Mexican Government and protected by it in the treaty of Guadalupe Hidalgo, by which this country and the allegiance of its inhabitants were transferred to the United States."

Phillips's lengthy discussion includes the following pertinent remarks:

> But in regard to the question which I now present to you, it can make no difference so far as the position of the United States is concerned whether the Mokis have a paper title to their land. They still hold them as they have from time immemorial in full right of property, and the

fact that no patent may have been issued to them does not affect the question whether Congress intended that the allotment act should be applied to these people. If so applicable, then Congress has done what the Supreme Court has declared they had no right to do, that is, treat the Pueblo people as Indian tribes.

. . . The act . . . provides for allotments in any case where a tribe or band of Indians is located upon a Reservation created for their use. This cannot be applied to the Pueblo people for they, under the decisions of the Court, have not, like other Indians, the use merely but have plenary ownership of their lands which they possessed for many centuries.

. . . I am informed that the allotments have been made without the knowledge of the Mokis, who are totally unacquainted with our language or our usages. Owing to this they have not protested, but I do not think this any reason to prevent you from taking notice of the matter and executing justice to this interesting and ancient people. . . .

Upon receiving an unfavorable reply, Phillips wrote again on November 15, 1893. His tone was sharp and his remarks concise:

. . . It is singular that the Department should feel itself obliged to apply the law *to the Moki Pueblos but not to* the other Pueblos.

. . . The rights of this people antedated the annexation of the country . . . and were not derived from our government, but were guaranteed protection by it when the country was acquired from Mexico. Those rights, as regards property and ownership, had been recognized and confirmed by the Spanish and Mexican laws. The people were not treated by the former sovereigns of the soil as were treated the wandering wild tribes which surrounded the pueblos. This was because they had a fixed habitat, a firm possession of the soil and its continual use, while their affairs were administered by an admirable local system. By peaceful arts they had attained to a position of more than self-support. The fact that for so many centuries they should have preserved their autonomy and reached a degree of culture encompassed as they were by warring tribes, is a marvel. . . . They have never asked anything from our government, *and if any people ought to be let alone they are the Mokis.* Right demands this and policy suggests it. To treat them as other Indian tribes are treated would be deplorable. To compel them to abandon the life which they have always led and the leading of which had preserved them would be entirely destructive of the national spirit of the people. It would be to reduce them to the level of other Indians; to disintegrate and finally make paupers of them. . . . *The avowed object of officers of the Bureau in Arizona is to make the Mokis desert their pueblo* and as individuals to settle upon the land so allotted. . . . They are entirely ignorant of the fact that their lands are being partitioned off and parceled out by our Government. . . . If some new man in the confidence of the Bureau could be sent out to the Mokis, he might be able to make a report showing the true state of affairs, and the policy of carrying out a system which I regard as unfortunate and needless. . . .

It was not long before the Hopis at Oraibi became aware of the land allotments to be made. The news that the government was going to give them land which they already owned seemd at once too ridiculous, insulting, and tragic to believe. Undoubtedly they never did understand it. Nevertheless work was begun to break up the land and allot to each man forty acres of farming land and sixty acres of range land.

A start was made in the northern part of Oraibi Valley, in a fertile section traditionally held by the Eagle Clan. The agent and his surveyors immediately found themselves in trouble when they attempted to allot lands to other clans. Having restricted allotments to members of the Eagle Clan, they then found there were not enough members to claim all the land, but they would not increase the individual allotments. Again the Hopis protested, explaining that they had to "move with the soil" as the sandy soil held water longer than the clay soil and was not always covered in the same place by the floodwaters from the wash.

The next allotments were made in the Crow Clan holdings just below, and the important Lance or One Horn Clan holdings farther south. Again there was a surplus of land after allotments to members of these clans.

The surveyors then moved south to the area between Sun Shrine Cliff and Porcupine Hill. These sandy hills and wastes were held by the Sand Clan. All altars for Hopi ceremonies were set on sand gathered by the Sand Clan, for the earth was alive and breathed, and moved with the prayers of the ceremony. This sand symbolized the Mother Earth, and the Sand Clan was the traditional custodian of the earth. But there was no earth here to be flooded during the rainy season; no arbitrary division into farming and range land could be made.

The problems kept multiplying. The Bear Clan's choice holdings lay along the eastern edge of Oraibi Wash, so each member was given forty acres classed as cultivated land. None of the Bear Clan was allotted grazing land until the Side Corn Clan was given allotments below, on its insistence that it helped the Bear Clan conduct the most important ceremonies. The Bear Clan members were then given pasture lands near Masipa [Gray Spring], Tuvootukpu [Rabbit in the Sack], and Kachina Point.

Allotments in this latter section, claimed by the Kachina Clan, caused more confusion. Otto Pentiwa of the Kachina Clan recalls that his family was allotted farming land near Gray Spring, but that their grazing land was ten miles farther south, forcing them to travel thirty-five miles from Oraibi. "My father and my brother start to build our home at Gray Spring. For several day we work on rock gathering. We had the walls up to three feet and over when the Navajos came and attack my father and brother and others. They broke our tools and we soon beating each other with our tool handles. By evening we have not tools to work with and most of the men were hurt. Some were badly beaten and cuts on the head. My father was kicked on the body, what cause him to lost his life from that injury. At that sad news Lololma at once notify the Agency, but the same was the result. No response in correcting of the trouble."

By the time the surveyors reached Red Lake, forty miles south of Oraibi, everything was confused and the Hopis were in an uproar. Upon establishing their villages centuries before, they had followed the land pattern marked on their sacred tablets, apportioning land holdings to each arriving clan according to its ceremonial importance, and reserving all grazing land outside these religious land holdings for the animal kingdom upon which they depended for food. The arbitrary allotments in severality thus broke up the whole religious and social structure of land tenure. No provision was made for the surplus land in many sections, nor for outlying grazing and wooded sections over which the government now assumed control. Many people were forced to occupy allotted lands far from the village only to be driven back by encroaching Navajos.

Confronted by such hopeless problems, the agent and surveyors gave up their first abortive allotment efforts in 1894. But the bureau, still wedded to the allotment theory, resumed its attempts. This time the farce of the proceedings was evident to all, and finally in 1911 they were abandoned.

THE SACRED TABLETS

During these crucial times the sacred tablets that confirmed the Hopis' religious rights to their land were brought into prominence. There were four of these tablets, as we recall: one given to the Fire Clan by Másaw, spiritual guardian of the earth, and three tablets given to the Bear Clan.* Lololma kept morosely brooding upon their meanings. Night after night he would bring out the tablets from their hiding place in his corn stack, set them before the leaders of other villages, and patiently explain their markings.

---

* All four tablets are sketched and described in Part Two, Chapter 1.

The small tablet with the figure of a headless man engrossed him most. It prophesied that a time would come when the Hopis would be forced to develop their lives and land at the dictates of a new ruler. They were not to resist, but to wait for their lost white brother, Pahána. Fitting the missing corner piece to the tablet, he would deliver them from their persecutors and work out with them a new and universal brotherhood of man. But if the Hopi leader accepted any other religion he must assent to having his head cut off. This would dispel the evil and save his people.

Lololma believed that the time had come. Was he the leader to have his head cut off? Or was it Yukioma, who was now challenging his leadership? Which was the leader with the strongest faith? All Oraibi began to echo his queries and knew that a test between the two men would have to be made.

It came soon with a troop of soldiers.

"There were many soldiers, foot soldiers and ones on horseback," relates Sengnogva. "There was one thing the Hopis saw for the first time. It was something that was shining, a cannon, and the barrel was eight feet long, and they fired twice to show how powerful it was. The captain of the soldiers then produced an instrument that opened with a big snap and closed the same way when he pulled the handles. He asked Lololma and Yukioma which one wanted now to have his head cut off. Neither Lololma nor Yukioma were able to fulfill the prophecy of the tablet and lose their head. Thereby each leader proved to their own people they did not have courage to sacrifice themselves."

The incident is also reported by Charles Fredericks, Tuwahoyiwma, the nephew of Lololma: "I was a young man and I was there when the time came for the cutting of the heads to take place. All the people had assembled at the *Tipkyavi* when the soldiers came. One of them brought out a shining scissor-like instrument that had a strong force when he snapped it together. When he asked Lololma if he is willing to have his head cut off, he said, 'No.' And the same one asked Yukioma, and he also said, 'No.' Since they were not willing to do this, they both lost out. For the leader according to tablet prophecy will have his head cut off that in the future all good things will come to the people. And all the land will be returned to him."

Baldwin Polipkioma, whose mother was the daughter of Lololma, states further: "All the Hopis know that Lololma and Yukioma were to test one another as to who would be the one with strong faith and is good for the good people. Those of one heart. If Lololma had been willing to have his head cut off, he would be the highest and respected man of our time and of this world. Because there was principle behind what he said he understood, and that is the writing on the tablet he possessed. Since neither man was willing to have their head cut off, it was the beginning of other trials for the Hopi people. It was this shame or disgrace that killed him."

Betrayed by the whites, shamed by his own people, and unable to bring true the prophecy of the sacred tablet, Lololma died of a broken heart. And one by one the tablets disappeared until the time when they would reappear to assert the Creator's promise of peace and justice.

Apparently the first to disappear was the first Bear Clan tablet—a small tablet showing the pattern of land holdings on one side and two bear tracks on the other side to indicate that the Bear Clan was the custodian of the land. This was an important tablet. For the Fire Clan, the Spider Clan, and the Sun Clan had been admitted into Oraibi, but had been given no land holdings because they had no religious ceremonies to contribute. Ever since then the three clans had "cried in shame" because of what they had done to the Bear Clan at Palátkwapi, because they still had no religious ceremony of their own, and because they had no land holdings. They wanted to steal the tablet so it would not show their lack of religious land holdings. This is the way it was stolen.

In the Spider Clan was a young woman who belonged to the Mumchit [Sword-Swallowing Society]. She kept trying to marry into the Bear Clan in order to secure land. The Bear Clan, recognizing her trickery, forbade marriage with her. Nevertheless she finally took gifts to the home of a young man she had selected. His distressed mother, fearing the Mumchit, accepted the gifts and arranged the mariage. Fortunately the couple had no children. But the woman learned where the tablets were hidden, and one day the small tablet disappeared.* The Bear Clan did away with the Mumchit, but the Hopis knew that because of her treachery Oraibi was doomed to disruption.

A few years after Lololma and Yukioma refused to have their heads cut off, when the Bear Clan was still trying to find this missing tablet, Yukioma was taken to Washington to visit President Taft in an effort to curb his hostility. With him he took the Fire Clan tablet secreted in his clothes, it being so small that "you could hold it in your hand." On his way back home, he stopped off at the Carlisle Indian School in Pennsylvania, where several Bear Clan members had been sent as students. These young Hopis, thinking that Yukioma might have the missing Bear Clan

---

* The description of the markings, as given by several Bear Clan leaders who conducted the Soyál ceremony, is believed to be accurate because the traditional meanings were always retold on the fourth day after Soyál. The tablet is now said to be held by the Spider Clan in Hotevilla.

tablet, grabbed Yukioma and searched him. They found the small Fire Clan tablet tied to his loincloth and took it from him. So for a time this tablet too disappeared.*

Upon the death of Lololma the two remaining Bear Clan tablets were given to Tawákwaptiwa, who succeeded him as village chief of Oraibi. Shortly afterward the second Bear Clan tablet disappeared. The Hopis say that it is still in Oraibi, but that it is not yet time to reveal who took it and who now keeps it in custody.

Upon the death of Tawákwaptiwa on April 30, 1960, the third Bear Clan tablet was given to John Lansa's wife, Myna, of the Parrot Clan in Oraibi, who still has it in custody.**

But the time will come, and soon, it is said, when all these tablets will be brought out again.

---

* The tablet briefly appeared in Phoenix in 1942, at the beginning of World War II, when several Hopis were on trial for refusing to register for the draft. It was in the possession of the son and nephew of Yukioma, who showed it to other Hopis, all of whom have described it for us. The tablet is now said to be in the custody of James, the ordained Fire Clan leader, in Hotevilla. It is also said that at the proper time the tablet will be split open to reveal other markings on the inside which will reveal the identity of the Hopi people.

** And who allowed us to inspect it, as described in Part Two, Chapter 1.

7

The Split at Oraibi

Following Lololma's death, one of his nephews, Tuwahoyiwma [Land Animals], was first selected to replace him as village chief of Oraibi. He refused because "at that time I did not have the full knowledge of our religion which was Soyál." Perhaps he had other unconscious reservations about living in strife-torn Oraibi and filling so difficult a post. An intelligent, sensitive man, he had been first put in school by Lololma, where he was given the name of Charles Fredericks.* He was then sent to the Indian school in Phoenix and returned to carry mail for the agency at Keams Canyon. He later adopted Christianity and moved down to New Oraibi.

A second choice was then made among his five brothers, and Wilson Tawákwaptiwa [Sun in the Sky] was appointed chief in 1901. Tawákwaptiwa was young, illiterate, and regarded as having been favored by Lololma. His appointment was resented by Yukioma, who now assumed more leadership of the Hostiles, and it widened the breach between the two factions beyond repair. Each began to hold a Soyál ceremony of its own, splitting clans and families along ceremonial lines.

Yukioma welcomed some thirty dissidents from Shongopovi to strengthen his forces. Tawákwaptiwa sent for reinforcements from his own faction in Moencopi. By the summer of 1906 it was evident that another bloody catastrophe—like that at Awatovi—was imminent. Crowds of Hopis began to gather in Oraibi.**

Four times Tawákwaptiwa requested Yukioma and his Hostiles to leave Oraibi. Four times Yukioma refused, daring Tawákwaptiwa and the Friendlies to force them out. Minor skirmishes began on the morning of September 6. Friendlies went through the village, searching out men,

---

* He is the father of Oswald Fredericks (White Bear).
** Made up of 324 Friendlies and 298 Hostiles, as estimated by Mischa Titiev.

women, and children of the Hostile faction, whom they herded together on the rocky, open mesa top. In the midst of the confusion several trusted whites, including Mr. Epp, the assistant to the Reverend Mr. Voth, and Miss Kate, the field matron, went among the men, begging them to remember that they were Hopis, the People of Peace, and to settle the matter without the use of guns, knives, clubs, and bows and arrows.

The Hopis agreed. A line was marked across the rocky mesa top. Yukioma agreed that if Tawákwaptiwa could push him across the line, he and his followers would leave Oraibi. Crowds of men gathered to back up their leaders, and next day the "push of war" began.

"I took part in the split with all my brothers," relates Tuwahoyiwma. "Tuvehoyeoma [Butterflies Hatching], Sakwaitiwa [Animals Run in Green Pasture], Tewahoyeoma [Animals Born out of Ground], Laahpu [Cedar Bark], Seque [Flesh], and Tawákwaptiwa. I did not know anything about this split to take place until I came back early in the morning after hunting my horses near Blue Canyon. So at once I start cleaning my 44 pistol and putting bullets in its six chambers. I also clean and load my 44 rifle. I put the pistol round my waist and tied the rifle on the saddle of my horse and went up to my brother's house [Tawákwaptiwa]. Just then a man came and said, 'You had better put your gun away. We were told we are not going to use that kind of weapon, and Miss Kate said that the Hopis should not do this to themselves.' At that moment Tawákwaptiwa came out and said, 'Today I shall face in this world what is to be done that was told in the prophecy.' So he began to lead the men out toward the plaza.

"Then all at once I saw the Moencopi men dragging Yukioma's people. So we march out to where Yukioma's people were gathered together on the foot trail that leads toward the Hotevilla spring. There Yukioma and my brother came face to face. Yukioma said, 'I have drawn a line here on the ground that when you people drive me across this line I shall leave Oraibi. But if my men push you across the line, then you must leave Oraibi.' So Tawákwaptiwa and Yukioma put their hands on each other's chests. The minute they started pushing each other all the other men that belonged to Tawákwaptiwa helped to push him across the line, and all the Yukioma men helped to push him across the line. Yukioma was so thin that sometimes he was pushed above the heads of the men and was gasping for air. Then his head would disappear again into the men. This continued for several hours.

"When the big push started I was just about at the edge of the fifty to sixty men pushing. Somehow the anger got a hold of me. I saw this man Kochventewa and I picked him up and threw him down on the ground very hard. He at once pick up a big rock and was ready to throw it at my head. Then someone shouted above the noise, 'Stop that!' and I saw a person grab him around the body. Then finally somebody shouted, 'It is all over! It is done!' and everybody stopped."

Yukioma's son, Dan Qöchhongva [White Cloud Above Horizon], Sun Clan, also relates his participation in the push-of-war "on that day of continued rough handling of us Hopis who do not wish to follow the government plan.

"The warning that my father, Yukioma, had pass on to his people was that we were to be removed to Hukovi [Windy Village, a deserted ruin] if the true plan is carried out by the followers of the government. Someone might forget that we are the same people fighting one another and someone might be seriously hurt. If this happened he was to be left there. No one was to touch him or bury him.

"We who helped one another were closely related. There were two who belong to the Coyote Clan. The names of the brothers, one Polyesva [Butterflies Settling on Flower], Poliyumptiwa, and Kuyumptiwa [Sun Comes Up Beautifully], and my brother and I.

"I was the one who was hurt when I was hit on the head and stomach. I was unconscious for some time. I was carried bodily through the street. It was while I laid on the ground unconscious the ones who fought said in a loud voice, 'It is done! It is complete!'

"There I kept laying on the ground. No one pay any attention to me, as my father ordered. I was hurt by the earth, not by the gun. So after long period I came to life. Then I made my oath that from then on I will bring to an end the evil among the Hopis. I will work to bring good for those who are humble, and bring to an end all trouble among us who are wicked. And I said out loudly, 'Thank you for coming to life! I shall live now for One Heart!'

"For it was my father, Yukioma, who established Hotevilla. And all the knowledge of the past will be brought to Hotevilla, who will bring about the prophecy even though the others said all prophecies are dead, buried the length of an arm, and sealed with *ahpelviki* [glue]. So it was said to me, 'It is fortunate you are the offspring of the Sun and Fire Clans. For the Sun Clan is the sign of leadership. Out of this clan shall rise a leader to fulfill future events if the rightful leader [the Bear Clan] has sidetracked the belief.' "

So it was that after several hours of bloodless struggle a voice rose above the din: "It is done! I have been pushed over the line!" The voice was Yukioma's.

Still today one can read the words scratched into the rock next day: "Well it have to be done this way now that when you pass me over this line it will be DONE, Sept. 8, 1906." Near the inscription are marked an outline of Másaw, deity of the Fire Clan, and the footprint of a bear, the signature of the Bear Clan.

By nightfall all Yukioma's followers had packed their belongings, food, bedding, and a few household articles on the backs of their burros. Unmolested by their victors, they filed slowly out of Oraibi forever.

THE FOUNDING OF HOTEVILLA

In leaving Oraibi, whose rituals and customs had been contaminated by the government and the whites, Yukioma was avowedly upholding the traditions of the Hopis. The line that had been drawn ran from east to west and represented the Colorado River. In being pushed across it to the north, Yukioma read an augury of his final destination. His route was also marked by prophecy.

He was to lead his followers, comprised largely of the Fire or Ghost, Sun, and Spider Clans, down the southeast trail to Sekyahyah [Yellow Stone]. Here at the shrine to Másaw he was to see standing the figure of the deity. Assured by this vision, he would turn south and proceed around Oraibi through Hononsekyah [Badger Valley] to Owakuntaka [Stone Standing Out], where he would see the vision of another ghost. From there he would lead his people up to the high butte known as Hukovi [Windy Village]. He would be accompanied by the vision of the two spirits assuring him of their protection, for they possessed the power of killing people with nothing but ashes.

After resting at Hukovi for several months, the people would move farther north to Kawéstima [North Village] in the ancient ruins that had been their last stopping place before they had concluded their migrations at Oraibi.* Here they would live for a number of years.

Resuming travel, they would then return at last to the original Kawéstima up near the Arctic Circle, symbolized by these closer ruins.** Yukioma and his followers, having abandoned all their religious ceremonies at Oraibi, were to depend here solely on the spiritual guidance of the two manifestations of Másaw, who would initiate again a pure and uncorrupted form of ritual. Under no circumstances would they go out looking for their lost white brother, Pahána; he would come to them with the missing corner of the Fire Clan tablet. Nor would they ever return

---

* Betatakin, founded by the Fire or Ghost Clan; Keet Seel, founded by the Spider Clan; and Inscription House, founded by the Snake Clan. See Part Two, Chapter 2.
** It was here at this northern *páso* of their migrations that the Ghost or Fire, Sun, Spider, Snake, and Blue Flute Clans were turned back. See Part Two, Chapter 2.

to Oraibi; they would merely watch to see if Oraibi would die out or continue to exist.

But again Yukioma failed to fulfill prophecy. That night he and his 298 weary followers made camp at the Hotevilla spring, eight miles north of Oraibi. Without adequate supplies and means to travel, and facing a severe winter, with women and children to take care of, they began erecting rude shelters for protection. Hotevilla had been established.

ESTABLISHMENT OF BAKAVI

Little wonder that dissension broke out that winter among Yukioma's followers, ill fed, clothed, and sheltered as they were. Night after night they sat and talked. Kuwanneumtewa [Land Covered with Beautiful Flowers], whose Spider Clan wife, Qömamönim, was Lomahokenna's niece, kept asking Yukioma, "Where are you taking all of us who were driven out from Oraibi?"

Yukioma assured him that they were going as far north as possible, being guided by their two spirits and the rock writing left by their clans centuries ago.

Kuwanneumtewa recalled that these clans—the Fire, Sun, Spider, Snake, and Flute—had reached the northern *páso,* but had failed to melt the Back Door with all their powers and had been forced to return. How was it possible now for these old people, women, and children to make such a journey? No; he would go no farther with Yukioma. Tired and aging Lomahokenna supported him in his stand.

After months of privation and bickering, Kuwanneumtewa and Lomahokenna with some sixty people returned to their old homes in Oraibi.

Meanwhile, a month after the split, the government had decided that Tawákwaptiwa should be temporarily deprived of his chieftainship until he learned the English language and American customs. Accordingly, in October 1906, he and another Friendly with their wives and about twenty Hopi children were taken to Sherman Institute at Riverside, California. The Commissioner of Indian Affairs decreed that in his absence Oraibi was to be governed by a commission consisting of the schoolteacher and a judge from each faction. Before leaving, however, Tawákwaptiwa put his brother, Bert Fredericks (Sakwaitiwa), in charge.

When the news of Kuwanneumtewa's and Lomahokenna's return reached Tawákwaptiwa in California, he angrily protested to government authorities. They in turn threatened him with permanent loss of his chieftainship unless he signed a paper offering peace to the returned Hostiles. His brother, Bert Sakwaitiwa Fredericks, ignored the paper and took the lead in driving the small party of returned Hostiles back out of Oraibi again.

This time, in the fall of 1907, they settled at Bakavi [Reed Spring], a mile southeast of Hotevilla. Having secured government help in building homes, they established the new village of Bakavi with Kuwanneumtewa as village chief.

The Oraibi split, followed by the Hotevilla split, thus helplessly followed the pattern of Hopi disunity set during the clan migrations. It was not marked by bloodshed as had been the destruction of Awatovi. But it was as tragically disastrous to a people now thinned by disease, encroached upon by the ever-increasing Navajos, and demoralized by government restrictions and control. If ever the Hopis needed to be consolidated by unity of purpose and endeavor into an integrated tribal whole, it was now. Instead, the inherent faults and weaknesses of their clan system cracked under the cumulative strain into a rupture that could not be healed.

The Oraibi split was more than a social schism between two factions. It was a psychological wound no Hopi can forget, that bleeds afresh whenever he talks. In Yukioma's avowed retreat back into the prehistoric ruins of the past, back into mythology, we read the retrogression of a living tradition unable to confront the future. And even this retrogression was a failure.

When Tawákwaptiwa finally returned from school in 1910, it was no longer Oraibi, the paternal home of Hopi ceremonialism, that upheld ancient tradition. Yukioma was the traditionalists' leader, and new Hotevilla was becoming the religious center. Already in these few short years it had established an almost complete cycle of ceremonies.

But in the same year that Chief Tawákwaptiwa returned to Oraibi, there came a new Indian agent who was to dispute Yukioma's growing influence in Hotevilla.

8

The Imprisonment of Yukioma

Beginning in 1824, when the Bureau of Indian Affairs was organized by the Secretary of War, all Indian agents were under the jurisdiction of the Department of War, and many of them were Army officers designated to place Indians under strict military rule. The bureau was then transferred in 1849 to the newly created Department of the Interior, but its civilian agents still had Army troops at call.

As late as 1892 the Indian Commissioner in his annual report included the significant statement: "The Indian Agent now has almost absolute power in the Indian country, and so far as the people over whom he rules are concerned, he has none to contest his power. . . . There is a striking contrast between 'ministers plenipotentiary' appointed by the United States to treat with powerful Indian nations, and an army officer, with troops at his command, installed over a tribe of Indians to maintain among them an absolute military despotism."

The Indian agent, then, was the government's spearpoint of contact with the tribes being swiftly diminished. Upon his capacity for judgment, the width of his perspective, his courage and kindness, rested the fate of his helpless wards. The average agent, ill-educated, underpaid, and stuck in remote and disagreeable surroundings, was far from being a disciple of their lost cause. Little wonder, then, that the Indian agent, good, bad, or indifferent, developed a reputation that did not sanctify his high calling.

The Hopis still keep with infallible memory a detailed record of every Indian agent sent to them from the respected Hugh Flemming and the loved Ralph Collins to the present incumbent.

Tuwahoyiwma says simply: "These first white government people treat us like fierce tribe because they been taught that all Indians are war-like people and you must treat them in rough way to have them understand. Our people know it was predicted that the white man would come in one of two ways. One with understanding and love, treating us with

307

respect when we meet. The other with force and terrible manner, showing us he had lost his good religion.

"When we were treated unkindly by the government men, our religious leaders began to be suspicious. Is this who was foretold would come with understanding and love? The elders who kept our sacred documents realized that something was wrong with the white man's belief. We, the people, began to check into his manner and conduct. Some of the white people were good, like Miss Skeets, who would come into our homes and take care of our illness without considering us a dirty Indian. They accepted us as human with feelings, also. But different were those who had other concept of us Hopis."

The new agent who came in 1910 stayed until 1919—six years longer than most of his predecessors. His name was Leo Crane. Around him revolved the events of the crucial period following the Oraibi split. He relates them himself in an entertaining and significant book that gives an unabashed account of the Hopis from the general viewpoint of the Indian agent of his time.*

Agent Crane was an energetic man with a sense of humor and a great love of the country which he always called the "Enchanted Desert." He also possessed the racial prejudice against Indians then current, for he quotes Section 3837 of the Civil Code of Arizona: "All marriages of persons of Caucasian blood, or their descendants, with Negroes, Mongolians, or Indians, *and their descendants,* shall be null and void." And he adds, "Arizona and its people have no desire for a population of half-breeds; and it is a pity that not all the sovereign States of the Union have been filled with equal pride."

Arriving at Keams Canyon, he was confronted by the fact that the 2500 Hopis had a reservation of 3863 square miles but existed on less than one-fifth of this land because the remainder was overrun by the Navajos, who had 30,000 square miles of their own. There was no patrolling the land with the three native policemen assigned to him, so Colonel Hugh L. Scott with an escort of 125 men of the Twelfth Cavalry was called to review the situation. Colonel Scott reported, "The Navajo are aggressive and independent. There is no doubt that the majority of those on the Moqui Reserve have come in from all sides with a deliberate purpose of taking the grazing land which rightfully belongs to the Hopi. *When a Navajo sees a Hopi with anything he wants, he takes it,* and there is no recourse." He recommended that Crane be given twenty-five well-paid policemen with a white chief. Crane was eventually given five more

---

* *Indians of the Enchanted Desert.* Boston: Little, Brown, 1925.

policemen, and the Hopis continued to be "quite as helpless as Judea between Egypt and Babylonia."

With his first close look at their villages Crane was completely disenchanted. Entering Oraibi, he found many houses abandoned and crumbling, the streets filled with rubbish and offal, burros and half-starved dogs standing in the doorways. "Here was a perfect picture of the senility of a one-time civilization that had been decaying for many centuries, and in this our day had reached very nearly to utter devitalization. . . .

"The contentious pueblo of Hotevilla," he observed, "was simply a dirtier duplicate of the other pueblos without their picturesque setting. And if there is a place in America where aroma reaches its highest magnitude, then that distinction must be granted Hotevilla on a July afternoon. The sun broils down on the heated sand and rock ledges, on the fetid houses and the litter and the garbage, and all that accumulates from unclean people and their animals."

One by one he met their chiefs. Tawákwaptiwa he always regarded as a politician. "As his Indian Agent, however, I tried for eight long years to make a sensible human being of him, and failed for lack of material. After having tried him as an Indian judge, and then as an Indian policeman, in the hope of preserving his dignity and authority as hereditary chief, he was found to be the most negatively contentious savage and unreconstructed rebel remaining in the Oraibi community, so filled with malicious mischief-making to his benefit that a group of his own people petitioned me to exile him from the mesa settlement, in the hope that they might then exist in peace."

Yukioma, "an American Dalai Lama," he found "in the medicine-man and prophecy business about seven miles to the west, in his new and already odorous town of Hotevilla. . . . My predecessor told me how . . . at great expense he had taken Youkeoma and several of his retainers on a trip to and through the East. At Washington they were honored by an audience with President Taft. . . . He might as well have taken a piece of Oraibi sandrock to see the Pope. Not even the size of President Taft impressed the old spider-like Hopi prophet. Youkeoma returned as sullen and determined as before . . . and sat down in his warren of a pueblo amid the sand and the garbage, to await whatever the white man might see fit to do about it. . . .

"Kewanimptewa, a third Oraibi factionist, who headed the weakest band of all, had trekked in another direction, a second upheaval having resulted in his eviction and retirement from the political field. His allies went to a little-known canon, Bacavi, where but for the prompt assistance of the Government Agent the whole lot of Ishmaelites would have perished."

Of them all the sullen and stubborn American Dalai Lama was most impervious to supplication, bribes, and threats. On July 28, 1911, Crane sent for troops. After a long delay, Colonel Scott with a hundred cavalrymen, extra mounts, and a pack train arrived early in November. For ten days the colonel argued with Yukioma, who in turn recited the whole Hopi Creation Myth to support his stand. In despair, Scott and Crane decided to remove all the children to school without further regard to this old religious fanatic. A few days later orders were received from Washington, and the cavalry troop marched into Hotevilla.

Reports Crane: "I do not know how many houses there are in Hotevilla, but I crawled into every filthy nook and hole of the place, most of them blind traps, half-underground. And I discovered Hopi children in all sorts of hiding places, and through their fright found them in various conditions of cleanliness. It was not an agreeable job; not the sort of work that a sentimentalist would care for. . . . By midday the wagons had trundled away from Hotevilla with 51 girls and 18 boys . . . nearly all had trachoma. It was winter, and not one of those children had clothing above rags; some were nude. During the journey of 45 miles to the Agency many ragged garments went to pieces; the blankets provided became very necessary as wrappings before the children reached their destination."

Next day the same scene was enacted at Shongopovi, "dominated by one Sackaletztewa, a direct descendant of the gentleman who had founded the original Hopi settlement after their emerging from the Underworld. Sackaletztewa was as orthodox as old Youkeoma, and it was his following that had given battle to a former Agent and his Navajo police." After some resistance, the cavalry troops removed more children. "They were nude, and hungry, and covered with vermin, and most of them were afflicted with trachoma, a very unpleasant and messy disease."

The children spent four years at the school in Keams Canyon, without vacations. They then elected, reports Crane, to attend the Phoenix Indian School without returning to their homes.

Before leaving with his troops, Colonel Scott gave Agent Crane his brief and pithy advice: "Young man! you have an empire to control. Either rule it or pack your trunk!"

Crane took his advice. When Yukioma protested the enforced dipping of sheep, Crane promptly jailed him for a few days. A year later, when more children at Hotevilla came of school age, Crane erected a new school close to the village. The children were dug out of their hiding places as before and properly enrolled. That night Yukioma threatened the school principal and the field matron, Miss Sarah Abbott. This time Crane showed no mercy. He rounded up Yukioma and his supporters and carted them back to the agency guardhouse for permanent residence.

All the men except Yukioma were put to work cutting weeds, tilling small fields and gardens, and mending roads. One by one they were released for good conduct. Yukioma remained—as mess-cook for other prisoners, where he could be watched. Yukioma did not complain.

"I shall go home sometime," he would tell Crane patiently. "Washington may send another Agent to replace you, or you may return to your own people, as all men do. Or you may be dismissed by the Government. Those things have happened before. White men come to the Desert, and white men leave the Desert; but the Hopi, who came up from the Underworld, remain. You have been here a long time now—seven winters—much longer than the others. And too—you may die."

In 1919 Crane was transferred to another agency. His last act was to release Yukioma for a forty-mile walk back home after his years of imprisonment. Two years later Crane returned for a brief visit—"and lo! Youkeoma was in the guardhouse again. He was squatted on the floor, sifting a pan of flour for the prison-mess, his old trade." With him was Colonel Scott, who had spent ten days listening to him ten years before. Yukioma was again reciting the legend of the Hopi people—"a deluded old savage, possessed by the witches and kachinas of his clan, living in a lost world of fable . . . the last of the Hopi caciques."

THE DISINTEGRATION OF ORAIBI

The imprisonment of Yukioma left Tawákwaptiwa in an enviable position of authority he could not fill. Having been indoctrinated into the mysteries of the English language and American customs during his four years in California, he was now a confirmed Progressive. Yet as the Bear Clan village chief of Oraibi he found it incumbent upon him to uphold the traditions of his people. Tawákwaptiwa was unable to serve either master or even straddle the fence between them. Hopis and whites alike found him quarrelsome, treacherous, and vindictive.

One story is told by Charles Tuwahoyiwma Fredericks, who had some trouble with his brother, the chief, over Bear Clan land. To get even, Tawákwaptiwa chose a devious way. Another brother, Bert Sakwaitiwa, was then in Santo Domingo and Santa Fe, exchanging with Tuwahoyiwma handicraft and trade goods, which each sold. He soon received a letter from Tawákwaptiwa saying that Tuwahoyiwma was cheating him. Sakwaitiwa immediately sent Tuwahoyiwma a letter instructing him to be in Oraibi on a certain day, for he had put up eight hundred dollars to have him killed by the chief and some friends.

Tuwahoyiwma showed the letter to the school principal in New Oraibi, Mr. Myers. Myers laughed and wrote on a piece of paper: "I, Tawákwaptiwa, Chief of Oraibi, and all those who are responsible for what has happened, hereby choose the way we want to be punished for this crime: (1) solitary confinement for the rest of our lives, or (2) by hanging."

Myers handed the paper to Tuwahoyiwma. "Take this to the chief in Oraibi on the day you have been instructed."

"But how will you know I have been killed?" asked Tuwahoyiwma.

"You won't be killed," said Myers, laughing.

Tuwahoyiwma went to Tawákwaptiwa and his friends and confronted them boldly. No one answered his accusations, so he walked out. Later he met Sakwaitiwa, who confessed that the letter Tawákwaptiwa had written him was a lie. Therefore they were good friends. But Tawákwaptiwa always harbored a grudge against Tuwahoyiwma because he had been first chosen to be chief, and he later tried to expel him from the Bear Clan because he had turned Christian.

Another incident far more serious occurred on the evening of the fifteenth day of the Wúwuchim ceremony. On this dread and secret Night of the Washing of the Hair, as we may recall, all priests and initiates are confined within the kiva until they have been ritually confirmed to the pure pattern of Creation. All roads into the village are closed, and pairs of One Horn and Two Horn guards patrol the deserted streets to protect the initiates against contamination by any mortal. If anyone breaks through, their fate is sealed. No initiate or priest will be allowed to come out of the kiva alive.*

On this particular night the dreadful unpredictable happened. A pair of One Horn guards carrying long lances glimpsed a man stealthily creeping toward the sealed kiva. They immediately rushed toward him to stab him with their lances, dismember his body, and secretly bury the pieces, according to tradition. At the same moment a pair of Two Horns saw the man and rushed to protect him with their *mongkos;* for, being of a higher order than the One Horns, they were empowered to hold him captive until his fate could be ceremonially decided. Fortunately they reached the intruder first. It was Tawákwaptiwa. Horrified, they grabbed him up bodily, rushed him to his own kiva, flung him inside, and stood guard outside with their sacred *mongkos.*

Why the village chief himself had attempted to flaunt tradition, to

* See Part Three, Chapter 2.

desecrate one of the most important of all ceremonies, and to endanger his own and many other lives, no one ever knew. Yet paradoxically he decreed that any villager who adopted American ways and accepted Christianity would have to leave Oraibi.

Little by little Oraibi's ceremonialism began to break down; one by one the great ceremonies were given up. One of the most dramatic instances involved Tuwaletstiwa [Sun Standing Up], the head of the Bow Clan, which controlled the rituals of the One Horn and Two Horn Societies. It is related that he and a companion were riding horseback to a dance when he proposed that each of them break a leg and heal it to test their powers. Apparently his companion refused the test. But a few moments later Tuwaletstiwa's horse bolted, throwing him off and breaking his leg. He was unable to heal it and thereafter limped stiffly through the streets. A few years later he turned Christian and moved down to New Oraibi.

Then a strange and dreadful thing happened: he was seen carrying into the street, publicly exposed to everyone's view, the Bow Clan altar, the two huge elkhorns, the six-foot-long *mongko,* the one-foot-long *mongko,* and the most sacred tiny *mongko* made of wood in the preceding Third World. Heedless of the gathering Hopis and the whites and Navajos watching from the trading post, he set up the altar and all its ritual paraphernalia in perfect order in the middle of the street. Then he lit a match to it.

Lorenzo Hubbell burst out of his trading post and offered him five hundred dollars for the altar. Tuwaletstiwa refused. Hubbell then offered him three hundred dollars for permission to photograph it. Again he refused. The fire by now was taking hold. All the Hopis, frightened and horrified, rushed home and closed their doors. The flames mounted and died, changing to a pillar of smoke, all that remained of an altar and a ritual that had been at once the most famous and infamous in all Hopi ceremonialism.

Today this last leader of the Bow Clan, known as the mysterious Mr. Johnson, is an old, crippled man with a tortured face—a strange man, still believed to have mystic powers, who limps down the street with a cane.

By 1933 Oraibi was practically through. Depopulated by people moving to New Oraibi, Moencopi, and other villages, it held only 112 people, over whom Chief Tawákwaptiwa still ruled—an aging man, eking out a living by selling *kachina* dolls at his tiny store, and complacently regarding the disintegration around him as a confirmation of prophecy.

9

The Indian Reorganization Act

Upon the death of Yukioma in 1929 there were three claimants for his position as village chief of Hotevilla and virtual religious leader of all Hopi traditionalists. One was his son, Dan Qöchhongva of the Sun Clan, who had experienced a religious awakening when he was injured during the Oraibi tug of war in 1906. The second contender was James Pongya-yanoma of the Fire Clan, the son of Yukioma's sister. The third was Poliwuhioma of the Spider Clan, a nephew of Lomahongyoma and the leader of the Soyál ceremony.

Pongyayanoma's right was most secure, as it was based on the traditional clan system, he being a member of Yukioma's Fire Clan. A series of events occurred, however, which took him out of the running for a time. It began to be said that his wife was having intimate relations with another man, whom gossip held to be Qöchhongva. Denying this, Qöchhongva took Pongyayanoma to confront his wife, threatening to expose her lover unless she cleared him. This she did. Pongyayanoma, having lost face, determined to leave Hotevilla and take with him all the "substance" of the village.

"In other words," relates Qöchhongva, "all the seeds of the plant life around Hotevilla, so all the vegetation the Hopis depended on for food would disappear. So he went secretly out in the field and took every kind of seed and plant and pollen." He was dissuaded from taking the seeds, but left anyway to live in the pueblo of Santo Domingo, New Mexico, for many years.

"Here," according to Qöchhongva, "he got himself into trouble with a woman who bore him a son. But when he was called to account he denied many things in front of the people of that village, and its religious leaders had to gather to straighten out the trouble. A letter was written to another man from Hotevilla, asking him to help with this matter. When he got there, this is what he found the trouble was.

"James's son had grown to a young man and had fallen in love with a girl older than he. His father, James, had been going with this one also; and as he did not want to put shame on himself, James denied his own son, saying he was not his. So the leaders find that James denied his son to discourage him so he would not have the girl and James would have her. And the question was put to him if he would only grant his son to marry this girl all matters were to be settled, but still he did not say anything.

"At last the leader of the Santo Domingo people made his last talk and told him he was a Two Heart person and he knows the penalty that lies ahead of him. And it will be up to him to decide how long he will go on this kind of life. With this word he left him.

"I know James very well. I taught him many things in the way of prophecy of his clan, and he has been a leader of our Two Horn society while he is yet young. But he does not quite understand the meaning of all the things our ceremony stands for. So he gave me the power to speak for his clan when the deep matters come up, particularly from the government."

Whatever happened, James Pongyayanoma was away in Santo Domingo for some time and Dan Qöchhongva was commonly recognized as the traditional leader in Hotevilla. Meanwhile, under government direction, there was established a new institution that was to split all the villages into the same old factions, known by different names.

THE TRIBAL COUNCIL

With the election of Franklin D. Roosevelt as President and the appointment of John Collier as Indian Commissioner, the United States' repressive and restrictive policy toward Indians was finally changed. The Indian Reorganization Act passed in 1934 was directed toward the preservation of Indian culture and the encouragement of tribal organizations. It planned for self-government of the tribes under special constitutions, and made provisions for loans to Indian community organizations for adequate schooling, medical service, soil conservation, development of arts and crafts, and other benefits. It also contained a requirement that each tribe should accept or reject the act by popular vote.

The Hopis by referendum accepted reorganization in 1935. A tribal constitution and by-laws were then drafted by a government anthropologist and a lawyer-anthropologist, in consultation with village leaders. The constitution authorized the establishment of a tribal council and a tribal court. The council was to be comprised of representatives from each village, thus forming the Hopis' own democratic government, empowered to undertake all needed reforms and improvements. This was explained to all villages through an interpreter named Otto Lomavita.

Old Oraibi, Hotevilla, Shongopovi, and Mishongnovi—the most important villages and the strongholds of the traditionalists—condemned the act immediately as another trick of the government to secure tighter control over them. Their leaders remembered too well the betrayal of Lololma, the imprisonment of Yukioma, the arbitrary establishment of a small reservation already being taken over by the Navajos, and the farcical allotment system. Moreover, each village had its own chief and elders, its own clan system, and its own lands. Never in their long tradition had these independent villages entered into an organized relationship with one another. The new plan was a white man's concept, utterly foreign to their nature and background. They could not understand it or accept it.

Two villages were persuaded to support its offered advantages: New Oraibi, largely comprised of schooled and Christianized Hopis; and Walpi, with the Tewa-speaking people of Hano, which had always been the first contact of the whites and was close to the agency at Keams Canyon.

The small villages of Bakavi, Shipaulovi, and Moencopi were divided; lower Moencopi, home of traditionalists, opposing the act, and upper Moencopi, just off the highway, supporting it.

Despite the preponderant sentiment against the constitution, the matter finally came to a vote on October 24, 1936. There were only 755 votes cast by the 4500 Hopis—651 for the provisions of the constitution and 104 against. This indicated not only the Hopis' utter unfamiliarity with the white man's voting concept, but the ingrained Hopi trait of shying away from anything that smelled of government control. However, this acceptance by less than 15 per cent of the Hopis was enough to warrant adoption of the constitution and by-laws and the establishment of a tribal council.

This immediately precipitated rivalry between villages. Shongopovi claimed the right of decision on all important issues because it was the first Hopi village to be established. Old Oraibi insisted on its leading position as the parental home of Hopi ceremonialism, as did Hotevilla on the basis of its present importance. Walpi in turn claimed precedence because of its proximity to Keams Canyon, its long familiarity with whites, and its custody of the Navajo *tiponis*. The tribal council, then, instead of welding the villages together according to the Anglo-American concept of democracy, only brought out into the open the inherent rivalry and lack of unity among villages that had been controlled by the traditional Hopi system of government.

Another source of contention was the selection of the members of the tribal council. It was natural that those appointed came from among the supporters of the act, and that the most influential was the Christianized interpreter Otto Lomavita. Never well liked, he was later jailed for misconduct and then sent to the relocation settlement at Parker, Arizona. Soon afterward another tribal council leader who aroused the anger of the Hopis by his prejudicial actions, Karl Johnson, fled to Parker as a social worker. It soon became an erroneous belief among Hopis that Parker was a government refuge for all tribal council members when their betrayal of their people was exposed.

Almost from the start the tribal council was boycotted by the traditionalists of all villages. None of them would serve as a member, attend meetings, nor even discuss the issues brought up before it. Nor were they informed. The tribal council was an organization composed solely of the Friendly or Progressive faction, which now merely took on the new name of "tribal council." Uneducated because of years of neglect, totally unfamiliar with white procedures, and often greedy for whatever small recompense they could manage, the members were generally regarded as rubber-stamp stooges blindly obeying the dictates of the government's local Indian agent and the tribal lawyer appointed to handle their affairs.

Such is the situation today. After two decades of trial, the tribal council is a complete and abject failure, a white concept of democratic self-government operating against the traditional background of Hopi belief and custom, and dividing the people into irreconcilable factions.

A HOPI QUAKER

Idealistic as the Indian Reorganization Act was in its intent to aid the remaining tribes to preserve their own cultures, its provisions were largely negated in practice by the still current prejudice against Indians.

The United States in 1924 had granted citizenship to the Hopis, as to all Indians. The Hopis as citizens then became subject to federal taxes and to compulsory military service in World War II. But for nearly a quarter of a century they were denied the rights of citizenship, the vote and the benefits they were called on to support, because Arizona did not ratify the federal ruling until 1948.

Again the land controversy came up. For nearly a century, as we recall, the Hopis had protested to the national government against continual Navajo encroachment on Hopi land. By the executive order of 1882 a Hopi Reservation of 3863 square miles or 2,472,320 acres was established, with the government's solemn promise to protect it from further Navajo encroachment. That promise had not been kept, although Agent

Leo Crane and Colonel Hugh L. Scott had protested in 1910 that four-fifths of the reservation was overrun by the Navajos, who forced the Hopis to exist on one-fifth of the land legally reserved for their use. Meanwhile the Hopi population had doubled since 1882, but the also increasing Navajos were still pouring in with their flocks of sheep.

Hence in 1943, nine years after the Indian Reorganization Act had been accepted by the Hopis but rejected by the Navajos, the government designated the area in which the Hopis were now permitted to graze their own flocks and herds. Known as District 6, or the Hopi Grazing Unit, it comprised only 624,064 acres, plus 7130 acres designated as farm land. This officially compressed the Hopis into one-fourth of their own reservation, the remaining three-fourths being tacitly left to the Navajos.

The tragic effect of all these new government promises, innovations, and restrictions—the tribal council, citizenship, and further land reductions—on one Hopi is dramatically illustrated in the case of Paul Siwingyawma [Corn That Has Been Rooted], Eagle Clan, Hotevilla. A big man in body and heart, embodying all the tenets of his own People of Peace, he is a true Hopi Quaker. His dictated story covers more than twenty-five pages. These are its essentials:

When the United States entered World War II in 1941, Paul and five other Hopis at Hotevilla refused to register for selective service in the armed forces and were arrested by the county sheriff, who had come from Holbrook at the summons of Indian Agent Seth Wilson.

"No one of our elders or of our people give us advice or told us not to sign," explained Paul. "It was our own belief that we do this. We realized the time had come to stand on our religious belief. For when we came to this continent we promised our Guardian Spirit to never show our weapon to anyone to destroy him. If we did show our weapon we would not inherit any land when the next world was established and would lose our chance.

"I had talked with my wife and told her I must stand on this principle. I was very unhappy to leave my family and my child at that time. We have some stock I got from my grandfather and father. This was my means of supporting my family. My father was getting old, and it would be a hardship for him and my wife to take care of the stock. How long I will be in prison I do not know. But the very thought of this old saying, that we must not fight anyone that comes to our land, gave me a great vision to the other world, that we have a right to be here."

The sheriff and his officers arrived at Hotevilla early in the afternoon, waited till the men came in from herding stock, then took them to New Oraibi. Here they were given soda pop and crackers for supper, handcuffed, and taken to Keams Canyon to spend the night in jail. Next day they were driven to the jail in Holbrook.

"One of the big officers in the Army told us that if we sign our name we do not have to go to prison. All of us told him that if we did sign our name and go to war we might not have a chance to live in the next world. This was our main purpose for not wanting to fight. We are doing this for the Hopi people, not for ourselves. I look at those who were with me and I feel a great strength, but yet sad. These men represented different clans of my people."

After spending several days in jail in Holbrook, the Hopis were taken to Prescott, where they were kept in prison for three months. "We are outdoor people," Paul continued, "and to look at the four walls for three months wears the spirit of anyone. I thought there was law that when you kill is when people are put in jail, but now I believe you make a mistake for not wanting to kill anyone."

Finally they were taken to Phoenix for trial. One by one each man was put on the stand to affirm his belief and his refusal to register. "When we were led back and forth between the jail and the courthouse the people look at us like we were criminals because each two men were chained to each other. We could not get them to understand that what we believed in was much stronger than the chains we were bound with."

The trial ended with the adjudgment of the Hopis as guilty—evidently on the basis that they could not be exempted as conscientious objectors because their Hopi belief was not a recognized church or religion. They were sentenced to three years' hard labor and taken to the prison camp at Tucson to work in a gang bulding a road up Mount Lemon.

The six Hopis were the only Indians in the gang of some three hundred whites, Negroes, and Mexicans. Some of the men were Quakers, many others simply did not believe in killing because their Bible said, "Thou shalt not kill." This encouraged the Hopis, but just the same they were sad; life in the barracks was miserable and the work was hard. Every night at nine o'clock, when the lights went out, Paul would gather his companions in a corner and talk to them. "We are not in this prison camp alone," he told them. "With us is our Guardian Spirit to whom we promised not to fight or kill any white man that would come to our shores. For we knew even then that our lost white brother, Pahána, would come. If we fought any white man we would fight our own brother. And we do not want our own brother's blood to be shed on this land which we have promised many, many years ago. Remember I said 'our brother,' and not just 'our friend.'"

Later, when all were asleep, Paul would go outdoors with his corn-meal. He would pray that their Guardian Spirit would show them in some way that he was still with them if they were doing right.

Finally one night the sign came: a ball of fire coming from the north. All the Hopis were awakened to watch it. The great fireball moved through the forest without burning anything, passed through the gap in the mountain, and went south to the mountain east of Tucson. Then it slowly returned on the same route. Four nights in succession the vision appeared. Then the Hopis knew it was the manifestation of Másaw, the Guardian Spirit of the land, and a great strength entered them.

At that time the gang was clearing large boulders from the roadway. Holes were bored with a compressed-air drill, dynamite was inserted, and the rock blown up. One of the drills became stuck so fast that it could not be removed even by a big-muscled Negro. Somebody shouted, "Give the Hopis a chance!" Everybody laughed, because the Hopis were comparatively small. Paul stepped up, ordered the compressor started, and began working with the drill. "At the same time I was praying in my heart, not for myself, but for others to know that we are human beings too. All at once the drill was loose and they all holler when the drill came out."

From then on the Hopis were accorded marked respect. Life became easier. They were taken off the hard rockpile and sent to work on farms. This was work they loved to do, and every Hopi was in great demand. Hopis could be trusted. Paul obtained permission to weave belts at night and on Sunday. These he sent home to be sold by his family. On the day the Hopis were released, Paul presented one of these belts to the man in charge of the prisoners.

Arriving home, Paul found that the Great Spirit had increased his sheep to more than a hundred. But a government agent came, saying that as District 6 was so small his flock would have to be reduced. Paul refused to comply with the reduction. So again he was arrested, taken to Keams Canyon, to Holbrook, to Prescott, and to Phoenix. Once more he stood trial and was sent back to the prison camp at Tucson for not allowing to be taken from him the sheep that the Creator had given him in answer to his prayers. Here he spent another year.

While he was away, the Hopi stock reduction was enforced. Paul's wife, Janet, heavy with child, and his old mother, were taken to their sheep corral near Bear Spring, about nine miles away. The government men took away about half their sheep. The two women were left to drive the remainder back to Hotevilla. On the nine-mile walk back through the hot desert Janet lost her child.

Shortly afterward a man from the agency brought her a check for the sheep—about a hundred dollars. Janet wrote Paul, asking him what she should do with the money. Paul instructed her to give the check to the school principal at Hotevilla to return to the agency. This was the last they ever heard of it.

That winter all their remaining sheep had to be killed, for Paul's parents were too old and his wife too weak to take care of them. So when Paul was finally released, it was to come home to an impoverished family and a wife who had lost her child. Still he could say, "I am glad we have suffered these things because we are going to continue to follow our life plan and religious teachings. We are working not only for ourselves, but for all the people in the world, and we hope we never lose this life."

Today, twenty years later, Paul has lost the sight of one eye because of an infection that was not treated promptly enough at the agency hospital. He has two small children whom he will not allow to go to school. They will grow up uneducated in the jet age, fortified against the tribal council, the government, and the white men who have betrayed their father. Who can say they are not right?

10

The Flag Still Flies

Today the People of Peace are still compressed upon a tiny Hopi island in a great Navajo sea bounded by the continental shores of white supremacy. Despite pressures from without and discord within, they still maintain their traditional concept of full sovereignty.

In a letter datelined "Hopi Indian Empire, March 28, 1949," and signed by six chiefs, four interpreters, and sixteen other Hopis, these spokesmen wrote the President of the United States to declare their stand on five vital issues:

1. A request from the Land Claims Commission to file a claim to any land to which they believed they were entitled before the five-year limit beginning August 13, 1946, expired: The Hopis refused to file any claim on the ground that "they had already claimed the whole Western Hemisphere long before Columbus' great-great grandmother was born. We will not ask a white man, who came to us recently, for a piece of land that is already ours."

2. A request from the agency to decide whether they should lease land to oil companies to drill for oil: The Hopis refused to lease any part of their land for oil development. "This land is not for leasing or for sale. This is our sacred soil. Our true brother has not yet arrived."

3. The sum of $90,000,000 appropriated by Congress for the rehabilitation of the Hopi and Navajo tribes: The Hopis refused to accept "any new theories that the Indian Bureau is planning for our lives under this new appropriation. Neither will we abandon our homes."

4. The Hoover Commission's proposal to convert the country's 400,000 Indians into "full tax-paying citizens" under state jurisdiction: The Hopis questioned the reason for such a proposal because "ever since its establishment the government of the United States has taken over everything we owed either by force, bribery, trickery, and sometimes by reckless killing, making himself very rich. . . . There is something terrible wrong with your system of government because after all these years we are still licking on the bones and crumbs that fall to us from your tables."

5. The North Atlantic security treaty which would bind the United States, Canada, and six European nations to an alliance in which an attack against one would be considered an attack against all: The Hopis refused to be bound to any such treaty or to any foreign nation on the grounds that they were an independent nation and all the laws under the Constitution of the United States were made without their consent, knowledge, and approval. "We want to come to our own destiny in our own way. We will neither show our bows and arrows to anyone at this time. . . . Our tradition and religious training forbid us to harm, kill and molest anyone. We therefore, objected to our boys being forced to be trained for war to become murderers and destroyers."

In summing up, the spokesmen declared to the President of the United States:

> The Hopi Empire is still in existence, its traditional path unbroken and its religious order intact and practiced, and the Stone Tablets, upon which are written the boundaries of the Hopi Empire, are still in the hands of the Chiefs of Oraibi and Hotevilla pueblos. . . .

> The Hopi form of government was established solely upon religious and traditional grounds. The divine plan of life in this land was laid out for us by the Great Spirit, Masau'u. This plan cannot be changed. . . . We cannot do otherwise but follow this plan. There is no other way for us. . . .

> This land is the sacred home of the Hopi people and all the Indian Race in this land. It was given to the Hopi people the task to guard this land not by force of arms, not by killing, not by confiscating the properties of others, but by humble prayers, by obedience to our traditional and religious instructions, and by being faithful to our Great Spirit, Masau'u. We have never abandoned our sovereignty to any foreign power or nation. We are still a sovereign nation. Our flag still flies throughout our land (our ancient ruins). . . .

> We speak as the first people in this land you call America. And we speak to you, a white man, the last people who came to our shores seeking freedom of worship, speech, assembly, and a right to life, liberty and the pursuit to happiness. . . .

> Today we, Hopi and white man, come face to face at the crossroads of our respective life. . . . It was foretold it would be at the most critical time in the history of mankind. Everywhere people are confused. What we decide now and do hereafter will be the fate of our respective people. . . . Now we are all talking about the judgment day. . . . In the light of our Hopi prophecy it is going to take place here and will be completed in the Hopi Empire. . . .

> Now we ask you, Mr. President, the American people, and you, our own people, American Indians, to give these words of ours your most serious considerations. . . .

THE COURT OF LAST APPEAL

In the fall of 1960, after protesting for more than a century the encroachment of Navajos on Hopi land, the Hopis brought suit against the Navajos to settle the matter. The suit was filed during the time Dewey Healing was acting as chairman of the Hopi Tribal Council, and Paul Jones was serving as chairman of the Navajo Tribal Council. Hence the case was known as *Healing* vs. *Jones*. Hearings began in the federal court at Prescott, Arizona, on September 26, 1960, before three federal judges.

The suit was filed solely at the instigation of the Hopi Tribal Council and the attorney it had engaged. The leaders of the traditionalist faction opposed it from the start on the grounds that the land had been given the Hopis by Másaw long before the arrival of the Navajos and the whites, and they would never assent to having a white man's court decide whether or not it belonged to them.

As early as February 20, 1960, in a letter datelined the "Hopi Independent Nation" and signed by Andrew Hermequaftewa, Bluebird Clan, spokesman for the Chief of Shongopovi, a group of traditionalist Hopi leaders wrote to Paul Jones, chairman of the Navajo Tribal Council, requesting him to bring his leading Navajo chiefs for a meeting with them on March 12 to settle the land dispute. They wrote:

> . . . You are aware that there exists a suit against you and your Navajo Tribe initiated and encouraged by the so-called Hopi Tribal Council in collaboration with their attorney, John S. Boyden of Salt Lake City, Utah, to settle a so-called "Hopi-Navajo Land Dispute" in a Federal Court by three Federal Judges.
>
> As Traditional Hopi leaders we are strongly opposed to the idea that a White Man or the Federal Government or the State decide for us what land we should have. The land belongs to the Hopi and all other Indian tribes. This land matter has been settled long ago by our forefathers and not by White men. . . .
>
> Our Traditional chiefs and religious priests are our real authorities on our Hopiland and they have never recognized nor authorized the so-called Hopi Tribal Council to bring suit against you or your tribe. In fact, the majority of the Hopi people did not know or were aware of this suit when it was initiated. Our land and way of life is at stake. The time has come for us to meet together.

It was believed that now was the time for the Hopi leaders to bring out the sacred bundles given them as hostages by the Navajo leaders nearly a century before and settle the matter between the two tribes on religious grounds. No answer was received, and no meeting was held. According to

Hopi belief, the Navajo Tribal Council withheld the letter from knowledge of the traditionalist Navajo leaders who were dissatisfied with its
administration of Navajo affairs.

Obviously the outcome of the case rested on whichever tribe, the
Hopis or Navajos, could prove prior occupancy of the land in question.
Hopi occupancy could be proved by the existence of ancient ruins, rock
writings, and secret shrines that had been established long before the
arrival of the Navajos. But the location and meaning of most of these were
known only to the Hopi traditionalists, who opposed the suit and who
either refused or did not volunteer to impart the information. The Navajo
Tribal Council, on the other hand, had prepared its case well. Enormously
wealthy from oil, timber, and uranium royalties, it had employed a corps
of lawyers, ethnologists, and witnesses to testify that Navajos had occupied
the land long before the Hopis. That some of this testimony was not above
suspicion seemed evident to several Hopis present at the hearings.

A Navajo witness named Kavento testified one day that he had been
living for some time in a certain part of the disputed land area and that
he did not know any Hopis. As he walked out of the courthouse four
Hopis whom he had known for years caught up with him and asked him
why he had lied. The Navajo admitted his perjury, saying that he had been
paid to lie. One of the Hopis was Bob Adams. Asked later if he had
reported the perjury to the court, he replied that he had reported it to
the attorney for the Hopi Tribal Council. He was then asked if he would
be willing to tape-record his knowledge of the Navajo over a period of
nearly fifty years. He assented and did so.

The hearings were concluded and the case submitted to court on
August 2, 1961. Judgment was rendered on September 28, 1962. It was
decreed, in brief, that the Hopis were to have exclusive right and interest
to the area embraced by Land Management District 6 lying within the
Executive Order Reservation of December 16, 1882; and that the Hopis
and Navajos were to have equal rights and interests to all the Executive
Order Reservation of 1882 lying outside the boundaries of District 6. The
case was then appealed by the Navajo Tribal Council.

Meanwhile, on November 18, 1960, at Grand Canyon, Arizona, a
hearing of Hopi land claims against the United States began, a United
States Land Claims commissioner presiding as judge. Hopi witnesses were
presented for questioning by the Hopi counsel, by the Navajo counsel,
and by a counsel acting for the United States. It was apparent that this case
was closely related to the previous suit and depended also on the establishment of the earliest occupancy of the land by Hopis. And again the lack
of cooperation from the Hopi traditionalists, who had opposed this suit,
was obvious.

Three witnesses held the stand for two days: one old man of one hundred, another aged ninety-four, and one seventy-two years old. Their memories were faulty. They seemed unable to answer specific questions. The interpreter had no knowledge of the Hopis' religious background; no one knew, for example, the name and significance of Chaikwaina, one of the Hopis' principal deities. And the witnesses were further confused and upset by the constant and irritating cross-examinations of the attorney for the Navajo Tribal Council.

Court was recessed over Sunday, and the case was resumed Monday morning. Bob Adams, a Hopi, was put on the stand to testify where he had grazed stock as a boy. Each location he called by a Hopi place-name. And each time he did so, the Navajo counsel interrupted to demand that he give the location its correct Navajo name. Adams refused, saying there were no Navajos there at the time; they had moved in later, forcing the Hopis out. Within a few moments the courtroom was in an uproar, with the Hopi counsel objecting to the Navajo counsel's procedure. The presiding judge immediately adjourned the court for an early lunch, during which time he and the three counsels telephoned the Land Commissioner in Washington.

The court was promptly reconvened after lunch, for the judge to announce that the hearings were postponed until the following spring. The reason given later to members of the Hopi Tribal Council by their attorney was that only four witnesses had been put on the stand in three days, and that it would cost too much to hear the remainder of the nineteen witnesses.

No decision on the case has yet been announced.

These two suits pinpointed, after more than a century, the two prime forces of evil that had beset the Hopis: the Navajos and the United States Government. The Hopis had no doubt of the outcome. Months before the hearings the Hopi religious leaders prophesied defeat and the loss of their land. It seemed realistically inconceivable that the government and its courts would decide in favor of some five thousand poverty-stricken, ingrown, introspective, and frustrated Hopis against ninety thousand rich, aggressive, and adaptative Navajos who had expanded into the largest Indian tribe in the United States, with nationwide publicity and with the backing of the Bureau of Indian Affairs.

Yet these two suits were based merely on secular laws established by a government which had assumed the power of the Creator but had lost all sense of moral values. Therefore the Hopi leaders saw in the suits the trial of the government itself before the court of world opinion and the highest tribunal of all—the Creator himself. According to both precedent and prophecy, the Hopis would lose their land by secular law. Then the higher forces would inexorably mete out justice. World War III would break out. The United States would be destroyed by a foreign nation just as it, as a foreign nation, had destroyed the Hopi nation. Land and people would be contaminated and destroyed by atomic bombs. Only the Hopis, on the homeland granted them by the Creator, would be saved to make an Emergence to the future Fifth World.

Still another action attested to their belief.

On February 6, 1960, a public meeting was called in the old school building below Shongopovi to discuss the welfare benefits being received by some 175 Hopis. The meeting was attended by the Commissioner of the Arizona Department of Public Welfare and four of his staff members and a crowd of Hopis from all three mesas. All traditionalist leaders protested against Hopi acceptance of state welfare money for two reasons: that the state would take Hopi land in return for the money, as had been done in South Dakota under a lien law; and that such dependence was destroying the faith of the Hopis in their own independence and reliance upon their Creator.

The commissioner assured the Hopis, confirming it by a letter signed by the Attorney General of Arizona, that Arizona did not have a lien law; and under existing state and federal law no agency could take over tribal lands or property in repayment for welfare assistance received by members of the Hopi tribe. Also, should Arizona pass such a law, it could not be applied retroactively.

Nevertheless, many Hopis at the meeting immediately canceled all welfare benefits being received by the members of their families.

CLOSING THE DOOR

All these current actions attest that the flag still flying above the Hopi nation is hoisted largely by the traditionalists rather than by the government-supported tribal council. Who is its present leader?

For a long time it was rumored that controversial old Tawákwaptiwa had been reminded that to avert catastrophe to his people he should have his head cut off or jump off the highest cliff, according to prophecy. The old village chief of Oraibi did neither. He died peacefully on April 30, 1960, and was buried the same day by John Lansa, in whose home he had been living. The sacred tablet in his keeping was turned over to Lansa's wife, Myna, of the Parrot Clan, until a Bear Clan successor was appointed.

With Oraibi gradually falling into ruins, Hotevilla is indisputably the stronghold of Hopi traditionalists. Its chief contenders for leadership, however, are of traditionally minor clans. They are, as previously mentioned, James Pongyayanoma of the Fire Clan, the son of Yukioma's sister; and aging Dan Qöchhongva of the Sun Clan, Yukioma's son, who was commonly recognized as the religious leader during James's long absence.

Dan apparently claims that he has been leading the people according to the beliefs of the Fire Clan, but he is not of that clan and has not assumed formal leadership. James is of the Fire Clan but still faces criticism for having abandoned his people for so long. Hence he is said to be waiting for Dan to die or for Dan's influence to wane before showing the Fire Clan tablet in his possession and assuming his inherent responsibilities.

Meanwhile several others have been taking advantage of the situation, including an ambitious member of a minor clan, which has no standing whatever. All these would-be contenders run to a type—exhibitionists with an itch for power who pose vociferously as traditionalists, yet curry favor with whites and the tribal council, ready to fall off the fence on the side that will benefit them most.

The true course of future leadership, however, is marked by long tradition. The Fire Clan was dominant in the First World, the Spider Clan in the Second World, the Bow Clan in the Third World, and the Bear Clan until now in the Fourth World. Now the Bear Clan rulership is over, and the Bow Clan is also dying out. There can be no reassertion of Fire Clan or Spider Clan supremacy, for they have had their chances and failed; and this is the reason why Hotevilla's days are numbered as the stronghold of Hopi ceremonialism. According to tradition the Parrot Clan ranks next to the Bear Clan in ritual precedence, and it is from this clan that the next religious leader should come. If one does not appear soon to claim the chieftainship, a member of the Tobacco Clan may claim the right. But despite current fears, another split does not seem likely. The time is too late and too short; the Hopi star is waning. There remains to be fulfilled only the ancient prophecy that a member of the Coyote Clan, which has always brought up the rear, will "close the door" at last upon the Hopis' tenancy of this Fourth World.

11

Recommendations and Prophecies

After reviewing for us over a period of nearly three years their complete Creation Myth, the legends of their migrations, the meanings of their ceremonials, and their entire history during modern times, our thirty Hopi spokesmen were asked what suggestions they could make to improve the present Hopi situation. Their recommendations are summarized as follows.

1. PROTECTION OF RESERVATION FROM NAVAJO ENCROACHMENT

Whatever the outcome of the two existing suits, the Hopis must be protected against further Navajo encroachment on whatever land is finally designated for their use. The Navajos not only have swarmed in and occupied three-fourths of the original reservation granted the Hopis by the executive order of 1882, but are pre-empting land within the District 6 or Hopi Grazing Unit designated in 1943. Recently the Navajo Tribal Council has posted a sign warning off all trespassers, including Hopis, from the great Inscription Rock on which for centuries all Hopi initiates making the salt pilgrimage to Grand Canyon have inscribed their clan signatures. Similar signs have been erected on sites of Hopi ruins. Today Navajos are trespassing at every Hopi spring, at every Hopi shrine, in every Hopi field, and are swarming into every Hopi village to steal every article left unguarded at Hopi homes. The Hopis feel that these transgressions are made with the tacit consent and approval of the Bureau of Indian Affairs, because its agents do nothing to stop them.

2. ABOLISHMENT OF THE TRIBAL COUNCIL

The tribal council, patterned on white concepts, has been proved a failure after twenty years of trial. It is not a local government representing all Hopis. It represents only a group of Progressives who are nominally opposed to traditional Hopi beliefs and customs which block progress. But it actually functions only as a puppet government to rubber-stamp decisions made by the local Indian agent and the attorney engaged to handle its affairs. "No one knows what it does." The tribal council should be replaced by some other form of self-government truly Hopi in concept.

The suggestion is made here that it be based upon the age-old Hopi clan system which links all villages, rather than upon the arbitrary tribal-council plan which sets one village against another, irrespective of clans. The new governing body would be comprised, not of a representative from each village as at present, but of a representative from each Hopi clan. The elected representative would be a traditionalist or a Progressive, depending upon the majority composition of his clan. The governing body would thus be controlled by a majority of clans reflecting either a conservative or liberal outlook. This would eliminate all splits between clans and villages, as the division of opinion would be resolved at the grass roots, within the clan itself. The status would be constantly changing as the older traditionalists died out and were replaced by younger Progressives, providing a gradual transition.

3. BETTER INDIAN AGENTS

Hopi Indian agents, as a rule, have been unsatisfactory. They have included old-time Civil Service employees merely sitting out the period until retirement; government bureaucrats exercising petty tyrannies; men lacking sufficient education, knowledge of the people, kindness, and tolerance. Men of better quality as persons, and administrators of higher professional standing, are required. A prerequisite, before their appointment, should be a thorough knowledge of Hopi myth, legend, and ceremonialism, upon which all Hopi secular life is based. Without this, an Indian Agent has no understanding whatever of the Hopi viewpoint on even the most seemingly insignificant matters.

4. EDUCATION

It has been more than fifty years since the first Hopi children were forcibly carted away to school by Army troops. Indian schools have been government tools for breaking down Indian culture. This has been particularly true of Hopi schools, still a bone of contention. Most Hopi children have emerged with their faith in their own culture broken, but without any respect for the alien culture enforced upon them. Cultural orphans, they have not been able to make a transition to modern times. The lack of education and the inability to manage their own affairs is reflected today in the tribal council members. It is time now that education for the Hopis should be geared to meet the demands of the next fifty years.

5. HEALTH

Almost all spokesmen deplore the lack of an adequate health program. They bitterly condemn the location of the new Public Health Service hospital just completed at Keams Canyon, east of First Mesa. It is not easily accessible to Hopis of Second and Third Mesa, who must travel, often by wagon, as many as forty miles to reach it. The hospital, however, is readily available to Navajos, who fill most of its beds. Hence Hopis generally regard it as a Navajo hospital built on the Hopi Reservation by a prejudiced government without their knowledge and consent. They believe a clinic on Second and Third Mesa, staffed with an adequate doctor and nurse to administer a general health program, is necessary.

6. BUSINESS CONCESSIONS

The Hopi Reservation is being opened up to tourist travel over paved roads. Business concessions—filling stations, hamburger stands, and curio shops—are beginning to appear. Permits to open them are granted upon application to the tribal council—but only to members of the tribal council faction. Numerous examples of such favoritism are a common cause of dissension. The Hopis, poor as they are, need to be encouraged to develop small businesses and sales outlets for their arts and crafts. This encouragement should be fostered by an impartial local self-government.

A bone of contention for many years is the trading post at New Oraibi, operated by outside white interests. Its retail prices for staples are regarded as exorbitant; a weekly refrigerator truck from Flagstaff, 125 miles away, sells vegetables far cheaper. Recent managers of the trading post have not been liked by Hopis, who believe that they have been prejudiced in favor of the Navajos who come to trade. They would like to see this trading post and others taken over by the Hopis in the same way that the Navajos have taken over so many industries and small businesses on their own reservation.

7. PUBLIC UTILITIES

Even in New Oraibi there are no electric lights for homes. No one can send or receive a telegram. There is only one public telephone. It is mounted on the outside wall of the trading post, where in emergencies one must stand in darkness, snow, rain, or dust for as long as an hour while waiting for the operator to answer in Holbrook, a hundred miles away. Is the mighty Bell Telephone System so poor, say enterprising Hopis, that it cannot afford a little booth for it? There is not a lodging house on the Reservation where one can get a room or bed for the night. To buy a hamburger one must drive to Keams Canyon, thirty miles away. If the government forces us to go to school to learn about all these things, Hopis say, why doesn't it give us telephones, a way to send a telegram, an electric light globe when we get back? White people give these things to themselves, all right.

8. CHANGE IN ATTITUDE

All these suggestions for improvement are summed up in the plea for a change in attitude toward the Hopis by all whites dealing with them—agency staff members, schoolteachers, doctors, government officials of all kinds, and representatives of private interests who conduct business with them. They should understand that the Hopis have never protected themselves from Navajo and white aggression because their religion forbids fighting and killing. They need help badly in all fields—self-government, education, health, ways to make a living—if they are to continue to exist as a people. So if the government at last really wants to help them, as it has not in the past, it should send "true peace-loving people who are Christians in their heart. These people will not want to subject us to a different way of life which is not good for us. They will consider those who want to live according to their own pattern given them by their Creator, an inherent right confirmed them by the Constitution of the United States."

9. ORAIBI—A NATIONAL MONUMENT

It has been proposed by many people over many years that Old Oraibi be created a national monument. Early American settlements elsewhere, such as Williamsburg, have been reconstructed by great private foundations. State and national monuments have been made of archaeological sites whose ruins have been excavated and reconstructed for view by future generations. Oraibi is even more important. It is the parental home of perhaps the first people to inhabit this country, the oldest continuously inhabited settlement in the United States, and a living pueblo built on the pattern of prehistoric ruins. It should be preserved as a priceless national heritage.

It is now almost deserted and falling into ruin. Steps should be taken to preserve and reconstruct it while its original walls and foundations still exist, with inhabitants who still remember the locations and functions of all rooms, kivas, plazas, and shrines. Such action, if taken now before it is too late, would serve many necessary purposes.

It would preserve for generations to come the most historic of all pueblos, complete in every detail. It would help to restore the Hopis' pride in their own culture. And it would be the best means at this crucial time of bettering their economic position.

The restoration of Oraibi would be done by Hopi workmen, providing a work project on a reservation which has no industry nor business to provide jobs for a needy people. As a tourist showplace, easily accessible by the present paved road, which is being converted into a main transcontinental highway—an alternate Route 66—Oraibi would attract the same thousands of visitors that now visit such pueblos as Zuñi and Taos. It would stimulate the sale of Hopi arts and crafts—*kachinas,* weaving, pottery, silverwork—which are already world-famous but difficult to obtain because of lack of public sales outlets. The complete annual cycle of Hopi ceremonies would be rejuvenated, enabling visitors to view the *kachina* dances and other public spectacles now largely restricted to the view of ethnologists and a few hardy persons fortunate enough to find accommodations and meals with Hopi families.

A restored Oraibi, in short, would offer a Hopi Williamsburg—but one entirely authentic, populated by its own people carrying on their own life with self-respect and pride in a tradition that is the oldest on this continent.

"There is no need to mention this in our book to interest anybody," adds a spokesman with Hopi pride. "It will all come at the right time by the right people without asking, according to prophecy."

HOPI PROPHECIES

The end of all Hopi ceremonialism will come when a *kachina* removes his mask during a dance in the plaza before uninitiated children. For a while there will be no more ceremonies, no more faith. Then Oraibi will be rejuvenated with its faith and ceremonies, marking the start of a new cycle of Hopi life.

World War III will be started by those peoples who first received the light [the divine wisdom or intelligence] in the other old countries [India, China, Egypt, Palestine, Africa].

The United States will be destroyed, land and people, by atomic bombs and radioactivity. Only the Hopis and their homeland will be preserved as an oasis to which refugees will flee. Bomb shelters are a fallacy. "It is only materialistic people who seek to make shelters. Those who are at peace in their hearts already are in the great shelter of life. There is no shelter for evil. Those who take no part in the making of world division by ideology are ready to resume life in another world, be they of the Black, White, Red, or Yellow race. They are all one, brothers."

The war will be "a spiritual conflict with material matters. Material matters will be destroyed by spiritual beings who will remain to create one world and one nation under one power, that of the Creator."

That time is not far off. It will come when the Saquasohuh [Blue Star] Kachina dances in the plaza. He represents a blue star, far off and yet invisible, which will make its appearance soon. The time is also foretold by a song sung during the Wúwuchim ceremony. It was sung in 1914 just before World War I, and again in 1940 before World War II, describing the disunity, corruption, and hatred contaminating Hopi rituals, which were followed by the same evils spreading over the world. This same song was sung in 1961 during the Wúwuchim ceremony.

The Emergence to the future Fifth World has begun. It is being made by the humble people of little nations, tribes, and racial minorities. "You can read this in the earth itself. Plant forms from previous worlds are beginning to spring up as seeds. This could start a new study of botany if people were wise enough to read them. The same kinds of seeds are being planted in the sky as stars. The same kinds of seeds are being planted in our hearts. All these are the same, depending how you look at them. That is what makes the Emergence to the next, Fifth World.

"These comprise the nine most important prophecies of the Hopis, connected with the creation of the nine worlds: the three previous worlds on which we have lived, the present Fourth World, the future three worlds we have yet to experience, and the worlds of Taiowa, the Creator, and his nephew, Sótuknang."

PRELUDE

Victor Hugo said: "There is no such thing as a little country. The greatness of a people is no more determined by their number than the greatness of a man is determined by his height."

These few Hopis, isolated for centuries on their remote mesas, have been a great people. Now their wheel of life is finally turning full circle. We are seeing today the last full Hopi moon and their ethnic eclipse as an independent race and society. Their only hope, as that of every other race and nation eventually, is to take their place in the one great body of world humanity, translating their values into universal terms.

To achieve it they must first integrate as a social whole, not as separate clans, religious societies, and villages. They must overcome their prejudice toward accepting outside help in the fields of self-government, education, health, sanitation, and economics as an impetus toward self-development. They must free themselves of the fear of witchcraft, of their paralyzing frustration. These weaknesses are not theirs alone; they are the weaknesses of every nation, great or small, on a larger scale. The Hopi nation, in minuscule, is the world at large—a world of nations split within themselves by rival liberal and conservative factions, preyed upon by their own pseudo-scientific witch-doctors, suffering the tyrannies of leaders whom they mistrust, and paralyzed by a frustrating fear of their neighbors.

These ills will not be cured, either for the Hopis or for their larger neighbors, on the lower levels of economics, politicis, and daily expediencies. They must be viewed at this great verge of mankind in greater perspective. The history of the Hopis lends us this perspective to see ourselves through uniquely indigenous American eyes.

It shows us a people with immemorial tenure of their homeland ruthlessly dispossessed by an invading people whose cultural premise was the primary sanctity of property rights over all human rights. It exposes the falsity of armed might over moral right by revealing to us a true People of Peace willing to die for their belief. It proclaims the failure of national governments to abide by their solemn international treaties; the hyprocisy of orthodox churches in betraying by their actions the religions they proclaimed; the juggernaut march of the dollar and the ever-mounting tide of rational materialism following in its wake; and finally the cataclysmic split widening between the spiritual and material, the conscious and unconscious, in us all.

It is not a pretty picture if we can face it; and in relating it to us, the Hopis speak not as a defeated little minority in the richest and most powerful nation on earth, but with the rising voice of all that world commonwealth of peoples who are affirming today their right to grow from their own native roots. Hopi time, unlike our own, is not a shallow horizontal stream. It does not flow out of a conveniently forgotten past through the present into a future we are hurrying to reach. All Indian time has a vertical dimension that cups past and future in a timeless present that forgets no injustices and anticipates all possible compensations.

Our shallow rationalization cannot be permitted to discount as primitive nonsense any aspect of Hopi mysticism and symbolism. We too below our smug and placid surface are swept by powerful and invisible forces. In our psychotic racial prejudice against peoples of darker skin, we did not see the Indians as human beings like ourselves. They embodied for our pioneers all the enigmatic and inimical forces of the unknown wilderness, the mysterious spirit-of-place of the new continent itself. So upon them we projected our own dark fears, only to destroy them, but not our fears.

The Hopis succumbed to a similar but opposite illusion within themselves. They saw in us their long-lost white brother, the mythical Pahána, and projected on us the sublimity of him who would establish at last the universal pattern of Creation. It was not we who betrayed them, but the frailty of mankind, which has not yet summoned courage to live up to its one common high ideal. So it is that we both, the dark and the white, have projected upon each other the repressed aspects of our dual natures.

The coming of the Hopis' lost white brother Pahána, the return of the Mayas' bearded white god Kukulcan, the Toltecan and Aztecan Quetzalcoatl, is a myth of deep significance to all the Americas. It is an unconscious projection of an entire race's dream of brotherhood with the races of all continents. It is the unfulfilled longing of all humanity. Yet it is not enough for us to render due homage to the immortal vision the Hopis have brought us. We and they must question the paradox that the very perfection of the life-pattern expressed in their ceremonialism has itself been one cause of the present Hopi dissolution.

The popular author of a number of rather sentimental books about the Hopis quotes a Hopi as stating that it is better for the Hopis not to have a written language to express their religion and beliefs. When a religion is written down it engenders arguments and quarrels. It is better to transmit beliefs orally and in secret as has always been done.

But Hopi religion is not a religion orally transmitted and as universally Hopi as this would lead us to believe. As we have seen, it is a belief whose core is not spoken, but expressed by the abstract ritualism and symbolism embodied in the great annual cycle of intricate ceremonies. This is what has made it almost impossible for whites to understand, and also so difficult for the Hopis themselves. For each ceremony is the "property" of a certain clan or society to whom it is their special religion, and the members so speak of it. Hence there are a number of Hopi "religions" jealously guarded from the knowledge of all Hopis. This lack of religious unity has set the pattern of clan disunity in secular matters and has been largely responsible for the rifts and splits contributing to the breakdown of Hopi morale.

Hopi religion has been both the one great strength and weakness of the Hopi Nation. Upon it the Hopis must depend to lift them out of their present rut, just as we must rely on the acceptance of a higher level of perception rather than on political and economic expediencies to lead us out of our present world crisis.

Is this too much, or too late, to hope for?

The courageous and cooperative effort of our thirty Hopi spokesmen in recapitulating here for the first time all their myths, legends, history, and meanings of their ceremonies is an indication of the answer. They have spoken freely for all to hear in the hope that their words will give to all Hopis today a full expression of the grounds on which they stand and thus provide a means for unifying all dissident groups. They hope it will give whites too a knowledge of their background and beliefs that will prevent future misunderstandings.

It is an effort on the part of a small nation that could well be emulated by greater nations in the shrinking time before this one small planet extends its pattern of unity or disunity to still more planets in outer space —a prelude to another Emergence to another stage of evolutionary development along our common and continuing Road of Life.

KEY TO HOPI PRONUNCIATION

GLOSSARY OF HOPI WORDS

Key to Hopi Pronunciation

ALPHABET

a, ā, ch, e, ē, f, h, i, ī, k, kw, l, m, n, ng,
ngy, ö, öö, o, ó, p, q, r, s, t, u, ú, n, w, y, '.

DIPHTHONGS

ai, oi, öi, öw, ui, aw, ew, iw, uw.

PRONUNCIATION

a—father
ā—father, pronounced long
ch—exchange
e—met
é—met, pronounced long
f—for
h—how
i—pin or machine
ī—machine, pronounced long
k—skate
kw—queen
l—low
m—man
n—no
ng—sing
ngy—sing your song

ö—purple
öö—purple, pronounced long
o—open
ó—spot
q—curve, pronounced in back of throat
r—measure
s—she, this sound is between s and sh
t—stone
ú—put, pronounced very close, with re-
    tracted lips
u—put, pronounced long and very close
    with retracted lips
v—very
w—wet
y—you
'—a glottal stop, a catch in the throat

PRONUNCIATION OF DIPHTHONGS

ai—aisle
oi—moist
öi—purple and machine
öw—purple and wet
ui—put and machine

aw—how
ew—met and wet
iw—machine and wet
uw—put and wet

341

Glossary of Hopi Words

A

Ahaliya: uncle of the *kachinas*

Aholi: Kachina, deity of Side Corn Clan

ahólki: clan house of Aholi

Ahööla: Name of Soyál Kachina at Walpi, Mishongnovi, and Shongopovi

Ahóte: The Restless One—warrior *kachina*

ál: a horn

álo: spiritual guide

Alósaka: Two Horn Society deity

álwimi: Two Horn Society ritual

Angwushahai'í: Whipper Mother Kachina

angwusi: a crow

Angwúsnasomtaqa: Crow Mother Kachina

ánkinamuru: house of the ants

ankti: repeat dance

á-pa: sheepskin

ahselviki: glue

Apónivi: Where the Wind Blows Down the Gap, place name

Asnyam: Mustard Seed Clan

Astotokya: Night of the Washing of the Hair during Wúwuchim ceremony

atkyaqw: below, down

atu'u: cape

átvila: on the slope

Avachhoya: Spotted Corn Kachina

Awatovi: Place of the Bow, ruin of village on Antelope Mesa

Awatwunga: Bow Clan

ayáwamat: one who follows orders

C

Catori: Kachina

Cha'ákmongwi: Crier Chief

Cha'kwaina: One Who Cries, name of a *kachina*

cha'lawu: to call out, make known

cha'risa: elk

Cha'tima: The Caller

chavátangakwunau: short rainbow

Chéveyo: Spirit Warrior

Chípiya: Home of Animal Kingdom, ancient village now known as Aztec Ruins, New Mexico

chivókya: deposit of new soil or silt

Chiyáwwipki: Narrow Hair People— Isleta Pueblo, New Mexico

Chochap: Purifier *kachina*

Chóchmingwu: Corn Mother

chochmo: mud mound

chochokpi: throne for the clouds—formed by the branches of the spruce

chochuschuvio: whitetail deer

Chööchökam: Stars that Cling Together —the Pleiades

chöövio: antelope

chöpki: antelope house

Chosnyam: Blue Jay People

chosóvi: blue bird

chosposi: bluebird eye—turquoise beads

chöviohóya: young deer

Chowílawu: Joined Together by Water, name of deity of Badger Clan, *kachina*

chu'a: a snake

Chúchip: Deer Kachina

chu'hongva: snake standing up

chu'knga: snake medicine

chu'mana: snake maidens

chunta: cheating, adultery

chu'öqwpi: snake vertebrae, plant

Chu'ovi: Snake Mountain

chu'si: snake flower

Chu'tiva: Snake Dance

Chu'yútu: Snake Race

Cio: Zuñi Pueblo or people

E

eamunkinpi: guns

equilni: burden of weight

Eototo: Kachina, deity of Bear Clan

eskyaro: a parrot

H

háhálviki: cornmeal wrapped in corn husks and baked between two hot stones

hakidonmúya: time-of-waiting moon

"Hakomi?":   "Who are you?"

"Halíksa'i":   "Listen, this is how it is"

hanányaha: loose sand around a badger hole

Hánia: Spirit Warrior

Havívokaltáwi: song of awakening

Hawiovi: Going Down the Ladder—name of a kiva used during Wúwuchim

Heheah: Crooked Mouth Kachina

Héhewúti: Warrior Mother Kachina

hekwpa: oak tree

Hemis: Far Away Kachina

hochichvi: lightning design

höhöqya: harvesting

hohoyawnga: stinkbug plant
honani: a badger
hónaw: a bear
Honnyam: Bear Clan
Hopaknyam: Reed Clan
Hópaq: White Cloud People of the North
hopaqa: large reed
hóta: the back of a person
hótachómi: arrows held together
hótanga: quiver of arrows
Hotomkam: Three Stars in Line, Orion's Belt
Hótoto: Warrior Spirit Who Sings
hovakpi: a medicine plant with a strong odor
hövatöqa: cut in the cliff
Hówungwa: Arrow Shaft Clan
Hóya: Ready to Fly off Nest—name given to a dance
Hu': Whipper Kachina
Húhuwa: One Who Hoes Kachina
Huiksi: Breath of Life
huknga: gray plant
hurúsuki: white cornmeal dough

I

istaqa: coyote man
Isumúya: Whispering Noises of Breezes —March

K

ka'aichokti: skin disease
kachada: white man
kachina: spirit of the invisible forces of life
kachinki: *kachina* house
Kachinyungta: Kachina Society ritual
kakwangwa: bitter
kasknuna: warmth
kataimatoqve: the spiritual eye or "third" eye
Kátischa: Pueblo Indians living along the Rio Grande
katoki: medicinal plant
Káto'ya: Guardian Snake of the West, black snake
Kawéstima: Village in the North, name given to three ruins in Navajo National Monument
kékelt: hawk fledglings, neophytes not yet initiated
Keleva: Sparrow Hawk Shrine
Kélmúya: Hawk Moon, most respected moon—November–December
Kelnyam: Red Hawk Clan
kevepsi: plant—With Abundance
Kikmongwi: Father of the People—the village chief
kísi: evergreen shelter which houses snakes during Snake Dance
kisonvi: open place or plaza in front of kiva

Kísiwu: Spring in the Shadow, a sacred shrine
kiva: underground ceremonial chamber
kivaove: above-surface portion of the kiva
knákwsuni: beginning to talk
Knayaya: Swaying Heads Kachinas
kneumapee: juniper tree
knukquivi: stew of lamb and hominy
Koa: High Pillared Clouds Kachina
Kókopilau: Humpback Flute Player
Kokopilmana: Humpback Locust Woman
Kókopnyam: Fire Clan
kókostawis: borrowing hot coals to build fire
kókotave: field between two fires
Kókoyemsin: Mud Head Kachinas
kokuiena: character
Kókyangwúti: Spider Woman at middle age
kolíchiyaw: carrier of hot embers, skunk
Kóninki: Home of the Coconina people —the Hualpais, Supais, and Wallapais tribes in western Arizona
Kononpaiochi: People of the North, who do not comb their hair
kopáchoki: decorated design carried on head
kópavi: crown of the head, the "Open Door"
kopölvu: tree stump
koritvi: holes in sandstone—the shallow rock basins where people gather rain water
kotoki: plant with small berries
Kotori: Screech Owl Kachina
Kowáwaimave: ancient word meaning Kachina House
Kowáwaive'e: Village That Is Always There. Both of these names are given to the ancient village now known as Kuaua whose ruins are near Bernalillo, New Mexico
kúivato: greeting the sun
kuiwanva: view of Oraibi, place over the horizon
kuiwánva: coming over the ridge
kúnya: water plant
Kuskurza: Third World
kúskuska: ancient or outmoded word meaning lost
kuwanlelenta: to make beautiful surroundings
kuwánnumtiwa: beautiful rolling green hills
kuwánvenioma: earth painted with green plants
kuwánventiwa: painting *kachina* masks
kuwányamtiwa: beautiful badger going over the hill

kuwányauma: butterfly showing beautiful wings

kwáhu: an eagle

Kwákwan: One Horn Society

Kwákwankyam: One Horn Society

kwákui: plant with red seed

kwána'pala: eagle sickness—twitching of head and body

Kwáni: Lance or One Horn Society kiva

kwántiva: One Horn Society dance

Kwátoko: Bird with Big Beak, deity of Eagle Clan

kwávaho: eagle prayer stick

kwávasa: eagle land—the area reserved by each clan for gathering eagles

kwáwiki: feathers tied together

Kwíkwivit: "Proud" *kachinas,* any group of *kachinas* unusually well costumed

Kwiníngnyak: Yellow Cloud People of the West

Kwiyamúya: Windbreaker Moon—April

kyaro: parrot

Kyáshnyam: Parrot Clan

Kyashva: Parrot Spring

Kyáshwungwa: member of Parrot Clan

L

Lakón: a women's religious society

lansa: a lance or spear

lápu: cedar bark

Lavaíhoya: mythical bird called "The Talker"

léhu: plant with black seed

lénmongwi: wild seed chief, millet grain

Lenyam: Flute Clan

Lepénangtiyo: Icicle Boy

loma'asni: head wash

lomáhongva: beautiful clouds arising

M

máchakw: horned toad

machínapna: glove

máhu: katydid bug, a mythical character

makwanpi: asperger—stick with feathers tied to end for sprinkling holy water

mámó'a: jar with several openings

mana: man dressed as woman for ceremony

má'övi: rabbit brush or *chamisa*

maráwmongwuti: member of Marawu, women's society

Márawu: Painted Leg, name of women's religious society

masákwaptiwa: corn plant holding out its arms

Másaw: Guardian of Underworld

masáwistiwa: wing spreading over earth

Masíchu'a: Guardian Snake of the North, gray horned snake

masíchuvio: gray deer

masimahu: gray flute bug

Mastöp: Kachina

mátu'uvé: ceremonial ear of corn

máwyavi: picking cotton from pods or bolls

móchi: awl

mochni: talking bird

mokee: dead

móki: deer

monakvi: flooded area

mong: pertaining to chief

mongko: chief's stick or emblem, the "law of laws"

Mónglavaiti: Priest Talk

mongwau: owl

mongwi: chief

móngwikoro: sacred water jar

monha: black paint

mötoü: dart game

muha: milkweed

Múi'ingwa: deity of germination

Mumchit: Sword Swallowing Society

mumurva: watergrass place

munqa: large field

Munyá'ovi: Cliff of the Porcupine

múte: Coconina name for a fast runner

Muyíovatki: where the Flute Ceremony takes place

N

nacha: wooden tongs

na'chi: standard planted on kiva during ceremony

nakwa: mark of identification

nakwách: symbol of brotherhood

nakwiáyestiwa: life feather tied to hair

Nalöönangmomwit: The four directional, spiritual leaders of the Bear, Parrot, Eagle, and Badger Clans

namátucham: invitation to the home

namósasavu: covering for leg from knee to ankle, legging

nánanha: face blackening of corn rust

nánapwala: purifying from within oneself

nanáyö'ya: emetic

nánmuru: sand drifts

nasílewi: corn covering itself with its green cape

Natá'aska: an ogre *kachina*

natnga: four-year period of initiation

Nátupkom: Two Brothers, Castor and Pollux stars

nátwanta: a practice dance

Nawáivösu: Cliff Runs in Two Directions —place name

ngákuyi: medicine water

ngölapki: The crook of longevity (Walpi)

ngölúshoya: small crook

ngömápi: juniper leaves

nöngántani: going out

nööna: wild grain

nöönkoa: large patch of grain

nöösioqa: nourishment, food

núkpana: evil

núta: thatch cover for kiva opening
nútungktatoka: the beginning and the end
nuvákosio: singing bug
nyöqwivi: meat cooked with corn

O

ómawki: cloud house
omawnakw: cloud feather
ómiq: above, up
Öraivi: Rock on High, Old Oraibi
Ösömuya: First Green Plant Moon, March–April
Ötöpsikvi: Valley of the Strong Plant, Canyon Diablo
óva: white cape
owa: rock
owákunqa: projecting stone
Owaqlt: Scattered Rocks—name of a women's society
Öwngtupka: Salt Canyon (Grand Canyon)

P

pa'ama: large bamboo reed
páchayanpi: water sifter, water sifter ring
pachu'a: feathered water snake
páchavu: bean plants, the Bean Dance, ceremony
Pahána: One from across the Water, the lost white brother
páho: prayer feather or prayer stick
pahómoki: sack for cornmeal
pahosvi: crown
Pákapngyam: Reed Clan
pakwa: frog
Palákwaio: Red Hawk Kachina
Pálangwu: Red Cliff near Canyon de Chelly, rendezvous of witches
Paláomawki: Red Cloud House
palásiva: red metal, copper
palátala: red light of sunrise
Palátkwapi: Legendary Red City of the South
Palöngawhoya: one of the sacred Twins
Pálulukang: Guardian Snake of the South, water serpent
pamistuhya: rheumatic fever
pamösi: fog
Pamösnyam: Fog Clan
Pámuya: Water Moon
Panaiyoikyasi: Short Rainbow, name of wu'ya or deity
pángwöla: water wheel ring
pangwú: bighorn sheep
pangwúvi: where the bighorn sheep climb
páqala: where water is held
pasíqölu: ground covered with water
páskwapi: decayed clay, used for color; blue earth clay from Grand Canyon
páso: where land meets water—seashore

pasopna: sweet water root
pásu: salt water
pasúyangasona: icicle
Pátkinyam: Water Clan
pátuchaya: magic water hoop
pátuwvota: water shield, flying shield
pa'uchvi: closed water with sand
pauipi: water-planted place
pavásio: conclusion of ritual, deepest concentration and singing of sacred songs
Pavásiya: Song of Creation
pávati: clear water
paváwkyaiva: water dogs
pávisa: brown clay from Grand Canyon
páwisavi: water mucus, scum
pawuchpi: throwing out the water
pele: scratch
pík'ami: sweet cornmeal baked in a pit
piki: thin wafer bread
píktotokya: day for making piki
pikyachvi: place of hard surface rock
píkyas: side corn
Píkyasya: Side Corn Clan
"Pinú'u": "I am I"
piphö: perfect rounded feather
Pisísvaiyu: Where Water Flows, commonly used for name of Colorado River
Pisísvayu: West Water That Keeps Rolling, the Pacific Ocean
píva: tobacco
pívane: weasel
Pivánhonkyapi: Weasel Ruin
pochta: sounding board
pohoki: shrine where prayer feathers are planted
po'ki: dog shrine
poko: animal who does things for you
pókoi'ta: pet, usually with reference to a snake
Polatkwua: Red Hawk initiation rite
políhongva: butterfly dancers formed in line
políkwaptiwa: butterfly sitting on flower
polípkoi'ma: male butterfly dancers followed by butterfly maidens
pongáletstiwa: altar set up for ceremony
pongnya: altar
pongovi: circle
Ponóchona: One Who Sucks from the Belly, the Dog Star
Pöqánghoya: one of the sacred Twins
pósi: eye
pósiotuiqa: where the black seed girl sings
pösövi: canyon corners
Póvolnyam: Butterfly Clan
Powamu: purification ceremony
powámúya: purification moon
powáqa: witch or scorcerer
púhui'ma: renewing of grass life

puhúkwaptiwa: new feathers tied to *kachina*

Púpsövi: legendary Seven Caves or Villages

pusivi: big cave

Q

Qaletaqa: Guardian of the People

qanu: liver

qaqletaq: several guards

Qoaquakleum: Kachinas

qöchásiva: white metal, silver

qöchata: white man

qöchatuwa: white sand

qöchventiwa: white painting

qóchyestiwa: animals that live in land of snow

qöiyangyesva: gray light of dawn

qöiyáwisioma: gray low cloud

qömi: cornmeal kneaded into dough

qömmaqtu: black paw

qöyangnuptu: purple light of the dawn

Quiquikivi: Kachina

R

rohona: coyote that runs on three legs

rúpi: mineral

S

sakapa: evergreen village

sakngöisi: one who runs after green plants

sákwaitiwa: animals running in green pasture

sakwlenvi: Blue Flute Clan kiva

sakwáosa: blue

Salapa: legendary village said to be Spruce Tree House, Mesa Verde

salápqölu: spruce forest

salavi: spruce tree

Sáqtiva: extinct Ladder Dance

Saquasohuh: Blue Star Kachina

saquavitkuna: blue kilt

Sáviki: deity of the Bow Clan

Sawungwa: Yucca Fruit Plant Clan

Shongopovi: Reed Spring Village, largest village on Second Mesa

sihu: flower

sikángnuqa: yellow light of dawn

sikwi: meat

sikyáhonaw: yellow bear

sikyangpu: yellow

sikyápala: mixed mineral

sikyáqöcha: yellow-white

sikyásvu: yellow mineral, gold

sikyátavo: yellow rabbit

Sikyatki: Yellow House, ruin of ancient village near First Mesa

sikya'wa: yellow rock

Siliómomo: Petal of Yucca Plant, name of legendary character

simocho: squash flower before it opens

Si'o: Zuñi Pueblo

Siova: Onion Spring

sipápuni: small hole in floor of kiva, represents Place of Emergence

sísivu: many jars

sivaki: iron horse, train

siwíkwtiwa: pumpkin stem

siyámtiwa: object disappearing over flowers

Somaíkoli: deity of the Ya Ya Society

somíviki: cornmeal tied up in corn husk

söngnomi'ta: a standard

songó'qaki: reed covering

Söqömhonaw: deity of the Bear Clan

Sósokmui: Pueblo people along Rio Grande River

Sótuknang: God of Universe, nephew of Taiowa, the Creator of all ceremony

sowi'ngwa: black-tail deer

sowungwa: yucca

sowiwa: shortest ear of corn, length of newborn rabbit

Soyál: Winter Solstice ceremony

Soyala: time of Winter Solstice

Soyálangwul: re-establishing pattern of life, Soyál

So'yoko: ogre *kachinas*

So'yo'kwúti: Ogre Mother-Talker Kachina

súkop: sixteen-day period

suongknah: covering of small reeds

suta: mineral paint

T

Tablita: tiara

Tahohuna: uncle of the ogre *kachinas*

Taiowa: the Creator, the Sun God

taítoinaka: the solar plexus

Taknokwunu: spirit who controls the weather

tálachiro: hot-weather birds

Talá'múyaw: Summer Moon—July–August

talánumtiwa: sun covering the land

talasi: pollen

talásiva: pollen water

talásveniuma: butterfly carrying pollen on wings

talásvenka: painted with pollen

talásyamka: corn tassel bearing pollen

Talátawi: song to the rising sun

tála'ti: hottest part of summer

Taláwsohu: Star Before the Light of Morning, Morning Star

tálawva: red light at dawn

Talpak: Red Cloud People of the East

tamöchpölö: muscle pulling back of the knee

tangákwunu: rainbow

tangave: religious plan

Tapnyam: Rabbit Clan

tápu'at: mother and child, Creation symbol

tásupi: before the sun has pulled down all the light, twilight

tatachpi: painted ball

Tátawkyam: Germination Society, Flute Society

Tatkyak: Blue Cloud People of the South

Tauzaza: deity of the Fire Clan

távank: southwest

Tavasuh: Navajo

Táwataho: Guardian Snake of Above, sun snake

taweyah: magic shield

tawtóma: where the sun ray goes over the line

tenyam: hard wood

tépchomo: plant used for making planting sticks

Tepnyam: Thorny Stick Clan

Tíkive: Day of the Dance

Tíkuiwúti: Spiritual Mother of the Animals

típoni: child of importance, clan fetish

típkyavi: womb, symbolic shrine

Títaptawi: song of happiness

tíva: dance

Tócha: Humming Bird Kachina

toho: mountain lion; black paint

Toho'osmúyaw: Harvest Moon—July–August

tohopko: wild beast

Tókchi'i: Guardian Snake of the East

Tokpa: Dark Midnight, Second World

Tokpela: Endless Space, First World

tótóko'wa: rock formed by many bodies of plant life

tókya: midnight dance

tosi: sweet cornmeal

Totokya: Day before the Dance

tovókinpi: rolling thunder—bull roarer

tovósi: smooth wood

Tövúsnyamsinom: Smoldering Wood Partners

túawta: vision; one who sees magic

túchvala: saliva

túhikya: medicine man

tú'ihi: wedding robe

tuma: white clay

Tunúkchina: Careful Walker Kachina

túoinaka: stack of corn, also ear jewel

túpevu: cooked dried corn

tupkya: safe place

Tupqölu: Hell

tútuskya: stones placed in circle with opening to the east shrine

tutúventingwu: clan symbols marked on rock

túvi: to throw, game of throwing

tuvola: wedding robe

tuvósi: animals with horns

tuvottast: sun shield

tuvumsi: burned wood

Tuwáchu'a: Guardian Snake of Below, sand snake

tuwahóima: butterflies hatching

tuwáhoyioma: hatching and growing on the soil

tuwaki: shrine in the kiva

tuwálanmomo: bee which protects the hive

Túwanasavi: Center of the Universe

Tuwápongtumsi: Earth Mother of the Animals

Túwaqachi: World Complete, present Fourth World

tuwksi: complete cycle of life

U

Uimúya: Planting Moon

úisti: planting time

urúhu'u: expression of fear

V

Ventisóma: Name for Montezuma

W

waítioma: running away

wáki: shelter, place of escape

Wénima: ruins of ancient village near Springerville, Arizona

wikima: being guided ahead

wíkwavi: sagebrush

wikvaya: one who brings

wisoko: fat-eating bird, buzzard, vulture

Wúchim: religious society

wúkotuchkw: long island

Wupávatki: Deep Well Clan

wúti: woman, female

Wúwuchim: first ceremony in annual cycle

Wuwuchpi: The Sprayer; pouring water on dry land; paddling

wu'ya: clan deity

Y

Yahoya: deity of Bear Clan at Shongopovi

yalaha: brown mineral paint

yamo'osta: mother people

Ya Ya: extinct ceremony on which modern witchcraft is based